BLOOD CURSED

ERICA HAYES

St. Martin's Paperbacks

This is a work of fiction. All of the characters, organizations, and events portrayed in this novel are either products of the author's imagination or are used fictitiously.

BLOOD CURSED

Copyright © 2011 by Erica Hayes.

All rights reserved.

For information address St. Martin's Press, 175 Fifth Avenue, New York, NY 10010.

ISBN: 978-0-312-62471-2

Printed in the United States of America

St. Martin's Paperbacks edition / August 2011

St. Martin's Paperbacks are published by St. Martin's Press, 175 Fifth Avenue, New York, NY 10010.

10 9 8 7 6 5 4 3 2 1

Praise for The Shadowfae Chronicles

"Steamy urban fantasy...magical [and] fast-paced."
—*Romantic Times BOOKreviews* (four stars)

"A thrilling and darkly erotic tale of betrayal, passion, and redemption that will ensnare the senses with lush prose and a deadly vision of the Fae that conjures fairy tales of old."
—Caitlin Kittredge, bestselling author of *Second Skin*

"A mind-bending blast into a darkness that enfolds and ensnares you from the first page...Pure magic from the word go."
—*Bitten by Books*

"Weaves rich sensual imagery and dark eroticism into a breathless thriller plot...Hayes's characters have distinct and delightful voices, and she's developed considerable skill at blending the gritty and the supernatural."
—*Publishers Weekly* (starred review)

"Seductive, dark, and wild."
—*Romantic Times* (four stars)

"Hayes's debut and series opener exemplifies erotic urban fantasy at its most visceral, illuminating the splendor and squalor of life on the edge. Fans of Laurell K. Hamilton's Merry Gentry novels and Caitlin Kittredge's Nocturne City books will enjoy this tale of sex, violence, and the supernatural."
—*Library Journal*

"Readers will thoroughly enjoy this entertaining tale of forbidden love. Erica Hayes has a great future ahead of her as a bestselling author."
—*Genre Go Round Reviews*

"Hot, spicy, and well rounded...awesome. I'm waiting for the next round!"
—*Tynga's Urban Fantasy Reviews*

ST. MARTIN'S PAPERBACKS TITLES
BY ERICA HAYES

Poison Kissed

Blood Cursed

1

"Where do you want it?"

Hot vampire lips caressed my shoulder in a fall of sweaty nightblack hair, and his salty breath burned me. I swallowed, sick. *Please, just let this be over quickly.*

Smoke and nightclub lights dizzied me. Bass vibrated my lungs, guitars and a screeching electric violin, the raw melody of fairy desperation. Around us, dancing bodies writhed, rainbow limbs and wings and glazed faestruck eyes. Sparks shimmered in the air, the glassy fairy glamour that hides us from human eyes, and the scent of flesh and kisses fired sweet temptation into my blood. A typical midnight at Unseelie Court, the dark and notorious club where Melbourne's shadowy underworld came to play. But tonight, I had an unpleasant job to do.

The vampire licked sweat from my collarbone, searching with his iron-pierced tongue for my pulse, and my guts twisted.

It'll be easy, Emmy, Jasper, my boyfriend, had whispered. *Show him some skin, tease him a little, give him a quick taste, and he's yours. Just get me my gemstone.*

I didn't want to. Not vampire bait, not me. No matter

how Jasper charmed or persuaded or disarmed me with his dazzling fairy smile.

But saying no to Jasper was a trick I'd never quite gotten the hang of.

The vampire nipped at my chin, playful, and I shivered. He wore black leather and lace, diamonds flashing, and behind ragged sable-dyed hair, his eyes glinted, drunken sapphire blue. His white shirt lay half-open, glowing purple in ultraviolet rain, and on his chest a fat scarlet gemstone glowed on a chain, shot through blue and green by wicked nightclub lasers.

My wing veins swelled. There it was. My prize. All I had to do was say yes.

Just one bite, and the gem would be mine.

I grabbed his coarse locks and tugged his kisses onto my throat. He groaned and crushed me against the mirrored wall, licking a warm wet trail up to my chin. The glass slicked my wings, warm and clammy, offering no comfort. I squirmed inside, but I didn't wriggle away.

He nipped at my bottom lip, stinging. He tasted of meat and bourbon, salt and fire. "I said, where do you want it?"

I let my lips part, my breasts heave and swell. My long crimson hair tumbled invitingly, showering him in my spell-lured scent. I'd dressed for the occasion in silver stilettos and a glittery dress with a tight skirt, a scooping neckline, and no midriff. Plenty of succulent bloodfae flesh on show, my dusky skin beading with scarlet-tinged sweat.

Vampires love bloodfairy juice, see. Bloodfae are special. To vamps, it's like the smoothest, slickest drug, heady and fragrant, sliding down their throats like opiumlaced honey. What's more, the phases of the moon rule us, and the near-full moon that lit the sky silver outside only made me tastier. It dragged like a tide in my pulse, igniting my blood with excitement and intoxicating flavor. Vampires can't resist.

And unless they've had the vampire virus long enough for their bloodfever to reach equilibrium, they're always hungry.

Always.

Which made a pretty bloodfairy like me the perfect bait. This guy—whatever his name was, kinda cute if you liked emotrash bloodsuckers—didn't stand a chance.

I gave him a sultry whore's smile, my nerves thrumming tight with danger. *Look, vampire. Candy. Come get it.* "Anywhere you like it, baby."

He growled like a hungry beast and drove hot fangs in hard.

Pain clawed my throat. I squealed, but no one heard. Lights flashed, uncaring, and deafening music rolled onward, wire grating on steel. My blood splashed the mirrors, running in a sticky ruby glow. No one cared. Just another bloodfae slut, taking her medicine.

God, it hurt. My own bloodscent made me retch, but I couldn't break free. Couldn't get away from his steely grip around my waist, his hot tongue pressing my skin, his crunching teeth forcing ever harder into my throat.

He sucked, and faintness washed my head bright. My skin tore off in his mouth, agonizing. He groaned and rubbed against me, tense and hard, a gruesome parody of sex. He swallowed, sucking harder, dragging the blood out against the current, a horrible suction that pulled all the way down to my guts.

Dizziness stuffed my skull like cotton wool. His heartbeat thudded through my chest, alien, stealing my body's rhythm until we throbbed together as one. He shuddered, helpless, and drove deeper, swallowed faster, a tortured cry spilling out like he couldn't take any more.

My rubyshine blood gushed from his mouth, over my breasts, a hot sticky mess. His body jerked against mine in release—okay, that was gross—and I fought crippling nausea and forced cramping fingers under his neckchain.

His hot wet body sickened me, the guttural growl in his throat as he came disgusting. At last I found the little metal knot, and I flicked the spring open and pulled the chain free.

Got it.

He didn't care. Didn't even notice I'd ripped him off. He'd gotten what he wanted, and he slumped panting against the bloodspattered couch with a groan of pure pleasure. Sweaty black hair fell in his face. Glowing fairy blood—my blood, hot and fresh—splashed scarlet down his chin. He'd orgasmed sharp and hard just from my spellrich taste, and his leatherclad thighs gleamed black and shining from the feverpink mess we'd made.

My head swam. I stumbled, and hid the bloody chain behind my back. Blood trickled between my breasts and clotted there. Drowsiness tugged my eyelids, but I fought it and gave my glamour a clumsy kick. Whiteblue spellsparks glittered the air between us, invisible to anyone but me, my innate fairy magic messing with his mind. *Don't see me, scumbag. Don't see what I did. Only the blood, hot and rubysweet . . .*

Spellwrought confusion swirled green in his eyes, and he gave a dripping crimson grin. Panting, he searched in his pocket and tossed me a folded wad of cash. "Thanks, darling."

"Any time." I fumbled the catch, shaking. The money slicked foul in my hand. I wanted to throw it back, scream, claw his face off.

But I forced myself to fake another smile, wink at him, turn. *Don't let him see. Never show them how they've hurt you.*

I pushed through the shimmying dance floor crowd. Heat stifled me, thick with sweat and blood and sex, and I burned to scrub my claws over my skin, rip away the horrid feeling of being fed upon like a dumb beast.

Shaking, I dug a handful of tissues from my bag and wiped at the blood, over and over until my hands were a wet red mess. A hot lump crawled up my throat to choke me. I could still taste the vampire's fleshy breath. Still feel his lips creeping on my skin, his teeth slashing my muscle, blood's dizzy surge away from my head.

The ragged hole he'd made in my throat burned. Soon it'd be healed, his vampire spit already thickening my blood like sticky acid. But the humiliation mushrooming inside me flamed hotter.

God, I hated this. I'd sworn I'd never stoop this low. I'd seen firsthand what selling your blood did to you: Always light-headed, always sick and dizzy like a permanent blacksparkle comedown. Desiccated skin, brittle hair snapping, rabid thirst that never ceases, hallucinations, waking nightmares, gnawing on your own fingers for protein. It's an addiction, cruel and sweet and deathless, and eventually, it kills you.

Once, I'd had a friend who bloodwhored. Now he was dead. I should know better.

Yet here I was, prostituting myself on my dark fairy-boy's say-so.

Rage burned my eyelids, and I flung the stinking money aside. The notes spilled on the floor, and colored fairy hands scrabbled for them, claws scraping, voices squealing their delight. Sickness bloated me like rotten food. They were welcome to it. After all, I had Jasper, didn't I? To keep me, feed me, dress me in nice clothes. All I had to do was say yes to everything.

You liked it, Ember. The unseen moon's warm whisper pierced my heart. *You liked that vampire's kiss. You wanted his mouth on your skin, those slick fangs digging in, splitting your delicate flesh, tearing you open, sinking deep inside. It felt good to be wanted. So dreamy and free. So right. Isn't this what you're meant to be, bloodfairy girl?*

My stomach heaved, and I covered my mouth and ran.

Music cackled accusation like a witch's laughter. Lights glared, flashing on my luminous ruby bloodstains, showing me up for everyone to see, and though I was lost in a perfumed crush of bodies and wings, I'd never felt more exposed. Like everyone stared at me, a muscled green troll's black-eyed stare, a blue waterfae girl's disdainful glitterpainted lashes, the scornful flicker of a firefairy boy's flaming wings. *Look at me, everyone. Look at the worthless bloodwhore.*

I stumbled on shaking legs. I felt hot and sick inside, like a scolded little girl. I needed to pee. I wanted a shower, to take a scrubbing brush to my filthy wet hide and scrape those greasy vampire fingerprints off my skin forever.

Not yet. Jasper first. I clenched determined fists, and the vampire's chain sliced my knuckles. I shook it free, and the crimson gemstone flared, as if coals ignited within.

I eyed it warily. It dangled from its chain, strobes flashing blue and yellow, but something definitely glowed inside.

A trick of the light? Surely.

I leaned closer, the gleam attracting my covetous fairy eye. Pretty, all shiny and sugarynice. Jasper and his mates were businessmen—selling fairy drugs and collecting protection money is business, see, and you don't say the word *gangster* around here, we're all businessmen or entertainment professionals or security consultants—and part of Jasper's business was getting things that didn't belong to him. He and his boss, a cocky glassfairy freak called Diamond, worked for the city's ruling vampire ganglord, and ran all sorts of shit in and out of all sorts of places. But I didn't know why Jasper wanted this. Childish envy warmed me. Maybe, once he'd finished, he'd let me keep it.

I peered into the gem's center, mesmerized by the tiny dancing flame. An eerie whisper slid into my head, ghostly and cold like mist. *Free meee . . . ssspare meee . . . take mee awayyy. . . .*

Mmm. Pretty thing. I hummed softly to it, and the light flared brighter.

The air juddered, and erupted with a jagged scream of agony.

I yelped, and jerked backwards, letting go. The vile thing clattered away, and the scream slashed to silence.

Shit. I scrambled for the gem on the dirty floor, dodging high heels and bare clawed toes and boots. At last, my clawtips brushed cold facets. I grabbed the chain and hopped to my feet, glaring at the dangling gem with suspicion licking my nerves cold. "Shush, nasty."

It sparkled at me, threatening, and something black and forbidding swirled deep inside.

I glanced around. No one was looking at me. They hadn't heard a thing.

I sniffed, doubtful. I'd hallucinated that. Jewels don't scream. Or light up by themselves. Right? Just because I'm a fairy doesn't mean I believe in ghosts and woo-woo.

A dry murmur wormed into my ears, cold like rustling leaves. The glow inside swirled, flaring like a firestorm, and swiftly I stuffed the nasty thing into my bag before it could scream at me again. Where the hell was Jasper? He'd promised to meet me here once I was done.

A cold hand clamped my aching shoulder and spun me around.

My wings sprang taut. I stumbled, pierced by pale green eyes shaped with golden glitterliner.

A tall blond woman smiled, fangs sharp on scarlet lips. "You for sale, pretty?" She wore a short red dress over long pale legs, her faded eyes hard. Beside her, a dark-eyed fangboy in leather pants and no shirt winked at me, his tangled dreadlocks a shock of dusty blue. Sharp studs glinted in the collar that chained him to her wrist, and he sniffed in my direction like a hungry dog.

Great. Paris Hiltonvamp and Tinkerfang the Chihuahua. More horny vampires out for bloodfae candies. Story of my life.

But I was alone, with no Jasper to protect me, and my throat shriveled.

I cocked my hand on my hip, faking nonchalance. "I'm sorry, do I know you?"

"You smell nice." Tinkerfang ghosted his damp palm

up my cheek, a feverwarm caress. He smelled sour, of meat and sweat.

"Look, don't touch me, okay? I'm not selling."

"No need to be shy." Paris grinned and grabbed my elbow.

I struggled, but she was too strong. Vampires were all too strong. "Let g—"

"We watched you feeding our friend," cut in Tinker. His black-smudged gaze draped over me, relishing the bloodstains, the sweat, the clotting fangwounds. He leaned over and licked a hot slick trail up my cheek.

Yuck. I squirmed, my wings thrumming tight with dread. Had they seen me steal their friend's gemstone? Was I busted?

Tinker's whisper burned my ear, bittersweet with cigarettes and lemon-drenched sparkle. "You were so fucking hot. I wanna drink you dry, baby. I wanna slice you all over and lick it up. Come play?"

I shrank back, disgusted, but Paris held me, and suddenly I was trapped in a cage of hot vampire limbs and invading fingers. Tinker stroked me, licked me, nuzzled my neck where the blood still trickled. Flesh-scent stuffed my nostrils, and my pulse pumped harder. Unseen moonlight tempted me, dragging on my fluids like a swelling tide, drawing me to wild fairyspelled desire. Blood throbbed between my legs. Let them feed on me, eat me, suck me dry. . . .

I jerked away and ran, horrid vampire laughter scraping in my ears like sandpaper.

I forced through the packed crowd on the dance floor, where fragrant sweat slicked on rainbow muscles and wingdust glazed the air like candy. Glamours clashed and sparked, the air alight with the dazzling fairy magic that made us look normal to humans. Lights glinted on

jeweled earrings, shining fangs, glowing fairy eyes
smeared blue and green with glitterpaint.

Sweat slid down my neck. My hair stuck to my bloody
chest. I glanced over my shoulder, my pulse burning.
Couldn't see them following. Didn't mean I was safe.
The sooner I found Jasper, the better.

Above, the mezzanine loomed, dark and backlit in
ultraviolet. Pounding music shimmered like heat haze
as I forced beneath the iron railing into the shadows. A
drooling blue fairy sprawled head downwards on the
stairs, violet curls dangling, eyes gleaming dully like
dead orbs from too much cheap sparkle. Telltale green
dust still sprinkled his face, and a scrawny green spriggan girl licked it up eagerly, slurping her long black
tongue over his nose, his lips, his pointed blue chin.

Drugsmoke shone in eerie purple light, green lasers
flashing shadows from bodies, crawling wingbones,
limbs contorted in pain or delight. Back here, the floor
lay littered with crunched foil and dusty mirror shards,
the sickly gleam of broken syringes smeared with green-
metal fluid. My sharp fairy ears twitched, and even in
the crunching din I heard sighs, heartbeats, wet rasping
breath.

I sidled into flashing blue dark, stretching onto my
tiptoes to look for Jasper. The tip of my nose whiffled,
searching for his distinctive honeycomb scent amongst
cologne and candy and the dark flowery cream of fairydust.

And there he was. Lounging against the iron wall, a
long lean shadow sparking with static charge, the heavy
glamour that turned him ordinary if you didn't know
how to look. Long lean legs in his habitual black, his
pale arms and face a bitter contrast. Wild, crisp black
hair, fresh with glitter and perfume, golden rings flash-

ing in his ears. His velvetdark butterfly wings shed dust that glimmered and swirled in purple-shot lights.

I swallowed, and walked in his direction.

He leaned one steel-bangled forearm against the metal, muscles roped tight. Talking to someone, one of his sleazy friends or a mark, I couldn't see. And then his wings swept back, and his long hair tumbled forward over a narrow green shoulder slick with blue waterfae sweat. Lavender lips, wet neongreen wings, a slow tempting smile.

I halted, my heart thumping.

A female smile.

Her green arm slipped around his waist, and he tugged her rippling golden hair back and kissed her.

My skin burned cold. I didn't want to look. But horrid steel spikes jabbed my muscles, pinning me in place, and I could only stand and stare.

Kissing another girl. Not just a *hello, darling, wanna buy my drugs?* kiss. A slow, deep, wet, tongue-on-tongue, *let's get naked* kiss. Bodies rubbing together, his thumb pressing her chin upward the way he liked, holding her so she couldn't escape even if she wanted to. And she already melted in his arms. I could tell by the way her eyes closed, her head fell back, her neon wing-veins glowed brighter. I knew that hot, helpless dizziness, how he made you feel wanted, beautiful, the sexiest woman in the room. His hand crept up her skirt, between her thighs, caressing, and she moaned and pulled him closer.

Numb, I turned away, and that old clockwork denial wound its creaking springs tight in my heart. It was okay, wasn't it? Just kissing. Stupid to be upset. I knew Jasper wasn't a saint. Hell, he sold drugs and stole stuff for a living. What did I expect? And I wasn't exactly blameless, right? I'd just been kissing another guy. It didn't mean anything.

Crazy laughter burst from my lips. Tick, tock, wind the clock, pretend it isn't happening. Only I could come up with an excuse like that. They weren't just kissing. The fucker was cheating on me. After everything I'd done for him.

Music throbbed, stirring in my guts. I felt hot and sick, impotent anger chewing me raw. I'd followed his rules, put up with his temper, made myself into the girl I thought he wanted. And now I'd sold my blood for him, the one thing I'd sworn I'd never do. Whored my dignity. Let some horny bloodsick beast chew on my throat and come in my lap with my blood running down his throat. I'd humiliated myself for Jasper, and he didn't care.

I swallowed, sniffling, but my throat cramped hot, and the tears just flowed faster. Not because Jasper lied to me. Not because he'd treated me like an idiot and it hurt deep inside like a poisoned blade.

Because I knew. I'd always known. I'd just never seen with my own eyes before.

I was besotted, but I wasn't dumb, and fear and puppy love hadn't dulled my sense of smell. Sometimes he reeked of cheap perfume and sex, fruity kisses in his mouth that weren't mine, and like an obedient little wifey, I never complained. Only smiled and did my best to forget about it, and cried later in the bathroom where he wouldn't see.

I had only myself to blame. Too pathetic and weak to do anything about it.

Well, not anymore.

Blindly, I walked off, fisting my tears, blood and makeup smearing glitterbright. My sharp heels scraped welts in my ankles as I stumbled. I didn't care. This was the last time Jasper would humiliate me like this. If he wanted to screw other women, fine. He could do it without me to come home to.

I plonked my ass onto a bar stool, my bruises aching. The neonglass bar glowed blue, vibrating under my palms as the music throbbed, and my blood invigorated, strength flowering in my muscles.

Conviction hardened like iron in my heart. Yes. He could have his precious gemstone—whatever the horrid thing was for—and then I was dumping his dusty fairy ass.

But the cowardly worm in my stomach quailed and shivered, chewing its tail in mocking fright. *But you've got no cash, Emmy. No stuff. Nowhere to go. Whatcha gonna do, get a job? You're just a useless bloodfae bitch. Who'll protect you? How will you ever survive in that big old nasty world?*

I clenched hot fists on the glass, sparking my courage. "Shut up. Screw him. I'll get by somehow."

But that sniveling fearworm just coiled there, a greasy smile on its fat face. *Sure, Emmy. You keep telling yourself that.*

I ordered a vodka and lime, and as I sipped the tart chill through a straw, determination ebbed uneasy in my heart. I could do it, right? I wouldn't let Jasper charm me this time. I'd forget his absent tenderness, the heady flavor of his kiss, the safety I felt in his arms. Instead I'd remember all the times he'd hurt me, all the thoughtless assumptions, harsh asides, and jokes at my expense, and I'd give him his gemstone and take off before he could work his sultry spell on me.

Get your hand off it, Emmy. One glance from those hot hellviolet eyes, and you'll melt. You really think you can stand up to him? Remember what happens when you piss him off.

My courage wavered, the twin tangs of vodka and dread sour on my tongue. I still had aches from the last time he'd taught me a lesson, and the old justifications slid comfortably into my veins, warm and oily from constant use. I should just forget about it, the way I forgot all the fights and slaps and nasty words. Most of the time, it was okay between us. Maybe this time he'd change, stop snorting so much of his own product, treat me better. . . .

Yeah. And we'd all get ice-skating lessons in hell.

No, it was over. I was leaving him. I'd give him his lousy gemstone and walk away, and I'd never let anyone rule my life like that again.

Uh-huh.

In a minute.

I gulped my drink, trying to suck confidence from alcohol and sweat-drenched air.

"Ember? You okay?"

That crystalchime voice rang sweet alarm in my head. The smell of roses rolled warm and tempting over my skin, and on the blue glass before me, my shadow's edge glowed pink.

Shit. Not Jasper. Worse.

My heart sank.

2

Behind the club, the alley shrivels in parched summer moonlight. Heat shimmers above black pavement, hovering over a rusted Dumpster, stacks of empty kegs, crates, garbage dusted in lost fairy glitter. Hot concrete and sweat lick the air with the scent of salt and tar. And beneath an awning pooled in blackness like ink, a cunning glassfairy named Diamond waits to make a killing.

He flexes tense muscles, sharpglitter wings slick in the heat. His glassfae glamour fades him dim, not quite invisible but translucent like a ghost, shedding a faint rosy glow that barely casts a shadow in the dark.

Adrenaline and anticipation wet his tongue sharp, and his pulse throbs hot and swift. After weeks of sly faedazzle and trickery, it's here. And it's a lovely hot night for a murdering.

Footsteps ring in harsh moonlight. His crystalsharp ears prickle, and he crouches tighter, fading deeper into shadow. Two people: one large, one small. A limp's uneven cadence, one foot scraping. A dark laugh, a snatch of conversation in bastardized Sicilian.

The rotting scent of ancient bloodfever aches Diamond's delicate fairy sinuses, and his nerves screw tight like tinfoil. Vampire. Sure as sugarplums. And not just any vampire.

Angelo Valenti, Diamond's gangland boss, the vampire prince of Melbourne and the meanest gangster in town. Tight dark curls, hard eyes gray like slate, heavy-built but calm and graceful like a cunning panther in his expensive charcoal suit. Flanked as always by LaFaro the lizard, his hunchbacked faeborn confidant with the splayed hipbones and double-lidded yellow eyes.

Striding coolly along the street like the world owes them obeisance, which around here, it does. Ange and Tony, the Valenti boys. Favorites of Kane, the reigning demon lord, whose gang rules Melbourne's underworld with rage and demonfear. Powerful. Impeccably connectified. Untouchable.

Hatred burns cold in Diamond's iceglass heart. Angelo. Stealifier of girlfriends. Spreader of vile vampire virusicality. Ange fucking Valenti, soon to be the deadest vampire asshole in town.

Diamond's translucent fingers clench, and in his palm a half-empty poison vial glitters emeraldine. The poison is strong, he made sure of that, a nasty flesh-rotting brew designed especiamally for vampires, crafted in a stinking underground laboratory by a mad fairy spellworker. And he's bought the sickest faecrazy killers he knows, with cash and sparkle and frightful promisicalities that make even a hardened deceiver like Diamond shudder and sweat.

He slips the vial away carefully. All in a day's treachery.

It takes cunning to kill a 350-year-old hellcursed vampire ganglord. Cunning, and some serious balls. Both of which Diamond has in plentification. He's had eyes on Ange's empire for a long time. Kill the boss, take the spoils. That's what gangsters do. But now, Diamond has reasonicality plus to want Ange dead.

Sweet vengeance thrills his blood. Angelo didn't just steal the woman Diamond loved. He corruptified her. Made her dirty. Fed her virustainted blood until the vampire infection took hold. Killed her, or as good as. Rosa was beautiful, dazzling, an earthly goddess. Now, she's a ravenous monster.

A life for a life. It won't make his rosepetal girl well, or bring her back to him after what happened. But that's not the pointificality. Ange deserves to die.

And then . . . well, the demon lord already likes Diamond's sense of funnification. Owning the town is a tough gig, but someone's gotta step up. And then Diamond will be as untouchable as Ange was.

After so many years of untruths and tricksprings and dirty gang politics that end in death, Diamond has to win. Otherwise, it's all for nothing. Without Rosa, it's the only way to make his sordid life worthwhile.

Ange and Tony round the corner. Tony flicks away a cigarette, ash glowing. Behind them, three silent fairy shadows loom and grow.

Diamond's mouth dries, and before he can swallow, the assassins strike.

It's swift, soundless, brutal. In an instant, Tony slams facefirst into the ground under a mess of flaming fire-fae wings. The firefairy laughs, shaking copperbright hair, and straddles Tony's neck, grinding his flat lizard nose on concrete. Tony grunts and whips misshapen legs, but he's overpowered.

Angelo tenses, spins fluidly like a dancer. His vampire reflexes are sharp like icicles, those hard gray eyes afire with danger. The second fairy assassin dives for

Ange's legs in a clatter of steely blue wingbones. The third one leaps, spearing down like a crazyass vulture, her greasy black hair streaming. Oily black wings stretch rubberlike, petrolscent spraying, and moonlight glints on her evil green-tinged blade. Poison drips, hissing on the pavement.

Diamond watches, his nerves glass-sharp. Just one slice. One splash of greenified death. That's all.

The cackling blue one aims a sharp elbow at Ange's kneecap, missing by a fraction. Angelo growls and kicks back, but the oily vulturefairy lands on sharp black haunches atop Ange's shoulders, her long feet curling in tight. She yanks the vampire's head back by wet dark curls, and snakyquick she slashes with her knife, bright-green steel blurring across Ange's throat.

Diamond sucks in a triumphant breath. Angelo snarls, the hole in his throat gushing crimson.

It doesn't even slow him down.

Ancient vampire anger roasts the air like a furnace. Ange ducks like a charging bull, the fairy still yowling triumph on his shoulders, and runs headfirst for the wall.

Bones crunch wet. Vulturegirl screeches like a wounded bird, and the blade clatters to the concrete in a scarletgreen spray.

Ange bounces off, blood still spilling down his chest. Kicks the one chewing at his ankles in the face. Grabs the shattered vulturegirl's wrist, and yanks.

Her slender arm cracks like kindling. She howls, fighting limp legs, feet flapping uselessly. Ange hauls the broken fairy from his back, throws her on the ground with a foul curse that blisters Diamond's palms, and rips her shiny black throat out with his teeth.

Oily blood sprays black. Angelo chews, flesh tearing like paper. Shakes his head like a sleek dark dog. Wrenches the vertebrae free with a pop, black fairy meat hanging in shreds. And spits the dripping head out onto the concrete.

Splat.

Diamond's guts wrench tight. Fuck. Fight's done. Chance is lostified. No point leaving any traililfication.

With a sharp crystalline flash, he sheds his dark-glamour.

Rosy light flares, stinging his skin raw. He dives for the dropped knife, glass wings clattering along the pavement as he rolls, and springs shrieking into the fight. The poisoned blade flashes warm in his hand, and he crashes like crystal on steel into the cackling blue fairy.

Limbs writhe and tangle. An elbow rams into his guts, retchworthy, but he cracks the blueshit's pointy chin upward with a glasshard fist. Stabbifies the clumsyfae in his skinny blue throat before he can talk and give Diamond's traitorfication away.

Blueberry blood squirts into Diamond's face. The fairy chokes and dies, blueshine draining from his skin. Diamond rips the knife out and heaves the body aside.

Two down. One to go.

The firefairy holding Tony down scuttles backwards like a flame-drenched crayfish. Ange leaps after him, but Diamond reverses the knife and switches on his shimmering fairysight with a crackle of static. The alley telescopes, his directionicality homing in. He lets fly. The knife cartwheels, bloody steel shining blue, and plants itself in the firefairy's eye socket.

Schlllp.

The fairy crumples to the ground, and his wingflames hiss out.

Silence. Just moonlight, and labored breath, and the trickle of blood from corpses.

Diamond sucks in air, fights to still his racing pulse. Three dead fairies. No prisoners. No one left to talkify.

Tony clambers to his feet, his face a mess of slimy lizard blood. He plants both hands on his broken nose and jerks it straight with a crackle like splintering wood. "Mother*fucker.*" He aims a kick at the dead firefairy's face, and broken teeth scatter.

Angelo cracks his neck viciously, the shallow wound in his throat already healing, and rips off a handful of the blue fairy's shirt to wipe his face clean. "Jesus Christ on a racehorse. Can't a man walk the street in peace?"

A frustrated scream wells cold in Diamond's throat. No trace of poison. Stupidfae missed her shot. Opportunity wastified.

He spits, casual, pinkshimmer stained with blue fairy gore. Blame their rival gang. Ange'll believify. "DiLuca scumfuckers."

"Most like." Ange prods the girl's greasy black wings with his toe, cold eyes calculating. "These assholes are freelancers. I've used 'em meself." He claps Diamond's bare shoulder. "Appreciate you coming by. Nice bladework. Find me who bought these dickheads and I'll let you kill him, too."

Diamond grins sickly. Usually, the vampire virus makes them faintly warm, like a fever. But Ange's fingers are cold, his palm stony hard. "On it. Appreciamated, boss."

Tony spears him on a suspicious yellow glare. "What you hanging out back for, anyway? Jerking off?"

Crippled lizardman doesn't trust him. Diamond's worming himself into Ange's confidence, undermining Tony at every deceitalicious opportunity. Diamond's chewed his way up the hierarchy lately, played some wicked sly fuckery on snaky Joey DiLuca, Ange's top gang rival. Ange liked Diamond's work, even if Joey and his bloodthirsty vampire funboy, Vincent, are still alive.

Discomfort spikes his wings, the delicate leading edge aching. The panes are only just healing where Joey's minions smashified them to shards, and it still fucking hurts. But no matterfy. The DiLucas did him favors in the end. They killed Ange's mean-ass cousins, and now, Diamond's the best Ange has left.

All in the plannification, see. Get close. Make Ange trustify him. Get even closer. And strike.

He winks back at Tony, glitter flashing. "Nah. Looking for a horny lizardboy to suck my cock. Wanna try?"

Tony scowls. "Or maybe checking up on your handiwork."

Diamond returns his stare, level.

But Ange just laughs and shoves Tony's shoulder. "Give it a rest. Let's get drinking. Coming, D-man?"

"Sure-sure." Diamond shoves nonchalant hands in his pockets. But as they skip the queue and walk into the club, the hidden poison vial burns accusation in his palm, and he seethes with frustration.

Fuckity shit. Vampire not dead. No idea if the poison works. And now LaFaro the Lizard suspectifies. Already, Tony slinks off through fragrant smoke, beady yellow eyes tracking Diamond from across the dance floor.

Diamond flashes his glamour in threat, sparks showering, and Tony slips him a sly two-lidded wink and skulks away. Tony is faeborn, one of those weird human–fae hybrids. Nasty lizard freakboy, senseless taunterizer of fairies and slipper of sexdrugs in girly gin fizzes. Jealous of Diamond for stealing Ange's favor. For his part, Diamond's got nothing against faeborn. It's assholes he doesn't like.

Music's heavy vibration heats his muscles, the delicious smells of flesh and alcohol a teasing pleasure. Angelo drags Diamond to the bar, and the girl brings him glowing fairy wine, chilled, rising apricot mist and a sparkly dusting of hallucinogen.

"To dead DiLuca fuckwits." Angelo clinks glasses, his own a bourbon and blood on a chili chaser, and drinks deep.

"Amen." Diamond forces a smile, the wine starry on his tongue and pleasantly warm. Already, his sinuses twinge, a sparkalicious rush. Flashes of color and breath, a cool caress, soft sighs.

Ange grins, a hungry predator. "Oh, hello, love."

Diamond chokes.

Feathersoft dark hair, smooth on creamy shoulders. Red satin dress, luscious hips swaying, a flash of dark violet eyes.

He swallows wine and acid, sick, but can't tear his eyes away.

Rosa slides a slim arm around Ange's neck, and they kiss, lingering, his hand creeping up her curving thigh, her long scarlet nails sliding into his hair. But her eyes flicker open, and her gaze locks on Diamond's. Hot. Sultry. Mockifying.

His fist jerks tight, and the glass splinters in his hand.

Wine splashes, and glowing pink blood oozes hot. The pain is delicious, stroking his desire. Bitch. Traitor.

Vampire's whore. Ange infected her, sure. But virus-sharing takes two.

Ange darts him a cool, *dare you to complainify* glare. "Darlin', you remember Diamond?"

Rosa licks ripe lips, and props one hand on her hip, showing off that glorious body he can no longer touch. "Of course." Her voice, deep and husky like a whore, a hot caress on his cock. "How could I forget?"

Diamond nods, twitches a smile, shakes broken glass from his bleeding hand. But his blood slithers hot. He hasn't forgotten, either. Not her body slick under his, her spicy kisses zinging his mouth, the intoxicating chiliwarmth of her breasts. Not her flesh so smooth and tight around him, her soft moan, her hair's freshmint whisper on his face. Not the thrill that tingled his bonehollows when he wrapped her in a gentle glowing embrace and whispered *I love you*.

Not the coldsick betrayal when he found vampire marks on her thigh. The empty heartshock that whatever it takifies to keep this gloryvibrant woman—the only woman who ever laid siege to his glass-walled heart and won—he doesn't got it.

Diamond isn't used to feeling inadequate. Always magical, strong, beautiful, rich, charmified. None of that means shit now.

Things disintegrated, that night. Rosa tauntified him, flaunted her scars. He . . . hurt her. They can't ever go back.

Rosa grins, wicked, and her flashing fangtips make his skin crawl. He forces another smile. "Gotta go, Ange, see my boy Jasper about a score. Letcha know about that thing outside. Have a good night, Rosa."

Aching, he turns and loses himself in the crowd. Laser lights glint off his glassy wings, shedding shatterfied rainbows on the floor, and his bleeding fingers clench tight around the poison vial in his pocket. No, she's a nasty lying whore. He doesn't want her back. And the part he does want—the part where he still had some self-respectification, when he'd never touch a girl in anger and still believed he deserves to be alive—well, that part can't be recovered. Ever.

So let it go. Revenge is all he has left. Hell, what else is there to do? Angelo stole her. Angelo infected her with his filthydirt virusicality. Angelo made her a monster, and deserves to die.

Diamond has worked for Ange for years. They're practicamally family, and without family loyalty, who can you trustify? Gangland is a vicious backstabbing swamp of untruths, and enemies are fair game. But you take care of what's yours. Right down to the lowest sparkle-grubbing puke or skanky faeborn muscleguy.

You protectify your own. You don't seduce his girlfriend and turn her into a ravenous beastie. Even if she wants you to.

He shoulders to the bar at the other end, stretching his wings carelessly to make room, and crunches frustrated elbows on the glass. The warm surface reflects neonblue, the ghostly echo of his envy. Determination burns like firefae oil over his heart. He'll think up another plan. Another tricksy vampire deathtrap.

But Ange is too clever, too vampire-strong for a knife. Three dead fairy assassins prove that. And he can't just slip the greendeath in a drink or creep up while the hypersensed prick is sleeping. He'll be caught in an instant.

He'll just have to thinkify another way. A fabulicious, Ange-proof way. The ice-hearted bastard's gotta be vulnerable somewhere, and Diamond's crystalline faetalents have a way of winkling out weaknificality.

He scans the crowd, making sure no one's watching. Across the room, there's Vincent DiLuca, his enemy, crazy-ass vampire, slurping blood from a glass and giving Diamond a cheeky wave. Diamond flashes him a glamour-rich scarlet fuck-off. Rabid bloodsucking asshole. Rules sayem no gangfights at Unseelie Court. Only reason Vincent's still breathing.

Over by the steps, Tony LaFaro's already chatting up girls, oblivious. A giggling drunk fairy with bright nectarine wings leans against his misshapen shoulder, and her lips slur and dribble with whatever faedrunk poison Tony's slipped her. His slanted yellow eyes shine cruel, sly claws wandering onto her dress. Scorn burns Diamond's fingertips. Dirtified little rat.

But Ange and Rosa are still at the bar. Stealthy, Diamond inhales and reaches out invisible glassfae talent.

Colors leech like waterpaint. Shapes waver and fade, translucent, a glassy matrix of lines and glowing shadows, and he weaves his senses among them, ghostlike. Closer, caressing the air like velvet, the soft whisper of hair, warm desire tingling, a fairy girl's haunted breath. The bar, damp glass aglow with neon, slick plastic cash, icy moisture trickling on a drink. Creep closer still, and here's Ange, dark and sinister, his cold gray eyes burning black in this strange shadowview.

Diamond leans against the bar, casual, and feels his cautious way, his skin tight and hot with magicweird sensation. Smooth, ageless vampire skin, no feverheat. Heartbeat steady and cold, even though Rosa is whispering her hand in his lap and nibbling his ear with her tiny sharp teeth.

Acid froths in Diamond's throat at the scorching bitterness of her desire. Since he lost her, he's felt nothing except disgust and contempt for himself, so clueless and unable to keep her. He can't forgivify.

In his shadowy magicsight, Rosa slips her finger over Angelo's lips, tempting him. Ange nips her, blooding his tongue in a hot burst. She sighs in pleasure, and smears her bloodstained finger on her own lips before leaning in for a kiss.

Ange nudges Rosa's chin up and strikes. Teeth flashing, skin ripping, the dulcet squelch of tearing flesh. She gasps, lost. Angelo drags her head back to bite deeper, claiming her body and blood. God, it's so primitive, so sensual, and pain and desire echo like dark music in Diamond's body. He wants to scream, be sick, touch himself.

But Ange's skin doesn't twitch. He doesn't get a hard-on. When he sucks deep and swallows, his pulse jumps slightly.

That's all.

Diamond pulls back, and glass shatters in his ears as the magic dissolves.

Every time, it's same-same. No doubts, no flaws, no weaknificality. The hunger's there—oh, it's there, all right, the need screaming in Ange's ancient blood like the dirty virusfever it is, and it isn't pretty inside Ange's head, not after 350 years of slaughterfication—but his passion is cold, calmified, wrapped in the icy straitjacket of centuries-perfectified control.

When Ange loses it, it's explosive. But it happens only when he wants it to.

Diamond's nerves tweak sharp. Can't sneakem up. Can't distractify. It'll take something specialicious to put Ange off guard.

Something Diamond doesn't have.

Just like he didn't have what it took to keep Rosa. All the one-night-stands in the world can't change that. Sometimes they cling, those nameless girls. He always shakes them off. They're not her. None of them ever will be.

Melancholy lurks at his mind's edge like a black crystal ghost. In his pocket, his little mirrored case tempts him, square edges tracing a seductive trail against his thigh. Forget. Drift away. Go somewhere else.

His mouth dries in anticipation of the nectarsweet crystals inside. He pops the shiny case open, cuts a tiny glitterblack line with one practiced claw, and inhales.

Lemonbombs burst fresh and cold in his sinuses. Things jolt brighter, clearer, closer, like chemical contact lenses slipped over his eyes. His blood rushes tight in his veins, glowing under his translucent skin like a pulsing scarlet web.

Energy, pure excitement, stolen on a kiss from some unsuspectifying creature by a lie-bright fairy spellworker. Or maybe not so unsuspecting. Sparkle is crafted from emotions, memories, dreams, and some people will sellify anything for what the fairies offer, pleasure, blood, a few moments of dizzy oblivion. Sparkle is Diamond's business, and he knows where it comes from. Tonight, he doesn't care.

He shakes his head like a dog, silvery tears spraying, and slides the case back into his pocket with ultrasharp movements. Already his muscles tighten, itching for action, touch, pain. In a few seconds, he'll have a hard-on. Shouldn't be difficult to get it attended to. And maybe screwing some random flirtgirl will take his mind off *her*. . . .

Sweet female sorrow fires his tongue electric.

He glances along the bar, compelled. The bloodfairy girl next to him is crying, lovely red hair messified with cherryblood and tears. Teethmarks pierce her slender neck, a bruise shadowing her chin. Blood streaking those luscious swelling breasts.

Pretty thing. Maybe a vampire boyfriend, or some asshole trying to get lucky. Seems everyone's in a mood tonight.

Diamond's eyes water, dazzled with hot druglaced focus. She isn't Rosa. None of them are. But the same anger flows in his bonehollows like lava. Dirty virus-rats, chewing on this girl's perfect milk chocolate skin. She's so delicate, her sparklygreen eyes jewelbright with tears. And those luscious cherrypop lips . . .

He eyes her speculatively, taking in endless tanned legs, narrow waist, delicate papery wings. He's a mind to kissify those bruises away. See if he can't make her forget her tears for a while. Mmm . . .

But waitify one second. He knows her. Isn't she—?

Fuck.

He glances around for his boy Jasper, but the lying weaselfae is nowhere in sight. He sighs, but he can't pretend he didn't seeify her, and that old covetous instinct caresses the back of his neck with seductive fingers. *Mine. Want. Mine.*

Pretty girl, covered in blood, crying into her vodka. Desperation flooding her eyes. Velvet helplessness richifying her scent.

His sensitive nose twitches, his drugstung flesh hot and deeply aware, and he swallows a dark twinge of conscience. Obvio-liciously, the pretty lady needs his helpification. In gangland, you protectify your own, right? Even if she's your own boy's woman and the sexiest girl in the room, trouble-icality in a juicy bite-size package.

Especially if Jasper can't be bothered to take care of her. But Jasper's temper is notorious. So who the hell was dumb enough to bite her? Curiouser and curiouser.

Diamond's skin prickles, warm and dangerous with intent, and he swallows and skids his stool over to her.

3

"Ember? You okay?"

Cool voice, crisp with bellchime harmonics. His rosy glow warmed my skin, and I glimpsed sharp gemstone claws, a crystalline jaw, fiber-optic hair shimmering in laserlight rainbows.

My stomach twisted. Jasper's weird glassfae boss. Who taught Jasper everything he knew about pushing sparkle to teenagers and kicking the shit out of gang pukes and screwing cute little fairy tarts behind his girlfriend's back.

I sniffled, dragging my hand across my eyes. Too late to pretend I hadn't seen, that I didn't care. "What you want?"

No doubt he expected trouble for Jasper from me. Likely he'd try to placate me, soothe my temper, shut me up.

But he just studied me distantly, taking in the blood, the cuts, the smeared tears on my cheeks. A weird creature, this Diamond. Clearly flesh and blood—nothing made of glass could smell like that, all warm and rosefresh—but his translucent skin glowed like faint pink neon, the shadows of his muscles curving underneath. Slanted crystal cheekbones, liquid berry eyes, lashes long and glitterbright. Glassfibered hair, long and shining like rain in sunlight. And eerie, luminous wings like fine quartz, a few broken edges glinting sharp. Nightclub lights glittered over him like jewels, reflecting in ripples over the shadowed floor.

Dangerous, sharp, ironstrong yet fragile. A perfect roseglass angel.

Pity he was a violent kiss-ass gangboy like all the rest.

He blinked, and faeweird prescience slid grasping fingers into my skull, stripping me of guile. "Eww. What happenated you?"

I shook myself loose with a sharp crack of glamour. I didn't like him. Didn't like how he saw through me with insidious glassfae talent. How he flirted with me in front of Jasper, careless and condescending like he was doing me a favor. How he looked at me sometimes, those intense ruby eyes raking shivers down my spine, like he knew something I didn't. And he was sparklefucked. I could tell by his wet gleaming eyes, his quivering fingers, the glowing pulse throbbing in his throat.

I ruffled my wings, like I had it all under control. "Nothing. I'm just great, Diamond. Like you give a shit."

He leaned strong, graceful wrists on the bar, showing off glasscarved muscles. His flashy fashion sense almost made me smile. Only an arrogant glow-in-the-dark fairy boy could carry off a sleeveless limegreen shirt and soft plumpurple leather pants and not look totally queer.

His claws jittered across the glass. "Have it your way. Just polite-ifying."

I wiped away scarletstained tears. His weird English

was kinda cute, all the same. He talked too fast, like his mind sprinted ahead of his mouth, and his words jumbled and flowered new syllables. It was annoyingly disarming. "If you're running interference, you suck at it. You're supposed to intercept me before I see him?"

A blank. "Seeify who what?"

Laughter snorted wet from my nose. "Screw you. Like you didn't know all along."

"About what?"

"About that, smart-ass." I stabbed my finger over my shoulder and chugged my drink dry, cool moisture dripping from the glass.

He glanced back, stainedglass wings rippling, and I couldn't help but stare. He was decorative, I'd give him that. Half a head shorter than Jasper, but none of Jasper's narrow fae slimness. No, Diamond was all hard glassy muscle, his weird translucent skin smooth and tight, faint scarlet veins an intriguing web beneath. When he moved, muscles stretched and bunched, fluid in a warm rosy glow.

Curiosity tingled my palms. Glassfae were strange. Improbable. Those churchwindow wings looked so delicate. For him to fly, all that dangerous muscle had to be fairylight. What would that ultrasmooth chest feel like under my fingertips? Blown glass? Cold, like crystal? Or soft, like skin, warm, slick, inviting? . . .

I swallowed and dropped my gaze, my cheeks warm. Like trouble, that's what. All the same, these cocky gangboys. Too damn intriguing for their own good.

He spied Jasper and turned back, elegant for such a bulky guy. He had the grace to look embarrassed, gold glimmering deep in his ruby eyes. "Oh. That."

Was that sympathy? Warmth spilled over my heart,

and I quenched it. Everyone knew Diamond went through girls like toilet paper. Use 'em up and flush 'em when you're done. "Yeah, *that*. Seriously, am I invisible or something?"

"It's nothing. Just biznificality." Rainbows danced in his long glassy hair.

His *fairy boys will be sluts* insouciance tickled warm indignation through my limbs. I plonked my glass on the bar. "Oh, sure. That makes me feel better, coming from you. Where's your tart-of-the-evening? Broken her already? You get them from vending machines, or what?"

"Moron."

"Excuse me?"

His gaze caught mine again, glowing violet. "Jasper. He's an idiot. If you were my lady, I wouldn't be fucking some other girl. I'd be fucking you."

Stupidly, I blushed. He flashed me an unreasonably scintillating smile, and before I could collect my wits, he'd tilted my chin up, exposing my wounds, already half-healed by virus-soaked vampire spit.

I jerked back, but he held me, ducking to peer at my cuts. "Let me lookify."

Mortification stained my sweat bloody. "It's nothing. Let go."

He tugged me closer, probing my slashed skin with surprisingly gentle claws. His voice clanged, discordant. "Who did this?"

"No one." I twisted, but he stroked me, soothing my bruised skin, easing the wound open to look for corruption. More a caress than an examination. His hair tumbled on my arm, not sharp but springy and soft. He leaned closer, his rosy warmth inflaming me, and I wanted to squirm away.

My wings tingled, aware. His tenderness embarrassed

me. I didn't care what he thought of me, but somehow I didn't want to tell him I'd done it for a strange fiery gemstone and one of Jasper's smiles. I swallowed, feeling his fingers move on my skin. Maybe he wasn't the thoughtless puke I'd imagined. "It doesn't matter, okay? It was an accident."

"Not on my patch. You're one of ours. Tell me who bit you, and I'll rip the skanksucker's fangs out."

My blood iced. So matter-of-fact. That was all he cared about. His patch. His possessions.

They were all the fucking same. If some guy gave me a hard time or looked at me the wrong way, Jasper would invariably break the guy's nose. Not because he cared how I felt. Because he owned me, and no one else was allowed.

Why did I expect Diamond to be any different? I shouldn't be disappointed.

But I was.

I grabbed his shining pink wrist and yanked my chin away. "Leave it, okay? It's nothing. Jasper told me to. He wanted me to steal from the guy. I swapped my blood on purpose. You got a problem with that?"

He broke my grip, his effortless fairy strength both threat and promise. Shiny contempt flashed his eyes silver. "Hey, it's your choosings, angel. You wanna put out for favors? Go right ahead. But don't fucking cry about it when they stick it in."

His scorn ripped me naked, a razorsharp mirror of my own shame. Fury burned my moonrich blood bright. Before I could hold back, my hand flashed out and I slapped him.

Right across his beautiful crystalline cheek.

My palm stung hot. His face glowed brighter, and

shock lit magenta flames in his eyes, but I didn't care. I was too incensed at his goddamn attitude. "Don't you judge me, sparkleboy. You don't fucking know anyth—Ugh!"

In a rosy flash, he grabbed my forearm and yanked me off my stool.

I stumbled against his hot glassy body, and my breath squeezed tight.

I wriggled, but he held me. I tried to look away, but he captured my gaze with his—not cold and contemptuous, but hot, intense, curious—and my guts melted.

His breath scorched my lips, warm glass and roses, only an inch or two away. "Do that again, and I'll do it back."

His glasschime murmur tinkled through me, dark and warm with promise. His bunched muscles slid on my limbs, damp with his rose-perfumed sweat, and damn it if his skin didn't feel nice on mine. Improbably smooth, inviting, that beautiful hair pouring over my arms like a hot sparkling waterfall. His pulse against my breasts, a shock of pleasure. His arousal against my thigh a temptation, though doubtless that impressive hard-on had more to do with a snort of glittering black-jewel than it had to do with me.

Rebellion fired my blood. All my fear, my sorrow, all that energy I'd stored up tonight begged for release. I wanted to run, fly, scream my rage at the stars, do all the naughty crazy things that being weak and blood-fae and Jasper's girlfriend forbade me.

I bared my pointed teeth, wickedness flaming like magnesium in my veins. "Dare ya."

His eyes glinted violet with challenge. "So kitty's got claws after all. Wanna showify?"

God, he was so fucking self-assured. His lips curled into a smile, and I thought I'd snap in two with rage.

But I didn't. Instead, a tingling ache flared in my wingjoints, and suddenly my mouth dried. Lights prismed through his translucent wingpanes, shadowing me in dark rainbows that smelled of roses and hot male skin, and the images that flooded my head weren't sordid and violent but hot and sensual.

My skin zinged fresh, alight, and I tried to stop staring at his mouth.

This wasn't happening. Moontide waxing in my blood, right? Making me horny, careless, indiscriminate. Just a little harmless rebellion. No way was I attracted to some cocky pinkglass gangpuke who called me a tart. Even if deep down, I feared he was right.

But my body wasn't listening. My pulse thudded, demanding things I didn't want to give. I tried to talk, but only a whisper came out. "Get off me, asshole."

He just gripped me harder, his breath tight against my breasts. "Name-calling? Fine. You're a whore, Ember. Sellifying yourself for safety. You blame Jasper but you're a big girl."

Too close. His sparklesharp scent dizzied me, the play of his muscles against mine a hot confusion. "Bully," I whispered. "Picker-on of little girls. Can't take it if you're not in control."

"Coward. Scarified little hider. Afraid to take what you want." His hot ruby gaze caressed my face, my hair, slid downward to my lips.

Heat pooled between my legs, slick and hungry. His fingertips played wicked games in the sensitive place between my wingjoints, and my voice dried to nothing. "Don't do that."

He didn't stop. "Why? Afraid you might likify?"

I'd like it, all right. I licked my lips, tempted. "You afraid I wouldn't?"

His tiny hot chuckle caressed my mouth. "Mmm. Sounds like a challenge. I'm in if you are."

Moonshine flamed in my blood, and I leaned in.

And my nose twitched with the familiar, tingling honeyscent of Jasper.

Diamond released me in a swift ripple of glamour that shocked me breathless. His rosy glow dissolved, and he *dimmed*, leaving only a shimmering ghost and a faint scarlet shadow on the floor. Jesus. How did he do that?

How *did* he do that? He'd barely touched me, yet my body still ached. My skin still tingled, frustrated, my lips stinging wet.

I tossed my hair straight and wiped my mouth, flushing. I knew the glass-ass freak was still there. I could see him, hiding in the crowd, a faint pink outline that could have been an illusion, a reflection. He flicked his shadow-wings casually, caught his breath with a swift sigh. Looked anywhere but at me.

Pretending nothing had happened.

Well, nothing had happened. Nothing would ever happen. Cocky glow-in-the-dark prick. Taking advantage of me like that.

Jasper's wirestrong arms slipped around me, his long-muscled fairy body hard against my side. Deep violet eyes curled in wild blue lashes, gorgeous death-white skin, long charcoal hair torn artfully jagged, the most perfectly curved, mauvesweet lips in Melbourne.

Lips that just made love to another girl's mouth. His honeyspice scent weakened my limbs, and my pulse lurched. For all I knew, he'd gone down on her right there in the dark.

I shivered, and behind him I spied shadow-Diamond sidling nonchalantly away. Like he'd done this before. Bastard.

But Jasper's embrace sank me into familiar fearful territory. Guilt flushed me damp, and I hated it. I hadn't done anything bad. But instinctively, my confidence sank, my mind racing for something, anything I'd done wrong, any small action or movement or thought that could have raised my lover's ire.

Like, I dunno, nearly kissing his boss? My skin burned at the memory. Jesus in a jam jar. What was I thinking?

Jasper's kiss brushed my cheekbone, and I jumped, my heart melting at the same time. I wanted him to comfort me, stroke my hair, tell me everything was okay. I wanted to slam my fist into his face and fly away.

"Did you get it?" His voice sparkled down my spine, dark and sultry with dirty earthfae come-hither.

Not *Emmy, hi, how's it going?* or *Are you okay?* or *Gosh, I'm sorry you had to bloodfuck some random guy just because I said so. Let me make it up to you.*

Just, *Did you get it?* like I was some gang puke he ordered around. Like I worked for him.

I swallowed, the half-healed bite on my throat hurting like poison. "Yeah, I got it."

"Show me, pretty." He captured me for a kiss, and I fumbled the clasp of my velvet clutch bag. The curve of my back tingled under his palm, and my sensitive wingjoints ached. Damn him.

I pulled back and popped my bag open to pull out the gemstone. My blood still slicked it, vampire spit trailing in a sticky string. I wiped wet hair from my throat, my gaze slipping. "Here."

Jasper took it, a greedy red spark lighting his eyes.

"Oh, that's good. That's most wonderfully good. Did I tell you lately how special you are?" He wrapped me in his arms, his body pressed to mine, and danced me lightly backwards on a flutter of soft blackvelvet wings.

His embrace dizzied me, made me think of chili hot chocolate, a crackling fire, deep silken fur caressing my back. Not for the first time I wondered what wicked spells lurked on his scent that he affected me like this. I licked dry lips, his honeycomb taste still tempting on my tongue. I was leaving him, remember? "Umm . . . look. We need to talk—"

"How precious you are?" He kissed me, tilting me backwards so I had to squeal and flutter to stay up, the blood washing rapidly to my head. "How beautiful?" Another kiss, dark and smoky with excitement, his lips trailing to my gorestained throat. "How deadly, tasty gorgeous . . . mmm. God, Em, you make me hot, you bad girl." His arm crushed my waist, my wings trailing on the floor. He nuzzled aside my flimsy wet top, and my treacherous nipple sprang hard in his mouth. I gasped at the sensation, hot and raw deep inside, and my limbs flushed weak.

"C'mon, Jay-jay, can't screwify around in the gutter all night."

That guiltwrapped roseglass scent invaded my stupor. I struggled, my whisper rough. "Let me up!"

Diamond grinned at us, glowing as brightly as ever, a magenta-haloed angel. He'd wiped my blood from his fingers, straightened his hair where I'd messed it.

My wings crawled with embarrassment. As smooth a liar as Jasper, and as arrogant. Obviously, he thought we had something to hide.

Jasper swept me to my feet, but he didn't cover me where he'd bared my breast. As if he showed me off, his pretty bloodfae prize. He slung his arm around my neck and nuzzled a laughing kiss below my ear. "Watch what ya say about my girl, shitbrain. Darlin', don't you mind him."

Flushing, I tugged my top into place, trying to swallow my awkwardness. "Umm . . . hey."

"Evening, beautiful." Diamond took my palm and kissed it, his usual meaningless flirtation. His warm lips teased me, but his eyes were glacial, contempt flashing clear like ice.

My stomach squeezed hot, and I snatched my hand back.

Diamond smiled coolly. "You meeting Ange, Jaspy-joo? Better lose your candy."

Angry ants crawled under my skin. More insults. As if his own profession—that'd be sticky gang puke and sparkle pusher—was so goddamn noble.

I wanted to stare him down, say, *Who the fuck are you calling "candy," crystal boy?* but my treacherous gaze kept sliding aside. Snarky glass-ass bastard. Still, gotta give him points for attitude. Anyone who called my hot-tempered boy Jaspy-joo had guts.

Jasper opened his mouth to retort, but settled for a sharp-toothed grin. He twirled one of my red curls in shiny black claws. "In a second. Just doing some doings. Gotta get me some Ember-time."

Diamond wrinkled his cute pointed nose. "Better get in line."

My heart clenched tight, but Jasper just giggled, rich. He thought it a compliment. Trusted his boss implicitly not to fool around with his girl.

Their stupid machofae code made me sick. I wanted to jump up and down, claw at my hair, scream, *What is wrong with you people? You're gangsters. You'd sell your own legs if you thought it'd make you fly faster. What's with the got-your-back bullshit?*

Diamond winked at me, dripping irony, and I scowled, my wings bristling. This asshole really pushed my buttons. Everyone thinks we bloodfae are bimbos, good for nothing but pleasure, but his condescending stare maddened me beyond sense. One minute he's about to kiss me; the next, he goes out of his way to make me feel worthless.

Well, screw him in a pile of pickles. I didn't care what he thought of me.

But my skin still prickled hot. I wanted to squint my eyes shut, disappear into the background. Angry breeze ruffled my wings, and I shot him the darkest glare I could muster. "Screw you, jewelboy. Fucked up any kids with sparkle lately? Hear you sell it cheaper to the youngsters."

"Hush it, Emmy." Jasper squeezed my shoulder in warning. His claws dug in painfully, and the old fear speared me cold. *Naughty Emmy, annoying the boss. Be quiet, or I'll have to punish you.*

But Diamond just draped his hot claret gaze over my chest. "Nice bloodstain, candygirl. Chargify by the mouthful?"

Shame scorched my nerves, but I raised him a coquettish eyebrow. "Why? Want some?"

A crystalsharp laugh. "No, thanks. Like me a girl who can make up her mind."

"Whatever." Asshole. I tried to look away, keep it casual. But my gaze kept dragging back to his perfect, narrow face, those sharpglitter cheekbones, his ripe beestung lips, and it occurred to me that maybe

Jasper had only the second most beautiful mouth in Melbourne.

A silent windchime chuckle tinkled in my ears, and my nerves strung taut. Glassfae had weirdsight. No doubt he'd heard everything I was thinking.

Well, the dirty eavesdropper wouldn't need weird-sight to hear this. I opened my mouth, vitriol searing my tongue loose.

But strange images flooded hot, wobbling my knees, and the words caught in my throat. His gaze fixed on mine, distant but inescapable. Grasping fingers of glassy shadow slid into my skull, and I could do nothing to stop them.

Blood, sloshing over my vision in scarlet waves, sliding down my neck's taut sinews. The vampire's cruel teeth in my throat, digging, raping, feeding until I squirmed with disgust and horrid longing that made me ache. Jasper's crueler kiss, unnerving, claws teasing me, velvet wings a dark caress that shivered my skin. His pale strong limbs entwining with mine, his hardness filling me, mouth on my swollen wingjoints, double-jointed fingers wrapped around my wrists, the echo of our urgent pleasure spearing deep.

I choked, and fought, my glamour rippling hot on my skin, but the flood wouldn't stop. Despair, loneliness, constant terror that Jasper would leave me for a prettier, more compliant girl. Doubt forcing like cold wire into my skull, leaving me grasping for affection, attention, one tiny sign that he cared for me.

And a flush of reluctant rosetinted compassion warmed my heart like sunshine.

It shocked me rigid. Diamond watched me, relentless, scorn tainting his sulky rose lips. But for a moment, his accusing gaze slipped.

My glamour recoiled, sharp and electric. Now the fucker dared to feel sorry for me? Far too much like Jasper, this Diamond, cocky and dominant and charming like the devil when he wished. I'm a sucker for the charming ones. Look where it's gotten me.

I wriggled, frantic, desperate to escape, and with a final glassy crack, Diamond's magic broke.

Mirrors flashed, cold and real, my own reflection jolting me from my trance. I ripped my gaze away, flushing. No fair. He knew far too much about me. Damn him and his vulgar glasstalent. It didn't make him special or desirable. Without his fairy tricks, he was about as sensitive as a punch in the face.

Anger ripped my skin raw, liberating, and I spat through gritted teeth. "Don't do that. Don't you *ever* come near me again, you crystalbrain prick."

Jasper grabbed my arm, claws digging in deep and dangerous. "Shush now, Emmy. Won't be a minute, Diamond, just some little seconds for darklysweet fun." He squeezed my arm cruelly, and pain speared up the bonehollow into my shoulder. "Just gotta see a man about a thing. Catchya in a flash."

And he dragged me off, but not before Diamond's gaze caught mine once more, a dark ruby glare mixing pity and bitter disdain that scorched deep into my soul like a rusty brand.

4

Diamond watches the pretty bloodfairy go, sympathy and disgust coiling his nerves like wire.

She's beautiful, all right. Sinfully long legs, brown thighs, her dusky back smooth and rich like meltified chocolate. That cherrybright hair, so crisp and crushable. Long graceful wings, so delicate and fragile. And the sweetest ass he's ever seen on a woman, so ripe and round, it'd pop fruitylicious in his teeth like a peach. . . .

Ploonk.

A vile idea pops like poison.

He stares, wings itching with delicious deceit. Candy blood. Big innocent eyes to drown in. Long smooth legs, succulent breasts, lips begging for a kiss.

Tasty bloodwhore who looks like an angel.

If anyone can tempt a jaded 350-year-old vampire to carelessness, it's Ember.

Slip her the poison. Feed her to Angelo. Scream-bleed-die, vampire—and good riddimance, too.

Crafty delight throbs in Diamond's blood. Perfectification. Ordinarily, Ange is cold and restrained. It's how he got where he is. But every now and then, like a man who hasn't gotten off in too long, his hunger gets the better of him.

A sexy little ingenue like Ember—her dusky skin glowing with tastylicious bloodfae nectar—Ember is the perfect bait.

And that's a reallytruly foul idea.

He rolls his wingjoints, sweating. The poison won't hurt her, right? It's especiamally for vampires, or at least that's what his mad fairy pharmacist toldified. Just a little fever, a headache, a dizzy skull. Maybe a few other side effects. She won't be hurt. What the hell does he care for his conscience? That weak-willed wormything bled out on the floor and died, the night Rosa tore his heart out.

But it's not right. He can't feedify a pretty girl to a vampire. Can he?

He grits sharp teeth and shakes his head to empty it, rainbows flashing on the floor from his hair. But the plan's there. He can't unthinkify it. And she's already selling herself, right? He'll just make her a business propomasition. An offer she can't refuse . . .

But it isn't just her angelic face and tastylicious body that haunt him. Fuck it if he can't still taste her desperation, a bright honeyache on the back of his tongue. Still smell her, rich and warm and womanly, her earthydark scent of blood and kisses watering his mouth. Still feel the shock on his cheek where she hit him, the delicious press of her pulsing thigh against his cock.

But also tension, tight and trembling, her liquidgreen eyes hyperaware. His glassfae talent stripped her bare, the way she longs for Jasper's approval, her utter despairification when it's lost. Diamond's sympathy mocks him. He knows that feeling. But he didn't need faesight to see she's frightened.

Acid compassion stings holes in his heart. She's

terrified. Screaming for help. Scrabbling to escape, like a scarified rabbit caught in steeltrap jaws.

Well, that'll learnify her to feed a vampire. Right? Rosa fed a vampire, and broke Diamond's heart. Ember's no better.

But his gaze follows her as she twirls across the floor in Jasper's embrace, and his claws jitter across the glass bar, his nerves wired tight. He protectifies his own. He should be helping her. Not using her as a murder weapon.

Already Jasper's fingers crawl onto her back like a bony white spider, his tongue curling around her sexy little pointed ear. Her pretty silver skirt stretches tight around those lickable thighs as they dance. She smiles, the tip of her tongue teasing cute sharp teeth, and for one hellscorched moment, desire dizzies Diamond blind.

He struggles for breath, his body a tense, hot demand. So he wants her. He wants lots of girls, the way other fairies covet jewels or gold or shiny things. Ever since Rosa, he's drowned himself in meaningless liaisons, hunting for something that'll make him care.

And now here's Ember, a luscious, feisty angel he can't have, and it's not just the hard-on making him shiver. It's the old burning need to protect, possessify, spreading over his skin like a feral scorchrash.

If Jasper's hurting her, he'll rip the dusty bastard's toeclaws out.

Except he won't. She's not his to look after. She never will be.

Foolish guilt scrapes Diamond's nerves raw. Ember's not the first prettyfae to fall for Jasper's charmifications, and all along he's known Jasper's lying to her, sleeping with other girls, his dusty earthfae fingers creeping places they shouldn't.

He slices shardlike claws into his palms, itching to be rid of this stupid compassion. Pain slides hot and relaxing into his veins. Luminous pink blood pools, his thoughts shimmering clear like quicksilver.

Focus, D. Don't softify. It'll only bite your ass later.

He breathes deep, calming, savoring the nighttime taste of sex and flesh, and stalks away from the bar. The crowd filters around him, fragrant bodies, tortured breath, deathmetal's razor chords. His shadow glows and ripples in the dark like bloodstained water.

Absently, he licks his bleeding palm clean, and the drugrich blood fires his defiance like stars. Ember's not his problem, right? Not enough hours in the night. He's got sparkle to sell, gangpuke ass to kickify, vampire mobsters to murder, a squillion and twelve things to do and none of them involve screwing . . . umm, pauseify, rewind . . . none of them involve rescuing sexy damsels in distress.

It's none of Diamond's biznificality. Not his can of wormatrons to sidle up to her, slide her pretty hand into his, say, *Hey, sugarplum fairy, you know your boyfriend's sticking his cock in other chicks? There, now, don't cry. Wanna come home with me instead? Mine's bigger.*

Yessum. If she's living on Jasper's money, she can put up with Jasper's bullshit. Don't see her complainamating when he showers her in shinygifts and treats her like a glitterfairy queen. And here she is tonight, all bloodified and sweaty, holes ripped raw in her throat by some greasy essence-sucking monster.

It's not Diamond's problem. If candygirl wants to whorify herself to filthyscum bloodsuckers, that's her cactus pie.

But for some reason, his anger won't fade. His tense muscles won't ease. Just the image of her doing it makes him hard. Tilting her luscious brown throat back for the monster's bite, that sexy hair slipping off one shoulder, her dark lips parting in pleasure, her long throaty sigh . . .

Yeah. None of his biznification. Right.

His heart aches, stubborn remnants of guilt, and he sighs. Fuck it. He can't use Ember for bait. It's not right. Have to thinkify something else.

A warm finger of scent caresses his cheek, and he snaps back to here and now, sweat fresh on his palms and a throbbing ache in his cock.

Spice and honey. Dark, familiar, frightening.

Rosa.

Hot rocks tumble in his guts, and he twitches his nose and snaps himself dim.

His vision shimmers and clears. Colors pale, shapes lose their reality, fading to translucent windows. In his dark glamourshadow, he's ghostly, almost invisible. Normally, it's soothing, this darkglass world where no one can see. Metal gleams gemlike, the air smells clean and unsullied by his violence. Even the noise falls uncluttered, each harmonic tinkling clear like glassy chimes.

He doesn't care. He just needs to get out.

"Diamond, don't. Please."

Rosa's voice vibrates his bones, low and husky and full of pain that stabs straight to his aching balls. She could always see him, no matter how dim he flickered. Warm fingers catch his sharp wing edge, and that too-familiar spicy scent snaps his spine tight.

Not her. Not now.

But he can't help but turn.

Blueblack hair, crisp and sculptured on pale shoulders. Slim body adorned in elegant crimson satin, hips swaying as she walks, drawing every glance in the room. Extraordinary violet eyes, lashes long and strokeable. And god help him, that mouth, soft and berryrich, so damned sexy, he nearly forgets they hate each other and drags her into his arms for a kiss.

She's more classically beautiful than Ember. Ember is girlflesh and kisses, quirky, luscious, mouthwatering. Rosa makes him feel unworthy, a perfect goddess he can never deserve.

Heat floods him, and that tiny glimpse of vampire teeth only makes him harder. Anger. Shame. Lust. They're all the same.

He swallows, parched. "Rosa. Hey."

"Long time. I mean, it's good to see you." She tries a smile, but it gutters like candleflame. Fangmarks flush crimson on her throat, matching the ruby necklace Ange gave her. A bruise yellows her smooth cheekbone, the imprint of fingers fading on her chin.

Vampires don't bruise easy, or for long.

Troublesense itches like allergy on Diamond's palate. Something's not right. He glances over her shoulder for Angelo. Nope. Good. He shoves his hands in his back pockets, arrogance he doesn't feel. "Uh-huh. Sure. What you want?"

"Can't I say hello to an old friend?"

Sick laughter bubbles. "You've got to be kiddifying. Just fuck off, okay? You took what you wanted from me. Sorry I boredified you. See ya."

"Please, just a moment. I need to talk to you." She touches his arm, and electricity tingles deep.

Stay. Kiss. Smell her hair. Pull her into the dark, slide the clothes from her body, kiss her breasts until she moans, ease his cock inside her and lose himself. Forget she shatterfied his heart, that he did raw and ugly things to her in anger. Pretend he still believes she loves him, and everything's like it was before.

He shakes her off, and turns.

But her fingers crush his forearm, effortlessly vampirestrong, and she pulls him into hot neongreen shadow. Their sweat mingles sparklebright, dizzying.

His wings tingle. The virusblood scent on her breath intoxicates him. His blood burns jagged. He's backed against a wall. Can't escape. Run. Scream. Kiss her.

Her pretty lips tremble. "Diamond, I'm in trouble. You have to help me."

The goddamn magickated words. Inwardly he curses, rich and raw. She's lying. It's a trick. But fear glitters her eyes wild, and her lashes fill with bloodstained tears.

Stupid compassion swells his heart golden. *Fuck. Don't go there. Don't touch her, hold her, wipify her tears. She'll only tear your heart out.*

But his throat parches tight, and he can't help but lift a shaking hand and brush her brimming lashes clean.

She slides her fevered hand into his, and before he can think *Diamond, you fucking idiot,* she's swaying closer and brushing her body against him and they're kissing, thirsty, her lithe little tongue in his mouth. Her sharp teeth slice his lip. Blood tingles, and she groans, and he can't help but kiss her harder, slide desperate hands into her hair, over her shoulders, down her luscious curves.

Her tears slide into his mouth, so salty and hot. His thoughts skid and stutter, useless. Is she playifying him? Maybe. Maybe not.

Who the fuck cares? His body burns. His cock aches, swollen tight, so hard with sparklethick lust that he can't think, can't reasonify, only smell her, taste her, touch her. Forget the shame, the emptiness, the bad things he did to her. Pretend it's real, that she wants him back, and adore her, gentleslow and breathless, lay her down in pinklit wingshadows and love her until sunrise.

She gasps between kisses, her fingers curling in his hair, rubbing her ripe breasts against him even as she's pushing away. "Someone'll see. He'll kill me. Don't—"

He grabs her chin and forces her away, his nerves wired tight. He's breathing hard. They both are. "So don't. What the fuck, Rosa?"

"I've no one else to go to." Now she's sobbing in his arms, tears spilling bloody on flushpainted cheeks. "God, it's awful, Diamond. Ange is so cold. He . . . he doesn't care for me like he used to. He makes me do things. Things I hate. I can't do it anymore."

"So leavify." His tone slices a jagged edge, but her misery slashes deep inside him, and he doesn't add, *It's what you're good at.*

She wipes her face. "I can't. I'm frightened. He watches me all the time, him and that lizard freak."

"Did he do this?" His fingers shake on her bruises. Too many memories he doesn't want. Vampire marks in her thigh. The back of his hand hitting her face. The way she looked at him, dark hair spilling over her bleeding mouth. Lost. Frightified. Disappointed.

"Diamond—"

"Did he?"

Rosa wipes her eyes, flushing. "He's so jealous, he just . . . If he finds out I came to you, that I still . . . he's gonna kill me. You have to help me. You have to get me

out of th— Oh, shit." Her gaze darts aside, and her
voice slides into panic, her eyes wide. "They're coming.
They'll see. Take this. I'll call you." She snaps something warm around his wrist, sharp edges cutting, and
she's gone.

He blinks in hot confusion and looks down. A violet-
dark jewel flashes up at him, rimmed in silver chain
that clips tight around his wrist. A woman's bracelet,
almost too tight to fit him, lozenge-shaped links scal-
loped sharp. Never seen it before.

He turns it to the light. The edges slice his wrist,
and a tiny drop of his hotpink blood slips over the silver. Restless flame shifts inside the jewel, eddying
like scarlet smoke.

Is she gifting him? Bribing him? A memento of
times gone?

Her words sear his heart like a jagged iron. *If Ange
finds out she still . . .* what? Stealifies jewels? Kisses
random fairy boys in the dark? Or something else?
Something wishfully, wildly deeper, a connection that
never truly died?

Diamond yanks his hair straight, her silkalicious
skin still tingling his palms. Whatever. He doesn't want
her back. What's the pointificality? He couldn't please
her before, and nothing's changed. He's still the same.
A cute fairy bauble, pretty and useless. It's not a life.

But he's crossed the line. Knows that. Can't go back
now. Cursify his weakness, but the memory of Rosa's
distress—and the lingering heat of her kiss—stabs irresistible compulsion deep into his veins. She's ma-
nipulating him, truthful or not, and he can't help but
fallify.

*Just like Jasper and Ember. Only this time, you're
the whore.*

The whisper taunts him raw, and he ignores it. *Nope no never. Not like that at all . . .*

Sharp lizard fingers crush his elbow, and he jerks back.

Tony LaFaro glares up at him, a satisfied smile on his dryscaled lips. "I knew you was up to something. Keep your shitfae hands where they belong. Them's Ange's pickings now."

Diamond shakes him off, suppressing dark longing to smash his palm into the little freak's flat-nosed face. "Chillify, mate. Didn't do nothing. Set her straight. She's just sparklefucked, or something."

"Like that ever stopped you."

"Screw you, okay? The bitch already dumpified me once. Think I'm gonna play there again? Riddified her skanky ass."

"Bullshit."

"C'mon, let it slidify. You see me fucking her?"

Tony laughs, yellow eyes cruel. "I seen Ange fucking her, that's for sure. You should come watch sometime. That woman's titties make a man's mouth water. And the things she can do with her tongue, sweet Jesus. But I guess you already kn—Mph!"

Diamond's glassy veins burn molten, and he slams the lizardman's pointy chin upward and jams him against the curtained wall, teeth crunching an inch from the bastard's nose. Rosa's spiky silver burns his wrist, pain pulsing in harmony with his rage. His blood flows faster, hotter, trickling down his forearm. "Don't scumtalk a lady like that, you fucking insect. You're grit between her goddamn shower tiles."

Tony just giggles, triumphant. "Yeah. You're over her, all right. See through you like a fucking window, mate. No pun intended."

Fury crackles Diamond's wings aglow. "Like your blood, lizard? Fuckshut up and you might keep some inside y—"

"Yeah, whatever, glassboy. One chance, since I like you so much. A guy should be allowedta think with his dick the one time. But touch her again, and I'll tell Ange you're boning his girlfriend on the sly. On top of the fun you had trying to kill us tonight? Your life won't be worth the spit in his mouth."

Diamond crushes harder. "He won't believify."

Tony chuckles, wet. "Think he might."

Diamond laughs, but dreadification seeps into his muscles like hot lead. Ange has three and a half centuries of brittle male vanity stacked up. He'll believify in an instant, *zip zap,* and then a little pile of pinkglass dust on the floor that used to be called Diamond.

Disgusted, he flings the little shitball away and stalks off, a rasping lizard chuckle grating in his ears. He fucked up. LaFaro saw. And now there's only one thing Diamond can do.

Screw conscience. He's got a plan. And Ember's not an innocent, no matter her pleadifying eyes. She's exactly the kind of no-shame bloodslut he needs. It's not like Rosa can just leave. Nothing less than Ange's hot screambleeding death will do.

Find Ember. Friendify. Feed her the poison. Kill Angelo. Get Rosa out of there. And then . . . what? Take her back?

His wrist stings, and he works Rosa's tightjeweled bracelet looser with a sweatslick finger and shakes the blood off. *Why d'you give a shit, D? Why don't you hate her? She usified you. Untruthed you. Tell her to fuck off.*

But guilt sparks his conscience alight.

Can't let her suffer. Can't let her stay with Ange and die. Even if it means Ember has to take a little discomforticality. She won't get hurtified, not really.

And mayembe, if he can help Rosa now, it'll make all the vileblack things he did and said okay.

Nothing else he can do. Choicem off.

Cynical laughter chokes him dry. Christ on a moldified cheeseburger. One day, his goddamn bleeding heart's gonna get him killed.

Compelled, Diamond glances back for Rosa, but she's already melted into darkness.

In hot clubsmoke, Vincent DiLuca lounges on his barstool, cradling a bloody bourbon cocktail and watching with vampiresharp eyes as Diamond slams LaFaro against the wall.

He inhales, flesh and perfume and hot fairy glamour, and his fangs ache as he grins. He's enjoying the show. Always fun to watch Valentis backstabbing each other. The Valenti gang are DiLuca's enemies. With any luck, LaFaro and Diamond will kill each other and save Vincent and his boys the trouble.

Vincent laughs, the dark bass beat throbbing pleasure into his fevered blood. "C'mon, ladies, just fuck and get it over with."

Beside him, Joey DiLuca snickers and sips his scotch, blond hair falling over his cheekbone. Joey is Vincent's boss, a snake-shifter with venomsharp instincts and an icewalled temper. "Can't fault the entertainment tonight. My money's on the lizard. Glassfairy'll trip over his own swollen fucking ego before long."

"Heh. You're on. I pick the fairy. Snotty prick's got balls, if ya know what I mean."

Joey shrugs, silent. Vincent gets a lot of silence from

Joey these days. Vincent has been a vampire for only a few weeks, since he contracted the virus in a little accident involving one very drunk Vincent and a vampire threesome. Since then, his transition to vampire has been . . . untidy. Bloody. Conspicuous. And if there's one thing Joey doesn't like, it's unnecessary mess.

At last, Diamond shoves LaFaro backwards and stalks off, and the fury frothing from the fairy's skin ignites Vincent's veins with desire and loathing. Just looking at all that musclebound fairyflesh makes him feel dirty.

And hungry. But these days, he's always hungry.

He gulps the last of his bourbon and blood, sweat dripping from his elaborately messy hair. Alcohol burns his throat and warms his belly. But it's not enough, never enough anymore, and his fingers itch and curl, longing to scrape, pierce, kill.

Sure, he's stronger now. Faster. His senses more alive. But being a vampire is one long torturefest of screaming famine.

Hah. That's fucking poetry. They should put that in the safe sex brochure, underneath *Rethink your fifteenth swallow* and *Bathing in that shit is a really bad idea*.

A golden-winged earthfae girl floats past on a cloud of sugary girlsmell, and Vincent's mouth waters hard. Her flimsy dress wafts around long sunburnished legs, her wings' trailing edges delicate and crushable. Her breasts are small and succulent, tantalizing beneath translucent fabric that shows the bronzed shadows of nipples. She smiles at him, her lips so soft. . . .

He tries to unstick his gaze, but he can't. He can't stop smelling her blood, so earthy and rich, the pulse throbbing in her neck, her wrists, her licksyrup thighs, an evil drumbeat in his veins. His fangs ache, the blood pressure rising like a tide until his skin burns and his muscles swell and his cock jumps hard with unslake-able thirst. . . .

"Sit the fuck down, Vincent." Joey's hellgreen serpent eyes flash warning.

Vincent shudders, hard. He didn't even realize he was standing, and he jerks back down, trying to erase that throbbing pulse in his ears. Sweat runs inside his crisp white shirt, soaks his torn jeans, drenches him in feverbright lust, and he grits his teeth on bloodfresh hunger. "Gimme a break. You said I could."

"I said you could eat. I didn't say you could gorge yourself. You've already had one tonight. Order a pizza." Joey lounges elegant and relaxed on his stool, one foot hooked in the rung, a faint sheen of luminous green sweat on his pale skin. Intense, unblinking. Snakes don't blink.

"Who the fuck are you, my mother?" Vincent lights a cigarette with shaking hands and tries to concentrate, reason, think of anything except bloody meat ripping between his teeth.

"Put on this earth to kick your girly ass. Get used to it." Joey grins, the sharp, confident smile of a guy who knows he's won.

"Whatever." Vincent blows smoke aside, irritated. What the hell's Joey got that he doesn't? Mina, Joey's kick-ass banshee girlfriend, that's what. Mina wouldn't sleep with Vincent, and not for lack of him trying. Vincent's nerves tighten with envy. One more reason to feel left out.

The other reasons—the indiscriminate bleeding,

the rape, the torture—the rest of it wasn't Vincent's fault. No way. He was newly infected, crazy with fever and bloodlust. Once, Mina was his best friend. Now, she eyes him askance, like he's dirty or wrong, and Joey circles like a vulture, waiting for him to fuck up.

And he will fuck up. The insatiable fever gnawing his blood makes that a certainty. Only a matter of time.

Gotta get some love back before it's too late. Mina's in the ladies', powdering her knives or polishing her nose or whatever. Vincent sidles closer. "Seriously, boss. Gimme something here. What I gotta do to show you I'm better?"

"Be better." Joey's glance is cold, unsympathetic. Like he doesn't have his own monster, waiting just beneath the skin. Vincent can smell it, scaly black skin cold and smooth like oil.

He sucks down more smoke, but it doesn't calm him like it used to. Only one thing calms him anymore. He exhales, bitter. "Hey, I'm doing okay. Gimme some credit. C'mon, Joey, we used to be good together. What can I do to show a little faith?"

Joey shrugs, sipping his scotch like he couldn't care, but he doesn't say, *Fuck off, Vincent, you crazy flesheater*.

Encouraged, Vincent stubs out his cigarette. "I can get you some fairy product. Good stuff, fresh emotions. I know some cookers, we can get it on the street before them Valenti assholes even lay hands."

Again, Joey shrugs, unimpressed.

"No? Okay. How about . . ." His mind scrabbles for something, anything he's good at. He's the guy who gets things. But now Joey has Mina, Joey's got everything he wants.

And then, over the boss's shoulder, Vincent spies a flash of rosetinted glass wing.

He leans over, a warm whisper of promise. "Diamond."

Joey's fingers whiten. "What about him?"

Vincent grins. Joey suppresses his hatred well. He's had years of practice at wearing two skins. But Vincent's known him too long, knows that narrowing eye and bunching thigh. Joey has one intensely personal reason to loathe Ange Valenti's favorite glassfae minion, and she's over in the ladies' room putting on her face.

He shrugs, casual. "I'll kill him for ya. Just to show I care."

"I don't need him dead." Joey's tone clips tight.

The hell. "But you'd like him dead. He fucking shot you, Joey."

"I lived."

"Not by his choice. And . . . well, I don't wanna burst your bubble, mate, but he did fuck your girlfriend." Vincent licks his teeth, satisfied, and waits for the explosion.

Shiny black fingerwebs burst from Joey's knuckles, and the glass in his hand shatters. "Not while she was my girlfriend, he didn't."

Inwardly, Vincent laughs, bloodfresh. "Doesn't soften the sting any, does it? And hey, you know what they say about fairy cock. Keeps us girls going back for more—"

Jasmine perfume tingles his nose, and he snaps his mouth shut. But he's said enough. Joey's insecurity will do the rest. Any idiot can see Mina's head over heels, but Joey's math adds differently. Diamond's a glowing fairy god, glamorous and beautiful, and Joey's a blackscaly serpent with ice for blood. To him, it's inevitable.

Vincent giggles inside, virusblood tingling his tongue. The thought of either of them touching Mina ignites foul rage in his heart. It's strange, compelling. Jealousy never consumed him like this before. But the vampire virus sharpens everything into a weapon.

Mina slides a graceful arm around Joey's neck, her skyblue hair falling over his shoulder. She's wearing tight leather pants with iron buckles and jackboots, and she looks fucking hot. She grins, ruby eyes shining. "You boys having a nice chat?"

Joey kisses her, and when he breaks off, he's gasping to catch his breath. He inhales the scent of her hair, that kill-you-crazy besotted look on his face, like he wants to fall on his knees and worship her right there. Snakeheart Joey's in love. It's fucking priceless.

Joey's fingers slide tight between hers, black skin caressing white. He sighs, closing his eyes with his cheek pressed to hers, and when he opens them again, his glare spears Vincent still, dark and burning cold with jealousy and everything he can't afford to lose. "All right. Do it. But I know nothing, understand?"

"You got it." Vincent lights another cigarette, delight twinging hot in his blood. Flashy glassboy is his. He'll track the pinkass slutfae down and carve himself a piece of tasty fairy butt.

Snicker.

And then Joey will take him back, and Mina will like him again, and everything will be like it was before.

Mina eyes them both blankly. "Do what?"

Vincent glances over her shoulder. Diamond is on

the phone, one long pink finger pressed to his pointed ear to block out the noise. No hurry. Not going anywhere.

He gives her his old handsome smile. "Nothing. Wanna dance, pretty girl?" And he winks sly triumph at Joey and twirls Mina out onto the floor.

5

Jasper tugged me away, slinging his arm around my shoulder, and I went, my nerves still jangling at Diamond's snarky insults. "What the hell's his problem?"

"Forget him." Jasper walked me down the steps to the main floor, where smoke hung sweet and the ground thudded with grinding electric chords. My moonsensitive blood hummed, every cell awake with magic and scent.

On the tables, fairy girls shimmied, showing off matchless bodies in tiny halter tops and hot pants, running long bony hands over lissome hips bare in sweaty heat. I flushed and tugged my tight skirt down over my butt. Blood still squelched inside my dress, trickling hot down my belly, and my skimpy top barely covered me. My boobs were practically bursting out of it. I wanted to go home and change. I liked to dress sexy, but not tacky and ridiculous. I felt false, like I wore a costume that neither fit nor suited me.

I felt like that a lot, no matter what I wore.

Jasper pulled me against the mirrors, nightshade hair tumbling over his gorgeous plumrich grin. "He's just jealous. You're my girl, and you done good, Emmy."

He leaned in for a kiss, and when his lips caressed

mine, so tender and warm, tears sprang to my eyes. I hated him for how I felt, shitty and miraculous at the same time. He tasted sugary and dark like spiced honey, the gentle sting of his teeth so much like home.

I wanted us to be like this all the time. Just wanted him to like me, care for me, give a shit how I felt.

But we weren't. He didn't care about me. I had to leave him, before I agreed to do something even worse, just for one dizzy moment of his affection.

"Mmm. You're a peach, Emmy. Got something for ya." He slipped the weird scarlet gem I'd stolen for him into his pocket, and came up holding something else.

My arm still hurt where he'd bruised me, and my wings ached. "Look, we need to t—"

My heart somersaulted, thieving my breath.

Another jewel sparkled in his pale fingers. Green like rainforest, flashed with gold, tapering to glittering points at each end.

And it was attached to a slim golden ring.

Jasper smiled, devastating, and dipped his forehead to mine in an intimate caress. "This is for you. Say you will."

My pulse thudded. *Say I will what—?*
Oh, shit.

I swallowed, dry, the mirrors suddenly cold against my shoulder. "Is . . . is that what I think it is?"

"I like having you around, Emmy. Say yes or I'll die." His earthy scent weakened my knees, and his lips drifting close to mine made me shiver. But something warm and sharp like a wire hook pulled my guts out of shape, and I realized it wasn't hope or love or a dream come true.

That shining jewel terrified me.

Already I could feel it, snug around my finger, tight

and unmovable. My future. Stuck there forever. No escape. And before I could speak—or run—he took my hand and slipped his ring onto my finger.

The cool band fit perfectly. The jewel sat oblique across my finger, so big, it brushed the knuckles either side, the golden setting curling like tiny leaves. I lifted my hand, fingers splayed, and smoky nightclub lights caught the facets, glittering blue and green and gold.

I swallowed, sick. "Umm . . . I dunno what to say."

Jasper caught my hand and kissed it, his gaze aflame on mine. "Same color as your eyes, cherry girl."

I bit my lip, and more tears leaked. He was right. The fucking thing looked gorgeous.

I tried to clear my eyes, to think. This was every fairy girl's dream. Family, love, babies, a real life just like a human.

But rebellion spiked icy shards in my heart. I didn't want to be a gangland wife. Didn't want to be That Poor Woman, always elegantly dressed, perfectly groomed, that dull glaze of denial in her smile, and people gaze at her with pity aglimmer in their eyes, and whisper behind their hands, *That poor woman, surely she can't not know.*

Jasper lifted my chin, caressing my lips with his thumb. "Hey, sugarpie, don't cry. I want you pretty."

My pulse skittered. *Last chance. Don't crumble. One moment more, and it'll be forever too late.* "Jasper, I can't—"

"It's okay. We can talk after. I'll take you out, we'll have a good time. But gotta go first. See a man about a thing. Wait for me?"

"But—"

"Sure you can." His consonants sharpened, his fingers tightening on mine. A subtle nuance, but I felt it in my bones, saw it churning restless in his eyes, the first tiny smolder of his temper.

Tiny anger-coals stirred in my heart. What could out-important this? Some drug deal with his smart-ass boss? Meeting his slutty girlfriend?

But I just nodded, confusion blotting like storm-clouds.

"That's my girl." He kissed the top of my head, his wings brushing my face with that wonderful warm velvet glow, and seeped into the smoky crowd like a shadow.

Frustration itched like mosquito bites. Missed that chance. Almost like he'd known what I'd say.

But Jasper was far from the marrying kind, and despite everything, foolish hope still shone on my heart. It wasn't the proposal I'd dreamed of, in that little girly part of me that wanted babies and puppy dogs and a petunia garden. He didn't go down on one knee or shower me with roses or treat me to a candlelit supper on the beach. But he did ask me, and for an instant, I dared to hope I'd actually touched him.

I swallowed, salty with unease. Could I really leave him now? Maybe this was it. Maybe this time, he'd change. Things would be different.

But things were never different. He never changed. And neither did I.

I peered into the crowd, but he was gone.

I wiped my sweaty hands and couldn't help glancing down at the beautiful ring. Most likely he didn't own it. The gem probably wasn't even real. It felt warm and slimy on my finger, sweat sticking in germs and dead skin. It trapped me, an invisible cage of acquiescence and silence and blind emotion that made no sense. I wanted it gone.

I wanted him gone.

I fingered the ragged hole in my throat, already healing but still sore to the bone with humiliation and rage. Urgency gripped me like hot vampire claws. No, this couldn't wait. I needed to say my piece, here, now, tonight. And if he lost his temper and hurt me, so be it. All the more reason to do it in a public place. So long as I could still walk away, I'd win.

Greasy fearfingers wrapped the back of my neck, but I tightened my mouth and pushed them off, and took one step into the crowd.

No lightning bolt. No giant boot crushing me from on high. My newly growing backbone didn't snap. I didn't even feel sick.

I felt great.

A smile tugged my mouth wide, and I wiped my tears and sidled through the dancing crowd, my damp wings tucked in safe. A sexy troll boy bumped my hip and threw me a jagged black-toothed grin, and I grinned back. I liked the glint in his eye. Maybe I'd come dance with him later.

Then again, maybe I'd swear off men forever.

Jasper had disappeared toward the back, so I went that way, sidling to get through. Beneath the mezzanine, the air rippled with heat, thick with sex and candy. My reflection floated along the mirrored wall, a tall shadowy ghost with smoky wings, her knotted hair bloodred. Her eyes burned, her face determined. She looked strange and wild, like the specter of a crazy big sister I never knew I had. A smart, kick-ass, take-no-shit version of me, without the fear. The Ember I wished I could be.

I crunched my nose in a smile and waved. "Hey, Big Em. You go, girl."

To my surprise, Big Em waved back and winked, eyes glowing red. And then she faded like a stain of breath, leaving only me.

I blinked. Weird. But good weird.

My silly heels clunked on the ribbed metal floor, and as I hopped down the stairs to the fire escape, my ankles ached. Sooner this was done, sooner I could get home, take a shower, dump this nasty outfit.

Assuming Jasper would let me take my things, of course, and didn't leave me with nowhere to go. But I didn't want to think about that.

The back firedoor lay ajar, its metal-hinged handle jammed down. I pushed, and it screeched open.

Hot dry air slammed my face, crinkling the blood on my skin to sticky lumps. I stepped into the alley, where garbagestink from the skip mixed with warm eucalyptus and stale beer. Moonlight glared yellow in my eyes, the brick walls a dusty rainbow of spraypaint and splashed vomit. Charming.

But my pulse sparkled, treacherous under the hot caress of the near-full moon. My body heated, warmth spreading, and I hated it.

Moonlight pleasures me. It's the same with all bloodfae, something about cycles and tides and monthly madness. And in a couple of nights, the moon would be full, so fat and round and juicy, just the thought of it swelled my heart and throbbed my blood with ancient pleasure rhythms that urged me to twirl, dance, fly crazy pinwheels in the moonlight, find a beautiful fairy boy and slide my naked body over his until I moaned.

But the last thing I wanted to think about right now was my blood.

The door banged shut, blocking out the noise. My

ears rang, clogged with cottony nightclub hangover, and I wobbled my head, straining for voices, footsteps, anything to show me where he'd gone. But silence, just the distant rough whisper of traffic and a screeching crow.

I flittered into the air and hovered, glancing left and right. Tire grooves lined the narrow asphalt lane, a few parched potholes left by last month's storms. At the end of the block, a tram rattled up the hill, a distant silver streak.

No one. Maybe Jasper didn't come this way after all. . . .

Scrape.

My eartips twitched. Behind me. I dived around in a breezy swish.

Scrape again. A metallic rattle. Maybe a voice.

I fluttered up the alley, summer air hot and strong beneath my wings. Garbage's meaty smell twitched my nose, and my ears hummed. Definitely a voice.

And then a slim dark body crashed out from behind the row of rusty skips.

Alarm tingled my tongue, and I darted into the shadows for cover. And then my heart jolted cold. Jasper. On his back. Bleeding, his lovely face a mess.

He rolled over with a wet gurgle of agony, trying to crawl away, but his legs wouldn't work. His soft wing membranes scraped the ground, dust shedding, and a jagged bone stuck out from one shoulder.

My pulse screamed. My feet hit the ground with a clunk, and my muscles jerked, urging me to jump, scuttle, run to him.

The monster in the shadows leapt out.

I recoiled, nerves squealing alive. A snarling hellbeast landed on all fours, black limbs gleaming like burnt toast, its birdlike legs folding backwards. Shining blue hair hung past its narrow waist, its lean black muscles wrapped tight over angular bones. Dripping needle teeth, monstrous black claws sharp as razors, flat yellow eyes dripping fire.

I hugged my knees to my chest, sweating. My pulse pounded. Already I could feel those teeth severing my tendons, feasting on me. . . .

But it didn't see me. It crouched over Jasper, saliva dripping onto the pavement in hissing steam, and growled like a pissed-off hound of hell.

And then it *changed*.

Limbs shrinking pale, teeth sliding into a rosy mouth, claws sucked back into elegant fingertips, slim hands, fingers ringed in gold. Iceblue hair shortening to a golden pageboy bob, sunflash eyes darkening to shiny black.

Jasper choked and groaned, blood bubbling on torn mauve lips.

The blond man adjusted his dark suit and crouched over Jasper with a sniff of distaste. Green flame leapt in his hair, threatening. "I want them all, Jasper. Not just one. All." He rested his wrist on one elegant knee and dangled something red and glinting on a chain before Jasper's bloodshot eyes.

The vampire's gemstone. The one I'd stolen.

It squirmed on the chain's end like a fishhooked worm, fighting blindly to escape, and that desperate squeal shrieked in my ears again. I stared, agape. What the hell was that thing?

Jasper flopped, broken bones grating. "Time. Just give me time, Kane. I'll get them. Promise . . ."

Disbelief blotted my vision scarlet. Black-eyed monsterblond was Kane? As in Kane, the prince of hell who ruled the city? Jasper and Diamond's ultimate boss, the guy who told even Angelo Valenti what to do? Kane, the demon lord of Melbourne, stalker of souls and master of temptation?

I bit my lips again, quivering. *Jasper, you fucking idiot. What have you done?*

Kane just looked at him, sparks crackling between his fingers. "Did you think you could betray your so-called friends to save your own soul? You're already mine, fairydirt. All five of you. You can't escape. Did you really imagine you could hide your souls from me with chunks of rock?" Kane gripped the wriggling gemstone and crushed his fist tight.

Jasper howled. Scarlet smoke hissed between Kane's fingers. The stink of charcoal rose, and he opened his fist and let bloody red chunks fall to the black pavement, mixed with mangled gold.

Kane licked his palm and smiled, blood smearing his scarlet lips. "Oops. Did I break your feeble spell? That was the vampire boy's, was it? Thanks so much. And now I'll hunt down the pretty liar and the burning girl and the shadowfairy, and have myself a tasty feast. But first—" He grabbed Jasper's bloody hair and dragged him close, his nails snapping out an inch and glowing scarlet. Cinders spat from his teeth and smoked on Jasper's face. "—first I want *yours*."

Cold sickness swamped me like salt water. Useless anger rippled my wings, urging me to jump, scream, do anything but let this creature eat Jasper. But fear froze my limbs fast, and I couldn't move.

Jasper laughed, bloodshot eyes swirling crazy, and wet crimson bubbles burst on his lips. "Find it, then, hellboy. Bring it on."

"Give it to me. Where is it, fairyshit?" Sparks flashed

from Kane's golden lashes, and hellcraft rippled the air black.

Ash stung my nose, and the ring on my finger burned cold.

I looked down, my heart racing. The cursed thing was glowing, not green like the stone but a dirty red gleam like fire.

Bile burned in my mouth. I wanted to scream. I wanted to be sick. I wanted to claw Jasper's eyes out for tricking me.

That fucking liar. He didn't want me, not really. Just needed somewhere to hide, and knew I was too love-struck and scared to question him.

I tugged at the ring, claws ripping, desperate to get the horrid thing off. But it burned colder, tighter, shrinking onto my finger with a clammy deathgrip that wouldn't budge.

Kane's handsome golden head swiveled around, razorblack gaze searching, elegant nose twitching for soulscent.

My guts squeezed tight. I needed to pee, big-time. I hunkered in the shadows, wrapping my wings tight, making myself as small as possible, that horrid ring pressed deep between my sweating thighs. My nerves yammered at me to flee. I should run. Get out and never look back.

But that black hellmagic seeped into my limbs, ca-ressing me, tempting me with foul come-hither. My lungs stuffed with useless air, and I gasped like a swamped fish and couldn't move.

Kane's gaze magnetized onto mine, and he dropped Jasper with a clunk like death.

My blood flooded cold, my wings crackling with ice, and something warm and sticky slid down my leg.

Kane licked soft red lips, mesmerizing. The air between us rippled like a darksweet sandstorm, and his voice crooned, rich and irresistible with hot demonic compulsion. He beckoned, just the crook of one elegant finger. "Come out, bloodgirl."

My mind tumbled, irrational. God, I wanted to come out. The magic slid deep into my veins like a creeping addiction, and I wanted to stumble out and fall at his feet, beg him to touch me, raise me up, take my hand.

But if I did, Jasper-the-dirty-rotten-liar-I-can't-believe-I-fell-for-his-crap would die. The demon would eat his soul, or whatever cringing part of it lurked in this strange, treacherous ring that still chewed my finger like a hungry rat. And who knew what would happen to me?

Then again, if I stayed here, the demon would just haul me out. Probably by a loose flap of skin. With his teeth. And Jasper would still get dragged off to hell, and with a pissed-off demon for my only friend, I'd be right there with him.

I squeezed my eyes shut, trying to resist. But Kane's magic licked the insides of my thighs, tempting me to dark surrender, and I knew there was only one thing I could do.

6

Trembling, I stepped from the shadows.

Kane smiled, beautiful like an angel, and the air grew colder. "Ember. How sweet of you."

How did he know my name? I shivered, the pressure of his black gaze an icy weight on my soul.

Jasper choked on the ground, broken legs twitching feebly. "Emmy. Christ. Told you to wait—"

"Shut up." Kane's gaze never slipped from mine. "Rest now, Ember. You've done enough. Come to me."

Unwilled, I stepped closer, my legs moving before I could stop them.

Kane reached for my hand, a greedy gleam staining his eyes blue, and his voice slithered warm under my skin and watered my will to mush. "Give me the gem."

"No." I backed off, hiding the jewel behind my back, but it was no use.

The demon grabbed my wrist, effortlessly strong, and dragged me forward. His smooth palm slipped over mine, and I fell.

Down into a swirling abyss of images, people, places, everyone I'd known, everything I'd ever thought I wanted. Girls who teased me, boys who blushed and dropped their gazes. I'd wanted to be friends, but I was always apart, always different, always *that bloodfae girl*. Ash, the bloodfae boy I'd shared a dingy apartment with years ago, who'd died selling blood to keep the two of us fed, leaving me with only guilt and a morbid fear of ending up like him. That hungry vampire tonight, his studded tongue a sweet pressure in my mouth. Dozens more like him, always hungry, always undressing me with their eyes and sniffing the air for my scent, and until tonight I'd resisted them all.

Diamond, magical, attractive, maddening, his ruby eyes glinting with scorn. Jasper, whole and laughing, violet eyes aflame with fun, his swanblack hair feathering over my fingers. The first time we made love, hot and breathless, pleasure like I'd never found before, his caresses resonating deep inside, his tenderness a revelation. Kissing in the rain, long and slow and soulful, our wet clothes plastered together, skin burning beneath.

The first night we argued, midnight in his sleek twelfth-floor apartment on Southbank, city lights twinkling over the river like stars. He accused me of flirting with his friends, only I hadn't, just smiled and made conversation like he told me to. I'm in tears on the bed, ears raw from the yelling. I snap one thoughtless word too many, and his knuckles curl white, that sickly smolder flashes in his eyes.

In the alley, my skin shrank cold, my bowels tight as the images flowed.

Only this time, Jasper doesn't grab me and throw me on the floor.

Instead, he swallows his rage, and says, *I'm sorry, just jealous, I love you so much.* And I say, *I'm sorry, it was stupid, I love you, too,* and we kiss, and have the best makeup sex ever, and that part of our relationship is over. It never started.

Kane's arm slipped over my shoulder, his breath an ashen caress on my cheek. "Do you want that, Ember? I can give it to you. Take you back there. Make Jasper whole again. All you need do is give me the ring."

The demon's body pressed against mine, gentle but compelling. My heart ached. I gulped in air, but tears blocked my nose. I did want it.

At least, I thought I did until tonight.

Kane's caress turned sultry, his sigh a sensual lure, his body no longer comforting but arousing. Desire stroked in my belly, on my breasts, between my legs. His fingers curled deeper in my hair to brush against my throat like a lover's. "Kiss me, Ember. Just say yes, and you and Jasper can have another chance."

My senses reeled, drunk on his heady scent of thunder. His succulent lips lingered at the corner of my mouth. I wanted to taste them, feel his hot ashen tongue in my mouth, his crisp golden hair trailing over my skin. . . .

Hellcraft sparked hot need deep in my flesh, and I fought for sanity. Another chance to what? Be that lonely gangland wife? Get tricked into wearing a hell-cursed soulstone? No, thanks.

But Kane's lips brushed mine, and his hot body pressed against me, his arm strong like steel around my waist. My breasts ached, that delicious tightness filling my belly. "Give me the ring, Ember," he whispered, and it caressed straight to my sex. "You know you want to."

I wanted to, all right.

I couldn't help but part my lips, and he stole a kiss, burning with charcoal. His mouth claimed mine, sensation splashing like hot honey all the way down my body, leaking deep inside to stroke me. My legs went flimsy with desire. God, his kiss was like fucking. Already I could feel him naked against me, his hot golden body a delight, our sweat mingling, muscles sliding together, his cock up inside me, heavy and hard and delicious. I longed to open my mouth, let him claim me, lie down beneath him and open my body to his, let him rip my heart out with his teeth and gorge himself on soulblood while I moaned in hellwrought pleasure.

But it wasn't enough.

Determination steeled my nerves cold. If Kane just wanted the ring, he could have taken it any time. No, he wanted my soul. And Jasper and I could never be the way we were. Not now. Jasper was already damned. But I could still save myself.

I squirmed from Kane's embrace and pushed him away. My voice crunched small, choked with tears, but strong. "You're pushing the wrong buttons, demon. Let me go."

I quivered, expecting wrath, thunder, gnashing teeth.

But Kane just smiled in childlike delight, ash drifting snowy from his hair. "Seems that way, doesn't it?" A crafty gleam crept into his eye, and dread numbed my bones, but too late. He leaned closer to whisper, his rich scent of charcoal and thunder raising hot bumps on my skin. "Fine. You want the ring so badly? You keep it."

He blinked, and a black wave of compulsion slammed from his lashes.

Angry flame flashed, and agony speared up my finger like hellfire.

I screamed. The ring glowed white-hot, searing my skin to blisters. The gemstone melted, running in a bright green river, scalding my hand to ash.

And then nothing. Cold. Calm. No pain. Gone as swiftly as it came.

I examined my hand, gasping for breath. No blisters. No weeping sores. Just the ring. Melted onto my finger, a deep indentation where the metal grew into my skin like a cancer. The gemstone winked at me, green like forest water, and deep within, a burning scarlet seed whispered and moaned.

And deep in my bones, the distant, relentless scorch of hellfire.

Kane's jewelblack eyes shone, impassive. "Do you feel that, Ember?" His voice was gentle. Conversational. Inescapable.

I wriggled and fought and flapped my wings, but the feeling wouldn't dissolve. "What have you done to me?"

"That's home. Hell. You belong with me now."

Terror watered my muscles, and I gasped for breath. "No. You're lying."

"Not this time." Warm, relentless.

Already, I felt the horrid firebeast inside the ring chewing at my soul. "But . . . but that's not fair!" The protest tumbled out, stained with tears and exhaustion and stupid rage. God, I was sick of being manipulated. "I said no! You can't just—"

"I didn't, Ember. You did."

I glanced behind him, furtive. Jasper wasn't moving. Wasn't breathing. I was alone. "What?"

"You took the fairyboy's ring of your own free will. His promise is yours now, and your soul belongs to me. If you want to be free, you'll have to pay his debt."

"Wh-what do you mean?"

Kane grimaced, exasperated, like he explained to a

child. "The prettyblack and his idiot friends gambled with me. They lost. But now they're trying to hide their souls in some silly gemstones. From me. Can you believe that?"

Jasper had been wandering around without his soul inside him? Well, that sure explained a lot. "What? Jewels with souls inside? I don't get it—"

"Not inside, cindergirl. Entwined. It isn't the same thing."

"Stop speaking riddles." Desperate tears burned my cheeks. "Please. Just give me another chance, and I'll—"

"But I am. Your boyfriend promised to get me his friends' souls in return for his. I do so enjoy treachery." Ice frosted his luminous hair like tiny moonlit jewels, and he gave me a scarlet grin. "But he's in no shape to deliver their gemstones now. Lucky for me you showed up, don't you think?"

"What? You want me to . . ." I swallowed, empty with despair. "But . . . they'll die, won't they? I'm not a killer. I can't—"

"Don't complain." Kane shot me a black glare that clamped my throat tight. "I'm in a generous mood, so don't spoil it. I'll give you your chance. Bring me my jewels, and I'll set you free."

"But this has nothing to do with m—"

Kane's hair flushed an angry blue, his razor claws sliding an inch longer. "Just bring me my jewels, cinder. You won't like me impatient."

My lip trembled, but indignation fired my belly, too. He wasn't so special. Just another man, ordering me around. "Get 'em yourself, why don't you, if you're so clever?"

He shrugged, sulky. "I'm busy. And it's more fun to watch you do it."

So I was to be a demon's plaything now? Palmed off from one manipulative bastard to the next? I took a deep breath, cold fear souring my mouth. "And what if I refuse?"

Kane licked his lips and smiled. "Then you can scream in hell along with him. Your soul is still fresh. You'll taste ever so nice."

My heart sank even further. Had Jasper known this would happen? That he'd damned me with his treacherous gift? Or was he just scared, hiding, desperate?

It didn't matter. I had no choice. Useless rage flamed in my moonlit blood. It wasn't fair. I didn't deserve this.

But it was happening.

I sighed and gave in. "Who are they? Where? How'm I supposed to—?"

"That's your problem. I don't make the rules." A wicked orange glint lit Kane's eyes. "Actually, I do. But I'll be fair, just this once. I'll even tell you who they are." He flipped a card from his jacket and offered it to me between two fingers.

I took it, my bones burning. His fingers brushed mine, and a delicious whiff of thunder dizzied me. I shivered, tugging my hand back. "How long have I got?"

"A while. Not soon. Not long. Let's say . . . when the full moon's at its brightest?" Kane glanced at my ring, where angry flame tumbled and spat inside, and cocked a perfect golden eyebrow. "Better hurry, cinder. Time's burning." And he straightened his tie and walked off, ash drifting like snowflakes from his hair.

I staggered, dizzy, and for a moment, Kane's absence tore into my bonehollows like a red-hot blade. My nose screamed for sensation as his thundery scent faded, and my mouth watered helplessly, searching for him.

The fire in my ring jumped and spat, static crackling on the facets like a tiny plasma ball. I gasped, trying to catch my breath, sate the raging need for the demon's voice, his touch, his ashen breath on my skin.

Was I his creature now? This cursed ring damning me to slavery?

My heart screamed, a frustrated wail of indignation and terror. *I don't deserve this. I didn't do anything wrong.*

But I had. I'd trusted the wrong man. Let myself be blinded by infatuation and false promises. Yessum, massuh, I'll drink the tasty purple grapejuice, no problemo.

I'd walked right up to the cliff and jumped with my eyes open. I mightn't be a low-down dirty sinner, but I was a fucking idiot.

I tugged at my finger, ripping it bloody, but the ring wouldn't budge. The metal had grown into my skin, seamless, the fine gold I'd admired now gloating at me with a supercilious liar's smile.

I swore, and sucked my bleeding knuckle. *Curse you, Jasper. You and your goddamn tricks. I'm over it, and I'm over you. . . .*

My heart stung cold. Jasper.

I scrambled to my knees at his side and skidded in a warm sticky puddle.

He wasn't moving. His soft black wings lay limp and bloody, drained fragile like a butterfly's. His pretty lips lay bitten, those fabulous violet eyes dull, indigo lashes caked with foul dust. His shoulders made horrible unnatural shapes in the dirt, his legs deformed. That blackcharred Kane-monster had slammed him into the ground, and he'd shattered like an inky china plate. Already, his rich dark colors faded.

Dead. Bled out, expired from agony and asphyxiation while I begged for my life with a demon.

My throat swelled. I couldn't swallow. I stroked crumbling hair from his face, smearing my fingers in blood and leaching black fairycolor, and something brittle and angry in my heart snapped.

He didn't deserve to die.

So he had commitment issues. Didn't everyone? We fairies aren't strong or tough or powerful, not compared to demons or vampires or the rest of the scum that festers in Melbourne's gutters. We have to fight with the weapons we're given, and all Jasper had was charm and lies.

He was just like us all, struggling for space in a human world that couldn't see or listen or care. Threatened, helpless, angry at life for dumping us in the shit. Just making his way, steeling himself bright so he couldn't be hurt.

And look where it got him.

I let my finger trace his curving mouth, that fine curlpointed nose, the shining jewels he wore in his ear, and I planted one last kiss on bloodstained lips and said good-bye.

I turned away, and tears blinded me.

A wretched howl ripped from my throat. I wanted him back, screw me if I didn't, cutting wit and bad temper and all. I wanted everything to be like it was before. It couldn't be worse than this. At least I'd had a home, a lover, a sometime friend. Now, I had nothing.

Nothing but a hellcursed ring and burning bones and the foulsweet taste of thunder.

If I didn't love him, why did this hurt so goddamn much?

I kicked angrily at the dust. I didn't understand any

of this. Everything was gray and smudged, where I'd thought it black and white. Nothing was certain.

Only that if I didn't get Kane his gemstones, I'd go to hell. When the moon was brightest. *Not soon. Not long.*

Foolishly, I snickered, tension giggling mad in my chest. Fucking bureaucrat, always fudging his dates. I bet hell was like that. Full of politicians and public servants.

I'd find out soon enough, if I didn't do something right away.

My giggles subsided. I knew exactly when the moon would be brightest. *Perilune,* it was called, when the moon came closest to earth, and this month perilune and full moon almost coincided. The brightest, fattest, hottest full moon of the year. It was in my blood. I could feel it. Not tonight. Not tomorrow night. Two nights from now. I had until then to make this right.

But what could I do? Call the cops like a good little human girl? Like they'd care about one more dead drug dealer and his skanky girlfriend. No, I had to handle this myself.

Slowly, I retrieved Kane's card from the dirt and dusted it off. The thick ivory paper felt nice in my fingers. His phone number in black print on one side—just the number, nothing else—and below it, he'd drawn a heart and two kisses in dusky red ink like blood. For some forgotten girlfriend? Or for me, his latest trick?

I flipped it over. Same ink, same round childish handwriting. *Scarletfire queen*, it said. *Famine in the dark. Bloodpetal girl.*

Despair burned my eyes like hot ash. This was supposed to help? Clearly this demon lord—*your demon lord*, that nasty ringfire beast hissed in my head, *he's your master now*—clearly Kane had a selfish sense of humor.

My heart quailed. Even if I could decipher his cryptic message, I didn't know anyone in gangland. Sure, I partied with Jasper's friends, but none of them gave a damn about me. I had no one to call on for help. Jasper always sheltered me from his business. Said he didn't want me to worry. Always watching his back, glancing over his shoulder.

Well, bad luck, Jaspie old thing. Your paranoia just got us killed.

But as I stared at his mangled body, wringing my hands like it'd make me think better, warm dark inspiration slipped into my blood.

Check his phone, cinder.

My bones burned, a blackcharred whisper from hell.

Or maybe it was Big Em, my inner superhero, with her wild hair and her screw-'em-all attitude, poking my sluggish brown ass in the right direction.

I blinked. Why didn't I think of that? Even paranoid sparklefreaks like Jasper had a phonebook. How else could he make his deals? Maybe Scarlet Queen and Darkly Famine and Bloodpetal Girl would be on there.

Thanks, Big Em. Or whoever you are.

Swiftly, I knelt and wormed my hand under Jasper's body. He was still warm underneath, spicy scent still drifting. I swallowed, and dug harder. My claws fumbled past the rolled edge of his jeans pocket, and tapped hard plastic.

I pulled the phone out and slid my finger over the bloodstained screen, scrambling to my feet. A text message flashed, his background a psychedelic smear. I ignored it and flipped to the phone book. Dozens of names. Lots of girls. Some had pictures, painted blue eyes or a curled wingtip or a naughty crimson lips shaped into a kiss. A few were naked.

Humiliation twinged, but I shoved it aside. The cheating weasel was dead. No need to rub it in.

Besides, I was just as pretty as those girls. Wasn't I?

I squashed the urge to flip back and check, and scrolled down.

Nothing useful. No names or pictures that looked anything like *famine* or *scarlet* or *petal*. My nerves skittered with frustration. The right numbers could be there. I just had no way of identifying them. And even if I could, what could I do? Call them up and say, *Hey, you don't know me, but d'ya mind if I steal your soul-stone and send you to hell?* That'd go down a treat.

I sighed and flipped back to the main screen. That message chimed at me again, and my finger hovered an inch from the glass, uncertain. Jasper didn't like me snooping. I'd had bruises to prove it. My eyes darted sideways, to make sure he wasn't watching.

Body. Broken and bleeding. Duh.

A lump clogged my throat, my eyes burning. But I'd no more time to feel sorry for myself. I dragged my gaze away and opened the message.

Where u @ JJ??

I read the caller ID, and my wings heated. Of course, I knew one person in gangland, if only slightly.

There was one rude, stuck-up glassfae asshole I could call.

I hesitated. Diamond was über-Jasper, stronger,

meaner, better connected. He knew things about people. He'd probably recognize in an instant who Kane's cryptic clues were for. And he was tough enough to make his way in the Valenti gang without getting his wings chewed off. With him on my side, I could have this done and dusted in a few hours and go home for a shower and a cool air-conditioned bed.

But I imagined asking for his help, and my guts coiled cold. He'd sneer at me with those contemptuous rosy lips. Throw a few more whore insults. Toss that shining hair at me and flitter his infuriatingly perky glass ass away.

My chin set tight, and I flicked the phone dark.

No way.

I didn't need Diamond. I was through asking for help. Relying on men to save me was what got me into this mess. Besides, Kane's hellspelled hourglass was running out. I didn't have time to quarrel with Diamond, to flirt and circumscribe and explain what the hell had happened. I had to do this now, tonight, on my own.

But you're insignificant. That nasty doubtvoice taunted me. *You're so weak and stupid, Emmy, how can you get through the night alone? You need someone to protect you. Someone to feed you and dress you and keep you safe.*

"Shut up." I sniffled, uneasy. "I can do it by myself."

No, you can't, Emmy. Don't be stupid. Go find another boy to take care of you. Diamond's cute, and strong. And he wants to fuck you. They all want to fuck you, Emmy. Didn't you watch those hot glitter-lashed eyes, licking over your body? All you gotta do is give him a nice hot blowjob in the dark and he'll give you what you need. . . .

"Shut up!" My voice grated in the hot silence, and I stuffed Jasper's phone into my bag with a vicious shove. No way. Coward-beast was right about one thing: In gangland, nothing got you nothing. If Diamond thought I'd lay one finger on his weird pinkglass body, he could bloody well think again.

In any case, the people I hunted were probably Diamond's friends. Once I explained what I needed, he'd tell me to get lost anyway.

No. I'd find another way.

I clicked my bag open again and poked inside, cataloging my meager resources. My phone. Jasper's phone. Mirror, dusted with blue glitter. Foil twist, opened, same blue glitter. Lipstick, cherry. Some loose change, a couple of crumpled fifties.

I fingered the bills, and an idea sparked. Money meant power. I might not have any friends, but that didn't make me helpless.

My stupid skirt rode up over my butt as I squatted. I yanked it down and carefully hooked Jasper's roll of cash from his front pocket with one finger.

I flipped it open and glanced through the bills. Like any suave purveyor of junk, Jasper was always either swimming in it or flat broke, and luckily for me, tonight was the former. The curled plastic cash slid smooth on my fingers, that lusty moneyscent crisp in my nose, seductive, beckoning. In the moonlight, the pale terracotta twenties shone wetblack with his blood.

My nose wrinkled, but I crammed it all into my bag anyway, inkstain smearing on velvet. Jasper's money always had blood on it. You just couldn't see it most of the time.

I stood, tugging my skirt down again. My thoughts fizzed, swirled, coalesced. I needed information, but if I poked my nose in too hard, it might get bitten off.

Can't imagine Jasper's hellbound buddies were too eager to be found. So I had to be careful. Subtle. Sneaky, even.

There were others who knew more than I. If I told Jasper's lick-ass drug-dealing friends he was in trouble, they might cough up. Everything was for sale. Maybe if I flirted a bit and laid down some cash, they'd help me.

I strode to the firedoor and yanked it open. Hot nightclub air drenched me in sweat and sound, the glory of dancing and sighs and wild abandoned grace mixing with heady moonlight until I swayed, drunk.

Screw Kane and his hellfire, Diamond's scornful looks, Jasper and his hateful lies. I didn't care. With moonlight racing in my blood and the dark pleasure of midnight sweat on my skin, I loved life. I didn't want to die.

Jasper's ring scorched my finger, the demonbound ache in my bones flaring scarlet. I sucked in a breath, trying to calm my pulse. *Easy, Em. Keep it simple.* I'd get Kane his damn stones, save my soul. And then I was leaving town forever.

A new start. No more excitement, no gangs, no drugs, no horny vampires or seedy nightclub demon deals. Thanks to Jasper, I had the price of an airfare and more. I'd go up to Brisbane, maybe, where it was warm and humid, big old rambling houses and no daylight saving and coffee down by the river in the scent of frangipani. Get a job. Keep my head down. Stay away from controlling men, find me a nice clean fairy boy who didn't know sparkle from sherbet powder. No more gangster boyfriends for me.

I thought of Jasper's beautiful apartment by the river, luxurious carpet and glass and shining white marble tiles. My pretty clothes, my jewels, all that expensive food and champagne, parties and candlelit cruises, nights spent in glittering casinos and bars. Sniffing luminous blue lines from golden mirrors, dancing slow and sultry wrapped in sugary fairy laughter, the rich drunken delight of sparkle-drenched sex. The hot velvet friction of his wings along mine, floating high on burning summer updrafts, midnight breeze a soft kiss in my hair.

Jasper was an asshole, sure. But he was a charming, cashed-up, fun-loving asshole who knew how to rock a fairy's world.

I'd miss that.

But not for me anymore the fast life, the money, that heady breathless flavor of danger. I'd get an office job. Wash dishes. Work at Starbucks. Anything but this. At least I wouldn't have to worry about being abandoned on the street to sell my blood.

Or dropped in a screeching hellpit with a ring on my finger.

I swallowed, tilted my chin high, and walked into the club to look for Jasper's friends. Just an ordinary, nice, simple, boring life. I'd be poor, but at least I'd be happy.

Right?

7

I shouldered up to the crowded bar in the warm smell of smoke and sweat. Music caressed my wings, a slow pulsing vibration. White neon gleamed under my elbows as I hopped onto a stool, between two kissing fairy girls and a stoned human kid with steel pins in his eyebrows and Inca tattoos on his half-shaven scalp. I ordered a champagne cocktail and craned my neck for a glimpse of Jasper's friends, my fingers itching to get on with it.

"Hey, baby." The tattooed kid offered me his joint, his crusty-lashed eyes glued to my cleavage.

I scowled. Smoking's banned in clubs. Those things'll kill ya.

Jasper's ring frosted hot on my finger, and I giggled, mad. Then again, what could go wrong from here? I took the lumpy cigarette and dragged. Clean, pale, a bitter opium twinge. I held it back out to him, the tart smoke croaking my voice. "Thanks."

He winked and shuffled closer, greasy hair tumbling. "Hey. You, ah, working tonight?"

"Huh?" The smoke made me dreamy, and I didn't really hear him.

He crept slick fingers up my thigh. "Wanna earn a little cash?"

"Fuck you." I exhaled into his face and pushed away, glaring. Talk about spoiling my mellow. I didn't have a choice how my glamour made me appear, but sometimes I wished it wasn't a big-breasted bimbo.

Grumble, boo hoo, so sad. Okay, it was nice to be pretty, and this slutty outfit wasn't exactly inconspicuous. But just once, I'd like to sit at the bar without some grubby guy thinking I'll blow him in the back room for twenty bucks. Was that so much to ask?

I found another stool, keeping my eyes down, and stupid tears crept into my nose. Jasper would've torn that guy's head off.

Yeah. Big Em, my ghostly better self, snorted at my shoulder, her matter-of-fact tone caustic. *Because it cost Jasper a lot more than twenty bucks to get you to suck him off.*

I flushed and wiped my eyes. *You know what, Big Em? Sometimes you can just keep your know-it-all mouth shut.*

The blond bar guy brought my champagne, and I drank deep, the alcoholic fizz warm and urgent inside. It didn't soothe me. Persistent male fingers slid over my shoulder, and I shrugged them off impatiently. Tattoo Boy didn't know when to give up. "Look, I'm not selling, okay?"

"Pity." Hot lips drenched my cheek in stale blood-scent, and fingers snapped tight like cruel jaws on the back of my neck. "Guess we'll just take it for free, then."

My pulse jiggled cold. Dark husky voice, dusty blue hair snaking over my shoulder. Tinkerfang, my new vampire buddy.

"Get off me, freak." Metal clattered as I shoved my stool back, trying to break Tinker's grip.

But I just banged into a hard shoulder. Paris snarled, teeth shining, golden fury glittering her eyes. "You murdered our friend, slutfae."

My nerves knotted cold. "What? No! I didn't hurt him, I just—Guh!"

Tinker gripped my throat, sharp nails slashing, and dived in to lick my blood from his knuckles with a lust-drunk hiss. "He's dead on the floor, bitch. What'd you give him? Huh? Cut your sparkle with drain cleaner?"

I struggled, sharp heels slipping on the metal floor. "No! Get off me. I didn't do anything!"

But guilt trickled like hot honey over my skin, and with an ugly jolt, I realized I had.

In my mind, that glowing scarlet jewel crushed once more in Kane's fist. That horrid deathly squelch, soul-blood's dark shine on his lips. *That was the vampire boy's, was it?* he'd said.

Jasper gave Kane the gemstone I stole, and now the vampire I'd stolen it from was dead. Kane ate his soul. Because I was too dumb to realize Jasper was playing me, some guy I didn't even know—some ordinary, horny, blood-drunk kid who never did me any wrong, only took what I was offering—was dead.

Tinker bared his teeth, a hungry dog's grin. "Oh yes, you did, princess. And I'm gonna chain you up and bleed you till you die. Could take weeks."

I choked and scrabbled at his hand, scratching his skin bloody. His meaty virus-stink wormed hot and sick in my mouth, but determination burned hotter.

Sure, their friend was a rude, dirty scumbag who bought blood from desperate girls. Didn't mean he deserved to die.

But neither did I.

I forced my jaw tight and jammed my knee into Tinker's balls.

He cramped over, gasping, and his grip faltered. I slammed my metal heel into Paris's shin. Skin ripped, a bloody splatter. She yowled like a wounded cat, and I pulled free and dived headfirst into the undulating crowd.

Fangs slashed at my ankle, but I kicked free and tumbled onto my face. The grimy metal floor smacked into my cheek. My teeth sliced my lips. A knee crushed my ribs. My hair yanked tight under stumbling feet, smearing in the dirt. I didn't care. I hauled myself up on nerveless wings and ran, shoving shoulders and limbs and trailing wings from my path.

Behind me, Paris and Tinker snarled, and metal furniture clanged. I fought a path through the sweaty crowd, between wailing fairies crazy on sparkle-drenched drinks, a pair of troll boys kissing, a lithe scarlet-haired firefairy on his knees, going down on his girl right there on the dance floor, her skirt wrapped around her hips and his lips shining wet. No one gave a damn about me. No one would help me, not a stupid bloodfae whore.

Sticky hair plastered in my eyes. I dragged it back. At last, I broke clear and hurtled toward the front door.

The skinny green troll girl at the counter speared me on a beady black glare as I stumbled by. I'd checked my jacket, a shiny silver one, my favorite. I didn't care. I forced out into the street, past a weaving blue waterfairy and a greasy pair of sniggering potbellied spriggans, and took a desperate gulp of hot dry midnight air.

Moonlight burned me, dancing sweet desire into my blood. The street was busy, cars cruising by in the shadow of motionless foliage, the plane trees on the median strip untouched by breeze. As usual for a midnight in summer, the queue stretched along the dirty footpath, a swath of dustbright wings, glowing eyes, rainbow limbs damp with fragrant sweat. Magical static sparked along the pavement, red and blue as glamours clashed and fought for space, and the air shimmered with spellcraft and moonlit heat.

But humans, too, excited and glassy-eyed, swaying dizzy on intoxicating glamour. Too many humans. My heart sank. I couldn't fly away, not in front of them. Too dangerous.

My heels raked my ankles bloody as I stumbled to the gutter and wildly searched the street. No cabs. Typical. Nearest tramstop blocks away.

Behind me, the door crashed open. I whirled, vision blurring, and hot needles stabbed along my nerves. Tinker hunkered and slavered like a chained dog. Paris sniffed, tasting the still heat like a cat, and her sharp gaze speared me to the wall.

8

I gulped a breath and ran.

Paris and Tinker hared behind me like hungry beasts. My stupid heels crippled me, my lungs a hot mess. That creeping hellfire cackled inside me, greasy with inevitability. I couldn't outrun them, couldn't hide. Couldn't fight them off.

Out of options. Out of luck. Out of time.

I scrabbled in my purse with shaking fingers. Dragged out Jasper's phone, moonbright blood smearing. Hit CALL BACK.

In a ring and a half, he picked up.

Club noise, harsh. His voice, impatient but harmonious like windchimes. "Where you lurkifying, Jayjay? Don't got all night."

I flung a glance over my shoulder, hair flying. "It's not Jasper," I panted. "It's me, Ember. Jasper's dead. They're chasing me, I—"

"Ember?" The noise faded, like he moved where it was quieter. "Whattaya mean, deaded? How? What happenated?"

"They're chasing me, okay?" Tears gripped my throat tight. I couldn't breathe. I gulped, wet. "They're gonna kill me, I can't—"

"Okay, angel. Chillify." Cool, authoritative, in control. "Where you at?"

"Outside, I'm out the fr— Ugh!"

Broken concrete caught my heel, and I tripped.

I flailed my wings for balance, but no good. My hips hit the asphalt, rattling my bones. I skidded, gravel scraping my midriff raw, and my chin slammed the pavement.

My teeth crunched, a mouthful of blood. Stars shimmied before my eyes like drunken jewels. Jasper's phone cracked on the ground and spun out of reach.

Fuck.

I shook my aching head, desperate to clear it. Dizzy, I tried to clamber up, clawing the dusty brick wall.

But Paris kicked my feet from under me, and I crumpled, wings flapping wet.

Tinkerfang sniffed me, grinning. "You smell good bleeding."

I kicked at him from the dirty ground, trembling. "Get off me, freak!"

Paris smiled cruelly, and she glanced cunningly at the watching crowd. "There you are, precious. Come on home, now. Don't be afraid." Her smooth voice soothed, placated, like a mistress to her naughty dog, and she offered me her hand, those vampire eyes seething with hot crimson death.

I shrank, my bruised flesh aching like the hellfire in my bones. "Get away from me!"

"Don't be silly, pretty. We're your friends. Come home. We won't hurt you."

Desperate, I searched the indifferent crowd. "Please, help me. She's not my friend. They're gonna kill me! Please!"

But no one moved or spoke. No one would help me,

not the gangster's skanky girlfriend. I'd probably brought it on myself, right? For dressing like a tart?

The cruel moon shone, careless, spilling the dark shadow of my new friends onto my body. They'd kill me. Drink every last slurp of my richcandy blood, and I didn't have Kane's stones and he'd drag me wailing to hell. Forever.

Paris leaned in. Tinker grinned, salivating, and dragged his hotslick tongue over my collarbone. Already my greedy moonpulse swelled hot and ready. I wanted to scream. I wanted to lie back and let them take me.

My guts clenched tight, but I didn't close my eyes. I stared them right in their faces. *Watch me die, fuckers. Look into my eyes while you kill me.*

Roseglass wings sliced the air apart.

Tinker stumbled, his chain suddenly yanked taut, and his grip tore away. Paris staggered and snarled, a flash of wet teeth and lustdrunk eyes. But a shining pink blur cracked her skull into the wall.

Blood spattered. She choked, her throat gripped tight in a fist that glowed like blood-drenched starlight, and Diamond's whisper sparkled the air with crystal. "Careful where you play, trashgirl."

I stared, detached, surprised he'd even bothered. Sweat shone on his bulging translucent muscles, and his glassy wings blazed scarlet as he jammed her against the wall.

One-handed. Three feet off the ground. Strong son of a bitch.

Especially for a guy who's . . . well . . . *pink*.

Mad giggles bubbled my throat, and I swallowed them.

Tinker whimpered, dribbling, and Diamond gave

his chain a savage pull, sprawling him facefirst to the ground. "Hush it, Fido, grown-ups are talkamating. That's my fairylady, petal. Hands off."

Paris snarled and kicked, struggling in his grip. "Don't see no lady. That bitch poisoned our friend."

"And you can take it up with Angelo. He says, we do-ify. Wanna get shitty with him? Be my guest. But she's my vampire bait, and you can't have her."

Indignation burred my skin, but I crouched small and kept my mouth shut.

Diamond flung Paris aside, and she landed in a snarling crouch, angry blond hair tangling. Tinker rolled over, quick as a snake, and dived for Diamond's ankles with a hungry howl.

Diamond skittered aside, wings clinking. Tinker grabbed his legs and chewed, sharp teeth slashing at leather, and Diamond hissed and yanked at Tinker's bluedusted hair. Rotting hanks ripped off in his hands, but the little rat screeched in famished delight and wouldn't let go.

"Get off, you sick little freak!" I flexed my aching thigh and kicked at Tinker's face.

My heel connected, a crunch of bone. Tinker howled again and let go, blood spurting from his cute button nose.

I scrambled up, my pulse racing. It felt good to stand up for myself, even if I wasn't tough enough to escape on my own. But still, my heart stung. Tinker was just a hungry kid on a chain, trying to please his mistress.

I knew how he felt.

I stammered, confusion melting my disgust. I wanted to claw Tinker's eyes out for threatening me. I wanted to put my arm around him, say, *There, there, sweetie,* and wipe his little nose clean. I just wasn't cut out for this gangfighting shit. "Yeah . . . that'll learn ya to chase me, weirdo. Take that."

Paris grabbed sobbing Tinker close and stroked his hair, soothing his whimpers. "Shush, now, pet. Mummy will make you better. Another time, shitfae." She shot us a hate-filled glare.

Diamond bared shining teeth, glassy claws aglitter. His fury burned rich around him like a raspberry fireball. "Whatever. Go on, piss off." And he swept me behind a redstained wing and stood there glowering until Paris gathered her bloodsoaked baby under her arm and stumbled away.

And then he swiped Jasper's dented phone into his pocket and dragged me up the street.

I pulled back, alarmed. "Hey—!"

His golden murmur burned my ear. "Trustify. Freakazoids got friends. You don't wanna hang here." He grinned, for our audience's benefit, and raised his voice a notch. "Come on, darlin'. Get you cleanified." And he tossed a casual arm around my shoulder and marched me off.

I swallowed, my belly warm. His protective act unnerved me. I was tall, for a girl, but his strength threatened me, his size intimidating. His elbow brushed my ticklish wingjoint, and I jumped, inadvertently pressing closer. His body felt hot, smooth, slick against my side. My pulse quickened, the moon purring on my skin. Mmm. That warm rosy scent lit my senses, dangerous and intriguing. God, he smelled fantastic when he was angry.

I flushed, shrugging his arm off. *Trouble, Ember. Don't go there. He thinks you're trash just like everyone else. He's only letting you hang around because you owe him.*

Graffiti snarled from the shadows, torn billposts hanging loose on grimy walls. Glass and black marble gleamed from offices and hotel foyers. Eighties music spilled from a redbrick pub, a corny saxophone solo, rows of lightbulbs under the cantilever shedding more heat into the scorching night. A tram rumbled by, sparks flashing in overhead wires.

Fatigue hit my limbs like a wave, all the tension of my escape exhausting me. I stumbled, and Diamond caught me, his fingers a warm temptation for a second on my waist and then gone. I swallowed, sick. "Where we going?"

"Rehydramate. You're pale, candy. Next time, don't let him drinkify so much."

Next time. Ha. That was a laugh. He still thought I was a whore. I turned my hands over, studying my skin, and frowned. I was brown. How could I go pale? Still, maybe he was right. I did feel strange, light-headed, that greedy moon dizzying me.

He tugged me around the corner, where traffic lights burned red and green and car headlamps flashed on polished shopfronts, and into a cheerybright café.

Wooden chairs and tables lay cluttered in the rich smell of coffee beans. The place was nearly empty, a few students sipping mochas on the stained brown sofa, a giggling blue fairy in torn jeans with his nose poked into a chocolate pudding. The soft orange spotlights looked warm, but overconditioned air parched my lungs. My damp skin already shrank into bumps. The bored boy behind the counter didn't look up from his dishcloth.

Jasper's ring burned icy on my finger. I pulled back, urgency nipping my toes like an angry crayfish. Jasper was dead. Vampires nearly ate me. I was going to hell, for god's sake. Was this really the time for a coffee date? "But what about—?"

Diamond pushed me toward a table at the back. "Just sittify."

Confused, I sat, and cool brown wood stuck to my butt with a squelch. I crossed my legs, tugging my tiny excuse for a skirt down. This dress was ridiculous. I rolled bloodsweaty hair off my neck, gazes real or imagined prickling my back. I'm used to being stared at, envy or desire or curiosity, and mostly I don't mind.

Mostly, I don't look like a desperate slut with a bloodfetish.

Still, my knight-in-shining-attitude didn't seem to care. He just flitted to the counter, flicking his bright wings gracefully this way and that so he wouldn't tip anything over. Electric glamour shimmered, and I caught a dizzying glimpse of his magical cover. Long pale hair, fair skin, deceptively gentle gray eyes, a faint blur where his wings should be. His chiselglass features were smoothed into inconspicuousness. Even his overt strength faded, his limbs slimming. He looked small, dull, the kind of unimpressive guy you'd brush past in the street without noticing or remembering.

Hell of an effort, considering the real thing.

I fidgeted, fiddling with my bag. He'd a lot more magicjuice than most. How effortlessly he'd read me, how viciously his faesight stripped me raw. And how softly he'd teased me into touching him, trusting him, taking his lead.

I swallowed, unwilled memory of a scorching almost-kiss drenching me in rosescent. Strawberry Boy was a threat, even if he'd just saved my skin.

Especially since he'd just saved my skin. His help me made me nervous. What would he ask in return?

Diamond perched his butt on the chair's edge opposite with a muffled crystal clunk, and slid me a tall sparkling pink lemonade. "Drink it, candy."

Great. Now he'd bought me a drink, too, even if it was just lolly water. I should refuse, pay for it myself. But my old obedient habit twitched my fingers toward the glass before I could stop them, and indignation prickled my wings hot. It wasn't his fault. But I wanted to throw the drink over him, shove it into his lap, yell, *Stop calling me "candy," you crystalwit freak!*

But perky sugarscent dried my mouth. I needed fluid after losing so much blood. Thirst clawed my tongue, and I dragged the glass to my lips and swallowed, ignoring the straw. Delicious chill poured down my throat, and my mouth sparkled, enraptured with glorious raspberry sweetness.

I stopped for a breath, and burped, bubbles frothing. Most unladylike.

Diamond handed me a bunch of paper napkins, glitter-lashed eyes unreadable. Downlights flashed on his rippleglass wings, eerie yet warm. He'd faded, calmed himself down, just a shimmer of rose caressing his skin. A strange angel indeed.

I took the napkins, self-conscious, and wiped clumsily at the clotted blood on my chest. I remembered how he'd stared at me in the club, contempt flashing rich in his eyes, and I flushed again, my wings sore and sunburned with embarrassment. I'd expected him to demand answers: *Where's Jasper, who killed him, why the hell did you just stand there and let it happen, you sillyfae bitch? You're useless, Emmy, you know that?*

But he said nothing. Like he trusted me to tell when I was ready.

My belly warmed. Either that, or he didn't expect

any sense out of me. Huh. Right. He already thought me a stupid tart, and my helpless girly behavior wasn't helping. Not that I cared for his opinion one way or the other.

I finished with the napkins and tossed them onto the table. They were sticky, a scarlet-smeared mess, but I was kinda clean. Pity about the dress, which was ruined. And I didn't have Jasper to buy me another one.

An ache swelled my throat. Jasper was gone. I was alone. Except for this mercurial glassfairy, who despised me one moment and guarded me with his life the next.

My skin prickled. I could feel him watching me, that hot rubycrystal gaze cataloging my every movement. I wished he'd stop. I didn't want the way it made me feel. Exposed. Vulnerable. Naked.

"Better?" He flashed me that blinding smile, and my skin heated. The scratches on my midriff stung like ant bites, the ring chopping my finger tight. I wanted to cover myself up, turn away, hide.

God, I hated it when he smiled. I crossed my arms, my breasts hot. "Uh-huh. Umm . . . thanks. I know you didn't have to . . . well, y'know. Thanks."

"No biggie." He wouldn't look away.

Jeez, just cut to the chase already. What did he want from me?

I tried to swallow my discomfort. I guessed I owed him an explanation, no matter how I distrusted him. Reluctantly, I offered my hand for inspection. "Jasper gave me this ring, see? I . . . well, I thought it was a gift."

Diamond bent to sniff at it, his sharp nose brushing my knuckles. He straightened, flicking his hair back. "Pretty. So what?"

"See that flame, deep inside? He and his friends did

a deal with Kane, and then they tried to hide from him with these gems. But Kane found out, and he . . . I mean, Jasper . . ." Tears choked me, and I swallowed hard. "He's dead. Kane crushed him. And now I can't get the stupid ring off and that flame's chewing up my bones, okay, and if I don't bring Kane all the jewels by big full moon, he'll drag me down to hell and yeah, I'm a stupid gullible bloodfae tart and you can just stop looking at me like that!"

Diamond's wings tilted in surprise. "What?"

My claws dug into my palms. "Like I'm dirt or something. Like you don't give a shit. I'm not an idiot, Diamond. You helped me when I called. You obviously want something from me, so give it a rest and stop calling me 'candy,' okay?"

The words spilled out before I'd had time to parse them for offense, and instinctively I cowered, making myself small and inoffensive even as my nerves fired like chili with impotent rage. *Go on, hit me. I'll be dead soon anyway. What the fuck do I care?*

But Diamond just blinked glitter lashes, and shrugged. "Okay, Ember."

I stared, bewildered. "Eh . . . Okay, then. Fine." I squared my shoulders, unaccustomed confidence glimmering in my heart. It felt so nice just to have someone to confide in, but I knew it wouldn't last. Nothing nice ever lasted. I waited for him to laugh, look askance, say, *Riiight, sure, thanks for letting me know. None of my beeswax, candywhore. Sort out your little demon problem on your own.*

He glanced at my ring, chewing his beautiful lip. "So you took Jaspy's gift, and now you're stuck with his owings, too?"

"Seems that way."

"Well, that sucks. Fucking demons. You got your-self a probby-lem."

I snickered, humorless. *You*. Not *we*. "Yeah. I sure do. Look, Diamond old buddy, I appreciate you saving my ass and everything, but—"

"Kane say who these morons was you're lookifying?"

I gave him a *whadda you care?* scowl, slurped more pink lemonade, and smacked my lips as loudly as I could. "Nice talking to ya, cutie. Don't let me keep you. Thanks for the drink. 'Kay. See ya. Bye." I pushed my chair aside.

But he caught it with his foot and dragged me back.

"Hey!" Now the table caged me. I wriggled, jerking my wings, but it only made my bare thigh rub against his under the table. Hot fairy muscle, too strong for me to shift. I sweated, seeping fragrant pink. "C'mon, no fair. Let go!"

He trapped my flailing hands against the table, light but firm. "Names, Ember."

Panic shuffled my wits like cards. I didn't want to owe him. Debts to sultryfae gangboys were danger-ous. Damn it, did he have to insist? "I don't need your help, okay?"

"Choice? Nope. Hushify," he added, a dangerous purple glint in his eyes when I tried to protest. "My boy made you a pretty mess. My job to unmessify."

"Yeah?" I glared, inches away. More stupid gang loyalty. He wasn't even pretending he cared about me. "And what do I owe you for your unmessification, huh?"

"A favor." His lips twitched, and inwardly I groaned. *Don't do it. Don't smile.*

Aw, hell.

Stunning. Hypnotic. Sparkling with promise, dark

with suggestion, wicked with the echo of kisses and laughter.

My belly melted, all warm and wobbly like treacle, and the moon howled wild in my blood. *I'm special. I'm wanted. I'm the only woman in his world.*

I wanted to press my legs together. And his thigh jammed between mine wasn't helping. God, a girl could die for that smile.

I swallowed, warm. "What kinda favor?"

"Hellfire cocktails and pitchforks in your butt, right? You care?"

"Maybe." I flushed under his scrutiny. Jeez, if he thought I'd do something cheap and dirty, he was dead wrong. I didn't care how tempting his smile was.

"It's just a favor." His musical voice dropped down a harmonic, mesmerizing. "Nothing grim. We're friends. That's all."

I knew what he meant. My friend, your friend, all that anachronistic mob crap. I'd owe him, and everyone would know.

Awesome. Just great. I rid myself of one controlling boy, only to glue like a suckerfish to another. Emphasis on the *sucker*.

He let go and leaned back, his blinding smile quirking into a sly shadow of itself. "Yes or no, Ember. Got better plannings?"

My bones burned deep inside, a tiny but growing echo of Kane's demonspelled will, and I scowled, but had no answer. Diamond was right. I had no choice. I didn't know who to look for or where, and the moon grew fuller and brighter by the minute.

"Okay. Fine. You win." I dug into my bag and tossed Kane's card onto the table. "Kane gave me this. Mean anything to you?"

He flipped the card over, and his melting ruby eyes froze azure.

I leaned forward, my pulse flickering. "What? You know those people?"

"Showify that ring again." His voice faded to a whisper, and his gaze didn't leave the card in his hand.

"What? Why?"

"Just do it."

Awkwardly, I stuck my hand out, splaying my bruised fingers like some fucked-up bride-to-be. The gemstone gleamed green like a wildcat's eye, hard and cold, that strange icefire dancing within. The metal seared like frost, and my finger ached.

He laughed, cynicism clanging like iron. "You've got to be shittifying."

"Excuse me?"

He shoved the card back to me and flitted to his feet. "Hangem here one second, can you?"

"Why? Where you going?"

He jerked his head toward the bathroom door, his knuckles crackling tight. "Gotta take a slash. Wanna come hold me?"

And before I could even wonder how I'd pissed him off, he'd left me there alone.

Across the street in hot dry shadow, Vincent DiLuca stares, bloodlust clogging his throat like hot honey.

God, she's delicious.

He came here to stalk Diamond, kill the skanky glass boyslut in some dark alley and get Joey's favor back. Now, Diamond's gone, out the back for a quick line or maybe even giving him the slip, but Vincent doesn't care.

He can smell the redhead from here, her darkrich

bloodfae scent swirling him dizzy until his knees go watery and he has to grab the streetlight post to stay upright. He hyperventilates, sucking in even more of her, and hunger boils his blood.

Long warm thighs wrapped in the thinnest silken skin. Roughpaper wings, those delicate veins swollen with hot liquid, a rich bloodscented cloud of hair. The tantalizing womansmell of her sex, as tasty as blood but sweeter, softer. She crosses her legs, muscles teasing beneath her skin, and her secret flesh slicks together under her skirt.

Desperation burns in Vincent's veins. Christ on a barbecued cross, she's sex on a stick.

He crouches, sniffing for her like an animal. He's seen her before somewhere. A gang groupie, someone's girlfriend, maybe. Em-something. Emma? Amber?

Where did Diamond find her, this plumsweet bloodfairy princess? Who the fuck cares? Vincent just wants to eat her, fuck her, slash her pretty body with a hundred jagged cuts and bathe in her blood under the moon while she moans and writhes, impaled on him. . . .

No. He grits aching teeth, fever flushing him sick. *Don't want to kill. She's pretty, it's okay to want her. Just not like that. Besides, Joey'll kick my ass.*

But he can't tear his starved gaze away. He's only ever tasted one bloodfairy, and never under the full moon, when their blood's richest and most delicious. Christ, even in the dark, it was glorious enough. Like the purest, smoothest heroin, easing into his veins, stroking him swiftly to the hottest pleasure of his rotten little life. And that was just a skinny black-haired boy selling it for sparkle, his blood undernourished and listless. This beautiful girl, pulsing with life and innocence, her blood swelled rich on midnight moontide . . .

Thirsty spit sloshes in his mouth, and he bangs his fist against the post until his knuckles split and bleed, but it doesn't erase the truth. He's tried having them without eating. It doesn't work. He's a monster.

Hunger scorches his veins, dragging his pulse tighter and hotter and faster. Sweat drips from his hair. His guts ache. He's shivering. He's so hard, it hurts, his balls aching deep like he's shoved a molten iron spike in there. Virus-chewed synapses misfire in his brain, and his drowning human reason gulps one last ragged breath and sinks beneath the surface.

His vampire vision homes in sharply, showing tiny lines between her brows, her soft curving lips, the crisp edge of her flamebright hair. The veins in her throat throb, a deep pulling tide. He stretches his jaws hungrily, and swallows to stop slavering, make himself presentable.

Just this once. She's only some Valenti groupie, probably a bloodwhore anyway. No one'll miss her. And Joey never needs to know.

But not yet.

He smiles, crafty. Diamond likes her, and that's worth something. She's good for more than a few minutes' bliss, this lovely girl with a few too many shithead Valenti friends for her own good. One more blade to stab Diamond with before he dies. She'll be worth waiting for.

Black delight fires Vincent's blood, and he rakes sweat from his hair and crosses the street.

9

Shaking, Diamond slams the bathroom door open and stalks in. No one inside, just rude white tiles and stainless steel, and when the door clangs shut, he strangles a screech.

Curse her. Cursify both of them.

His warm poison vial scorches his palm, accusing, and he unfolds aching knuckles over glittergreen glass.

He couldn't do it. He had the fucking thing in his hand over her berrypink lemonade and he just . . . couldn't. Couldn't poison this lovelybright girl. Couldn't spikify her drink like a sleazy lizard gangshit who can't get laid. It's not right.

But all that seems insignificant now.

Kane's bloodyscratched letters still scorch his eyes. The demon's riddling is laughafiably simple. Scarletfire, envied lady of shadow and flame. Famine, starved and insane, his heart clotted black with strange desires, an altogether more sinister beast. Simple to find. Harder to stealify from. Couldn't care a spit for them, black or white.

But the bloodpetal girl can be only one person, and bitter dread parches Diamond's mouth like ash.

Rosa has sold her soul to Kane. She'll die screaming

in hell. And she's trappified Diamond right there with her.

Ashen heat crackles already in his bones, and slowly, he turns his wrist to the light.

His dustypink blood still crusts the sharp bracelet, dried rosepetals caressing wicked silver thorns. The jewel gleams under bluesharp fluorescents, purple like Rosa's eyes, and the fire inside whispers sweet death. The bracelet's tight, razor edges threatening. No clasp, no spring, no hook where it comes apart.

Shoulda noticed that before. Shoulda guessed her gift wouldn't be harmless.

The memory of Rosa's tricksy kiss taunts him raw. A calculamated, distracting kiss. He wants to crack his fucking idiot skull into the mirror. Pretty girls in trouble are his weakness. He'll never learnify.

He digs his claw underneath to rip it off, and with a hiss, the metal flexes and tightens, piercing his skin until the blood seeps.

Yeow. The jewel winks, wicked, and an evil giggle whisks around the edges of his mind. *Mess with me, stupidfae? Cut your bloody arm off, see if I don't.*

He crunches glass claws hard on the sink. Demon lies. Hellfire. Rosa's trickified him, as smooth and sweatless as Jasper trickified Ember. Check-fucking-mate.

And now Diamond's torn between two unpossible endings.

If Ember doesn't get her gemstones, she'll die. But if she does get them, Rosa dies.

Never mind Diamond's own worthless life. No matter what he does, some prettylicious girl is gonna burn.

Impotent fury clangs in his bones, a discordant crystalchime, welling louder and louder. His ears ache and split, but he can't stop the sound swelling. His nerves stretch, impossibly tight. Evil resonance vibrates his body, glass glowing hot. The floor shudders beneath his feet. Tiles jiggle and crack. The air shrieks in pain, and the finger-smeared mirror judders and explodes.

Crash.

Abruptly, silence. Glintglass shards, scattered wall to wall. Blood running rosy in the sink where he's cut himself again, but this time the pain doesn't dissolvify his rage. He gasps, trying to catch his breath, muscles still aching despite the release.

He slams on the tap, and cold water rushes, soothing his bloody palm. His thoughts scramble wild. He doesn't know it's truthful, this soul-bindy-twiny-whatever. The stone could be tricksy lies, some elaborate swindlicality Rosa invented to tauntify him.

Or Ember could be falsing. Using her body and her luscious green glance to seduce him, grasping for another boy to keep her now Jasper's dead. He's only got her wordies that Jaspy's even gone.

But the hopeless fear in her eyes still slashes his heart like poisoned steel, and he spits a curse. His glasstalent doesn't lie. The hot, searching desperation in her touch wasn't fakified. She's telling real. Has to be.

And now he must choosify.

Pretty, brave, helpless Ember, desperate to trustify him even if she pretends not. Eyeball-deep in fuckup through no bad of her own. Or Rosa, dark, cool, sophistimacated, lies as venomsweet as her kisses.

One never did him a scrap of harm. The other tore his heart from his chest and ate it.

Can't save both.

He squeezes his eyes shut, calming his racing heart. Easy. Chillify. Stick with the plannification. There's still time to slippify the poison to Ember later.

Angelo dead. The city his. Rosa where she belongs. All he ever wanted.

Don't owify Embercandy nothing. She's not his problem. Never mind that she's clever and courageous and begging to be cared for in more luscious ways than one.

Or that her spicy girlscent makes him sweat, or that he can't peel his eyes off her sunfire hair or her smooth mochabrown thighs or stop imagining how those wispy-fine wings will quiver when he kisses them. How she'll moan, so rich and throaty, when he sucks her duskylicious wingjoint into his mouth . . .

Uh-huh. Like that's ever happening. *Here, Ember, drink this tasty vampire poison so I can send you to hell, wanna screw?* Even his glassbrittle conscience squeals at charming her into his bed now.

He snaps the water off and blasts his hands dry under the hot air machine. His sliced palm already scabs itchy. The memory of her trusting green gaze salts his mouth with remorse, and he ripples his wings taut and cracks the guilt off like tarnish.

Because that's what guilt is. Tarnish. Dirt. Useless verdigris.

Ember's troublemesses change nothing. He'll help her get her first two gems. Stealify her trust. Use the poison, one way or the other. Keep Rosa's gemstone safe and secret, just until the moon's ripe. And when Angelo's dead and Rosa's safe and everything's the way it should be . . . well, maybe Diamond can warptruth, connive, find some sneakalicious way out of this. Sweet-talk Kane, trade him something nice, convince him to let Ember free.

Yeah. Because demons like letting mortals squir-micate off the hook. Happens all the time.

Whatever. One probbylem at a time.

Practiced, he breathes. Calms. Relaxifies. Spreads steady hands out before him, lights glimmering silver on his pinksmooth skin. The clinging bracelet hurts as he flexes his forearm, and the hellpurple jewel winks him a wicked promise.

His muscles quiver, then relax. Not a tremble. Not a twitch. Nothing to offshow his deception.

Remorse twinges his nerves with a faint blue glow, and he shucks it off with a grimace. Fresh pink light flares, rimmed with gold, and his hair shimmers in the broken mirror like rainbows. He looks good. Fresh. Sharp.

Cynicism tweaks his mouth sour. Always such a pretty liar. It's why he's still alive. Pity what's underneath isn't worth spitting on.

He turns, and the door squeaks open.

"Are you here on your own?"

"Huh?" My glass tilted as I jerked back to the present. I'd been staring off into space, imagining it was all a dream. That no ring clamped my finger, that I'd never heard of Kane or Jasper or this disturbing Diamond. That I'd looked askance that moonlit night six months ago when Jasper hit on me in the club, instead of sparking my courage bright and slipping him a saucy wink and a smile. That I'd skipped away with my girlfriends, drunk myself silly on salty tequila shots and stumbled home at dawn, instead of letting Jasper take me back to his place and love me into heartmelting oblivion.

I sighed. Nice dream.

". . . saw you with someone else."

Smooth voice, low and casual. Not Diamond.

Orange lights glared. I slurped my drink dry, cold fizz tickling my throat. "I'm sorry, what?"

"I said, I thought I saw you with someone else before. Ember, right?"

I could see him now, crispy chocolate hair arranged in an elaborate mess, puppy-dog brown eyes, curling lashes. Jewelstud earrings, goldlink bracelets, too many rings on his fingers. Hot body, for a human, fit and shaped. He wore torn jeans and a white shirt with tiny ruffles, and light sweat caressed his olive skin in the heat.

Cute. Familiar. Could he see me? I thought so. His gaze was too direct to be glamour-dazzled. I squinted, trying to recall where I'd seen him before. "Yeah. Who are you?"

He sat in Diamond's chair, lean legs stretching. He had a young face, handsome, big beautiful boylashed eyes and a secretly dirty smile. Like your best friend's oversexed little brother, cute and harmless until you'd had a few too many drinks and he turned into a tempting ball of trouble. "Thought so. Listen, I wanted to apologize for my friends back there."

"I'm sorry, who?"

"Y'know. The, uh, sharp-toothed lady and her pet. That wasn't nice." He smiled, charming, and curved fangs glinted at the corners of his mouth.

I jerked backwards, my nerves shrieking warning, and too late the rabid rawmeat scent of bloodfever hit me full in the face like a dumping wave. "Get away from me!"

"S'okay." He grabbed my hand to halt me, his skin scorching. "You're safe with me. They were outta line, and I'm sorry. That's all."

Disbelief muddled with wonder. So this one hadn't jumped me yet. Didn't mean I liked him touching me. Still, he was polite. I tugged my hand back, less roughly than I'd planned. "What, you not hungry?"

"With you six inches away? Honey, I'm fucking starving. But that's no excuse for me to be rude."

"Oh." I fidgeted. I still didn't trust him, and something was so naggingly familiar. . . . "Okay. Uhh . . . thanks, I guess. For the apology, I mean."

"My pleasure." He winked, and memory scraped my nerves again. I'd definitely seen him before. "So, you here with someone or not?"

I glanced past him at the bathroom door. Diamond hadn't come out. "Kinda. Look, you should leave now—"

"I don't mean to cut in or anything." He leaned closer, so close, his feverheat warmed my face like sunlight, and again I scrabbled at memory's edge for that elusive connection. "But you seem like a nice girl, I can't just . . . Listen, how much d'you know about your new boyfriend?"

I flushed. Five damn minutes and the whole world thought we were screwing. "He's not my boyfriend, okay? And how the hell do you kn—?" In midsentence, wires connected in my head, and my skin jerked cold. "Shit. You're Vincent, right? Vincent DiLuca?"

The snake bastard's human minion, après virus. The worst kind of DiLuca troublemaker. I'd heard Jasper curse him countless times. Diamond would kick the crap out of him on sight. But he'd been sorta nice to me, even if he was a stinky bloodsucker and technically my enemy.

Vincent gave a dangerous cherub smile, charming except for the fangs. "Guilty, Your Worship. I'm flattered. So, how much d'you know about glitterboy?"

Loaded question, from him. But curiosity gnawed me. "None of your goddamn business."

"Kinda quick to pick you up, wasn't he? No offense or anything."

I lifted my chin, haughty. "Wow, you're a real charmer."

"You know he killed some fairies tonight? S'what I heard."

"Really. Why the hell should I trust you?" My thigh muscles twitched, begging to flee. I gripped my bag tight, determined not to show fear. The stinky little ferret was my enemy, charmer or no. If he jumped me, I'd scream. There were humans here. Violence got noticed.

But Vincent just laughed, handsome brown eyes glinting. "Don't be afraid. We're not all scumsucking morons."

"Who, vampires or DiLucas?"

"Ooh, that stung. This your dance card, sweetie?" And before I could stop him, he'd swept Kane's card from the table.

"Give that back!" I snatched for it, my heart skipping.

But he laughed and flipped it away, golden rings glinting. "Finders keepers. Tsk, tsk, bad Ember. That dirty fairy's leading you astray. Into Famine's kinky parties, are ya?"

My mind raced. Did he know something about this? "What do you mean? Who's Famine?"

Vincent cocked a sardonic eyebrow. "Whatever. I think it's hot. So what's Diamond want with Famine? You Valentis got weird-ass fairy sadists working for you now? Or is pinkboy just hot for rusty dungeon sex? Jesus, stop it with the heart rate, lady, you're giving me a hard-on."

I flushed, but I couldn't calm my pulse. Could he hear me? Feel my blood, hot and swelling with moonlust? "Look, you'd better leave. . . ."

"You know what? I'll ask him myself. Nice meeting you, Emm-berr." The way he purred my name made it sound like food. He grabbed my phone from the table, and before I could stop him or protest, he'd called himself and hung up after a single ring.

Great. Now he had my number. "Put that down!"

He winked and tossed it to me, making me fumble. "That's Vincent with a *V.* You ever want the lowdown on your fairytoy, you gimme a call." And he flipped my card back onto the table and sauntered off to the bathroom.

The bathroom door squeaks open, and swiftly, Diamond *blends,* hasty glamourflash clanging on broken glass. The magic stinks of rain and roses, but a human won't notice. Anyone else won't care.

Vincent DiLuca grins, jewels flashing in his ears. "Fancy meeting you here, glasshole."

Diamond bites down on a mouthful of rich insults. Snitchy little bastard ain't worth it, with his girly hair and *come hit on me* eyes. He's never sure if Vincent wants him dead or naked. Either way, no fight with him.

Yes fight with filthyskank vampire creepazoids who won't control their hunger. "Likewise," he mutters, and sidles for the door.

But Vincent clicks his tongue, cocky. "Who's your lady friend? Wouldn't mind a taste of her."

Rage shocks Diamond cold.

Before he can think or breathe, he's jammed Vincent against the shard-spiked wall, forearm crunching into his gold-chained throat. The vampire's body fights, fevered and fresh against him, and muscle tight on muscle slams his pulse wild. "Wanna scrap with me, missy? Come gettify. Just leave her the fuck out of it."

He sucks in a heated breath, blood pumping too fast. He's glowing bright like a flashlight. Chillify, for fucksake. Ratbrain didn't even say her name. Besides, Ember means nothing to him, right? And this is a public place. People care if gangboys kill each other.

But hearing Vincent threaten her enrages Diamond beyond sense or reasonicality. Shiteating vampire scum. Always taking what don't belongem them.

Not that Ember belongs to anyone. Least of all Diamond.

Vincent flicks up unperturbed eyebrows. "Jeez, no need to flip out. Just saying, she's one sexy bitch. You're a lucky guy. I bet she fucks like a goddess. Christ, just the smell of her pussy makes me hard. See?" He grabs Diamond's hand and pulls it between his legs, where his hard flesh throbs with sick fever.

Diamond fights the urge to jab cutting claws deep into Vincent's balls. Instead, he rips his hand away with a wet snarl. "You're all class, scumlicker. Stay away from her."

"No, seriously, is she selling? Because I can pay, and I'd just *love* to suck on her." Vincent flexes virus-strong muscles, and suddenly it's Diamond crammed back against the wall, Vincent's fangsharp grin inches from his mouth.

Diamond tries to jump back, but his wings are crushified behind him and the vile little ratweed is strong.

Vincent jams his fevered thigh in and yanks a fistful of long glassy hair. He laughs, and it stinks of meat and bourbon. " 'Cause that's what I'm gonna do, fairy-shit, once you're dead. I'm gonna eat your girlfriend. I'm gonna put my cock in her mouth and spread her legs and suck the blood from her pretty pussy. And you know what? She'll like it. I'm talented like that."

"Sickity fuck." Diamond claws for Vincent's eyes, but he can't reach, not in the vampire's stony grip. Fuck. How did the wormatron get so strong?

Vincent giggles, mad. "Sick fuck. Ha ha. Good one. You're a funny guy. She must really like you." He snaps at Diamond's ear, missing the point by a shard, and his whisper pierces deep. "She'll curse you to hell before I'm finished with her. And you won't be able to save her. How does that feel, Diamond? Gallant mother-fucker like you? Must really break your heart."

"Don't walkify the hall of mirrors with me, asshole. I live there." Diamond flashes out wild glassfae talent, sharp like a wasp's sting, and Vincent's jealousy and hunger and rich longing crush Diamond's breath tight. He laughs, cutting. "Feeling a bit left out? Deadify as many as you want, it won't make pretty Mina love you."

Vincent's eyes darken angry black. "Don't even go there."

"She'd rather screw a slimycated snake than lay a finger on you. Hell, she even slept with me. I think she liked it. Make you feel good?"

A wet vampire snort, ripe with fury. "Don't sleep, fairyshit. Don't even close your pretty eyes. You're both mine."

And in a whoosh of stinking laughter, Vincent's not there.

Diamond stumbles, his heart sprinting, and jumps for the swinging door.

Ember sits, starifying into space, fiddling with her straw. Alone.

Relief cools his pulse. He halts in the doorway, catching his breath. He sniffs deep, flicks on his shin-ing faesight. Shapes loom and fade, sounds melting into shadows, air currents like dark eddies in glass. No tell-tale heat signature from a fevered vampire body. Only foul virus-stink, lingering. Vincent's gone.

Diamond snaps his sight back to normal, colors flooding in. The idea of Vincent's filthified mouth on Ember's skin lights his rage faster than any threat to his own useless life. Images flash vivid and scarlet-drenched, of Vincent kissing her, licking that perfect skin, dragging sharp teeth over her hipbone. Parting those lovely thighs, nuzzling her there with his tongue where the hair's soft and red, her blood running neon-fresh on hungry vampire lips . . .

He yanks long hair tight around his fist, frustration burning. It's not right. If Vincent wants to pick some fighticality? Bring it on with tinkles. But to grubby-talk a sweet innocent girl like that . . .

Diamond curses, and more glass shatters. Vincent's up to no good. Never mind dreamlusting about Ember naked and breathless. He can't leave her unprotecti-fied and alone now.

Like it or spit it, she's Diamond's responsimability now. And deep in some cold, forgotten crevice of his heart, protecting her feels good.

Yeah. It's really gonna goodfeel when you have to choosify Rosa over her, too. Frosticate it, fairy. Don't let her get to you.

He whips his hair smooth, calms his quivering limbs—nothing he can do about the hard-on—and walks out into the café.

10

"I can help you." Diamond held out his hand, his bracelet glinting silver.

"Huh?" I hadn't seen Vincent leave. Hadn't heard a scuffle. Couldn't see any blood. Had they fought? Was Vincent dead on the bathroom floor?

". . . can take you to her—"

"Did you just see—?" We both spoke at once, and I shook my head. "Never mind. What was that?"

"Scarletfire. Real name of Crimson. I'll show ya." Irresistibly he lifted me to my feet.

I scrabbled for my bag, stuffing Kane's infuriatingly cryptic card inside. "What, now?"

"Sure. Why waitify?"

"Umm . . . righto. Good plan." I stumbled over my heels as we walked out, his fingers tight but comfortable above my elbow, like he was afraid I'd escape. "You sure? I mean, how d'ya know it's the right person?"

"Get it when you see her."

"O-kaay. And 'famine in the dark'? What's that mean?"

"That's where he is, silly."

My palms itched, frustrated. "And the bloodpetal girl? You know her?"

He shrugged, short. "Maybe. C'mon." He tugged me outside, where the sweating café boy was piling up menus and stacking aluminum chairs on the hot pavement. Molten moonlight puddled on the black asphalt, glinting on iron tram lines. A police car screeched past, red and blue lights flashing, heat haze eddying in its wake.

Already, midnight warmth seeped under my skin, my hair crackling crisp. This was one fierce summer. Even in the dark, the heat just didn't let up.

I glanced left and right. No sign of Vincent. I looked at Diamond, trying to recover my small scrap of confidence, but he just glanced back with hot liquidberry eyes and said nothing.

Suspicion settled warm and uncomfortable in my veins. Vincent could've dragged me into the dark if he'd wanted to, taken my blood and left me in the gutter to die. But he hadn't. Maybe he'd truly wanted to help me.

But why would Snakeboy DiLuca's pet vampire psychopath care about me?

Unless DiLuca were plotting against Diamond. Using me to get to him. That was a laugh. Like Diamond gave a damn what happened to me. But should I hang around, or leave? Was I helping him, or them? Jeez, this was all too fucking hard.

I sighed, arranging my bag strap over my shoulder. It didn't matter. I'd be dead soon if I didn't do something, and I still had no other options. "Okay. Where we going?"

Diamond eyed me critically, up and down and up again. "First, home to changify your clothes."

"Huh? What for?" Urgency clawed my spine, the moon igniting my blood like alcohol. I didn't have time to change. I needed to fix this now.

"You really wanna go out looking like that?"

"Screw you, okay?" I tossed my hair, defiant. "In case you didn't get it, I have just a *teensy* time-pressure problem here. I don't have time to go home and make myself *pretty* for a sexist glassbrained warthog like y—"

"You're bloodified, Ember," he interrupted, glossy wings flashing as he faced me down. "You stink of it. Your dress is ripped up to your ass and you're showing off your—" And he bit his bottom lip and hid behind his rainbow cascade of hair.

But too late. I'd seen the deep magenta splash in his cheeks, the veins swelling bright in his throat. A teasing smile tweaked my lips. Cockyfae was blushing. Fancy that.

Which meant . . . Oh, shit.

My wings heated, and I looked down.

Yeah. There they were. A nice rip in the underside of my top had left me . . . well, semi-naked. And not in a classy way.

I must have torn it when Paris and Tinker attacked me. Flushing, I tugged the fabric downward, but they only spilled out the top. I tugged it up, and the opposite happened.

My wings scorched, and my face felt like burnt toast. Now everyone was staring at me again. Even the coffee boy hid a smile. I crossed my arms over my chest, furious.

"Toldified." Diamond flicked me a heated glance, somewhere around the level of my kneecaps.

I scowled, and huffed my wings, but a laugh stole up my throat. The spectacle of Diamond losing his composure was too good to pass up. I folded my arms belligerently, breasts swelling. "What's your problem, loverboy? Never seen any like these before?"

He opened his mouth, and swiftly shut it again.

Speechless. Another score.

I grinned, and he gave me an exasperated glance. "C'mon. Take you home."

I followed him over the curb into the street, delight still feathering my step. Still, my blood itched, discomfited. I knew my boobs were up there with the best. Guys salivated for a glimpse. What was wrong with him? He hadn't even looked, not really.

Guess I still didn't rate, after that bully-whore-coward thing. I sniffed. Fine. He could be like that. Not like I was interested anyway.

We crossed the street, dodging an earsplitting motorbike and a bunch of yelling spriggans in a rusty old van, and I shot him a sarcastic smile behind his back to make myself feel better. "It's not so far. We can walk—" I stopped when I saw where he was headed, and giggles broke in my chest. "Or not. Is that your car?"

I'd expected him to roll flashy. It went with the territory. Jasper drove a sleek sports car, all shinymetal and tinted glass, stealthy and black like a ghost's breath. I didn't know what make it was. I don't care much about cars.

But this thing of Diamond's was stunning. Low, convertible, the inside soft and delicious, the outside a symphony of hot metal curves, smooth and sensuous like a woman's satinclad body. I wanted to lick it, run my hands over it.

It was also the purplest thing I'd ever seen. Glossy, orchidbright, smack-your-face purple. So purple, my eyes hurt.

He flitted onto the curb to open the door for me, crazyshiny metal flashing like his grin. "Like it?"

I stepped up beside him and peered inside, shielding my eyes from the glare. It smelled of him, warm and rosy in summer heat, the leather soft and dark like plumskin. It reminded me of his butt in those purple pants, all tight and velvety smooth. I giggled, warm. "Zero outta ten for stealth, partner. Tell me you don't actually drive this."

"Angel, girls have chewed each other's eyeballs out for a ride."

"No doubt. Doesn't it clash with your hair?"

"If ya got it, offshow it. Coming or not?"

"With you driving, sparklebrain? No way. How many lines did you suck back tonight?"

He sniffed, and grinned, devastating. "Just tightifies the reflexes, baby."

Moonlight slid sweet uncaution deep into my veins like a warm needle, and I yearned for thrill, danger, crazy laughter.

My pulse pressed hot between my legs, and I snorted, trying to shake it off. "Yeah. Double vision and a three-hour hard-on, more like. You are so not driving." I held out my hand, daring him. "Keys, please."

"Like you're not drunkified, moongirl." His ruby gaze flickered downward, and up again, darkening to violet.

I grinned inwardly. Yep, they're still there. Still, his gaze made me flush, and I fought it off with a mock-serious eyebrow. "Am not."

"Uh-huh. Then why'd you kiss me before?"

"I did not!" But heat caressed my nerves, annoying. Shit. Why'd he have to bring that up? Sure, my brain imploded when he gave me that look. But the last thing

I needed was another stupid infatuation. Couldn't we just pretend we weren't young and horny and eyeing each other off? Just for a few hours, until this was over?

"Did so."

"Did not!"

"Angel, that was so a kiss. We just didn't get to the liplocking part." He shot me a tiny smile, cool and self-assured. Not the screw-me-weak-at-the-ankles one. This one was his *You know I'm right, so stop arguing* smile, and it sliced just as sharp.

His confidence itched me deep inside, tempting and irritating at the same time. I glared, one hand crooked on my sweating hip. "Guess I'm sober enough to know what's good for me, then."

"Yeah?" He vaulted easily over me, and dropped into the driver's seat. He didn't bother to fold his wings aside. Just spread them out behind him, his rosy halo glowing. Like he didn't care who saw. He started the thing up, engine growling, and the dashboard lit neon-bright, spearing blue and purple shadows that glittered like laserlight in his hair. "Then screw sober. I liked you better crazified. Get in, grandma. Live it up."

Challenge thrilled my blood warm. I shook my head in mock exasperation and got in.

My body sank into the seat, the plumskin leather wrapping around me, his scent so warm and inviting, my moonstruck blood purred. I wanted to wriggle my shoulders, rub my wings in the softness, strip naked and stretch out like an amorous tabby cat to have my belly rubbed.

No doubt this worked on all the girls, and I checked surreptitiously for chewed eyeballs before I pulled the door shut, clunking it harder than necessary. "If you crash and kill me, I swear I'll crawl back from hell to haunt you."

He grinned, wickedlight. "Promise?"

"In a heartbeat."

"Better buckle up, then." He slotted the shiny metal shift into gear, threatening, and flashed me a glittery wink.

I'd barely clicked the seat belt home when acceleration flung me back into my seat.

We scorched out into the traffic, and he floored it, skidding around the corner on a drift that lurched my stomach light. Wind dragged my hair back, the hot midnight air a dazzling caress on my skin. He shifted gears, and the vibration thrummed deep in my belly. Lights dizzied me, streetlamps flashing overhead, the dashboard's digital jitter, the pulsing glow of his body next to mine, and my senses lit with the heady flavors of nighttime and city smoke and roses.

The cusp of his glasstalent caressed my skin, teasing like a wing's soft edge, and deep inside I felt him smile. My lungs swelled. My heart beat faster, and I stretched my pulsing wings to that greedy, fattening moon and laughed.

In the shadows across the street, Vincent wipes his mouth, smearing hungry spit. Lordy, she's perfect. He can't stop staring, her sweaty thighs gleaming as she hops in the car, her smile flashing, pulse flickering in her throat as she leans back and laughs, scarlet hair flowing like blood.

Ember pretends she's so noble, but she's just a slutty bloodfairy milkshake, begging to be sucked dry. And Diamond . . . Well, Diamond shouldn't have said those things about Mina.

The virus whips Vincent's jealousy to dirty fever. Just the idea of his lost Mina screwing Diamond makes his palms itch to scratch the smarmy pinkshit's glow-ball eyes out. Her lovely blue hair, spilling over sweat-slick raspberry muscles. Her pretty lips parting on a groan as that no doubt magnificent cock forces into her, sweat and fluid and pleasure mingling. . . .

Want her. Wanna be her. Vincent doesn't know. Story of his fucking life.

Fuck it. He was already gonna kill the lying glass-fae rat. Now he's gonna have some real fun first.

Fury and resentment boil to steam in his blood, and the hunger sucks it away, all-consuming. The car screeches off, a knife-edge purple splash. Savage thirst claws his throat, and he swallows wet hunger and digs out his phone to make a call.

A blonde and her Thai girlfriend walk by and block his view, holding hands, high heels teetering drunk-enly on the uneven concrete. Blondie is slim and perky, Thailand curvy and luscious, and their rich skinscent only enrages Vincent more. His ravenous gaze flicks between them, fiery hair and long lickable legs and scrumptious breasts all covered in skin and full of tasty blood. . . .

He leans against the jagged brick wall. "Famine. Hey, it's Vincent. . . . Yeah, it sure was a rockin' party, mate. Sorry about your carpet. I'll fix you up. . . . Yeah, shit happens, eh? Listen, I got something for ya. You know that gemstone thing you told me about?"

The girls strut past in a cloud of tequila and ladys-cent. Mmm. He ambles after them, casual. "Yeah, well, I heard about it, didn't I, so don't get the shits, bone-ass. I got the chick who's chasing you, and I'm sending her your way."

The girls turn the corner and stumble against the alley wall for a lipstick-smearing kiss. Vincent shadows them, already thirsting for their flavor, and drops his voice so he won't reveal himself.

"Because I like you, mate. Jeez, one little accident and everyone thinks you're a maniac. . . . Well, she's already got one on her finger. She's one of Diamond's girlfriends. Bloodfairy, red hair, legs up to here, calls herself Ember."

Low moans drift from the dark, and Vincent's mouth waters at the taste of slick female flesh as the girls slide fingers under skirts.

He chuckles. "Yeah, I know it's a full moon. Why d'ya think I'm calling? I'm the guy who gets things, remember? Your clients are gonna piss themselves over this lady."

He can see what the girls are doing, his virus-sharp eyes sucking in every morsel of light, and his balls ache hard. Christ, that girlsex shit should be illegal. "Yeah, well, don't go breaking nothing. I want her when you've finished."

Problem with two is, the second one'll scream while he's still working on the first. But he's got ways around that. A whiff of charm. A brush of hypnotic seduction. Something to stuff in their mouths. "Oh, sure. Mind-fuck her all you like, mate. It's her body I want."

Blondie bends to lick a stiff pink nipple, her fingers sliding between the dark one's thighs, coaxing out swollen flesh. Vincent's mouth waters, his pulse throbbing. *Go down. Please, go on . . . yeah.* On her knees, Blondie sucks and licks, her lips shining, and Vincent's cock aches rock hard. He'll do that to Ember, make her moan, suck hard on her ripe little clit and make the blood flow.

But for now, he's hungry. And hungry vampires eat.

He cuts Famine off in midsentence. Skinny white-boned prick always did talk too much. "Yeah. I'll let ya know. Look, I gotta go." A strained female voice groans and calls on god, and Vincent laughs in dark anticipation. "Mate, the pleasure's all mine." And he slips his phone away and slinks like a ravenous ghost into the dark.

11

We skidded sideways to the curb, the back end of Diamond's hellpurple machine sliding like an eel, and hurtled to a stop in the shadow of Jasper's building, facing the opposite way to which we'd come.

Diamond killed the engine with a cheeky grin, and I let out a pent-up breath, my pulse racing, excitement laced with terror. "You always drive like that?"

"Angel, I do *everything* like that."

I snickered. "Hard and wild and too fast? I've heard that about you."

"All lies, baby. *That* takes me all night." He hopped over me on a flick of wings, lighted on the pavement, and flipped my door open, an exaggerated courtesy. "Madam."

I unclipped my belt and climbed reluctantly from the bodyhugging seat, glancing surreptitiously downward. Blood throbbed tightly in my thighs, and I was sweating and kinda . . . well . . . damp. I sure hoped I hadn't left a stain. "Damned if I know how you've still got your license. You're a fucking maniac."

He stuffed the remote in his pocket. "Who said license? They askify your last name. They wanna take your picture. Screw *them*."

"I've got a license." Emma Sinclair, it said. Jasper knew a guy who knew a guy, and we got some human girl to pose for the picture. Cameras and glamour don't mix, at least not my glamour. Of course, Jasper never let me drive. He already took me everywhere he thought I needed to go.

"Course you do. You're a girl."

"What's that got to do w—?" I saw his teasing glance and shook my head in mock disgust, a giggle sweetening my mouth. "Shut up, okay? Just get in here."

We hopped up the grayslate steps. Above us, dark marble gleamed yellow in the moonlight. Our shadows fell short beneath our feet, one black, one haloed in pinkspun gold. In the distance, clouds gathered, and a flash of lightning split the sky. We were in for a storm, but for the moment, the heat hung thick and dry.

I popped my security card in the slot, and the blackglass door hissed open. Same card for the elevator, cool and white-lit fluorescent, my sweat drying to a crisp, and the foyer on twelve lay silent, rich dark carpet gleaming beneath golden downlights.

Jasper's apartment was dim and cool, the wide glass windows spilling moonlight over his sofa, his bookshelves, the dim flash of his television hanging on the wall. I stepped inside, and his cinnamon scent crawled over me, hot and accusing, a virulent curse I couldn't escape.

Dizziness punched me hard. I staggered against the wall, the same sick starlight shimmering in my eyes that flashed there when he hit me.

Why was I here without Jasper? Why was I alive, when he crumbled to fairydust in some greasy alley-

way? Gone only a few hours, and already I brought
some other guy home.

Guilt chewed my skin raw. Diamond had crept effortlessly under my radar, lurking beneath the surface
like a hungry crocodile, waiting for me to glance the
other way. I'd smiled at him. Laughed for him. Even
enjoyed some honest good time.

Jasper's hellviolet eyes glowed in my mind, sharp
and unforgiving. *You're a dirty flirt, Emmy. Hitting on
my friends like a gutter bitch. What kind of ungrateful
slut are you?*

My heart quailed, and I hugged myself, my throat
clamping tight. *Didn't mean it. Wasn't my fault. Not
what you think . . .*

"You okay?" Diamond's glassy claws brushed the
bare curve of my back in the dark, and tingles swept
my body. His rosescented glow heated my skin. It felt
nice. It felt wrong.

I jerked away and flipped on all four lights, until the
creamy walls gleamed like midday and the balcony
windows sparkled. "Uh-huh. Won't be a sec. Just . . .
just stay out here, okay?" And I stumbled to our bedroom, a few feet of corridor stretching like a mile, and
clamped the door shut.

I held my breath, my back pressed against the door,
my heartbeat thumping like a guilty drum. The bed-
side lamp had popped on automatically as I entered, a
dim golden halo showing our bed, dark and soft, the
ivory bathtub festooned with candles, the shining glass
shower. My mahogany dressing table with my jewelry
box on it, the carvenwood mirror, my walk-in wardrobe stuffed with dresses and coats and pretty things.
All my things. Everything Jasper had given me.

Everything I owed him slammed shut around me like a horrid metal cage. I couldn't do this. Couldn't stay with Diamond, trust him, let him near me. Jasper wouldn't like it. It wasn't right.

My legs shook, and I clutched the doorframe tighter. Jasper was dead. I knew it was stupid. That didn't make it any less real. I had to hide, run, get rid of Diamond before I made another really bad mistake.

That clammy fearworm slithered in my guts, and I swallowed hard, my skin tingling. The door had no lock. If he followed me, I'd scream, fight, claw his eyes out. Prove I was true to a dead guy who'd treated me like scum.

But Diamond didn't follow. Silence for a few moments, and then a glassy tinkle, metal sliding as he opened the balcony door, his voice a deep-pitched windchime on the phone.

Cautious relief twinged my nerves looser, and I released my breath silently.

Stiffly, I unbuckled my torturous heels. My sore feet cooed relief, sinking into the lambswool rug. I peeled off my torn dress and climbed into the shower.

Cool water sloshed through my hair, over my shoulders. I sighed and fluttered wet wings, blood and sweaty makeup swirling over the dark marble tiles. God, I'd been dying for a shower ever since that bloodsucker first laid his feverstank fingers on me.

But it didn't feel good. Wet hair stuck like peeling skin to my breasts, and water slimed over me like dead hands. Jasper's hands, cold and clammy, smearing wet dust as he disintegrated, caressing me to sick arousal. His wings dragging wet over mine, his cold rotting lips on my face . . .

I shivered and wrenched the hot water higher, but it

didn't help. Now the hands were Kane's, his smooth hot body claiming me, pleasuring me horrid. Liquid hellfire flooded my belly, my bones burning, and his blond hair rained blood over my skin, clots squelching and smearing on my belly, my breasts, my face.

I gurgled and fought, but it was all over me, dripping, sliding, stinking. Death's meaty stench clumped in my mouth. Ashen hellstink seared my lungs. The ring smarted on my finger, and I clawed desperately at it with scarlet soap suds dripping from my palms, but it wouldn't come off, wouldn't come free and I was dead, damned, poisoned by a demon's bonescorching kiss. . . .

"Ember? You cool?"

My forehead hit the glass, shock snapping me from the depths. Cool, clean air, gentle bathroom lights, trickling water.

My breath squeezed shallow and sour. Frantically I palmed my wet body under the spray. No blood. No hands. Just water. I was alone.

Surely, I'd wailed for help. Diamond's question was low, concerned, his claws a faint tickle on the door. He could've entered, but he hadn't.

I caught my breath, my pulse slowly calming. I leaned my forehead against the glass, and my reflection shone back at me, green eyes wide and wet.

And then they glinted scarlet, and Big Em grinned at me, ghostly, brimming with all the defiance I didn't have courage for. *Jasper's dead, Little Em. He can't touch you now. Get over it, and get on with it.*

I closed my eyes, sweating. Big Em was right. I couldn't let that stupid wetfaced fearworm paralyze me. No matter how vivid its lies. No matter how much Diamond was like Jasper, with his dominant will and heartshock confidence and sexy give-a-shit grin. Being alone scared me. But being with a man like that scared me more.

I knew how quickly I lost my confidence. It was too easy to get used to being protected, doing what I was told, doing anything to please him so I'd feel safe. And Diamond's "favor" sounded ominous. Could I stand up for myself? Keep my newfound freedom? Tell him no? Even if it meant he'd leave me, alone and vulnerable?

Determination fired me. My freedom was too important. I was over being owned. Enough with the flirting. I could let Diamond help me. Didn't mean I had to let him have me. Right?

Jasper had saved me from starving. Diamond might help save me from hell. But no one could save me from myself.

Except me.

"Ember? Everything righty?" Claws tinkled the iron doorknob, hesitant.

I pushed upright, rinsed my mouth under the spray, and wiped my sour lips dry. "Yeah. I'm fine. Won't be a sec."

And I turned off the shower and flittered out. Dried myself on Jasper's towel, combed my hair into a slick flamescarlet twist. Chose a dress and put it on, working my wings through the cutaway at the back. Sparkleblack silk draped respectably to just above my knee, and I slipped on a pair of low heels I could walk in.

I surveyed my reflection, uncertain. I hadn't asked Diamond where we were going. I'd no clue if I'd dressed right.

Put your face on, Emmy, Jasper insisted darkly in

my head. *You can't go out like that. Take some care with yourself. What will people think?*

My fingers crept automatically toward the mascara, and I yanked them back. No time for makeup. If we were gonna trick this Scarletfire tonight, we couldn't waste a second.

Jasper's ring glowed evilly on my finger. My bones burned, a searing echo of hell, and I crunched my fist tight.

Screw it. I wouldn't let him control me. I'd never let any man control me again.

I retrieved my bag, shivered my wings dry, and walked out into the lounge.

Diamond sat perched on the balcony rail like a careless crystal angel, knees folded to his chest. Hot moonlight flashed from his hair, and his outstretched wings glittered. A tiny updraft swelled, and his wings wafted to compensate, his thighs rippling, strong but featherlight.

My wingtips curled, hot and rebellious. Mmm. Those duds he wore looked . . . hot. The plumdark leather had worn soft, and it clung to his body like wet velvet, showing every . . . um . . . curve. And he sure had the jump on curves. That butt of his was epic. My mouth watered. Tight, muscled, the perfect shape for naughtiness.

He looked up from flicking through his phone and hopped down to meet me at the open glass door, a fluid flex of chest and leanmuscled thigh that left me breathless. Oh, how I longed for moonlight on my skin, that warm glow spilling over my wings. . . .

My hands wanted to twist together, and I forced them down, one finger coiling in my bag's strap. *Don't look. Don't flirt. Don't give him ideas. Just keep it business.* "Who you talking to?"

"No one." He clicked his phone dark and slipped it away. "Just business."

Right. I smoothed my skirt over my thighs, swallowing. "Do I look okay? I mean, is this—?" Great. That was cool and confident.

He swept me up and down, his gaze a hot caress of appreciation that made me shiver. "Baby, you're gorgeous. Readyfied?"

My cheeks heated. I hated him looking at me like that. But I liked it, too, and I hated that more. Was the heat in his glance an act? A tease? Genuine, even? I didn't care. I wouldn't act on it, no matter how he tempted me. If he could help me run from hell, I'd take the chance.

I met his gaze straight, barely a tremble in my voice. "Sure. Where we going?"

12

I gripped the card table's edge with both hands, my sweaty palms sliding on the smooth black leather. The ponytailed dealer flipped cards on green baize, her white shirt and golden waistcoat sparkling in flashy casino lights. One each, faceup. Blackjack, I guessed. I knew the rules, sort of. I had a ten of hearts. Was that good or bad?

I forced a smile, my whisper tight. "What are we doing here?"

Beside me, Diamond plucked a green melon-scented cocktail from a waiter's tray and slid it in front of me. "Relaxify. No one's gonna eat you."

"You sure?" I grabbed the glass and swallowed, green fizz and alcohol sparkling warm in my nose. Two in the morning, and the crowd was middling, but everywhere light, color, sound, the scrape and plop of colored chips, shiny cards sliding smooth on green and merlot baize, dice tumbling in metal cages. Beeps and chimes rang, the brash music of slot machines. Chips changing hands, cash pushed down the slot with plastic catchers, the roulette ball spinning red-black-white.

My head swam, a muddle of perfumes and alcohol,

the baffling mix of takeaway noodles and lobster bisque, fizzy cola and champagne. Heady human sweat a temptation, wingdust sugaring my tongue, the dizzy whiff of vampire blood. And like a poisoned undercurrent, the dark plasticgrime scent of money.

I swallowed. No clocks. No windows. You couldn't see either end of the room. Even the doorway vanished into clutter, like the money went on forever.

Normally, I liked the casino, Jasper leading me about on his arm, so charming and confident as he chatted and connived, doing the business with people I smiled at as if I remembered them, and then forgot about ten seconds later. When I was with Jasper, I liked everyone assessing me with covetous eyes. Men because they wanted me, an apparition in designer gowns and jewels he'd paid for in cash. Women because I was pretty and charming and *his* girlfriend, a queen to be lauded and flattered and kissed on the hand. It made me feel special like I never did when I was alone.

But tonight, I longed for Unseelie Court, dark and anonymous. I wanted to crawl under the carpet and hide. Even the lights dazzled harsh, glittering glass cascades flashing, stretching from the distant ceiling like electric stalactites.

And Diamond was no comfort, delicious and dangerous like a mouthwatering raspberry dessert I just knew was bad for me. Jasper was hot-tempered and careless, but he was the devil I knew. For all his taunts and irritating attitude, Diamond crept under my skin, and not all the uncomfortable warmth in my belly was fear.

Diamond sidled closer, absently pushing chips across the baize and tapping for another card, chancing on sixteen and losing. He played my game for me, keeping fifteen. "Roulette table, ten o'clock," he murmured, light like a tinkle of breeze. "Seeify?"

I glanced over, casual, sipping my drink like I did this all the time. But inside my pulse danced a crazy slam, bouncing off the walls like a mad-ass skeleton.

On my left, the low roulette table gleamed, green under golden spotlights. The yellow betting grid lay spotted with chips in all colors, and the croupier spun the wheel and tossed in the little white ball, his eyes vacant. Alongside hunkered a pair of grouchy black spriggans in dirty T-shirts and jeans, spiky hair gleaming, eyeing off some giggling human girls having a hen's night party. The bride sported flashing red demon horns and a white veil plastered in love hearts.

My heart warmed. Whoever her guy was, I hoped he actually loved her.

My ring tightened a notch, and I shuddered, moving my gaze on.

A tall dark human boy and his black-eyed fairy lover, hot glances and swallows, hands brushing together secretly. They were losing hopelessly, and didn't care. An old woman thick with jeweled rings, eyes glassy with fatigue and greed.

And then, at the far end, a bunch of guys.

Hot guys.

My mouth watered. Oh, my. This one looked like a jeans model, all tight muscles and tumbling brown hair and lashes to kill for. Identical vampire twins dressed in white, sleek strawberry blond hair swept back, graceful like twin tiger cubs and as gorgeous. A lissome blue waterfae boy, gleaming sapphire eyes and glossy wings like stormy rainbow sky.

Only it wasn't just guys. There was one girl, and as the group parted to reveal her, my breath stopped.

Tall, flawless pale skin, a long red sparklesatin gown wrapping whipslim hips and small ripe breasts. Face long and oval, uptilted amber eyes tipped with scarlet lashes. Dragonfly wings, delicate and graceful, the kind of wings I'd always wanted instead of my uncouth jagged ones. Hair like a volcano sunset, a bright orange-gold cascade that rippled alive when she laughed. Long redclawed fingers wrapped seductively around a martini glass. And those lips, so full and ripe, her smile a heady shock of desire.

My pulse tripped faster, and I didn't even like girls. Jesus in a jam jar, she was gorgeous.

But it barely registered, compared to her flames.

Long ghostly ribbons of underwater fairy fire licked her skin, dancing lovingly over her curves. Rippling orange and crimson, darkening to purple, flashed with green and blue as her light caught metal or dust. Warmth lifted her hair, tugging at her flowing gown, her fingertips fluttering over updrafts. Even her step was elevated, so graceful, like she danced on air.

I swallowed, envy warming my skin. How did she do it? Her glamour must work overtime to cover that up. I had enough trouble with red hair and wings. But firefae always had strong magic. It came with the blisters and the singed hair, though this Crimson looked like she'd never burned a wisp out of place in her life.

My fingers tensed around my glass. She was crazy-beautiful, an amazing freak of nature.

And I was going to kill her.

Steal her gemstone and send her squealing to hell, where she'd burn into a lump of ugly, charred, disgusting flesh, just like the rest of us.

Guilt stung me raw. Could I really damn her? Just to save my own pitiful skin? For all I knew, she'd fallen in with Kane through no fault of her own. And it wasn't only this pretty Crimson I needed to kill. It was *famine* and *flower* as well, whoever they were. My own imminent damnation didn't make it okay to turn into a serial murderer. Did it?

Diamond poked me back to reality. "Seeify?"

I edged my glass onto the table. My chip stack had grown. He'd won me a couple of hundred bucks while I'd been staring. Hell, how could he not stare at her, too? How could any straight guy not worship her?

His pinklit shadow reddened on my hands, a whiff of darkrose passion, and my wings prickled hot. I was used to being the prettiest girl in the room. No doubt he was drooling over her like a cow in hay. I scowled. "Yeah, I see. What about her?"

But he just wrinkled his nose, like he didn't like some taste, and slipped his arm around my shoulder, turning me. "Look again."

"Hey!" I wriggled in protest. But he held me tighter, pressing my back against his hard body. His hot flavor of wine and roses licked my tongue, delicious, and glassy chill clinked down over my vision like underwater lenses. "What the f—? Oh!"

The room telescoped into tortured black and white. Gray outlines loomed, translucent, ghostly charcoal cartoons. Lights flared icewhite and cold. The metal edges of tables and stools shone black and hard, their insides washed out to monochrome like watercolors in the rain. People stretched and writhed, ghoulish, insectoid limbs floating, their faces real but distorted with all the raw and unfettered emotion they tried to hide.

My wings crushed against Diamond's chest, damp and warm, and the sensation made me shiver. His cold glassy world swallowed me like an alien planet, the only reality his body against mine, his arms around me. I wanted to squeeze my eyes shut, let his scent fill my lungs, feel his gentle touch on my skin, be safe again.

"Look, Ember." His whisper caressed my name, sliding warm into my ear. "Seeify her now."

I lifted my gaze. There she floated, tall and ghostly, her flames a mirror-rippled shadow, gray and lacking substance. Those magical amber eyes shone dull, their color gone. Serrated teeth gleamed, her hair a torn frightwig. Her body contorted, wizened like a bird's bones. Her wings rotted with worms, and her skin wasn't smooth but crackled and old, her face disintegrating like a monster who'd far outlived her time.

I shuddered. Her spells fouled the air, wrapping like spectral fingers around those handsome boys who adored her. Their eyes gleamed freshgold with ambition and lust, their inflated self-image plastered on their ghostly façades like carnival masks. But they were still young and beautiful, the blue fairy's wings glossy, the human boy's hair a distant autumn glory.

They were real. She was a monster.

She reached out skeletal hands and drew the human boy's face to hers for a kiss. Their lips met, mingled, her grayboned mouth sucking at him like she ate something tasty. Color flooded down her throat like rich brown honey to melt into her belly. And when she broke away, the boy staggered, that gorgeous auburn hair fading. His youthful glow subsumed, dull, sickly like he'd been drained of life.

I let my breath out. "Holy shit. She's using them to stay young?"

"Uh-huh. Revenant, maybe. Some kinda juicetheft. Or just a wicked old bitch who won't dyify." Diamond shrugged and broke his glamour with a pinkstatic crack.

A mirror shattered before my eyes. I yelped, shards tumbling, and colors flooded in, the lights golden over green tables, pale carpet, black hair and a blue dress and red lipstick on a girl's mouth.

Water sprang to my eyes, dazzling, and I shook them clear. I'd never been so pleased to be blinded.

But my gaze crept back to Crimson, her façade tucked neatly in place. That stunning smile, that shimmering sunset hair and glorybright flame. All a lie. A predatory, insatiable lie that sucked the life from strong virile boys to survive.

My wilting resolve firmed like a rose stem sucking up water. Fine. If suckerbitch had traded Kane her soul— for beauty, immortality even?—that was her own pile of thistles. I'd be saving lives by killing her.

And Diamond's glassfae sight showed him all that. Stripped everything of illusion. A gift, or a curse? Would I prefer ignorance or reality? Not seeing the threat, or having to pretend it wasn't there?

And what did he see when he looked at me?

His warm body shifted against my back, and his lips teased my ear. "You feel real. I like realicality just fine."

My eartip curled, and hot tingles spread all the way down to my wingjoints. He still embraced me, smooth and strong, his hair a soft caress on my wings. My skin sparkled alive. I wanted to lean back in his arms, let him hold me, protect me. But his crystalsight crept cold and prickly along my nerves. I didn't want him seeing inside my heart. It was too barren there, too fickle. Too afraid.

My wings jittered, defensive, and I shrugged him off. "So. Umm . . . what do we do now?"

Diamond touched a finger to my lips and flicked glitter lashes upward.

I glanced up. Security cameras, black hemispheres like clams hugging the ceiling. No doubt they had audio, too. We'd already given away enough.

I smiled for the camera and slipped my arm into his. "Had enough?"

"Yeah." He scraped his chips into a cup and we wandered off, casual, eyes anywhere but on our redflame target.

The crowd wasn't thick, but it was noisy enough to cover us now we'd moved away from the tables. "So whaddaya think? Where do we start looking?"

He shrugged, stroking my hand and gazing at the lights as we wandered past endless neonflash slot machines. "Who knows? We can upturn her place if you want."

"Breaking and entering? You've got to be kidding." I ruffled my wings, uncomfortable. I wasn't a burglar. Then again, a lot had changed tonight.

"Choice? Think she's even got it on her?

I bit my lip, thinking. "Well . . . what would you do with a gemstone you'd wired your soul to?"

He laughed, dark. "Choicem on? Swallow the fucking thing, maybe. Smashify? Chuck it off the pier at South Melbourne?"

"Better hope she hasn't thought of that. But you'd at least keep it on you always, right?"

"Or give it to someone I trustified."

My face heated. *Wow, thanks for reminding me.* "She eats pretty boys for supper. She doesn't trust anyone. And she's wearing enough bling to crash a rocketship."

He stopped me under a low-hanging sign flashing

golden with lightbulbs, electric beeps chiming. "Okay. So how we gonna get it off her?"

I frowned. I'd swiped a gem from right under a vampire's nose. But I had an advantage when it came to vampires. I pictured her, surrounded by her boy harem, other players, the croupier. Not to mention a zillion security cameras. No way could we roll her in plain sight. "We need to—"

"—get her out of there somehow."

We both spoke at once, and I looked away, discomfited. I didn't want to think like a gangster. "But what we gonna do, wait for her to go home? Or head out the back with one of her snacks? It might take all night. It might never happen. . . ."

Unless we made it happen. But what could make her leave? Boredom? Run out of money? The munchies, a run to the food hall before it closed?

A trip to the ladies' room?

Bingo.

Diamond tilted his head, rainbow hair waterfalling, and I knew we'd had the same thought again. "What's she drinkify?"

Long red claws, a conical glass with a long stem. "Vodka martini. Olives, no ice."

"Sweet. What you got on you?"

"Huh?"

"How much you carrying?" He dragged a little silver case from his pocket and popped the lid, revealing a little mound of sparkling black dust.

I bristled, glancing around for cameras. "What makes you think I'm—?"

"Tell it to the angels, princess."

I sighed, and hunted in my bag for the foil. I handed

it over, and he untwisted it one-handed and dumped my blue on top of his blackjewel. The crystals crackled and glittered, slithering like they were happy to be together at last. He poked one claw at the mix, glitter puffing. "Should be strong enough."

Black for wicked pleasure. Blue for ennui. My mouth watered, hungry, and I looked askance. I wasn't addicted. I just liked it, the rush, the bright shiny laughter and the slow comedown to pleasant woolliness, the feeling that nothing could hurt me.

He pocketed the case, and we headed back to the gaming floor, where Crimson still held her twisted court. Diamond nudged me, pointing to the drinks waiter, who had one of her martinis balanced on his tray beside a Bloody Mary and a pair of glowing cosmos garnished with lime. "Go fall over that guy."

"What?" My mind stumbled, catching up slowly. Already Diamond dimmed himself, fading at the edges, not invisible but elusive, deceptive, don't-see-me. "Oh, I see—"

His whisper warmed my ear, and his strange glamour zinged, mixing with my own in a shower of seductive sparks. "Trip over him, make him lookify. Gimme five seconds." A hot, shimmering kiss teased my collarbone, a shivershock of delight, and before I could pull back, he'd stolen away.

Damn. I wish he wouldn't do that.

The waiter was already halfway to the table, sidling neatly around gamblers and hangers-on. His gold-and-white uniform gleamed, blond hair curling jagged around sharp cheekbones. He served the dark boy and his fairy their pink neon cosmos. Now the old lady and her Bloody Mary. Diamond lurked behind her in a ghostly blur of confusion.

I took a steadying breath, loosened my pinned-up hair with my claws, and shouldered through the crowd like I was late, gripping my bag tightly to my side. "Excuse me . . . sorry . . . thanks . . . oh, my goodness!" Casually, I stuck out my foot and hooked the waiter's ankle.

He dodged, spinning his tray high so as not to spill, and I stumbled to hands and knees at his feet.

"Oh, silly me, I'm so clumsy." I gazed up at him with girlywide eyes, heaving my chest more than was strictly necessary, and my hair spilled from its pins to tumble around my shoulders.

His tired blue eyes diluted with frustration, like I was just one more fuckup in a long, shitty shift, a snarky rich bitch who'd probably complain and get him fired. "Jeez, I'm sorry. You okay, miss?" He slid one hand under my arm, the other instinctively holding his tray level and out of reach, but his gaze lingered on my cleavage.

Just a few seconds, but it was enough.

Diamond wandered by, his long pinksilver hand trailing like an afterthought, and without looking back, he tipped a sparkling blueblack cascade into Crimson's martini. It bubbled, and the drug dissolved, a tiny wisp of blacksparkling steam curling up to disappear.

Clear. Transparent. No trace.

My pulse thrummed. I glanced sideways, up, around. No one had noticed.

I gave the waiter a shy smile, leaning into him as if by accident and kicking my perfume up a notch as he helped me up. "Thank you, you're very kind—"

"Can I get you a drink, miss? On the house, of course." My glamour glazed his eyes and hitched his breath tight, but discomfort still wrinkled his young face, like he thought I'd scream or accuse him of feeling me up or something. Sympathy twinged. It wasn't nice to be used.

"No, no, it's quite all right." I fluttered demure lashes at him and arranged my bag over my shoulder, and quite by accident slipped fifty dollars onto his tray. "My fault, I'm sure. You have a good night, sweetie."

He stared, flushing. I patted my hair smooth and hurried off. Poor kid. He'd have glitter in his eyes all night.

Diamond took my arm, and we faded into what would have been a dim corner but for dangling fiber-optics hanging low from the ceiling. Shadows flashed blue and green, the glowing strands rippling like a inky waterfall.

I peered out beneath the cascade, static jumping in my hair. Crimson took her martini from the tray with a gushing smile.

I held my breath. The walls shuddered and threatened, accusing me, the neon glaring like cruel blue eyes. I'd poisoned her drink. Me. As bad as some scumsucking date rapist. I could get arrested.

Crimson laughed, flames dripping from her hair, her shining red lips flirting over the glass's rim. I bit my lip, anticipation nipping under my toeclaws like ants. God, what did she order it for, if she wasn't going to drink it this century?

Diamond flicked through phone messages, composed. Not anxious at all. Didn't bother him, slipping that woman drugs. He and Jasper probably did shit like this all the time.

I swallowed. What the hell was I doing even talking to this guy? Never mind trusting him with my life. I shivered. Note to self: Don't let him buy me a drink.

Pity he already had.

Surreptitiously I licked my gums, checking for numbness. Surely he had more class than to drug me. If he wanted to get laid, all he had to do was ask.

Some other girl, that is. The kind who fell for lickable muscles and attitude and sexy rainbow smiles. Not a sensible girl like me.

Crimson stirred her martini, popping the olive into her mouth. Finally, she lifted the glass to her lips and swallowed.

My chest tightened. Surely, she'd taste that faint sparkle on her tongue, feel the fire-ice rush as her blood sparked alive. Spit it out, dive aloft screeching to hunt the culprits down, flame flashing from her hair.

But she just smiled and stroked her fairy boy's slick blue wings, and drank again, until the glass was empty.

I swallowed, dry. "How long d'ya reckon?"

Diamond coolly flipped his phone away. "Hard to sayify. Snort that all at once and you'd pop a valve. . . . Oop. Check it."

Crimson put her glass down and staggered.

I gulped. Just a tiny stumble, one elegant foot weaving into the other. But compared with her superlative grace, that was a headlong dive.

I clutched Diamond's wrist. "It's working. What now?"

"Give it a sec. Wait till she . . . There ya go."

Her pale face flushed, glamour or no. Her amber eyes glinted sickly gold. She cleared her throat, long fingers pressing her lips like she'd swallowed something unpleasant. The blue fairy touched her shoulder, murmuring something, but she brushed him off with a smile, tracing scarlet nails through his skybright hair.

And then she tucked her purse under her arm and walked off, a new and unsteady sway in her step.

I jiggled, wings rustling. "Look! She's going!" My voice rang loud, and I clapped a hand over my mouth.

Crimson circled the roulette tables, swaying in sputtering flames, and headed for the wide lobby exit. She weaved into the ladies' room, and the door swung shut.

My courage quivered, my thoughts racing in frightening new directions. I hadn't considered what to do now. What if the bathroom wasn't empty? If other girls were in there? How would I explain myself? I swallowed. "Umm . . . maybe we should—"

But Diamond gripped my hand like glassy steel, inescapable. "Chillify, cherrypie. It'll be easy. C'mon."

And he dragged me out across the floor.

My legs shook, and I plastered a smile on my face, hoping no one noticed us. Scarletfire's boytoys lounged and mingled, waiting for her to return. They hadn't noticed anything wrong with her, and for a moment, my sympathy warmed. Even a flamebright goddess was merely a toy, an object to be used for pleasure or status.

We all used each other. Even me.

Halfway past the roulette table, a feral screech split my ears.

My wings jerked, ready to flee. Diamond dug his phone from his pocket and flicked it bright. I sighed, nerves still tingling. "Tell me that wasn't your ringtone."

"I gotta take this." He stared at the screen, his jaw tight.

What phone call could out-urgent this? I gripped his hand tighter. "No way. I'm not doing this alone!"

He shook me off, his eyes glinting hard and silver. Sweatdrops glistened on his forehead. "Just gimme a moment, okay?"

His musical voice clanged discordant, ice on steel.

He was like a different person. All his charming fairy levity erased. Whoever was on the line, I didn't like them for spoiling him.

I shot him a filthy glare. "Forget it. I'm a big girl. I don't need you holding my hand." And I ruffled indignant wings and headed for the shiny black bathroom door.

I yanked my hair back as I walked, my fingers itching. I didn't get him. One moment he came on all machofae and protective; the next, he ignored me. Maybe he just did it to confuse me. Hooray for him, because it was working.

Whatever. I didn't need him.

I flung the door open and strode in.

13

Diamond picks up, shaking. "Rosa?"

Her voice quivers. "Diamond, thank god. I didn't know who else to call."

"Already seen this movie, petal. I'm bored. What you want?" But shame and stupid hope clench his fingers tight.

"Ange is creeping me out. He stalks me. Watches me. It's like a game to him. I'm hiding.... Shit, I'm scared, Di. I... I got a little drunk tonight, and I... I've been bad. He locks me up at night and ... He'll kill me, I swear." Tears thicken her words, and his stubborn heart aches.

He swallows. "Whatever, okay? I know what that shiny is. You trickified me. Why the hell should I spit on your ass if you burn?"

"I'm sorry!" A sob catches her throat. "Famine said someone was hunting us down. I had to keep it safe. I didn't know what else to do. Can't you just—? Oh, shit." Her voice rasps to a whisper. "Ange is here. He'll find me. Please, Diamond, I'm begging you, you have to help me!"

Fuckfuckfuck.

Across the room, pretty Ember stalks into the ladies' alone, tossing angry flamescarlet hair, and Diamond's pulse thuds, both accusation and hot distraction. The disappointment in her eyes when he left her alone stabbed hot blades in his heart. He was wrong about her. She's no bloodwhore, happy to be used. She's gentle, innocent, not up for a scrap. Too clean and precious for this dirtysmeared world. Should do the bad stuff for her.

He slips into shadow behind a fakeplastic garden, his wings twitching. "Chillify, petal. Where you at? I'll come get you later—"

"No! You can't! Not tonight. He's fucking furious, he'll kill us both. I think Tony saw you and me . . . you know, in the club?" Clunks, distant voices, the soft scrape of her hand over her mouth. "I can't please Ange when he's like this. He hurts me."

Diamond squeezes burning eyes shut, but vile pictures slice his mind ragged. Ange's ugly hands on her, forcing her naked body under his. Fucking her. Fangsharp mouth on throat, breast, thigh, feeding from her . . .

Disgusted. Envious. Confused. He smacks his head back into the wall, pain a bright splash, but it doesn't calm his racing pulse. "Then let me—"

"No, it's too dangerous. Look, Friday night there's a party. Ange'll be doing business, we'll be able to slip away. I can deal until then. But you have to get me out of h— Uhh!!"

Thud, the phone drops. A scream. Flesh smacking flesh.

Diamond's muscles snap tight. "Rosa, talkify. Jesus. Talk to me!"

"Sorry, Rosa can't come to the phone right now." That scaly lizard voice scars Diamond's ears, sharp with triumph, and rage wriggles burning tentacles under his skin.

He slams his palm into the wall, and plaster crumbles in a scarletflashed halo. "What you done to her?"

Tony chuckles, dark. "Oh, she'll live. For now. But I've got you cold, fairyshit. You and her, plotting against us. Ange is gonna peel your pretty pink skin off. Once he's finished with this little traitorbitch, of course."

"Don't you touchify her." Fury burns Diamond's skin violet. Useless words. But they're all he can do.

"Don't worry on her account, you smart-ass fairy faggot. Ange'll just fuck some sense into her." A cracked giggle. "Maybe I'll get to help. More than enough holes for two. I've heard she screams real nice. That true?"

"You dirty scumfuck, if you hurtify—"

But Tony's already gone.

Click.

Diamond kicks at a potted plant. Plastic cracks open, leaves and colored pebbles flying. Impulses tumble loud and discordant, twitching at his muscles to act. Scramblicate to Ange's place and kill them all. Tear LaFaro's scaly skin off and eat it raw. Scrub that dirty lizard stink from Rosa's body, make her clean again. Diamond's seen the sick torture games the stinky lizard creepazoid likes to play. Wire. Sharpyrazors. Dirt. Even Rosa don't deservamate that.

Fuck. Everything used to be so fresh and cleanified. His life. His conscience. His heart. Now, it's blackstained grime, and the filth will never wash away.

But deep underneath, a helpless glimmer of compassion still burns. And tryify till he drops, he can't put it out.

He jams his phone away, itchifying to call back, make sure she's okay. Like there'd be any pointificality.

Friday, she said. Two nights from now. Diamond knows Ange's parties. Colorful, rich, ostentatious, the vampire ganglord offshowing to his subjects. Lots of free booze and conspicuous gift-giving, no no, the pleasure's all mine, I assurify. Perfect for stealing a poor bruised girl away in the crush.

Perfect for feeding a poisonrich bloodfairy to a vampire.

Ember, shitwit. Her name is Ember, and she's brave and alone and smackdead beautiful. And you want to poison her.

He shrugs the guilt aside, but suspicion itches his wings. Something about Rosa's story doesn't chime true. If Ange is that crazyfied, why wait until Friday?

I've got you cold, fairyshit, Tony said. But one phone call provifies nothing. Angelo, so hot and reckless over pale suggestification? No no. Ange is cold, calm, collectified. Jump-skip at shadows, nuh-uh.

He knots loose hair around his fingers, frustrated. Even if Rosa is telling untrue, he still can't chancify. The gemstone molded to his wrist still binds his fate to hers. She dies; he dies.

Besides, if he can help her, maybe it'll make up for all the bad things he's done. Make him feel like a decent fairy again.

So why the fuck are you messifying here with Ember? If you care so much about Rosa, go gettify.

But the thought of Ember alone and frightened itchifies his skin with rage.

His thoughts spiral wild. Rosa playifies with his mind, twisting sweet and nasty together until he can't tellem different. Ember is innocent. How can he betray her, when—?

His lungs squeeze tight, and for a heartbeat, he can't breathe.

When he likes her. Cares about her. Gives a damn how she thinkifies him.

Fuck.

Glassfae calculation flashes cold warning in his heart. *Don't go there, D. It won't end well. You know exactamally how a decent girl like that thinkifies you. She's way over your horizon. Let it go.*

But he can't helpify. Watching her gasp and laugh and warble with excitement over a simple joyride was astonishing. She's like a fun-virgin, sheltered and clueless to the pleasures he could offer her. Jasper knew sex and drugs, sure. But Diamond does it better.

His wings swell tight, aroused. Besides, her wide-eyed courage impresses him. He wants more than a moment's delight with her. He wants to charmify her, make her laugh, free her from her prison of fear.

Bring her to life.

His blood heats. With a heady breath of chaos, she'd be magnificent. Helping her fly free wouldn't just be physical pleasure. It'd be . . . happy.

He doesn't remember happy. Not even with Rosa. Rosa makes him want to take, punish, possess, dark and violent needings sprinting free. With Ember, he wants to give.

His nose twitchifies. Christ. Hell of a time to crushify on some luscious angel he can't have. What is he, fifteen?

Fact is, Ember would be safer in his bed. And hell, would it be fun. Fever swells his cock hard just

thinkifying it. Kissing her chocolate skin all over. Her
honeyed moan as he sucks her nipples taut. Her sweet-
shudder when he enters her, fiery hair tumbling over
his knuckles, salty wingjoints hardening in his mouth
while he drives his cock deep into her willing flesh
over and over until she . . .

Guilt crunches bitter in his heart, and he flushes,
muscles stiff and aching. Shouldn't thinkify her like
that. It's not respectiful. Not when he's untruthing
her—

A woman's shout pricks his earpoints tight. "That's
her! I seen her! She done it!"

No time to figure it now. His pulse flips wild, and
he ducks out into the light.

Across town, in a dim ivory bedroom in Angelo's man-
sion, Rosa crouches in a corner, her heart skipping fe-
verstrong. Candleflame dances off the square panes
of the French windows, shadows leaping like angry
ghosts. Her bruises ache and swell, but swift virusblood's already healing them. It's the second best thing
about being infected. No lasting bruises. Ever.

Tony LaFaro winks his second set of eyelids and
hands the phone back to her, flat nose twitching. "You
think he bought it?"

"I dearly hope so. Hell, I bought it. Did you have to
hit me quite so hard?" Rosa sucks her swollen lip, blood
flowing.

"Sorry. Keepin' it authentic, y'know." Tony grins,
teeth black and broken, and offers her his misshapen
hand.

LaFaro enjoys this too much. She can see it in his
glinting yellow eyes, the way he breathes harder and

licks those scaly lips when he touches her. Vicious little bastard. For a moment, their pretense seemed frighteningly real, the secrecy, the brutality, the paralyzing fear of discovery. His shadow hulks over her, echoes of ill-forgotten violence past.

Genuine tears swell Rosa's throat, and she swallows, salty. She's a good actress. She has to be. Gangland is a man's world, and all she has is a hot body and lies. She'll do what she must to get ahead.

Swim for the light. Get your head above water. Keep kicking, no matter how many others drown as you push them under. Diamond was cute, but Ange is stronger, more powerful. And power's all that matters.

She grabs Tony's slippery hand and hauls herself up. Her bruises flare and fade as the virus does its work. "You got what you wanted. He'll come here Friday night, and you can do what you want with him."

"Mmm. Can I do what I want with you, too?" Tony pulls her in for a kiss, his forked tongue sly on her lips. His body is warm, his limbs tight and lithe. The dry smell of the sand he sleeps in sickens her, but she swallows and sucks his tongue in deep.

For a deformed faeborn abomination, he's not totally gross. And doing it in Ange's house always makes her hot. If Ange catches her, he'll tear her throat out. Rebellion and danger make the sordid things she does to survive fun.

It's liberating, this razoredge fear. Some guys are so damn protective, they stifle her. Not pointing any pink fairy fingers or anything. "Mmm. Maybe you can. You have to keep up your end of the bargain, though. The gemstone's still mine."

Another kiss, and Tony growls in guttural satisfaction, palming her breast. "Whatever."

"You promised." She slips her hand into his lap—that part's not from a lizard, that's for sure—and at his lusty groan, her blood thrills with power and desire. Men are so weak. Diamond's no exception, with his silly soft spot for damsels in distress. Deceiving him tonight turned her on, made her all tense and warm inside.

Famine told her about Ember, Diamond's little bloodfairy tart who's hunting them all down. But Diamond is Rosa's creature now. Shouldn't be hard to get him to turn on Ember, take the little bitch's gemstones and hand them over to Rosa.

Tony laughs as he kisses her throat, that weird tongue doing wicked things to the place where her pulse throbs tight. "Yeah, yeah. Don't worry. Fucking gemstone. Must be real sad for you, damning your soul and all."

"Screw you."

"Good idea. Think Ange'll mind?"

Rosa's breath catches as he nips at her breasts and pushes her against the wall. A mistake, getting involved with Famine and his crazyfae plan for immortality. She'd figured the demon lord, Kane, would be like any other man, his pleasure bought and sold at her whim. She'd figured very wrong.

Still, now she has her immortality, more or less. So long as she keeps eating.

And so long as some arrogant yellowface lizard doesn't wreck everything. Tony demanded she lay a trap for Diamond, or he'd take her gemstone and give her up to Kane. She agreed. What else could she do? Ange won't protect her from Tony. Ange and Tony go way back, and Rosa's just a drink and a fuck.

Tony drags her skirt up, greedily stripping her panties

away. He's shorter than she, and fits perfectly between her thighs. "I guess what Ange don't know don't hurt him, right?"

She laughs, breathless. "You've got no conscience, have you?"

"Ange's protection keeps me alive. He listens to my advice? Bonus. If he's too dumb to know I'm fucking his girlfriend, that's his problem."

Danger fires her blood, making her ache for release. She helps him, searching for buttons and studs. His cock is smooth and blunt, a bit weird, and she strokes him for only a moment before he hisses and pulls her thigh around him. She gasps in delight as he pushes into her, uncomfortable but full and good.

Tony thrusts deep, hard, faster, his breath short. "Christ, you kill me, woman."

"Careful. Not inside me. Ange'll notice."

"Not if I leave it somewhere he won't look." And he drags her from the wall, facedown on the bed with her bottom showing, and forces himself inside with a grunt. "Oh, yeah. That's fantastic."

Her vampire blood bubbles indignantly. She's stronger than he. She could throw him to the floor, tear his throat open and swallow as his lukewarm lizard blood fountains.

But he groans as he thrusts, and the ragged sound of his control slipping inflames her beyond sex or rich bloodlust. He grips her hips tighter, fucking her harder. Pleasure swells inside her, sucking her breath away, and it's nothing to do with friction.

Power is everything. These men own the world, take whatever they want, but still they're helpless in her grip. And all it takes is a little false surrender.

"Mmm," she purrs, "you feel so good," and when he jerks deep and comes, she does, too.

When the spasms fade, Rosa collapses sweating to the bed and crawls away, a smile on her unbruised lips.

Diamond tricked. Ange thwarted. Tony salivating for more.

A good few minutes' work.

14

The ladies' room door flapped closed behind me, and the casino noises faded.

Black tiles gleamed, floor to ceiling. A row of mirrors shone above half a dozen square white sinks. Opposite, cubicles with black laminated doors. No cameras that I could see. Uncleaned toilet smells wrinkled my nose. Guess they didn't employ too many cleaning staff so late.

A skinny blond girl with whitepowder wings leaned over the sink to apply mascara, glossy purple lips shining. I joined her, washing my hands and pretending to look in my bag for makeup while I scanned the reflections. Two cubicles occupied. No one in the corner or on the floor. No flicker of flame or shadow. I inhaled, faking a sigh to test the air, and pungent firefae incendiary stung my nostrils like petrol. Crimson was here. No doubt about it.

A toilet flushed. Coolly I flicked a stray lash from my cheek, pretending nerves weren't wriggling like crazy worms beneath my skin. A cubicle door opened, and a fat brown spriggan in a flowerprint dress waddled out. Her claws clicked as she stretched up on tiptoes to reach the sink, spraying water left and right and teasing her dirtbrown hair into an even ruder mess. The white fairy girl sniffed and flounced out, curls bouncing. The spriggan muttered and followed her, and the door slammed shut.

I fluttered aloft and poked my chin over the closed cubicle door.

There she lay. Crimson, curled like a fetus, sick yellow flame sputtering from her hair. Her breath heaved fast and shallow. Feebly, her wings jerked, slimy with sweat. Shiny drool slipped from her lips, but her glamour still held. She looked harmless, innocent, a beautiful dying bride, and my heart bled for her.

But she wasn't innocent. I swooped higher, and floated down inside.

I squatted, wrinkling my nose at her hypersweet sweat. Burnt sugar and blood, the smell of sparkle overspeed.

I swallowed, sick. I'd drugged her. Poisoned her like a coward. Didn't have the guts to meet her face-to-face.

My fingertips crawled cold at the thought of touching her, but I locked my jaw tight and pulled wet flameorange hair away from her throat.

Crimson's head flopped, her swanlike neck graceless. Her jeweled necklaces glittered, green and red and white. Tiny flames attacked my wrists, the remnants of her crippled magic, but they barely burned. She was at my mercy.

Unwilled, my fist clenched. I could put her out of it right now, crush my thumbs hard into her windpipe until she stopped panting. Save those pretty boys from a starving, fading death, and no doubt they hadn't been the first. I'd be doing the world a favor.

But I tried to imagine killing her, as easily and coolly as Diamond might eliminate some gang puke who'd trespassed on his turf or pissed him off somehow, and my guts hollowed cold.

I couldn't do it.

I'm not the angel of vengeance. I'm just a girl trying to stay alive. When I gave Crimson's gemstone to Kane, she'd die. Thanks to the stupid devil's bargain she and her friends had made, and the magic tricks they'd done in an effort to hide from the consequences, her soul was inextricably entwined within her gem, and Kane would delight in eating her up.

I couldn't help that. Didn't mean I should delight in her blood on my hands.

Cautiously, I poked at her jewels.

She didn't move. Just lay there and hyperventilated, blacksparkle vomit dripping from her lips.

My courage firmed. I bent closer, examining each jeweled strand. Pearls, gold, a row of red ones, a sparkling choker like ice. Nothing that burned like the stone in my ring. Her hair tangled in the chains, and I tugged it impatiently, wet strands gluing to my fingers. A pair of deepblue stones like tiny eggs in her pierced ears. I checked her fingers. Gold rings, a spray of garnets, nothing like mine. A single jade bangle. I even tugged her shoes off to search for a toe ring. No dice.

I ruffled my hair, frustrated. Maybe Diamond was right. She'd gotten rid of it, or kept it safe. Guess we'd have to trash her place after all. Great. I'll go home and get my ski mask.

She convulsed, rolling her onto her back. She gurgled, her throat filling. Guilt salted my conscience. I'd seen enough paralytic idiots to know that if I left her like that, she'd drown.

I shoved my hand under her hip to flip her onto her side, and a sharp point tugged her dress taut over her belly. I stared and poked at it, and my claw clinked on metal.

A belly ring. My nerves strung tight. Maybe she did keep her gemstone safe. Close to her body, where no one would see it unless she wanted them to.

She stirred, moaning, and fluttered a weak hand to her face.

My heart somersaulted. No way was I sticking my hand up her skirt. I already felt too much like a rapist. Instead I plucked at the silk, trying to tear a hole. The flimsy fabric was deceptively tough. I couldn't get my claw through, and my efforts made her wriggle in her stupor, trying to fend me off. She wasn't unconscious, just incapacitated. Probably hallucinating, her rational mind gibbering in fear. God knew what she thought I was.

Each wasted second itched the back of my neck. If she woke, I was screwed. And I had nothing sharp, not nail scissors or a knife. I tried both hands, stabbing my claw in. My left hand brushed her belly, and Jasper's ring clamped down on my finger like icefire jaws.

Hellfire flashed my bones white-hot. I yelped and yanked away. My ring caught, and the silk tore with a sound like rending flesh.

A ragged hole gaped, showing her smooth belly. A golden spike pierced her navel, and in it winked a glittering tiger's eye jewel.

Cruel demon laughter spun cackling psychosis in my head, and the echo of Kane's kiss filled my mouth with ash. The tiger's eye flashed at me, green and golden. Trembling, I fastened aching fingers around it.

Crimson screeched, her breath foul. A drooling death's head grin split her lips, and she whiplashed up like a zombie and clawed for my throat.

I yelled, and scrabbled to get her off me, the gemstone slipping from my grasp. But her horrid wet fingers bruised my neck, digging in where the vampire's cruel biteholes were almost healed. My skin tore, her sharp claws raking deep.

I fell backwards onto warm tiles. She tumbled on top of me, a dead sweating weight reanimated by foul demon magic. Diseased yellow smoke puffed from her wings. Her eyes rolled back, blossoming scarlet. She wasn't conscious. Just fighting blindly for her soul.

My wings crumpled under me like paper. I wriggled my knee between her legs to lever her off. She fought, and my skull clanged the tiles. My throat swelled in her grip. I grabbed her hair and pulled, but she didn't care, even when strands popped out.

My breath squashed to a tiny squeak. My chest heaved, but no air forced in, and I fought numbing nerves to think, plan, do anything but let her kill me.

But panic howled in my blood like a moonlit monster, obliterating my reason. Colors flashed, edges blurring starry. Wildly I kicked for her groin, but hit only muscle and bruising bone. Spit dribbled from her numb lips, splashing sugary into my mouth. I flapped my tongue frantically, but I had no air to spit it out.

My ears buzzed from oxygen deficit. Her weight crushed me. Desperate, I wormed one leg free and jammed my knee into her guts.

Her breath woofed out, lurching her off balance, and her grip on my throat loosened.

I gasped a welcome breath. Colored stars burst before my eyes. Blood and bile scorched my gullet, and I wound my hands in her long orange hair, thrust backwards with my wings, and kicked as hard as I could.

We tumbled in a backwards roll, a flail of limbs and

hair. My ankle smacked into the wall. Pain exploded, but I hung on grimly. Her limp wings stuttered, but she couldn't halt her fall, and I grabbed her around the neck and smacked her skull hard into the toilet bowl.

She jerked and lay still.

I panted, my lungs refusing to fill. Jesus Christ on a beanbag. I'd hit her pretty hard. She wasn't moving. My pulse skittered like a frightened rabbit. *Please, don't let me have killed her.*

Her hair knotted around my fingers, slick and horrible like sunset seaweed. I flapped my hands, wild. It wouldn't come off. My palms crawled, and I scrabbled at it furiously until it came free, but I could still feel her on me. Still taste her foul spit in my mouth, feel her cold feversweat smearing my skin.

A shiver rotted my spine. I wanted to scramble backwards, get as far from her as I could. But I fumbled with the jewel. Popped the stud open. Slid it out. A splat of bright blood came with it, oiling my fingers scarlet, and no matter how I wiped, it wouldn't come off.

My ring cackled, horrid demon laughter swirling in my head like ash until I couldn't see. Sickness salted my mouth. I scrabbled the doorcatch open, heels sliding in the sweaty mess, and burst out, stumbling against the sink in my haste to get away.

The mirrors showed me stark, my red hair disheveled, fresh bruises smearing my throat scarlet and black. Crimson's jewel squirmed, scorching my hand. I stuffed it into my bag, trying to ignore the tiger's eye's accusing glare. Great. Now I'm a thief as well as a murderer.

I straightened my dress and splashed my face, trying to regain some semblance of cool. I struggled for a few seconds to calm my breath and still my shaking hands, before I scraped my hair as neat as I could and walked out.

Lights glared. The gaming floor's business carried on without a hiccup. No one stared or pointed or yelled. They all kept playing, laughing, drinking, money changing hands under glittering lightbulbs.

Weak relief cooled my skin, and I realized I'd expected to be jumped on, pinned down in a hail of bullets like Butch Cassidy and the Sundance Fairy.

I straightened my bag, my new jewel whispering hot rebellion inside, and took a few tentative steps. No one looked at me. My heart thudded. I kept walking, around the roulette tables and away, peering across the crowd for the glitter of rosepink glass.

Where was Diamond? I'd almost forgotten he'd said he'd watch me. I snorted, indignant. Fine bunch of help he was. If he'd left me here, I'd kill him. Y'know, once I'd escaped from hell and all.

Behind me, a door crashed and a woman screamed.

My stomach leapt into my throat. Heads turned. I fought not to look around, and kept walking, clutching my bag to my lap. The woman kept yelling. "Help, someone, there's a girl beat up in here!"

A pair of human security guards appeared from nowhere, guys in dark brown suits with curly wires behind their ears. My cheeks burned, culpability painted all over my face in sweat and blood. They'd see it, stop me, push me to the ground. Crimson's blood scorched my fingers, and I wanted to tear my guilty skin off and scrub it clean.

Doors swung. Footsteps scraped tiles. And then another yell, a high-pitched voice that chilled my blood. "That's her! I seen her! She done it!"

My head whizzed around.

The white fairy girl pointed at me through the crowd, that silly purple lipstick a bright slash on her pale face. The security guys looked up and fastened twin black gazes on me.

15

I didn't think. I just bolted.

Colors blurred and melted. Tables and stools loomed at me from dazzling neon, and I tripped and banged into people but stayed on my feet. My heart shot rapid bullets in my chest. My earpoints twitched backwards, hunting for pursuit. Relentless footsteps, commands, voices talking into intercoms and radios. I threw a stool down behind me, hoping to obstruct them like I'd seen on TV. Did that even work? Who the fuck knew?

I flung my head this way and that, hunting for an exit. The gaming floor went on and on. Where the fuck was the door?

My throat swelled as I ran, my bag bumping my hip. I'd never make it out. They'd catch me and lock me up and some dirty prison bitch would rape me and scratch my face and rip my wings off strip by bleeding strip, only I wouldn't care, because Kane would drag my sorry ass to hell in a couple of days anyway.

A warm hand grabbed my wrist and pulled.

I swooped, tumbling on desperate wings into a half-hidden service corridor, and rammed against the wall into a hard rosescented body.

"Zero outa ten for stealth, partner." Diamond held me close around my waist, his wings glimmering violet.

I choked, my senses drunk. My body pulsed warm, his scent flowing over me in a hot caress. Damn it if I wasn't pleased to see the cocky lying bastard.

Damn it twice if I'd let him see it. I scowled, my pulse still racing. "Fine help you were."

"Got caught up. You okay?"

At least he asked, unlike Jasper. "Yeah."

"Get your shiny?"

"Uh-huh."

"Nice. C'mon, then. Scramblicate. These losers won't give up." And he grabbed my hand, and we ran.

Tables gave way to rainbow slot machines, gamblers mesmerized by flashing lights and burbling tunes. A few looked up as we hurtled by, but most kept on staring and punching buttons, backlit graphics rolling. I snickered, mad. *Never mind the murderer, Mr. Security Guard, I've got three bananas! Jackpot!*

Giggles tore breath from my lungs. Diamond tugged me between two rows of machines, where a door quartered the white wall with a red sign proclaiming EMERGENCY EXIT ONLY! THIS DOOR IS ALARMED!

I cackled, helpless. *Be alert, not alarmed!* "We can't go out that way. They'll know."

But Diamond dragged me to a steel panel on the wall, and I laughed still more. Fire alarm.

Diamond ripped the metal cover off and jammed glassy fingers into the exposed circuits. Current arced blue, backlighting his skin.

I gasped, my hair springing on end. "Jesus, don't—!"

But it didn't zap him. Current didn't flow in glass. And he forced his claws around a handful of sparking metal wires and ripped them out.

For a moment, nothing happened.

And then, all the lights in the room snapped out, and with a hiss and a happy thump of pressure, the fire sprinklers erupted.

Water splashed. Alarms wailed, electric. People screamed in the dark. And everyone started pouring for the exits.

Diamond grinned at me through a blinding mist of spray. I grinned back. And together we crashed our shoulders into the metal-barred door and tumbled out into the black marble lobby.

The door slammed shut behind us. The dark glass ceiling towered, three stories high and filled with a dazzling purple light and water display. Narrow water columns burst from the shining tile floor, spurting high in glittering arcs, and from above, light poured in elliptical patterns, shimmering violet and magenta on hanging sparkles and crystal sculptures. Bubbly aquarium music played, and fresh cool air caressed my fevered skin. Outside, the moon shone brilliant, almost perfectly round, illuminating the glass orangebright.

Inside, the evacuation alarm still screeched, a hellish discord piercing through the music. Around us, people milled, gamblers spilling into the lobby from the gaming floor.

Swiftly, we ducked into the thickening crowd. Security people ran and searched, their radios chattering overtime. Diamond pulled me close, his arm around my waist. We were both wet, and his skin slid warm on mine. My scalp prickled as his crystalline glamour settled over us, and we shimmered out of sight, a faint pink glow crisping my vision's edge.

I bumped into a brownsuit, and my pulse jerked.

But he just pointed and shouted directions, his gaze sliding over us without a blink.

Diamond's satisfied laugh warmed my ear, and together we hustled for the front door.

We darted across the street at the pedestrian lights, the bridge's traffic thin but constant even this late at night. Sweat broke on my skin in the heat, and the moon thrummed sweet delight in my veins. Already, the hungry dry air sucked the moisture from my sodden clothes.

Behind us on the wide gray pavement outside the lobby, people milled under spotlights, the tall glass façade looming overhead. The security people had apparently given up hunting the Ladies' Room Smiter and were concentrating on evacuating hundreds of people from the casino floor, and as we skipped down the graystone walkway to Southbank, twin red fire trucks screeched over the bridge from the city, sirens pealing and lights flashing red and white.

I giggled and danced, elated, Diamond's hand still warm in mine. My hair hung in sticky ringlets, and I shook my head wild. On our left, the river shone darkly, city lights reflecting orange and yellow, the footbridge's purple stripe arcing high toward the big blue cube of the aquarium. Ahead, Southbank lay almost deserted, the strip of restaurants and pubs closed for the night, the pavement cleared of chairs and tables.

Apartment blocks gleamed, tall and bright, the immense bladelike height of Eureka Tower stabbing deep into moonlit sky. I could even see Jasper's building below it, marble and shining glass. A few folks strayed, some kids on skateboards weaving their curves, a pair of naked fairies splashing each other silly in the warm dank river with garbage tangled in their hair. Distant thunder rolled, a storm flashing to the south.

All was normal. We'd escaped.

My moonrich blood still throbbed with excitement, and panic's rich echo tingled warm and seductive in my limbs. Tricking people was hard. Being chased was terrifying. Slamming that woman's skull into the porcelain made me want to throw up.

But getting away with it was exhilarating. The moon tempted me to wildness. I wanted to laugh, frisk my wings, hop and jump and shake my sweaty hair until it crackled.

Did that make me a bad person?

Crazy giggles frothed in my chest, and I couldn't swallow them.

"Nice work, candy." Diamond snapped his glamour off in a puff of glitter and laughed. I couldn't help noticing it lit his face, those perfect crystal cheekbones glinting.

"Toldya not to call me that." This was exactly the sort of naïve excitement that got me in trouble with Jasper, and I scowled, trying to brush it off. But his glee was irresistible, apparently, because I kept laughing, and some flighty and wicked creature twirled crazy orbits in my heart.

He poked my ribs, teasing. "Candy. You were fucking magnificent."

Stupidly, his praise blushed my wings tender. Like he knew anything about me, magnificent or otherwise. I tried another glare. "Like you saw anything. Coulda used your help in there, flash."

"Sorry. Toldya, I got tied up."

"Oh, yeah? Doing what?"

"Phone. Couldn't helpify." A violet flush darkened his face, and he wouldn't look at me. More evasion. Damn it.

A solitary banshee cruised past on in-line skates, crooning to herself, applegreen hair flowing in the night air. Her magical lovesong dragged fresh longing through my blood. I wanted to be mad at him, but it wasn't easy, not the way he flittered so close to me, all shiny and glowing and muscled up. Not the way he smelled, so dark and seductive, a mouthwatering feast I wanted to devour. Not with that damn moonlight caressing me slow and deep, hypnotic, stealing my soul like a demon lover.

"Oh, sure. That nastyfae cow nearly ripped my head off in there. Look." I cocked my chin up and pointed at my bruises, trying to ignore the pulse that pounded in my throat.

"Said I was sorry, didn't I? You handled it great. Got your shiny, didn't ya?" He grabbed my hand and twirled me, my skirt flaring out like a salsa dancer's, and instinctively I stretched my wings out to catch the breeze, wafting a few inches in the air on a gloriously warm updraft. I wanted to spin, fly, tumble somersaults in dizzy delight.

I landed with a flutter and scowled again, trying not to smile as he danced me backwards in his fragrant pink shadow. I wouldn't have escaped without him. No need to show him I knew that. "No thanks to you."

"But you did. And we escapamated, didn't we? Scarpered? Pissed off outa there under their silly human noses?"

"But they could still catch us—"

"Don't you ever stop worrying?" He spun me again and tipped me backwards over his arm, and uncomfortable Jasper-flash warmed me. But Diamond's shining hair rained over my face, so warm, so unexpectedly soft and fragrant, and his strong arm supported my back, and I knew this was different. For fun, not for show. For Jasper, everything was selfishness, calculation, done to make him look good.

Diamond acted on impulse, and to hell with tomorrow.

His prismed light dazzled me, and suddenly my head swam with the scent of roses and hot, willing male flesh.

He swept me to my feet, and dizzy temptation swirled. I stumbled against him, laughing, and when he tugged me back against the wall with him in a bright patch of moonlight and played idle fingers into my hair, I didn't push him away.

Delight warmed me, stained delicious with his tempting rosy scent. I felt like I'd done something naughty and fun for once in my life, and guess what? No one cared. No one disciplined me. No one slapped me or put me in the corner or sent me to bed without any supper. The rules I lived by had dissolved.

Including the one that said *Don't play with dirty-sexymad fairy boys.*

"Toldya it'd be fun." Diamond captured my fingers and kissed them, lingering on the soft places inside my knuckles, and tingles crept up my arm, dangerous.

"Umm . . . don't do that." But desire sprang alive deep in my belly. I shivered, cold and burning at the same time. I felt strange, reckless, fevered. Just the moon, playing sexy tricks in my blood, like the night I'd met Jasper. Right?

"Why not?" He kissed inside my wrist, and longing rippled so deep in my soul, I nearly cried out. I had a hundred reasons why not, and I couldn't think of a single one.

What was wrong with me? I'd only just ditched one controlling boy. I couldn't succumb to another. Was he casting some treacherous glamour on me? I didn't know or care. I just wanted to dance into his embrace and let him make me his.

Stop it, idiot. That cross, sensible voice scolded me again. *Walk away before you do something you'll regret. Your boyfriend died tonight, remember? You're exhausted, hurt, confused. You're in no state to know what you want.*

But I was.

I'd stopped loving Jasper the night he hit me for the first time. The rest was just habit and infatuation. For so long, I'd painted and prettied and molded myself into the girl someone else wanted—the girl I had to be to survive—that I'd almost forgotten there was a real me inside, one who wanted and hoped and dreamed for herself. But tonight, with my heart still pounding and the moon rippling sweet anarchy in my blood, I knew exactly what I wanted.

And I wasn't the only one.

"Kiss me, Ember." Diamond's whisper burned my collarbone, and I shivered with anticipation. "Know you wanna."

16

"Uhh . . . this is a bad idea." The words trembled on my tongue. But he curled his wings around us in shimmerpink shadow, and his hot-glass-and-roses scent poured melting need over my skin like honey, and I couldn't help tilting my chin up, inviting him on.

"No badness. Just this." He trailed kisses across my bruised throat and up to my chin, and it felt so naughty and dangerous, every featherlight caress a torture deep inside. My wingjoints ached hard, longing for more. He burbled darkly with faewarm desire, halfway between a sigh and a growl. "You make me reckless, Ember. Let's go home and play."

Moonstruck longing crippled my reason. God, it'd feel so good. To lose myself in his kiss, forget about tomorrow and demons and dead boyfriends and live here, now, in this glorious, triumphant moment.

"Can't," I murmured, but my eyes fluttered closed. His fairy weirdness pulled a magical riptide deep in my blood, and I wanted to melt in his arms and let him do whatever he wanted to me. Would it be so bad, to be captured? He was hot and male and so beautiful, I ached. He made me laugh, exult, shiver, howl inside to the greedy moon.

But he was also mad, careless and domineering, the same thoughtless arrogance as Jasper but a hundred times worse.

It'd be so easy to throw my freedom away.

Maybe Diamond did act on impulse. Maybe the way he teased his lips in my hair was a whim, his fingers sliding over my hips just a mad notion he was running with to pass the time. And maybe he'd forget me just as quickly, like a whimsical summer breeze whisking through his mind and clearing out the trash.

But I wouldn't forget. When I jumped in, it was with everything I had. And before I knew it, it'd be too late to climb out.

"Screw *can't*. You like me. I sure as hell want you. Who'll care?" His mouth hovered over mine, tempting me to come to him. Desire dizzied me, tingling through my body until my breasts ached heavy and my sex slicked wet for his touch. His nearness stole my breath, the pressure of his body on mine—how did we get so close?—his smooth muscles sliding against me melted my limbs to quivering. Different from Jasper. So big and hard-packed and luscious. Almost like a human . . .

God, this was crazy. But I couldn't help it. How would it feel, to slide my palms over his naked chest, that shining flesh mine to play with? Sit naked in his lap and ease him inside me, feel him move, thrust into me, pleasure me?

Perhaps he heard me thinking—or was it obvious, the way my body molded to him, the iron scent of my moisture fresh?—because he laughed, a soft crystal tinkle that drove me wild. "C'mon, then. Let's seeify."

He stroked the quivering curve of my back, and my knees nearly buckled, it felt so good. How did he know that? My wingtips curled in anticipation. Desire battled common sense in my aching body. God, I wanted to kiss him.

He leaned closer, and my nipples stung hard against his chest. He must have felt it. Must know I yearned for him. He was tempting me, easy as one of his tricks, and for a moment, fear oozed hot into my longing.

I liked it. Wanted him to overwhelm me, lead me, give me no choice. And the fear only spiced my desire.

He licked my bottom lip, a teasing promise, and when I murmured in sweet confusion, he claimed my mouth for a kiss, and nothing had ever felt more inevitable.

Mmm. Slow, hot, deep, tingling my nerves with pleasure. His tongue slipped into my mouth, filling me with his rosedrenched flavor, making me want more. He murmured, encouraging, and I threaded my arms around his neck, pressing closer, deepening the kiss at the pace I wanted. For a few bright seconds, I had control, and delicious power flamed deep inside.

But then he growled, a soft snarl of need deep in his chest, and he tilted my head back and effortlessly wrenched my control away.

Oh, lord. His lips caressed mine, hot and urgent, slashing desire deep into my veins. He cupped my face in his hands and claimed my mouth like he'd claimed me, first my curiosity and then my desire and finally my hunger, rich and ravenous like the heat that tortured me. He wasn't careful or gentle. He just took me, his tongue seducing mine and demanding my surrender. His hot summer taste flooded my mouth, spice and roses, dragging deep longing from my pores like blood. Lust swelled tight between my legs. I was wet, fresh, ready. God, it was like love, this utter longing, this insatiable thirst to please. . . .

He spun me around, back to the wall, and pulled my thigh around him, crushing me against his big body. I could feel him, hard, hot, bold, his big fairy cock pressing between my legs, searching for a home. My wings swelled, and when he pushed hot fingertips beneath my skirt, I groaned into his mouth, my excitement quickening. Hot moonlight caressed my naked thigh, all the way up to my ass. Anyone could have seen us. It felt wicked, dirty, a naughty thing good girls didn't do.

I dug my claws into his back, dragging him boldly closer. He teased the edge of my panties, tempting me, sliding those clever fingers closer and closer to where I was hot and slick.

Deep inside, I ached, empty. I wanted him to pleasure me, stroke my swollen flesh, play with me, torture me insane with pleasure. And it wasn't just because he'd feel so very good. It was disobedient. Bad. Rebellious. And I wanted to fuck the world and everyone in it who'd put me in this stupid predicament.

I whimpered and panted, pleading words far too close to the tip of my tongue. *Please, just a little closer. Touch me.*

"Like this?" He pressed my mouth open more, tilting my head to ravish me deeper, and at the same time, he pushed one long finger inside me to the hilt.

I groaned. So smooth, so tight. My body was so slick and warm, the friction delicious. Fairies have long fingers, that extra knuckle made for pleasure, and his were clever, practiced, demanding. Already my flesh hardened under his stroking fingertip, the tiny tingle of claw a dangerous delight. So perfect.

His halo darkened, a lusty violet, and he growled into our kiss, deep and rough with desire. "Mmm. You like that?"

"Uh-huh." My voice strangled, breathless, his rhythmic stroking dragging me hard and fast toward impossible pleasure. He knew exactly what I liked. I'd thought I could handle this. Use it. Control it. I was wrong.

"Don't fight. Let go for me. Showify how beautiful you are."

My fist clenched in his hair, my nerves raw and sparkling inside. He was so dirty. So bad. Breaking the rules excited me. I wanted to spread my legs on the concrete, pull his mouth between my thighs and let him lick me to heaven where everyone could see. I'd peel those silkysmooth pants off him, slide his cock into my mouth and suck him hard, savor that rosy sweetness. . . .

He dropped to his knees and swept hot lips up the inside of my thigh, tugging my panties aside. The summer night caressed my naked skin raw. I trembled, every nerve ragged. He'd never really do it, would he? Right here under the greedy moon?

He laughed, low and breathy, and it burned me. "Never tell me never," he murmured, and swept his long curled tongue right over my clit.

I clutched at the wall, muscles weak. He felt so sinfully good. He licked me, caressed me, made me shudder. Not too hard, not too gentle, the perfect spot, just how I liked. And then he sucked me into his mouth, and I moaned. So perfect, he had to be reading my mind. . . .

My thighs clenched. The prick was reading my mind. Using his dirty glassfae sight to trick me. Control me. Make me his creature. Just like Jasper, only Jasper hadn't used magic. He'd intimidated me into obedience. But this was worse.

This, I had no chance of resisting.

Denial burned like ash in my hellscorched bones.

Diamond sucked me again, his tongue torturing my sensitive tip, and hot tension coiled tight inside me, threatening to snap. God, I wanted him to make me come. But not like this. Not a nasty trick.

I gritted my teeth and shoved him away, my thighs quivering. "No. Don't. Get off me."

He stumbled, violet wings shining wet. His lips glistened, and he pressed the back of his hand to his mouth, my fluid still shining rich and wet on his fingers. "Sorry. I thought you . . . Fuck."

I averted my face, fighting for control. I was sweating, shaking, my legs a melted mess. "Just stay away from me."

"Ember—"

"Don't." My breath ripped hot welts in my chest, and I warded him off with trembling hands. No way. No matter how hard and hot the moonlight throbbed in my blood, how slyly it tempted me. No matter how much I longed to feel him naked against me, his smooth glowing skin on mine, his beautiful mouth having its sultry way with me . . .

He lifted my chin gently to make me look at him. "Hey. I'm sorry, 'kay? Didn't meanify—"

"Then what the hell did you mean?" I shook him off angrily and rearranged my clothes. My lips still swelled from our kiss. My sex still throbbed from his clever tongue. I could still feel his body, hot and tempting, his rosedark flavor madness in my mouth. "Stay the fuck out of my head, okay?"

"What?"

"Were you reading my mind?"

"Don't freakify. I can't mindread you. I get flashes, that's all—"

"Oh, sure. You call that 'flashes'?"

"I call it turning you on. Didn't take a genius to figure what you wanted."

I laughed, incredulous. "Lord, you've got an ego. I am not some girltoy you can play with!"

"Who's gaming? I've wanted you ever since Jasper first showed you off. Didn't you know?"

Unwilled pleasure flushed me. All those times he'd flirted with me, teased me, tricked me into checking him out when I thought he wasn't looking. I'd thought it flattery for Jasper's benefit. Had he meant it, then? Liked me? Imagined touching me, stealing a kiss, pulling me aside for some illicit wickedness where Jasper couldn't see? Tugging me into a dark corner, ripping my panties off and taking me roughly from behind, his mouth hot and wet on my wingjoints?

Not that I'd thought about it.

But the images wouldn't fade. My sex throbbed, still tense and frustrated from his caress. Oh, lord. How good his cock would feel there right now. So hot and smooth and hard . . .

I scowled and folded my arms, my heartbeat thudding. "Am I supposed to be flattered? How many girls didya pick up this week with that line?"

"So what? You're smart and funny and sexy. Isn't that enough?"

My skin heated. "Oh, yeah? What happened to whore? Liar? Coward?"

He laughed, crystaldark. "Didn't botherfy you just now."

"Screw you, okay? You don't trick me. I know what you're up to."

His wings flushed darker. "What's that meanify?"

"You know what I mean. Why are you really helping me, Diamond? And don't give me that gangbanger loyalty crap."

He didn't answer. Just looked at me, sweat glistening like quicksilver on his throat, those scorching eyes glowing scarlet with desire.

My guts tightened. I knew it. Sure, he wanted to fuck me. But he was using me for some shadowy purpose of his own, and I'd walked right into his trap like a stupid little bloodfae moron.

I scowled and pushed past him. "Yeah, that's what I thought."

He flicked his wings and landed beside me, flashing hair trailing in his wake.

I kept my arms folded. Kept walking, a treacherous flush still warming my face, my thighs sticky and sore. Pretended not to look at him, though my gaze kept sucking itself back onto him like wicked glue. "You can go now. Any time you want. Really."

"The hell." He stuffed long hands into his pockets and walked beside me.

That sexy rosefragrant glow on my skin irritated me. "Look, just leave me alone. I'll find Famine by myself—"

"Not going solitary, candy." He tossed glittering hair over his shoulder. "S'not safe. Crimson's got friendlies. They all got friendlies. If word's out, you're toasticated."

"But . . . oh." My voice trailed off. His infuriating *I know better than you* smile itched my palms raw. All the more because he was right.

My stupidity made me squirm. I never thought things through. Should've known from Paris and Tinker's attack that there'd be trouble. My blood chilled, even though the moon cast brightedged shadows on the concrete. I'd just made myself a target. And I wasn't finished yet. Still two gemstones to go.

Going it alone was all very well, but I wasn't a kick-ass warrior chick with superpowers. I couldn't fight vampires or demon minions, or who the hell knew what else this Famine person would turn out to be. But Diamond could.

I sighed. This night just kept getting better. "So what, you gonna follow me around?"

"That's the plannification. Complaints?"

He shot me a crafty golden glance, and I bit my lip in frustration. *Yes,* and I was an ungrateful skank. *No,* and I got myself an all-too-attractive escort I really didn't want. I sighed, defeated. "Guess not. But we're not sleeping in the same room, okay?"

He shrugged, tense. "Whatever."

We turned into the empty shopping center, flood-lights shining on deserted pubs, darkened windows, a parched fountain. I hopped up the steps to the other side, and stumbled as I fluttered to the top.

I held my aching forehead, dizziness blurring my vision. It soon passed, but I still felt hot and light-headed, the distant ache in my bones spreading through my muscles like oversweet honey. Guess I was more tired than I thought. A meal probably wouldn't go astray. I couldn't remember the last time I'd eaten, and my mouth watered just thinking about the contents of Jasper's fridge, leftover pizza or chocolate chip cookies or strawberry milk and cheese.

Well, maybe not the milk. Anything pink was off the menu.

We crossed the road and I headed left, toward Jasper's place. The familiar black marble invited, and I stifled a yawn and scraped sweaty hair off my neck. A shower, dinner, a few hours' sleep, pick Diamond's brains about this Famine character.

I guess it was nice of him to help me, even if I couldn't trust him to keep his hands—or his mind—to himself. No doubt he'd a squillion more important things to do. Kicking heads, selling sparkle, picking up girls who didn't know better. I might be a charity project, but better than no project at all.

The memory of his scorching kiss stirred again, my flesh still purring for more. I glanced up at the swollen moon, and it smiled back, seductive.

My blood thrummed. Hmm. Maybe I'd been a bit rude, brushing him off like that. He'd gone out of his way for me, after all. Perhaps it wouldn't hurt to give something back. Perhaps we could just . . .

I tripped on a loose tile, and common sense crashed cold.

God, did I really just think that?

So what if the moon made me horny? If he condescended to give me a few moments of his time? Didn't mean I had to let him touch me.

I flushed, and Big Em's rational voice addressed me curtly: *Grow up, Ember. Don't give me shit about owing him anything or the moon making you. You're a big girl. You wanna fuck him, you go right ahead. But don't blame everyone else for it.*

Diamond touched my shoulder, and I jumped.

Goddamn it. I still remembered how those fingers felt inside me, the hot melting pleasure when he—

"What?" I snapped without thinking.

He pulled me to a stop. "You can't go home."

"Why not?"

"Not safe."

Alarm rippled my blood. "You mean they know where I live?"

He wriggled his fingers, palms upward—*maybe, maybe not*—and flicked hair from my cheek with a cocky claw. "Safer with me, peachy."

Indignation burred my fingertips. That possessive caress drove me bugfuck. I liked him touching me. I hated it. Damn him. "No way. You're so not taking me back to your place."

"Okay. Wanna curl up right here, then? Nice gutter over there. Good comfy patch of dirt. Look, it's even got a tree."

"Don't be a smart-ass."

"Don't be a princess, then. Take some gifties for once. Not everything is business."

Golden sorrow melted his eyes, and for a bright moment, I believed him.

I puffed damp hair from my eyes—gosh, it was hot for three in the morning—and shrugged, knowing I had no choice. But I didn't like it. Didn't like the way he looked at me, like he was waiting for something to happen. "Okay. Fine. But just for the night, and then I'm leaving. And I get the bed. You do sleep in a bed, right?"

"Bed, yes. Sleep, no." He drifted a few feet into the air, an easy wingsweep, and tugged my hand twice, like a kid who wants ice cream. "Shortcut?"

I resisted. "Why, where is it?"

He pointed with his chin. "Upski."

I cocked my neck, moonlight shining in my eyes, and he took advantage of my lack of balance and pulled me aloft.

We shot up two stories, wind dragging my sweaty hair back.

I squealed, fluttering so I wouldn't fall. "Someone'll see!"

"Screw 'em. It's three in the morning. Prob-mally shitfaced anyway." And he tugged me higher on a powerful roseglowing slash. Muscled-up son of a bitch could really fly.

My skirt billowed around my thighs. Warmth soared beneath me, filling my delicate wing membranes with gentle upward pressure. The ground zoomed away beneath us. Laughing, I swooped into a dive, trailing my wings behind me and flaring them at the last second to catch myself. Diamond followed, arcing elegantly like a pinkglass dolphin, his hand still warm in mine.

I giggled, sublime. Fresh hot air swirled around me, and moonlight flashed from glossy apartment windows as we darted by. My damp dress plastered to my breasts and rippled in the breeze. Diamond's hair streamed behind him, billowing over his wings like a rainbow. He never left my side, and his rosy halo enclosed me like a fragrant bubble, filled with warmth and safety and the dark male smell of his skin.

I rolled onto my back, drifting, bathing in the warm updraft, pleasant vertigo swirling in my skull. My wings stretched tight like tissue paper, and it felt fantastic, little starbursts of delight firing in my pores. A smile tweaked my lips. It did feel good, floating beneath a summer moon, the lazy friction of our glamours rubbing together sparking the air.

We fairies don't get to fly much. Always too afraid some human will see us. It's every fae girl's nightmare. Trapped in a net like some stupid butterfly, wings peeled back or pinned to a slab, dissected alive by skinny dudes with bad breath and white coats, all in the name of science. Or worse, kept captive in secret by some lunatic with a fairy fetish, iron cagebars and worms for breakfast and grotty sex games in the dark.

Don't laugh. It happens. An airfae girl I knew went out for milk and didn't come back. They say some weirdo netted her for his collection, leaving only tufts of fluffy white hair and a pile of wingdust. They found her chewed wingbones in a Dumpster six weeks later. True story.

But if some grimy fairychewer wanted me, he'd have to come through Diamond first. At least, he would tonight.

He floated beside me, basking in the warmth, moonlight flashing off his weirdglass wings, and I had to admit it felt kinda nice. Jasper had protected me, sure, but always I'd had that nagging feeling he'd toast me in an instant if someone made him a better offer. Diamond . . . Well, he was hanging with me for some bullheaded reason of his own, and making Diamond change his mind if he didn't want to seemed to be right up there with bleeding stones and pissing into the wind.

Hell of a reason to feel safe. But I did. From fairychewers, that is. Not from Diamond.

He spiraled, pulling me around with him like two fish playing in the surf. Concrete walls lurched perilously close, and then we flitted over a tall glass balcony rail and he settled me to my feet, his arm steady around my waist.

I staggered, fatigue making me heavy. Too much action and excitement. Sure, I loved to party, but that didn't usually involve smacking some zombie chick over the head with a toilet bowl and sprinting through a crowded casino with the fire alarm going off.

Or kissing some naughty fairy boy in steamy moonlight.

"You 'kay?" His whisper warmed my ear.

"Umm . . . sure." He still had his arm around me, his body pressed hard against my side, slick with delicious fairy sweat, and mmm, was that his wing edge rubbing against mine? Dirty boy. My wingjoints swelled with pleasure, and I wobbled away, flushing. Enough of that tonight.

The long balcony glared silver in moonshine, curved around the side of the building, tiled in glossy black with dusty raindrops sprinkling the tinted glass door. In the corner sat a fat ultragreen potted plant, wrapped tight like a mummy with purple tinsel.

I peered over the edge, my heart thudding. On one side, a taller building blocked the view, but on the other, you could see all the way across the river to the city, skyscrapers knifing the sky, lights sparkling orange and blue and white. Beyond the park across St. Kilda Road, lightning flashed, too distant to hear the thunder. I inhaled, fresh eucalyptus and flowers, dirty underneath with smoke and distant rain we wouldn't get. The smell of Melbourne in summer, gritty and delightful.

Inside, it was dark, outlines of furniture dim. He slid the glass door open and walked in. Magenta light pooled around him, shadows flickering. I followed, envious, searching for obstacles with my toes. Must be nice to make your own light.

He flipped the downlights on, presumably for my benefit, and I stopped short.

Handy, too, when your place was such a fucking mess.

He had shit everywhere. And I mean everywhere. His coffee table was jammed between two couches, the whole thing piled up like a Mexican pyramid with magazines, books, DVD cases, empty chocolate wrappers, crunched-up tinfoil and discarded glassware smeared with suspicious glitter, green and blue and black. The floor lay ankle-deep in the same. I saw laptop computers, game consoles, tablets, a couple of MP3 players.

Even the walls were a furious clutter of paintings, photos, and drawings, hung crooked and cramped together in a mass work of chaotic art. He'd drawn on them, colored in and over with paint or crayon or glitter. And behind them, more spraypainted colors splashed the creamy walls. Even the ceiling hadn't escaped clean. It looked like some epileptic artist had partied with the Unabomber.

I stared, overwhelmed. This place was a riot. If this was what his brain was like, no wonder he had a few too many syllables tumbling off his tongue.

He shrugged at my bewildered glance. "What? If I'd known you was coming, I'd have cleanified."

I snorted. "No, you wouldn't."

"I mighta. Sometimes I even vacuum." His wounded look just made me laugh, and he relapsed into a dazzling grin and fluttered over piled books and paper flowers to land on the raised part of the floor. It was rich red timber, and you could see it, which was an improvement on the rest.

He swept an armful of paper and DVDs off his bed, which sported a neat bright purple quilt and looked like he hadn't slept there. "Homify yourself. Tasties in the fridge, eat what ya see. 'Kay?"

My mouth watered at his mention of food, and I fluttered to the kitchenette so I wouldn't trip over his stuff. Long time since I ate. His fridge looked all white and shiny underneath, but he'd fingerpainted it, tangled smears of blue and green and orange. I yanked the door open. Chocolate bars, iced coffee, bananas, cans of fizzy caffeine drink. Mmm. All the good stuff a party-fairy needs.

I grabbed a Kit Kat and a banana, and lighted on his glimmering quilt. Mmm, squishy purple goodness. I wriggled my wings and yawned, stretching as I peeled both banana and chocolate, and munched.

Diamond knotted shining hair in his fist, averting his gaze. "Umm. Gonna takem shower. You okay?"

I gulped a choc-banana mouthful. Awkward much? Here I am, in his apartment. On his bed. At three in the morning. Five minutes ago, this hot luscious fairy boy had his tongue between my legs. My body still tingled from his touch, the air still rich with the scent of my desire. Normally, I knew what to do now. It's the part where I strip to my lingerie, coax him onto me, figure out what he likes, make him gasp and sigh and worship me. . . .

Or not. "Um. Yeah. I'll just . . . get some sleep, I guess."

And I rolled over away from him, wrapping myself in the quilt. It smelled of him, roses and warm glass and hot spicy fairyboy and damn it if it wasn't sexy as hell. My nipples tingled. I wanted to rub my face in it, strip naked and feel him on my skin.

Awesome. Like I'd sleep now.

And the splash of running water as he started the shower didn't soothe me. It only made me imagine him, wet and delicious, rainbows glistening on his naked skin, wet hair plastered to his body, his powerful thighs flexing, the muscles in his butt clenching as he . . .

Yeah. Stay right where you are, Ember. He's not for you. Tomorrow, you're leaving.

I closed my eyes and drifted away into feverwarm dreams.

When Diamond tiptoes from the bathroom, Ember's sleeping.

Fuck. He drags damp hair from his neck, already sweating again. He didn't really need showerings. Only to get away from her.

Sweat shines her forehead, scarlet lashes fluttering softly on her cheek. She tosses and murmurs in her sleep, pretty lips quivering. She looks so . . . vulnerable.

His fingers hover over her hair, and static tingles up his wrist, where the prickly bracelet squeezes his tendons tight. The jewel glows brighter, dragging hot urgency from his blood. He wants to touch her. Brush that girlysoft hair from her face, glide his thumb over her lips, tilt her chin up for a kiss.

He recalls her honeyspice mouth opening under his, her little gasps tugging his breath away, her flavor so sweet, it ached his throat like sugar. And touching her, stroking her inside, her soft succulent flesh so wet and eager . . .

Irrational desire flushes him fiery all over again. God, it was hard enough to let her go once. And she's right here in his bed, her beautiful body so fragrant and warm and begging to be touched. . . .

This is usually so easyfied. Her desire is real enough, isn't it? Even if she's confused and crazyhot in her moonblood and has no reason in the world ever to trustify him again.

Even if her smile makes him all hot and reckless, burning to touch her, set her free, hear her glossychime laugh.

Fuckity shit. He's used people before. It's what he does. Prettylicious ladies no exception. He's untruthed dozens of girls. Used his talent to pleasure them, too. Never meant any badness by it. Why is this one so different?

He plops onto the couch in a pile of crunchy tinfoil and flicks on the TV. Mindless images flicker and swap, some old action movie with melting robots and a big guy in leather. But his gaze drags back to her, curled like a chocolatefrost angel in his bed, her sweaty wings ashiver. She tosses the quilt off, battling some invisible foe with twitching legs. Her skirt falls in her lap, and her thigh glistens, a single sweatdrop gliding over smooth brown skin, down into the tasty crevice between her thighs. . . .

He sighs, hot, and switches telly off. Not be here. Not watch her mutter and thrash in the grip of dirty-fever dreams. Not think about touching her when in two nights' time he's gonna feed her to a vampire.

He glances at her again, some achy-honest compulsion dragging his gaze to her face, and the dizzy flame in his blood ignites an agonizing truth he can't ignore.

Gotta tell her everything, D.

Can't not. Can't.

He squeezes his eyes shut, denial a sparkling ache in his heart. But it's no use. He can't untruth her anymore. Not when in his mind, they're already lovers, her sweetblood scent forever alive in his nose, her lost flavor an empty hollow inside where he hungers for her, in more ways than hot blood and a sparkle hard-on can accountify.

He snaps harsh teeth on moonswept memories of kissing her, tasting the dusky skin inside her thigh, exploring her deliciousness with his tongue, making her shudder. . . . He tries to think of Rosa, his real lover, dark hair and paledeath skin and . . . what color eyes again?

Fuck. He can't do this anymore.

Let her have sleepings. She's earnified. And in the morning, he'll tellify everything. Rosa. The shiny on his wrist. The poison he couldn't slip into her fizzies. And then he'll have to crafty up some way to make her stay.

Because he can't leave her alone now. Vincent could be watching. That bloodfetish bitch and doggy-blue on a chain from the club might not've given up. Hell, Rosa said Famine knew someone was huntifying those gemstones. How the hell did Famine find out anyway, the twisticated little boneworm?

Who the fuck knows? Diamond can't chancify. Half the town could be chasing his pretty candygirl, and he's not letting them have her. Keep her alive. Keep her safe. Worry about this souly-twiny-go-to-hell thing later.

Diamond stalks to the door and checks the locks. Bolt, chain, key, all in place. Fine. If they kick it in, he'll hearify. If they can magicate a door open, he's screwed anyway. Bring it, scumsuckers.

Ember murmurs soft confusion, her limbs shifting, and desire melts hot like chocolate into his veins. Tellify everything. Take her in his arms, run his fingers through that glorious fiery hair, hold her close and kiss her dreams away. Forget Angelo, Rosa, Vincent, forgettify it all and just take her away, fly on the moonlit summer breeze to some warm shadowy place where no one will ever find them.

Yeah. Right after she punches his nose to splinters and refuses to speakify him again. *By the byebye, your third gemstone is my psycho vampire ex-girlfriend, and I nearly toxicated you.* That'll work.

It'll never happen. Never anything between them but biznificality. She's a decentsweet girl, and he's . . . well, he's him. Broken. Rotten. Corruptified.

Discomfited, he flits over the junk toward the balcony, the only other place anyone can get in. The glass table gleams up at him, sparkles in blue and green tempting his tongue wet. But he's got no headspace for giggles and drifting. Not now.

Out on the balcony, warm breeze lifts his wings on the gritty scent of river water and darkness. Moonlight gloats on marble edges, the sides of buildings sharp in shadow and light, and in the distance, warm dawnfingers grope the horizon pale. Already the heat is oppressive. It's gonna be a scorcher. Urgency throbs in his blood, a useless compulsion to flee. Frustration zaps static in his hair. He wants to fly, but he can't, and with a hot shock, he understands how Ember feels.

Trapped.

If it wasn't his own stupidbrain fault, it'd be laugh-a-fucking-licious.

Sweat slicks his chest, and he twists his wings and shucks his shirt off. His glamourglow springs brighter, pink shadow spilling. Summer parches his skin. Only minutes till sunrise. Only a blink before she wakifies and he has to explain.

Somehow, he doesn't think *vampire bait* is gonna go down well.

His faesense brightens, monochrome outlines zooming sharp, sucking in traffic noise, breeze, the distant urban hum, filtering for creepings and murmurings, the sly slidings of encroaching wings. Anything out of place, a breath, a whisper, a sniff of sweat not his own.

He senses Ember's heartbeat, swift and hot, waxing moonlight a ripe lure in her blood. Unwilled, he inhales, and her sexy honeyflavor wraps hot fingers around his cock and drags his desire out hard.

She murmurs, her sleepy smile tingling his spine. His glassfae sight paints her outline so clear in his mind, her curving hip, her swelling breasts, the sugary softness of her lips, her sex's honey scent a glossy shimmer. She's dreaming, her pulse racing, a sigh quivering her lips.

Diamond's breath catches. So easy, to touch her, safe in this glassy cocoon. He doesn't have to move. Just let this sneaky, covetous faetouch do its work. Slide a shadowy caress between her legs, stroke her, fill her, make love to her in a darkbleeding glassy world where she'll never see. Never know it was real. Just a fevered dream . . .

He blinks, and the mindglass shatters, leaving only night and breeze and a burning ache he can't satisfy.

Let her dream. It isn't truth, this connection he feels. This compulsion to protectify her, please her, hold her close. It can't be real.

Real is, he can't have her. And she real as shit doesn't want him. What the hell has he got that a decent woman would want?

He pulls the glass door closed on her tempting sighs, hops onto the railing with wings tucked back like an owl, and settles in hot brightening dawn to wait.

17

In bloodstained darkness, burning hands claimed me. Ashen kisses swept my face, and something dry and loathsome stroked me, scaly like a worm.

I struggled. I didn't want it. The evil stink of charcoal swamped my senses thick. Hot moisture smothered me like boiling quicksand, wrapping around my legs, dragging me deeper into hell. My lungs filled with ash. Blindly I kicked, terror sucking me beneath the surface. I gulped and thrashed, air only a few inches away, but I couldn't reach. I'd stay trapped here forever.

Cool fingers brushed my forehead, distant like an echo. "Ember. S'okay. Me. Quietify, angel."

His bellchime voice resonated in my bones, so calm and confident, feeding my strength. With a scream and a thrash of wings, I broke the surface and gasped for air.

His arms wrapped me, smooth and damp, his rosepetal scent washing cool comfort over my limbs. I clung to him, my head throbbing. My pulse echoed in his chest, swift and terrified. The damp quilt tangled my legs, and blindly I scrabbled it off. I tried to talk, but only incoherent sounds came out.

"Time to wakify." His cool hair spilled over my face, fresh and alive. It felt nice. I wanted him to hold me, kiss my nightmare away.

But I sat up, pushing him off. Just Jasper's evil ring, poisoning my dreams. I wasn't dying. Not yet. And I didn't want Diamond to touch me. He'd tricked me last night. Tried to control me with his faetalent. I knew my fear was stupid, that if it weren't for Jasper's tricks, I wouldn't be so frightened now. But that didn't make what Diamond did to me okay.

My hair sprang tight and angry. Damn him. My palms itched at me to scream, demand an apology, ask what the hell gave him the right. But stubbornly, I kept it in. I didn't want to give him the chance to attack me with that knee-melting smile and talk me out of being pissed off with him.

"What time is it?" I wiped my damp face, still trembling. The air conditioner wasn't on, and the quilt lay rumpled, the sheets damp and sanguine with my sweat. The place was silent, lights out, daylight leaking under the curtains.

"Six-ish." Diamond knelt by the bed, a thick luminous knot of hair spilling over his bare chest. Magenta warmth shed gently from his wings, like he'd dimmed it to ease my eyes. It wasn't the only part of him that eased my eyes, and I flushed and dragged my gaze from all that glistening hard-packed muscle, the flat line of his hip, the way his stomach muscles flexed under wisp-thin skin as he moved. . . .

Ahem. Fairy boys should really keep their shirts on. It's a matter of public safety.

"Six? Is that all?" My voice croaked. My muscles ached rotten, and sleep furred my tongue. I felt like I'd drowned for an age.

"In the p.m., sleepybrain."

"No way." Urgency stripped my nerves, and I struggled up. The tiles were hot and dry under my feet as I stumbled over piles of his junk to the window and dragged the curtain aside. Outside, deep shadows angled, late afternoon sun throwing tall buildings into black relief.

Shit. I'd slept all day. Who the hell had time to sleep?

But hey, at least my clothes were still on, which I seemed to recall hadn't been a given in last night's delicious madness. My bag was still here, with Crimson's stone still inside. One down, two to go. And all things considered, I didn't feel too bad.

I stretched my neck with a pop. It all seemed a bad dream. The casino, ghoulish Crimson, that sick crack as her head hit porcelain. Running from stupid security guards. Kissing Diamond in glorious moonshine like an infatuated little girl.

I flushed, and my finger burned, icy metal tightening. It wasn't a dream. Jasper's cursed ring still wrapped my finger. My bones still scorched inside with ashen flame, and I was still going to hell if I didn't find this Famine and his friends.

"Jeez, why didn't you wake me?" I dragged damp hair back and aimed for the door. But I turned too fast and stumbled into the hot window.

Diamond flitted over to help me, setting me gently on my feet. "Easify. We got time."

"Easy for you to say." I wrinkled my nose. I needed a shower real bad. Must have been a stinker of a day. "You could at least've left the aircon on."

"No zappies."

"Huh?"

"Power's out. Too bloody hot, everyone puts the air on, poof. No more electricality."

I peered outside, tinted windowglass hot under my fingers. No lights twinkled in the skyscrapers, no spotlights or flashing neon signs. The whole city was out. Orange heat halo sizzled the sun-bleached buildings. Distant thunder growled. On the train tracks across the river, carriages queued motionless. Sirens echoed. Traffic still grated, but the noise was subdued, eerily silent.

I sighed. Great. Another Melbourne summer blackout. Now I'd have to find this Famine character with the lights out. At least for an hour or two, until they restored the grid.

I slid the glass door open, and heat slapped my face like an angry hand.

Sweat roasted my skin, the hot air drowning me like an acrid spa bath. Burning wind swirled my hair in my eyes. I inhaled, and my lungs seared, my mouth parching instantly. Smoke roughened the air, and beyond the city an ominous blood-orange pall filtered the sky, the telltale smear of wildfire. The stink of metal and hot tar hung heavy over curdled river water and salt, and under it all the crusty, cackling reek of hell.

I slammed the door shut. Lately, every summer we broke some record for Shittiest Weather Ever or Most Days in a Row Hotter than Hell. Last year, roads melted and train tracks buckled in the heat, with half the state either on fire or still smoking. I stayed inside for three days with the curtains drawn and a damp towel over my head. Some said the heat was what you deserved when you let a demon run your town. What else did you expect, with the city one step away from hell?

"Stinky, huh." His breath sparkled on my shoulder, warm and tingly.

I walked away, my nerves tight. I had only a few hours before the moon rose and sent me stupid. I had things to do. Better get on with it.

I straightened my skirt and tugged back my tangled hair. "Okay, I'm outta here. Thanks for the, uh, nap. See ya." And I braced myself for sucking heat and tugged the door open again.

Hot wind crackled my sweat dry, whipping my hair wild. I hopped my butt up onto the rail to swing myself over.

Diamond grabbed my wrist, wings glaring in the sun. "What you doing?"

"Power's off, dumbo. The lift won't be working." I tried to shrug him off.

But he held me, gentle but firm. "You can't leavify."

I ripped my arm away and jumped down, anger at last bubbling over. "Really? Don't you remember your little mindtricks last night? You practically date-raped me, you creep. I'm not spending a second longer with you than I have to."

"Ember, stop it. Really gotta talk to you—"

"You expect me to be okay with it? Christ, you've got an ego."

"Just let me explainify—"

"No. I'm not interested. I guess you must be out of practice. Who knows what I woulda done if you'd mindfucked me properly!"

I expected a flip-off, a saucy comeback, maybe a snap of teeth. But the ruby light in his eyes froze iceblue. "Angel, you don't knowem half."

I gaped. "Excuse me?"

"Will you upshut and hearify? Trying to explain you something. I . . . I haven't totally upfronted with you, Ember. I'm sorry."

My face burned, tight. Damn him. I knew it. But that deceptively tame little word of apology frightened me. Whatever he was about to say would hurt, and it pinched all the harder because I knew it meant I cared. About him, about us. That maybe there was an "us," despite everything.

Shit. I didn't want to have this conversation. I just wanted to get away from him.

But I hated it when people didn't listen to me. When Jasper lost it at me for some imagined misdemeanor without hearing me out. I couldn't do that now, even if Diamond was so full of shit, I could smell it. "Go on, then, astonish me. I'm listening."

"A friend of mine's got trouble. I came with you last night because I wanted your helpings." His voice cracked, pretty bellchimes discordant, and such strain twanged there that sympathy melted warm in my stupid girly heart.

I cursed under my breath. *You're not his girlfriend. You're not even his friend. His problems are not yours. He lied to you.*

But I stayed. I had to.

He peeled shining hair from his neck and knotted it. "I need you to do me a favor so I can help her. Okay? Choicem off."

My skin prickled. *Her.* A lover? So fooling around with me was just a game? Cheating bastard.

Like I cared, right? I perched my butt on the rail, exasperated. "Right. Sure. That makes it okay to control my mind, does it?"

"Ember, I didn't meanify—"

"I don't care what you meant!" I swooped down again on angry wings. "I want you to stop lying to me! You've said about three words I can rely on for the whole damn night, and two of them were *kiss me*. Maybe I'm an idiot, but how the flippin' hell does fooling around with me help your girlfriend? Because I'd really *love* to know that."

I glared at him, arms crossed over my chest.

For a moment, his gaze slipped. And then he sighed and pulled his hand from his pocket to show me a sparkling glass vial with a cork stuffed in one end. It glittered half-empty, an evil green liquid that spat and swirled. He looked me full in the eye, hot and ruby-red. "I was gonna poison you. She's in some vampire messes, and I wanted to toxicate your blood so I could use you as bait."

Scorching wind buffeted my face, and my guts tore hollow.

He wanted to taint my blood. Make me bait. Trap me on the burning cusp of a full moon, when my glamour sparkled bright and bloodscent poured off me in luscious scarlet waves.

He wanted me to feed a vampire. Give myself to some rotten bloodsucker who'd probably drink me dry.

And he thought I'd just go along with it. Like a good little bloodwhore.

"It's only poison for vamps." Diamond's voice gleamed hard with desperation. "It wouldn'ta hurt you. And I seen you feeding that kid for Jasper last night, and I thinkem—"

"You thought I was a whore." My throat cracked dry. He thought I did that all the time. That I could let some monster drink me and just laugh it off. "Well, I'm not, okay?"

Yeah. You just go on telling yourself that, Emmy.

"Knowify that! But I thought you could trickem without getting hurt. At the café, I . . . I was gonna sneaky the juice in your drink. But I couldn't. You were too . . ." He clawed his glittery hair. "Fuck."

Hot tears swelled my eyelids, and I blinked them back, hard. Diamond used me like he used everyone. Just like Jasper, only worse. I shouldn't have expected otherwise.

But for a few heady hours, I'd believed his bullshit. Thought he told the truth about helping me. Imagined that the desire flaming in his kiss, the urgency driving his touch was real, the attraction flowering between us something more than a cheap thrill.

Dreamed that he thought better of me than vampire bait.

Silly little Ember actually thought he cared.

Silly little Ember was wrong.

"Hey, don't—" Diamond reached out to brush my cheek clean.

I jerked backwards, a stupid ache swelling my throat. "No. Get away from me."

"I'm sorry, okay? I didn't knowify what else. But then you came all pretty and dangerfied and I . . . I liked you. I mindchanged, right up—"

"Were you gonna pay me, was that the deal? Blood for a pile of lousy cash?" Fury shot fire through my blood, and my heart raced. I heaved another breath, trying to stay calm, but the words wouldn't stop pouring out. "Or were you just gonna fuck me with your sleazy mindtricks and call it even? You disgust me. You and your fucking lies. At least Jasper was an honest asshole."

His glossy wings flushed scarlet. "What'd you want

me sayify? 'Oh, hey, sugarplum, sorry your boyfriend died, come drink this sparkalicious poison so I can murder a vampire, it won't hurt, I swear'?"

My fingers itched to claw his lying eyes out. "So you pretend to help me instead? How is that even close to the right thing to do?"

"No pretendings. Got your shiny, didn't ya?"

"Oh, so this is your favor, is it? Feed a vampire my blood? And here I was thinking it'd be a good old-fashioned blowjob. Pity you didn't stick with that." It fell out before I could stop it, and I flushed, thankfully hidden by the heat. Going down on him had just dropped way to the bottom of my list. From higher up than it ever should've been. The rest of him was so glassy-beautiful, I had to admit I'd wondered. . . . Hmph. Stupid full moon, putting ideas in my head.

"Please, Ember. I know it's shitful. But I said I'd help you find your gemstones and I truthed it. What the fuck would you have done? She's Ange's prisoner. She'll die if I don't get her outta there." He yanked his knotted hair in one fist, a pent-up flutter of frustration and no options.

He really believed it.

I shivered. I'd heard bad stories about Ange Valenti, Diamond's vampire boss. If Ange had this girl, she was probably toast. What would I do, if someone I loved was in mortal danger? Wouldn't I do everything I could to get them back? Even if it meant deception and untruths?

Right this very second, wasn't I planning on damning others to hell, so I could free myself? Hell, I'd already done it.

That didn't make it okay that I'd trusted him and he'd treated me like scum. Did it?

I swallowed, parched. "This girl really means that much to you, huh? I'm just bait? Is that all I am?"

"You know it inn't that." His burning gaze trapped me. The muscles in his bare chest corded tight, and his whisper shook beneath a distant burst of thunder. "She and me, we're . . . Fuck, it's no matter. But please, Ember. Believify. I never meant you harmings. But I need to help her. I can't just let her die."

Cruel sympathy warmed my heart, and I wanted to touch his face, stroke his hair back, tell him it was okay.

But it wasn't. And it had nothing to do with right and wrong, or my blood spilling over some dirty vampire's chin.

I'd liked him when I thought him just a sticky gang puke out for a good time. At least he was honest about it. I'd even liked him—too much—when he kissed me and touched me in public like the dirty fairy tempter I knew he was.

Truth was, I'd liked him when I had his attention. When I thought he was mine.

And now he wasn't. He had some other woman to rescue. Someone else to care for. And it didn't leave room for me.

My eyelids burned, and I turned my face to the sky to hide stupid tears. The wind buffeted my face hard, squashing me in on myself, and shadows loomed gigantic like I'd shrunk to half my size. Even catching Jasper kissing another girl hadn't hurt like this. This time, some other woman was the girlfriend, and I was the bit on the side. The one who wasn't fit to be seen in public. The whore.

Fact was, I was used to being the prettiest girl in the room, and Diamond had ignored me for someone else.

I was jealous, pure and prickly. And it cut me to the core.

I swallowed a hot lump, my face afire. "Fine. Go rescue her, then. But you can do it alone."

And I flitted onto the balcony rail in hot gusting wind and dived into fading sunlight.

18

By the time I reached the riverbank, sweat washed off me in rivulets. The setting sun glared on windswept concrete, and the footbridge streaked dim and neonless over sunglittered brown water. The moon hadn't yet risen, and relief smoothed sticky bumps from my arms. At least I didn't have rampaging hormones to deal with. Much.

I wiped my streaming face, pulled out my phone, and called the latest number back, trying to quiet my trembling nerves.

It rang a couple times before he picked up, and a smile tainted his voice. "Whattaya know? It's my new girlfriend. Didn't expect you so soon, beauty. Did Diamond dump you already?"

"Cut it out, Vincent." My spine chilled. God, he gave me the creeps. And not in a good way. This was insanity. Foolishness. I might not live out the night. Trusting my life to a known enemy vampire with hungry undress-me eyes and a potty mouth. Great plan.

But it beat spending another moment with a sexy rose-winged poisoner who made me want things I shouldn't.

I stuck my finger in my ear, trying to hear over the bar noise at his end. "Can we just be nice to each other? I need to find this Famine person."

"Uh-huh. Dude, look where the fuck you're going." Crashes, stumbles, distant swearing. Didn't sound like he was really listening.

I pressed harder. "I need Famine, Vincent. Can you help me?"

The click of a lighter, a deep exhale, the rustle of the phone held on his shoulder. "Fucking loser. Look, yeah, maybe we can sort something out. Let me make some calls, get back to ya—"

"No, you don't understand. It has to be tonight. I don't have time to wait!" My voice shrilled, and I bit my tongue, but too late. He'd heard my desperation. I sat on a concrete bollard decorated with seashells, but frustration crawled nipping ants under my skin and I hopped up again.

Vincent chuckled, dark. "Don't twist your G-string, princess. I'm just playing with ya. Since I like you, we'll expedite. Where are you? I'll pick you up."

My skin tightened. "You don't have to do that. Just tell me where I should go—"

"Nuh-uh. Wouldn't want a pretty thing like you to get lost on the way. You down by Diamond's? Cool. I'll swing by Princes Bridge and pick you up. An hour . . . no, make it an hour and a half. Famine never gets up before dark. Umm . . . you been to his place before?"

I swallowed, nerves shredding. No point in lying. Vincent had an unsettling knack for picking up on it. Besides, I needed all the help I could get. "Nope."

"Didn't think so. Listen, it's kinda edgy down there.

People go to Famine's to play games. You're either a boss or a victim, get me? You might wanna slip into something a bit more assertive."

My blood frosted. What did he mean, boss or victim? Images forced into my head, black leather, spiky chains and whips, cruel power games. "Excuse me?"

"Just saying. Gotta go, princess. See ya soon." And he hung up, a dull clunk like death.

I slipped my sweaty phone away, discomforted. I didn't like Vincent, his hungry gaze and snarky wit and self-satisfied laugh. I didn't like any of this.

But at least I knew where I stood with him. Might as well make the best.

Ninety minutes to get ready. Dinner, shower, change. Famine's sounded like one hell of a place. Something more assertive, hah. If Vincent thought to dress me up as his own private dominatrix fantasy, he could bloody well think again.

But the words *boss* and *victim* resonated in me like evil demon breath, and I tossed my head, defiant. I was through being a victim. I'd show this Famine and his sick slave-fantasy cronies just who was boss tonight. And I had just the wardrobe. Jasper liked me pretty, but he also liked me sexy, usually when he was in the mood for some rougher games. I could take it. If babyboy Vincent thought he could shock me, he was dead wrong.

Acid laughter spurted from my lips. Look at me, acting all tough. This was the dumbest, most futile idea of my life. I was gonna die, and scream in hell forever. Why didn't I just go out, party, get laid, have myself a rocking good time? Screw tomorrow. It'd never come.

Temptation licked my flesh warm.

But a little hard shiny place deep inside me glowed

hot and angry. I didn't deserve this death. I didn't want it.

I'd been weak, but now I had one last chance. Screw Kane. And Jasper, and Diamond, and everyone else who'd ever tried to control me. I was finally learning my lesson. I couldn't give up now.

I tugged my bag over my shoulder and headed for Jasper's one more time.

19

Good as his word, Vincent picked me up, and as we drove beside twin tram lines past the green quasi-cubic edifice of Federation Square toward Chinatown, the last scarlet ghost of sunset stole away, leaving the tree-lined street in thick hot darkness. As we turned under the bright-painted Chinese archway, open windows loomed close on either side of the one-lane street, restaurants and bars lit with red lanterns and flickering candles, drifting with the salty smells of Szechuan spices and chili. Humans and fairies and every shady creature crowded the sidewalks and lanes, sullen and dangerous, the redstained light glinting evil in heatgritted eyes. The heat had put everyone in a mood, for a party or a fight or both.

I clutched my bag in my lap, nerves crawling. Vincent's cute little black SUV smelled of cigarettes and spicy male perfume. The seat belt trapped me, the warm seat like a prison. Vincent grinned at me, hungry. It didn't help.

He stopped the car by the curb in a pool of shadow, sweat still slicking his hair tight. We hadn't gone far, and it was slow driving through the people spilling onto the road. The aircon hummed. It wasn't achieving any-thing. The temperature hadn't dropped with the setting sun. No, if anything the heat had intensified, and the air stank with smoke and hot tar. Streetlights lay dark and useless, and behind me the moon rose fat and sultry, only a sliver from full, throwing sharp silvery shadows under the cantilevers and threading hot tension through my blood.

I shifted uneasily, my bare thighs slicking the seat. "We here?"

"As promised. You gonna thank me?" Moonlight glinted danger deep in Vincent's eyes, and his gaze slid downward.

"Uh . . . sure. Thanks." I flattened my hands on my knees. Knew he'd get down to payment sooner or later. No use pulling my skirt down. It didn't go down any farther. I'd picked the tightest one I had left, a shiny halter dress in black vinyl that showed an acre of cleav-age and midriff, little buttons in the curves of my waist holding top and bottom halves together. It hugged my butt like glue and forced my boobs up high and full.

"Wasn't what I had in mind." Vincent's gaze licked up to my cleavage where my pulse jumped.

I flushed, my fingers twitching. I wasn't defenseless. Even I'm not stupid enough to get in a vampire's car without some protection. I had the little girly handgun Jasper gave me strapped in a holster between my thighs. It wouldn't kill Vincent, but it'd slow him down enough for me to get away. At least, I hoped so.

Still, the metal did strange things between my legs, sexy and uncomfortable at the same time. The smooth, warm, hard feel of it caressed my sensitive skin, the danger licking me wet. And I wasn't wearing any underwear. Remind me not to bend over when I get out. I swallowed. "Very funny. I gotta go. You're, uh, not coming in, are you?"

Vincent laughed, predatory. "No offense, princess, but I don't think you're bringing Famine flowers. Farther away, the better." He slicked a burning finger down my cheek, and leaned closer, teeth glinting. "Pity, though. Love the outfit."

His body heat swamped me in teasing vampire scent. Irrational moonfever heated my skin, rich and needy, and embarrassment only inflamed me more. God, he could probably smell my arousal. I could. I was tempted to let him take a bite. More tempted to let him kiss me, slide his tongue on my skin, graze me with those sharp teeth and ease out first one drop, then another. . . .

I scrabbled for the door handle, sweating. "Uh-huh. Look, thanks for the ride—"

"You always this shy? 'Cause it really turns me on." He twined a lock of my hair around his finger and sniffed it hungrily. "Mmm. I can taste the moon on your perfume, baby. Sure you don't wanna play? I'll be gentle."

I fumbled the door open and scrambled onto the curb, my pulse clattering. He hadn't locked me in. Hadn't grabbed me. He was letting me go, for some crafty reason I didn't understand.

Whatever his game was, it didn't bolster my confidence. A trap? Probably. But what else could I do?

Vincent laughed, and flipped me a wave as he drove off.

Asshole. I pulled my dress straight. My hair dragged wet on my wings, flushing me overwarm. Too hot to wear it down, so I'd pulled it off my neck in a high ponytail that spread in scarlet waves around my shoulders.

Along with the fetish dress, I'd picked shiny black stiletto boots up to my thighs and heavy black-and-silver makeup, and I'd sprayed my wings with dazzling crimson glitter.

So yeah, I looked like a hooker. I hoped I looked tough and arrogant. Boss, not victim. *Victim* sounded bad.

I wiped my forehead, discomfort frothing inside me for more reasons than one. I felt strange. Displaced, as if just for tonight, I was Big Em, a sexy Ember-shadow I couldn't control.

I didn't want to control her.

She was wild, sexy, free. As I'd dressed, the tight vinyl sliding over my skin, I'd stared at myself in the mirror in my candlelit bedroom, imagining Jasper bending me over the bed and spanking me, taking me from behind, hard and rough, his claws raking my hips. I saw myself on top, red hair smearing over him, my breasts ripe in his hands, riding him harder and deeper until my pleasure broke.

Then Jasper morphed into Vincent, crunching hungry teeth on my throat in a hot crimson splash, his cock moving deep in me, making me cry out in pleasure or pain. And then Vincent morphed into Diamond, loving me hot and slow on a warm updraft, crystalrose wings spread and my legs wrapped around him. God, he felt good inside me, his massive body straining into mine, his rainbow hair sifting over my face like water, and that's when I turned from the mirror and didn't look again.

What with that and the gun, I felt swollen and uncomfortable down there. This costume made me feel naughty and sexy. And the reckless moonshine caressing my skin wasn't helping. My pulse thrummed, desire's sweet melody singing in my veins. I wanted movement, laughter, touching, kissing, the feel of a man's flesh inside me, anything and everything to set my body afire.

I scowled, flushing. Damn that full moon. Pay attention.

I looked around, trying to orient myself. Asian supermarket, a convenience store, an Internet café, all darkened in the blackout. A Thai restaurant with a guy sizzling up a fragrant green curry on a little gas stove in the window. I sidled past an old troll in a raincoat hunched beneath a painted sign reading COMMIT NO NUISANCE, spit dribbling from his broken tusks. Kids zipped by me on skateboards, glamourbright fairy girls in summer dresses and high heels did late-night shopping in benighted alleyways, couples headed to restaurants and dimlit cafés. Like we were all pretending the lights weren't out, that this was normal.

A pair of vampire guys stalked for prey beneath the darkened neon lights of a karaoke lounge, leather jackets and shiny smiles, their hypnotic eyes tracking passing girls and luring them in. The blond one glanced at me and salivated, and he had to whip his hand up to stop it gushing down his chin and giving him away.

I snickered, and waved at him through the crowd. Keep it in your pants, sunshine.

Ahead, a sunken doorway beckoned, cracked plaster edged in broken tiles. A scrawny black fairy hunched in the door's lee. His manky teeth shone with spit, his ragged gray mothwings curled behind twistypointed ears and a shaven skull.

I stabbed my courage alive. Vincent dropped me right here. This must be it. Either that, or he'd dumped me in some bloodsoaked vampire den to get eaten.

But that seemed unlikely. Vincent wanted to eat me himself, not give me away.

Hell of a reason to trust him.

I felt for my clutch bag, a habitual gesture of comfort, and grasped empty air.

My heart sank. Great. I'd left my bag in Vincent's car. Now I had no money, no phone, no anything. Hooker-Em would just have to do it all herself.

Boldly, I strode up to the door, cocking one hand on my outthrust hip. "Famine sent me."

The fairy just crouched, scratching his bony butt through his jeans and stabbing irritably at the dust with a gnarled stick. "Yeti-skin britches. Whatever you say."

I prodded his ankles with my pointed boot tip. "He won't be pleased if I'm late. Special order, know what I mean? Client's waiting."

He poked his sharp chin at me, pale eyes gleaming. He was naked to the waist, his brittle black skin shining, and weak glamour crackled like plastic. He stank of crackers and moldy cheese. "Yeah? What's your poison, green-eyes?"

I leaned over, flashing him my ample cleavage. My dress pulled up over my butt, and I wrestled down the urge to yank it south again, hoping I wasn't flushing. I traced a suggestive finger under his grimy chin and gave my hardest *don't fuck with me* smile. "Whaddaya think, skinny? Any smart-ass makes a victim of me, I'll crush his balls." I squeezed his chin, hard enough to hurt, and leaned my painted lips closer to whisper. "With my teeth."

The fairy grinned. "Baby, you can crush my balls any time." He hopped up, tucking his stick under one scrawny black arm, and kicked the cracked door open.

Inside, dusty steps led down. A single light globe

buzzed and flickered, the distant creak of a generator echoing. He led me downward into the fresh fairy scents of lavender and jasmine. My metal heels clicked on each step, and sweat dripped between my breasts. The air heated as we descended, darkness swarming.

The skinny fairy pushed aside a motheaten velvet curtain, and fiery light dazzled.

I blinked, squinting. Low ceiling, mottled brick walls. On one side, a bar stretched, metal stools and a polished redwood bench with beer on tap and colored liqueurs shelved along the wall. A purple glossy-winged bargirl polished glassware, her frilly skirt frothing. Cherry alcohol and delicious perfume drenched my nose, making me want to inhale more. From somewhere, rhythmic music filtered. Air flowed gently, an unseen fan or window, and even the heat seemed bearable, welcoming.

Red velvet loveseats scattered the room, little alcoves for two or three with cushions, wooden tables, copper vases with single red carnations. It was only early, but the place was full, men and women, fae and human, and not all vinylfetish apemen like I'd expected. I saw jeans, evening dresses, sleek skirts and heels. Dampbright wings shone, skin of a dozen different colors gleaming in sweat, the crisp glint of clean vampire teeth.

I swallowed, smoothing my shinyclad hips. I felt overdressed. Had Vincent brought me to the wrong place? A couple of fairy boys kissed at the bar, green fingers twining in sootblack hair, and a girl and a guy danced in a clinch by the door. But that was it. No brawling or drunken revels, no puddles of vomit, no music screaming so loud, you couldn't think. No one taking drugs. Not even anyone screwing in the corners that I could see. Unseelie Court was far seedier than this. I liked it here. The kind of place your boy might take you on a date.

Unless your boy was a sparklefreak gangbanger.

Not that this was the pointificality, as Diamond would say. I just needed to find Famine. Steal his gem. Bug out. Easy.

An elbow jabbed my ribs. I jumped back. "Huh?"

Skinnyfae handed me a pair of pinkglass spectacles. "Take these. Don't put 'em on yet. They're for the client."

Confused, I took them. Wire-rimmed, thick oval glass lenses the color of diluted blood. The hinges were bent, the wire doubled over in loops. Looked like a mad professor made them. I held them to the light, peering through, but saw only a dizzy pink blur.

I snickered. Like I needed these. I was already winning Idiotic Optimist of the Week, imagining I could escape Kane's trap. "Rose-tinted glasses. You're kidding, right?"

Skinny's wetslug lips stretched in a smirk. "You'll see. Now wait here and I'll sort out your client. Drinks on the house for players. Back soon." And he unfurled limp gray wings and drifted away, down a dimming corridor out of sight.

O-kaay.

I folded the glasses and tucked them in at my hip, sliding one wire earpiece down inside my skirt. Urgency nibbled my toes. My time just started ticking. When Skinny found out I'd lied, he'd throw me out, or worse. Better get on with it.

I sauntered up to the bar, trying to keep it cool. My dress kept sticking to my thighs. Damn, it was hot. I could really use a drink. Champagne cocktail, for choice.

The purple girl smiled at me, long dragonfly wings flickering violet and green. "It's okay. No need to be scared. Champagne cocktail, is it?"

I blinked, and tried to toughen it up with a saucy sneer. I didn't look scared, did I? "Uh . . . yeah. Thanks."

Her blue ponytail bobbed as she filled a glass, long aubergine fingers curling. A pair of pink wire-rimmed glasses, same as mine, perched on her turned-up nose.

Curiosity prickled. What were they for? I didn't want to ask in case it gave me away. I sipped, thirsty, the fine bubbles tingling my throat. "Hey, uh . . . is Famine here tonight?"

She giggled and crossed her eyes. "Well, yeah. He's always here. You new?"

"Uh-huh. Client, you know. Special order. I kinda wanted to talk to Famine about that, actually. Make sure the, uh, payment's satisfactory. He around?"

But she just smiled and pushed me a plate of peanuts as she glided away. "Sit down, make yourself at home. Famine knows. He'll be out soon."

Damn. She wasn't revealing anything. Maybe I'd have better luck with the clientele.

I wandered off, sipping my champagne. Good stuff, too, not the cheap shit. Jasper had spoiled me for bubbly with too many giggly nights on the Moët. Anything less tasted like piss.

At the tables, couples chatted and laughed. I saw more pairs of glasses, on the table or in pockets or sticking out of bags. Everyone had them, but no one wore them, and intrigue tickled my spine. What were they for? 3D glasses? Some kind of light show?

I draped myself on a red velvet chaise longue, beside a green troll with polished black horns and golden earrings, sitting quietly alone with his beer. I grinned and tossed one boot over the couch's edge, showing off my thigh right under his flat bull nose. "Hey, baby."

Trollboy kept drinking his beer, vast shoulders hunched in a tight black T-shirt, but his gaze flickered to where my tiny skirt barely shadowed what was underneath.

I tried again, a coquettish smile, hooking one claw into my hair. "I'm a friend of Famine's, y'know. Special like. You looking for some company— Ugh!"

He gripped the soft inside of my thigh with a thick green hand, too hard, way too close to my crotch for comfort. He growled low, tusks gleaming. "Sure, honey. You've got a beautiful big mouth. Wanna swallow my cock?"

His fingers bruised me, and I wanted to roll my eyes. Great. A rude one. I'd heard worse, but this would never do for my image. I tried to laugh, but his claws ripped my skin, crawling upward to where it was tender.

My skin wriggled like wet caterpillars. Eww. If he touched me there, I'd punch his lights out. "Know what? I changed my mind. Get your lousy hands offa me, asshole."

He yanked my leg, pulling me onto my back with my knee crooked around his shoulder, and ripped my pistol holster from my thigh and tossed it to the floor. "You take a shit, you swim in it, bitch."

"Hey!" I kicked at him, but he held me fast. No one took any notice. What kinda place was this? I wriggled, furious. "How dare you, minion? Let me go and say you're sorry right now. What the hell do I look like, a victim?"

He slicked his rough tongue up my thigh, hot and slimy. My skin recoiled like a salty leech, and he gave me a lascivious grin. "Honey, that's exactly what you look like," he growled, and sank his blunt teeth into my thigh.

My flesh crunched. I jerked back, skin tearing with a spurt of pain. "Ow! Jesus fucking Christ—"

Electricity sizzled, a hot white flash, and the troll yelped like a girl and let me go.

I scrambled up, wary. Blood trickled down my smarting thigh, shining like rubies with moonfire and shock, and I flicked it angrily away. Yuck. That hurt. What next?

Skinnyfae poked at the troll with his bangstick, and dry white static crackled. "Tsk, tsk. Take it downstairs, bozo."

The troll gripped his singed cheek and growled, but backed off, his teeth still dark with my blood. Asshole.

Skinny flapped limp gray wings and aimed his stick at my nose. "You. Famine's girl. Come with me."

I bent for my gun, but he kicked it aside. "Bang-bang not allowed." And he darted away.

I stretched my burning thigh and followed, excitement and apprehension fighting like rats under my skin. I'd done it. He believed me. Or was I waltzing into a trap? Either way, too late to change my mind now.

Skinnyfae headed for a dim corridor that curved out of sight. I stumbled to catch up. "Hey, thanks. I mean, who did that guy think he was, chewing on the staff like that?"

Skinnyfae cackled, twirling his stick. "He's a client. Snap snap, always too quick to choose. Should be more discerning, yes yes. Come along, no wastie. Snap those heels. That's it."

The corridor curved to stairs leading down, lit by another single glass bulb. I hesitated. *Take it downstairs,* Skinny said. Right after that troll bit my leg in half. "Uh, look, are you sure the client's ready? Because I can just as well stay up here—"

"No time, special lady. Not a spare moment. Skip-skip." Skinny ran down the steps, his scrawny legs scything, and pulled open a heavy door.

Nothing scary. Just more brick corridor, dim orange light.

But the smell made me gag. So faint, I could hardly detect it. But visceral. Dark. Squishy like meat. The horrid, caustic taste of fear.

My ears pricked, and a distant scream kicked my heart into a gallop. I jerked back. "Look, I've made a mistake—ugh!"

Skinnyfae darted behind me on dry rustling wings and shoved me forward.

I lurched and staggered, panic swelling my blood, but too late. My heels tangled, and I tumbled into that fear-drenched doorway.

The door slammed behind me, echoing in dull silence. Light glared, watering my eyes blind. Terror slashed me with icy fangs, and I whirled, looking for Skinnyfae, anyone, anything that might attack me.

But I didn't see what grabbed my wrist and dragged me into blackness.

20

A rough brick wall slammed into my shoulder. Another door crunched shut. I staggered, breathless, my heart thumping wild. Total blackness.

I strained my eyes and blinked, but it was useless. Open or closed, it made no difference. I waved terrified hands in front of my face, scrabbling for light. Nothing.

Sweat dripped over my wings. Heat drowned me. I couldn't breathe. The air was so black, the heat so complete and horrible and empty, that with a horrid jolt, I knew.

I was dead. This was hell. It was over.

Dread writhed under my skin like maggots. My moonrich pulse hammered, my ears useless. Tears stung my eyes. I scrabbled for the wall, stumbling along for a few steps, but it reached no junction and offered no comfort. Hot blackness squelched down my throat like tar, and I screamed until my breath died.

The echo faded, leaving me in burning black silence.

"Put your glasses on." A cold voice clanged like dead bells, no echo.

I gasped, my tongue parched, and flung my arms

out, searching left and right. "What? Who's there? Let me the hell out of here!"

"Put your glasses on, Ember."

"What the hell for, you fucking idiot? I can't bloody see!" I slammed my fists against the wall at my sides, hot tears leaking onto my cheeks. *Rile up your captor. Good one, Emmy. Rule one for dealing with an unpredictable boy: Don't argue. Ever.*

"Just do it."

Blindly I scrabbled at my hip, and found twisted wire. God help me if they were broken. I unfolded them clumsily, my sweaty fingers slipping, and jammed them on my nose.

Scarlet light flashed, blinding me all over again.

I yelled and squeezed my eyes shut, tears dripping through my fingers. Crazy burn-in savaged my retinas, shapes, colors, figures, a crowded room full of outlines. What the hell?

Cautiously, I squeaked one eye open.

Pale colors greeted me, a wall, the outline of the door I'd come in by. I hooked the wire over my pointed ears and blinked my tears clear. Outside the rims of the lenses, blackness still suffocated. But inside, the light rippled, stained translucent red like bloody water, and I could see everything. Like some strange pink night-vision goggles.

Weird.

Figures moved and shimmered, outlined like scarlet ghosts. I saw a woman lying on a bench, a figure huddled in a corner, a thin person striding up and down. Over there, someone backed against a glimmering white wall, wings splayed flat, and another figure leaned over her.

I swallowed. "Who's there? I'm lost. Can you help me?"

No one answered. But those people were right there. They must have heard me.

"Excuse me?" I reached out, but my claws cracked on rough brick.

I jumped back, startled. I couldn't see a wall. I flattened my palms and reached again. There it was, solid, a brick wall between me and them.

Glasses that saw through walls. Light that wasn't there. This was too peculiar. But I could see the door, and that was enough. Leaving now.

I turned, and Skinnyfae grinned.

I jerked back, cracking my head against the wall.

He cackled, his own pink glasses hooked over greasy ears. In this strange light he looked like a weird cartoon, pink edges mingling with black. "Ha ha. Gotcha. Good trick, eh?"

Fury blew through me like a gale, and I shoved him backwards, my palms itching to rip his skin off. "You little bastard."

He whooped, catching himself on dusty wings. His bald oystershell skull shone as he tutted in mock displeasure, waving his stick. "Language."

"Screw language, grandpa. Let me the fuck out of here!"

" 'Fraid I can't do that."

"Oh, really?" I advanced on him, shaking. "Well, let me tell you something. People know where I am. Important people. They'll come looking for me, and when they've finished, you'll be a little gray birdshit smear on the wall. How d'ya like that?" It was a long shot. But I was so furious, I didn't care.

"Mmm. Sounds serious." He cackled, rubbing skinny

wrists together. "I'm quivering. Want a chewy?" And he actually offered me his pack of gum.

I smacked it out of his hand. "Knock it off, you freak! What is this place? And who the hell do you think you are, treating me like this?"

"You know, that's the first intelligent question you've asked all night." His gaze flashed up at me, cold and hard, and the air rippled white.

My membranes tingled in warning, and I backed against the wall, tensing to flee.

In a flash, his black eyes gleamed red.

Ozone stung my tongue, and magic lit the air like gunpowder. Glamour crystallized around him, an icy cocoon, and shattered.

His scrawny body grew, towering over me, his black skin bleaching white. Drybone hair crackled from his skull, brittle and corpselike. His face thinned, cheekbones hollowing, his bloodless white skin straining shiny over his skeleton like a starving thing's. Those floppy gray wings parched white, thin insectoid membranes torn with crumbling ragged edges.

He tossed his stick aside, like he'd no further use for it, and the same dazzling electric field zapped between his skeletal three-knuckle fingers like a toy. Pink lenses gleamed on his fleshless nose as he smiled, lips cracking like overdry paper. "So you deserve an intelligent answer. I'm Famine, and this place is mine. Let's get started, shall we?"

21

Famine strode up to me, static flickering between his starved fingers. He grinned, ravenous, withered gums exposing his teeth.

Cold sweat dripped into my boots. His body was emaciated, the wasted muscles in his chest contorted like wire. Famished indeed. Like he hadn't eaten for a month, and I was dinner.

He looked transparent and brittle, like spun candy. Like ice. Or glass.

Glassfairy. My stomach shriveled. If he could read my mind like Diamond did, I was in real trouble.

"Famine. Uh . . . hi. Look, this is a mistake." I backed off, feeling behind me for safety, but now where the wall had loomed dense and unbreakable, there floated only empty space.

Famine swooped beside me, a white blur. "No mistake, Ember."

His sick oceansalt scent coated my mouth. He knew my name. Knew I was coming for him. I tried to flap away, jittering. "Get away from me!"

But he was too fast. Like a striking snake, he grabbed my hair. Strands snagged in his bonebare knuckles. He dragged my head down until I gazed into his strange red eyes. I struggled, clawing at his flaking chest.

But his gaze drilled my eyeballs, boring deep into my skull, and my will melted like steam on the wind.

I gibbered, flailing for sharp defiant words, but my brain fuzzed over with welcome warmth like hot chocolate sprinkles, and a silly smile painted my lips. He was nice. I liked him. He was my friend.

Fear hammered inside my heart, yelling and banging its fists like a caged beast, but the noise was distant, echoing, not something I had to pay attention to. My belly warmed, the ache in my bitten thigh fading with a tingling caress of Famine-scented air. He smelled like the sea, stormy and fresh and delicious. Slow delight sparkled my blood like summer rain, and pleasure eased into my body until I murmured happily. I didn't want to escape. I just wanted to gaze into his lovely albino eyes and feel like this all night.

Famine released me, stroking my hair with one bony claw. He was so pretty, such delicate pale skin, such rich ruby eyes. I rubbed my cheek in his crisp white hair, and he smiled, so gentle, I ached. His whisper stroked my skin, relaxing. "Better. Step backwards."

Alarm sparked my nerves, but my legs were already moving, eager to please him. He slipped something warm and soothing around my left forearm, then my right, and I smiled and wriggled against it, enjoying the smooth sensation. I felt warm, safe, happy.

And then he broke his gaze, and my contentment shattered.

Black ice crystals tinkled to the floor, the residue of vile fairy spellcraft. I jerked away, but hot metal yanked my wrists, dragging my arms above my head and wrenching my shoulders back. Wildly, I swung my head around, trying to see, and my bones spiked cold.

Iron strips shackled my wrists tight, and fat chains gleamed taut, binding me to an unseen ceiling. Something hard banged against my legs, and I looked down. More shackles gripped my booted ankles, locked to the floor with wire, holding me fast. The chains crunched and yanked tighter. Dragging me to my tiptoes. Stretching me.

My shoulder tendons shrieked. My feet clattered on the floor, scrabbling for a hold, the bricks just half an inch too far away for comfort. I couldn't kick. Couldn't move. Couldn't get free.

My bowels watered, and I rattled my chains, terrified. "Let me go, you sick freak!"

Famine laughed, his dry lungs hacking.

Shit. I swiveled my eyeballs, frantic, hunting for weapons, blades, whips, and spikes and other nasty toys. In my strange pink-tinted vision, outlines of people still shimmered through the walls, and with bile lurching sick in my throat, I understood what my addled brain hadn't made sense of before.

Those people were hurting each other.

One held another wriggling one down while he did vicious things to her with a long thick object I didn't want to identify. A body screamed, spreadeagled on the floor in a shining wet stain, while another poked him with sharp needles the size of chopsticks. Someone dragged a limp body by the ankles, insensible or dead. A thin one shivered in a corner, moaning. No one did anything to her. She just trembled and muttered like her mind was broken, like they'd tormented her until her brain was spaghetti and she couldn't talk or think or endure any more.

The rich stink of suffering fouled the air like rotting meat. But that wasn't the worst of it.

In the light of my strange pink glasses, colored auras bloomed around each person, sick hues shimmering rancid. The ones in control glowed blue and scarlet with triumph and passion, their exhilaration burning bright. And around the tortured ones, the air bled black and silver, roiling waves of pain and fear and disgust, emotions spilling from their torment like blood from a wound. And the torturers sucked it up, drinking it greedily from the air, their grins splashed with luminescent gore.

Feeding on raw emotion. Gobbling up the suffering like hungry parasites. *People go to Famine's to play games,* Vincent had said.

My glasses gripped my nose, the wire tightening with glee. I thrashed my head from side to side, but I couldn't knock them off. I wanted to be sick. Ultimate power, ultimate submission, not just physical but emotional as well. It was disgusting. It was compelling. I couldn't tear my eyes away.

My skin rippled cold. Famine's dungeon lay a world from the sweet-tempered bar upstairs. He'd torture me, probably to death, sucking out my last drop of agony for a tasty snack, and with my luck, I wouldn't die soon enough.

I struggled, but my limbs felt watery, my strength drained by his nasty spell. I tried to bleed the tremor from my voice with sarcasm, but it came out wobbly and small. "Very clever, stinkweed. What do you want with me?"

Famine poked a taunting bony finger at my nose. "Should've thought that's obvious. Real question is, what d'you want with me?"

I'd almost forgotten why I'd come here. Find the gemstone, get free, escape this bizarre torture den. My dazed eyes skittered, trying to focus. He wasn't wearing any jewelry I could see, nothing around his neck or on his wrists. His pale shirtless body was clean.

His black persuasions still licked my skin, stroking me in places he'd no right to touch. His invisible spelldark caress numbed my wits. I wanted to bolt screaming into the street. But I also wanted to stay, be consumed, lie down and let this weird pain-vampire drink me up.

I licked wet lips, stalling. Find the gem. Only the gem mattered. "What do you mean?"

Famine jabbed sharp claws at my belly. "Fancy hunting me. How rude. We've never even been *introduced*."

He sounded genuinely incensed, and green mist sparkled from his hair, swarming like tiny gnats. My fingers tingled. Visible emotions. The glasses worked on him, too. I could use that.

I tried my charming smile. "Well, we can remedy that. I'm Ember. Pleased to meet you. I didn't mean to be rude. You frightened me, is all. Perhaps we can—"

"Not interested." Famine slapped my naked hip, scolding.

Ow. Sweat smarted over the spot. My blood heated, unkind memories of my mirror fantasy taunting me. "Huh?"

"I don't want your body, Ember, lovely though it is. So you can give up trying to seduce me." He grinned, exposing flayed gums. "Got any other tricks?"

I simpered. "Oh, I didn't mean anything like that. I just thought we could be friends. . . ."

His voice hardened, contempt flashing yellow on his breath. "You don't have any other tricks, do you? You're just a grasping little whore."

Memories of Diamond's insults sucked my mouth dry. It wasn't like that. Was it? "Screw you, okay—"

"Shut up." Famine's flat tone stopped me dead. "Just be *silent*. Your tart's tricks won't work on me. And you don't know any other way to get what you want."

He stroked drybone fingers across my forehead, cold like a skeleton. I recoiled, but I had nowhere to go. Famine hacked a laugh and scraped his palm over my temple, a gruesome parody of a lover's caress, and inside my skull something wet and sticky *pulled*.

Agony ripped my head raw. I yelled, horror stuffing my stomach with cold worms. God, it hurt, like skin flaying, ripping wet and bleeding from the muscle, only this was my *head* and the bastard was tearing out my *thoughts* and there wasn't a damn thing I could do about it. I'd thought Diamond's glassfae tricks were invasive. This was infinitely worse.

Famine sighed, satisfied. "Mmm. Thought so. You're useless. You're so dirtypretty and lovely to taste, but you've got nothing else. They all want to touch you but no one wants to talk, do they, because you're a stupid, boring, useless little whore. Yes?"

"Shut your face, boneweed." I bared my teeth, defiant. But his taunts attacked my heart, vicious truth-wasps that stung and stung.

I struggled, trying to shake off my dismay. It was stupid. What did I care what he said? But he drilled a brittle claw into my forehead, probing deeper, and his spellsharp perception scraped my mind's surface raw.

His gibes shouldn't hurt me. They weren't true. But despair carved me up inside like salted razors, smarting long after the wound was made.

I scraped my dry tongue across my lips. "I don't wanna talk about this anym—"

"You've got no friends, Ember. No one cares about you." He darted behind me, slipping a skinny arm around my waist, his jutting bones poking into my back. "Just liars and hungry boys. Because you're not worth it. If you were worth it, you wouldn't have to flirt and fuck to get attention."

"That's not tr—" I choked, tiny black gnats of spellcraft clogging my throat. It was true. My friends were all Jasper's friends. My girlfriends drifted away when I took up with him. And I didn't remember the last time a guy talked to me without his greedy gaze fixed on either my pulse or my cleavage.

Except Diamond. But only because he wanted something just as sordid.

Famine's stealthy mindtricks settled on my brain like evil black fog, and fight as I might, I couldn't shake them off. His spectral fingers tunneled deeper, darker, searching out the places that hurt and stabbing them sharp. God, I'd acted like such a desperate whore with Diamond. The fact that I'd wanted his attention sickened me. I'm a sad, pathetic, needy woman. A wisp of careless affection, and I'm anyone's.

"It's true, Ember. You know it is. Show me your fear." Famine's grip on my screeching mind-skin tightened, and self-disgust tore up my throat from deep in my heart. It burned, that self-loathing, bubbling through my brain like acid, chewing hungrily into my soul.

My heartbeat stumbled into a sprint. Sweat broke out in rivers, soaking my dress with the rotten stink of terror, and an evil green aura rippled the air, spreading outward from my body like ink.

I gurgled, sick. I knew what he was doing. Dragging out my deepest, most secret fears and desires so he could feast on me. But I couldn't stop him. Already he sniffed the air, drinking in the pulsing green liquid of my despair.

Frantically, I tried to tear my mind loose, think of something else, banish the fear and desperation from my heart.

But I couldn't help it. Everything Famine said was true.

Famine snaked in front of me, green ichor spilling over his chin. He stretched his parched wings with a sigh, and they swelled with glowing blue fluid, life pulsing inside, the crumbling edges plumping out to a silky taut edge.

Feeding himself. Growing fat on my misery.

He settled bony hands on my hips. "Mmm. That's it. Trust me. Feed me your fear. Show me what you're really afraid of."

He leaned closer, and my own green fearjuice splashed my face. He sniffed my lips, humming sweet oblivion, his hypnotic warble rooting me to the spot. My muscles cramped in terror. I couldn't move my head. Couldn't turn away.

He forced crunchy white lips onto mine. His tongue forced inside, cold and salty with insane hunger.

I gagged, my mouth filling. His mesmerizing magic flowed over me like water, warm and threatening, drink or drown. I wanted to scream and stab him dead with my claws. I wanted to open my mouth and take him in, embrace him, savor the faint as he stripped me raw and swallowed me.

Desperate, I kicked at my determination until it sparked. I wouldn't let him have me. Not like this, mind-raped and babbling. He'd have to kill me first, and then no one would get to swallow anyone. *Screw you, hungerboy. I'm not on the menu.*

Defiant orange sparks sizzled my hair, and the green fear-haze roiled black with my anger. But Famine just murmured in delight and kissed me harder, desire salty on his tongue.

Confusion yammered. I'd tried to swallow my fear. But it hadn't worked. He ate everything I gave him, fear and defiance and anger, too. I could feel his body heat growing, absorbing me, his thinparched skin swelling with glowing blue moisture. How could I ever escape?

Famine gave a hungry laugh. His lips slid over mine, no longer dry and crackling but succulent, pulsing with stolen life. "You can't escape. You're mine. Just give in to me."

"No." I fought, writhing in my shackles until metal sliced my skin. But the pain only sharpened my mind, casting off confusion, leaving my fear exposed and raw for him to taste.

I didn't want to die. I didn't want to go to hell. And try as I might, I couldn't pretend I wasn't afraid.

"Tell me what you fear." Famine's dark persuasion caressed me, hot magical fingers digging deep into my nastiest memories, and my mind reeled with dark, threatening images of everything I'd ever feared.

Dark places, a closet where they'd locked me in as a child, spiders black and hairy and crawling down my throat. Smothering, drowning, loss of breath, nightmares that wake me in freezing sweat. Vomiting and cowering in the dust as a kid, the gangly redheaded thing who got boobs before everyone else. Mean girls with flouncing wings kick me in the guts and skinny fairy boys pull my hair and slide long bony fingers up my skirt. No school for fairy girls, not if their glamour isn't right, and mornings I curl tight in my nest under the bridge with the torn blanket pulled over my head, quivering lest someone see what I am and hurt me.

Famine crushed my hair in strengthening fists. His skinny body hardened and filled out with muscle. Curves swelled, skin stretched, flesh forming fiber by fiber, tightening over bone. He forced his mouth onto mine, sucking in my breath. "Mmm. That's it. Show me more."

I tore my mouth away. "No. Stop. Please."

His growl rusted my mouth dry. "I'm starving, Ember. Feed me. Don't make me hurt you."

Green fearstain splashed between us, hot and sticky. I recoiled, but more images flooded, irresistible.

Older, fourteen going on twenty, a body I can't control and passion-crazy moonblood I don't want to resist. My first vampire, a gorgeous pewter-eyed maniac who promises me flowers, the pain and terror as his teeth tear my skin, the cold hollow inside as I think he's going to kill me, the shame afterwards that I never get over.

Jobs, interviews, scratchy human clothes that don't fit and my dirtyscarlet hair pulled back like a nun's, typing tests I can't do because my stupid claws keep catching no matter how I cut them, long walks home in tears because I can't afford the train. A greasy fat human boss with sour breath and dull, glamour-piercing eyes, who grabs my wings and pushes me over a desk and whispers, It's okay, young lady, I won't tell a soul, not if you're a good fairy girl and do exactly as I say. Carpet stings my knees, his vile skin scraping my fingers and

*his sweat's rotten stench before bile chokes my throat
and I scramble up and run.*

I whimpered, but Famine just swallowed my cries.
"More. Such sweet guilt, Ember. Show me why you
hate yourself so much."

"No." I shuddered and struggled. I didn't want to.
That one hurt too much. But Famine's kiss drenched
me in ugly self-pity and I couldn't help but drown.

*Ash, my darling bloodfairy boy. My only friend,
dying parched and drained to keep me safe. I cry, every sunrise in our grubby little room when he stumbles home bleeding, too exhausted to kiss me or talk
to me or eat the food I buy with his trick money. His
pretty brown skin bleaches and crumbles, night after
night, wingpanes riddled with cracking holes, and his
faded golden hair breaks off like yellow candy in my
hands as I plead with him to stop, it's killing you,
we'll find something else.*

Famine laughed, rich with desire. "But he didn't stop,
did he?"

I whimpered, lost. No, Ash didn't stop. And he
didn't die in my arms. I couldn't even offer him that
comfort. He sneaked out one night while I slept for
one more trick, and I never saw him alive again.

"But that's not the worst, is it?" Famine nuzzled my
throat, nipping me. "Tell me, Ember. Say it."

His will forced into my mind like a drugged needle. I choked and fought, but I couldn't keep silent.

"I never tried to take his place!" Tears stuffed my
throat like broken glass, and I sobbed, bleeding. "I
never tried to help. I could've sold my blood instead, so
he could recover. If we'd shared—"

"If you'd shared, maybe he'd still be alive." Famine's

voice chewed black holes my heart. "But you never did. Why not, Ember? Such a little thing. Why didn't you help?"

"I was frightened!" It spilled out stained in golden despair. Ash was a memory, but my guilt was alive and ravenous. "I couldn't bear it! Those horrible vampires—"

"What? Sucking on your blood? Like they did his?"

"Yes! Ash was strong. He could take it. But I . . ."

"But you were weak." Famine yanked my hair back, and green ichor splashed over his face. "You never insisted. He brushed you off and you let him. He died because you're a coward."

I sobbed in Famine's embrace, despair stabbing hot blades through my heart. His fingers crept over my waist, popping the buttons. He was peeling away my dress, sniffing hungrily at me. I didn't care.

Poor, besotted Ash. I'd said I loved him. What a dirty, lethal lie. I didn't love anyone. Especially not myself.

"Come on, sweetie. More. What did you do then? Why did you end up with that nasty Jasper?" Famine mouthed my nipple through my bra, sharp teeth catching. The sting jolted me forward, and my mind hurtled headlong, horrid memories spilling like black poison.

Jasper that first night, hot and passionate under the swelling moon, slinky black with lies. I'm desperate and vulnerable, my body weeping pleasure in his embrace. Later, when he thinks I'm asleep, I hear him on the phone, talking his dirty business of drugs and death, and I realize who I've hooked up with and I feel sick. I should smile, walk away, never come back.

"But you didn't." Famine licked my belly, tasting me. "You were too afraid."

I nodded, sobbing. Jasper had an evil, sunflash temper. I was scared of what he might do to me if I angered him.

But also because he might leave me. Because I needed protection, too weak and scared to survive on my own. Because this dangerous, selfish, beautiful fairy boy might be the last good thing I ever got in my life.

A shattering smile, some stolen kisses, a couple of scorching nights of passion, and before I know it, I'm living in his apartment, wearing clothes he bought me, jewels he gave me, the haircut he chose for me, living the decent life I'll never afford without him because I'm bloodfae, talentless, just a useless prettygirl.

Tiptoeing around when he's in a nasty mood, hoping I won't shuffle or sigh or drop something at the wrong moment and make him mad. Lying awake beside him at four in the morning, wondering how the hell I got here, if tomorrow he'll lose interest and throw me out and I'll be left on the street with nothing but a false candy smile and a body full of vampire-bait blood. I don't want to die like Ash. I have no choice.

Later, when he starts hitting me, I cry in the shower where he can't see the tears. I know he doesn't love me. How could anyone love me? But I'm too afraid of being alone to leave.

I spluttered, green fluid splashing my naked chest. Jasper kept me around because I made him look good and gave him all the sex he wanted, at least all he wanted from me. My girlfriends didn't talk to me anymore. I'd no time for them. I spent my hours shopping, getting haircuts and beauty treatments, desperate to be more beautiful, more fashionable, the perfect girlfriend. Jasper insisted.

Famine grinned. "Only he didn't, did he? Not in so many words."

I sobbed. No, it was that hot, calculating look in his darkviolet eyes, the one that said, *Better take care of yourself, Emmy. I can have any girl I want. Better make sure it's you.*

It was my own gut-numbing fear.

"Self-absorbed little tart." Famine's whisper savaged my soul. "Preening and cowering, wasting your life away to please a man who doesn't care."

"Because he'd leave me and I'd be alone!" The words spilled out, scarlet with despair and agony and tears. I was humiliating myself. I didn't care. I just wanted to scream it to the world, cut that horrid swelling disgust from my heart so it couldn't hurt me anymore.

"You're too scared to be alone, aren't you?" Famine's lips caressed mine, and he whispered between kisses to savage my soul. "Too scared to live. And now Jasper's dead and you're lost. Scrabbling in the dark. Offering yourself to any man who'll flatter and adore you and make you forget what a worthless piece of meat you are. Your fresh pink fairy boy, for instance. Pretending there's something more so you can lie to yourself all over again."

I howled, tears splashing. He was right. I hadn't just wanted Diamond because I was moonstruck or horny or infatuated by his smile. I'd wanted him because sex was the only way I knew to get him to like me. If he gave me the chance, I'd do anything to make myself into the girl I thought he wanted. And it'd start all over again.

I slumped, unable to fight any longer. My wings drooped limp with fatigue and pain. *You win, Famine. Drink me up. I don't care.*

Famine smiled, his breath ragged on my lips. "I know, sweetie. It hurts. It'd be a relief to die here, wouldn't it?"

His words pierced me like a poisoned blade, and for a horrible moment, all I could think was *yes.*

My heart screamed, but I couldn't unthink that cowardly thought.

I shivered and sweated, self-disgust hacking at my bones. I'd really rather die than face myself? After all I'd been through, trying to save my soul, I couldn't even fight this hellspelled madman off with a *no thanks*? I couldn't even scream, *fuck you, do your worst, you'll have to kill me first.* The only defense I had to Famine's ugly mindrape magic was to hang here and wallow in steaming self-pity.

I didn't respect myself. I hated my life. But I was too shit-scared to do anything about it.

And because of that, no one would ever love me. How could they? I'd never love myself. I didn't have to fail Kane's test to go to hell. I already lived there. And no matter how I lived, I'd die alone.

I sobbed, lost. Utter despair loomed black and smothering, a cruel specter of death. Famine had unearthed my deepest, most secret fear, and he'd done it as easily as a crazy pink fairy smearing fingerpaint on the wall.

Famine groaned, pleasure or tension shuddering his body rigid. "Yes, Ember. Feed me. Let me have it. Don't hold back."

His serpentine grip dragged harder, stronger, tearing my heart up my throat and out the top of my head. Bright agony flooded, and I couldn't help but give him what he wanted.

I screamed.

In the next room, Vincent crouches in the dark, rose-tinted glasses clinging to his nose in hungry sweat. Blackness swamps him, even his virus-sharp eyes detecting no light. But the fairyspelled lenses give him pain-vision, and through the wall he sees Ember, locked between floor and ceiling, her lovely wings thrashing useless. She's screaming as Famine does what Famine does, and dark passion quivers in Vincent's hungry heart.

She's so vulnerable. So tender inside. Just watching her makes him shiver, a hot frisson of hunger and sorrow. To caress her weeping body, kiss her trembling lips, pierce that coffeecream skin and ease her smooth rich blood into his mouth and swallow . . .

It's both sick and beautiful, and Vincent grimaces in the dark, his teeth aching hard. There was a time when he'd have rescued her. But this is the world he lives in now, he and the virus-mad beast in his blood, and the beast likes it here.

Screams rend the air like claws, and his mouth drips with hungry spit at the luscious scent of all this torment. Screw it. He's thinking too much. It's easier just to eat, and forget about it. One day he'll atone for his monstrous appetite in hell.

But not for a very long time.

The air crackles azure, his lust spilling out, and in the distance someone cackles and howls, overcome.

He sucks in hot breath, calming. Gotta keep it in.

Gotta keep it to himself. Famine's basement will kill you, and vampires don't die easy.

Let's just do what we came for. Ember, rich and delicious under the moon. But not before Diamond gets his fill of despair.

He slips sweaty fingers into his pocket. He doesn't have the pinkdick bastard's number. But Ember does. And she so thoughtfully left her bag in his car. Nice tiger's eye gemstone in there, too. He's not up on the whole story, but he gets the feeling Famine will like that. Demons, souls, gems, whatever. It's all just a game.

She has two phones, his and hers. Vincent picks the cracked one, and covers the screen with his hand so as not to break the blackness as he finds the number and calls.

Diamond picks up in half a ring, harmonics ripe with worry. "Candy? You okay?"

Vincent grins. "Oh, she's peachy. Guess where I am, asshat?"

Diamond's voice ripples cold. "Up shit creek in a razorwire canoe is where you are, buttwad. Let me talkify her."

In the next room, Ember writhes and moans, her dress ripping in Famine's hungry claws, and the air bleeds green like witch's oil with her torment. Vincent squirms, palms itching to touch. "Sure. Oh, wait, sorry. She's kinda tied up with Famine right now."

"Ooh, I'm gonna have fun hurting you."

"Hey, she asked me to bring her here, mate. What was I meant to do? Lie to her, like you?" Vincent pushes his glasses up with trembling fingers, fixated on the thrust of her thighs as she struggles, the glowing sweat oozing from her skin, her heaving half-naked breasts.

So lovely and vulnerable . . . "Can't believe you let a cherry pie like her outta your sight. Shoulda known better. Anyway, just wanna let you know she'll be late home. She's playing a double feature tonight. Hey, maybe you can help me. First date nerves and all. Does she like it fast or slow?"

"Just you keep on talkifying, moron."

Vincent laughs, sweaty desire prickling his skin. "What for? So you can feel like you're protecting her for a few seconds longer?"

A hot glassy hand clamps down on his throat.

His breath squeezes away. Hard fairy flesh slams into his back, ramming him facefirst into the hot brick wall.

Brutal scarlet fairylight refracts like sunflash in his lenses, scorching him blind. He sucks back an agonized howl, razors slicing his optic nerves ragged, and the phone drops from his numb fingers and smashes.

"No, fuckstick." Diamond's whisper scorches Vincent's ear, and gloating fairy fingers slide up his cheek like a kiss. "It's so I can find you in the dark."

22

I screamed, and the world screamed back.

Noise ruptured, flesh ripping and hearts breaking and feelings torn to shreds. Fear cramped my muscles, unbearable. My wings shrieked taut. My stomach wrung tight like a chamois, and it sucked my breath away.

But I still managed to scream, and scream, and scream again.

At last I squeezed my eyes shut, exhausted, but some malicious magic in the glasses dragged my eyelids open. The air glowed with my pain, a shimmering neongreen sunset. Fairy perfume clotted my nose, and I knew it came from *him*.

Famine hovered on glowing sapphire wings, his violet skin gleaming. Sweat shone on muscles no longer wasted but slim and tight, his long indigo hair sifting like darkspun glass. Only his red albino eyes remained, glinting sickly at me, a reminder that any life he retained, he'd stolen from me.

Did he do this every night? Starve white, so hungry he had to devour some innocent creature to stay alive? Or was he just a glutton, sucking life from others to feed his grotesque appetite?

I struggled, thrashing my head. I wanted to look away, but those horrid pink lenses peeled my eyelids back.

And a fiery blue gleam dragged my eyes front.

There. On his narrow chest. A lump swelled his skin, just a few inches below his throat. His newly fresh skin parted there, and a gemstone winked, seablue.

Jasper's ring muttered and writhed on my finger, and I gulped. Famine's gemstone. Embedded in his flesh.

My nerves hacked raw with razor certainty. I'd have to kill him. Or at least knock him insensible, so I could cut it out. No fucking loss. I'd felt sorry for Crimson. This guy deserved a rotten shock.

But that didn't make it any easier. Not chained to the ceiling with fearfever quivering my blood.

Famine swooped behind me, his fresh body heat taunting mine. He rubbed his cheek against my wing's edge, intimate. My membrane recoiled, and he laughed, warm and ripe with hunger. "We're not done yet, Ember. We've explored your fear. Now I want to taste your pain."

God, it was good to hear him say that.

Strange relief cooled my burning bones. Even if I wouldn't like what happened next, pain was so . . . ordinary. It made him more fathomable. Less dangerous. Like a common thug.

My blood thrilled, hopeful. I could already feel him, the sweet twisted hardness of his cock sliding against my bottom. Maybe Famine was like any other guy. Get him focused on his dick, he'll stop paying attention and I can get free.

I spat, even though I knew I couldn't hit him. "Screw you, sickfae. You're not special, you know that? Just another horny guy who wants to touch. Go right ahead. I don't give a fuck."

But my body trembled, writhing on panic's razorcut edge, and when he grazed a warm claw over my breast, I felt it deep down in my belly, and I knew with quivering certainty that this wouldn't be so easy. He'd already raped me, mentally at least. I didn't know if I could take it again.

He tweaked my nipple, and I couldn't help but gasp. It didn't feel good. But it sure as hell felt. Hard. Tense. Relentless. Magenta syrup flooded the air, stirring in with green, that squirmraw sensation mixing with my fear.

He did it again, cupping my breast and teasing my nipple hard. I cried out, helpless. My nerves strung taut like a marionette's strings, and Famine knew exactly how to play them to get the reaction he wanted. Not pleasure. Humiliation. The disgust of reacting to his caress.

"Get off me!" I thrashed, but the manacles held fast. My wings throbbed with hot blood. A thick ache swelled between my legs, not arousal but panic response, all those fight-or-flight chemicals screaming in my veins. I longed for relief, but I didn't want him to touch me. My body would react, and I'd scream and shudder and break apart, and he'd get every scrap of the evil self-hating emotion he wanted from me.

Famine's dark chuckle tingled through my wingjoints like sparkling blackjewel. My arms strained in their steely prisons, my wings jerking backwards on a taut knife's edge. And then he licked me, hot and deliberate, right where wing meets shoulder.

It felt horrible. It felt beautiful. I gasped, dark loathsome sensation rippling through my body, and squeezed my eyes shut on Famine's black laughter.

Diamond tears his darkglamour apart and flashes into sight.

Vincent howls, blinded by the glare. Diamond grabs Vincent's pink glasses and rips them off, ramming his knee into the skanky bloodsucker's balls for good measure. "Upshut, fuckweed."

Swiftly he jams the glasses on his own nose and blinks himself dim. His glow winks out like a dead Christmas tree. Now Vincent can't see.

Good fucking riddamance. Through Famine's hell-glasses, the air streams crimson with foul vampire hunger, along with all the other torn-up emotions that string the atmosphere tight like piano wire.

Diamond's anger stirs like rotten egg, and he longs to yank the lenses off and crush them. He sneakified in here dim in the dark, with nothing but glassfae tricksies to light his way. He'd prefer impenetrable darkness to this sick suffermad rainbow. But he must find Ember.

He tried to let her go her own way. Tried to let her walk out of his life. But he couldn't let her go. The idea of her facing Famine alone . . .

Vincent fangsnaps and struggles, but Diamond jams him tighter against the wall, flashing a glance left and right. Walls. Open doorway. More doors. Shadowfied people doing sick shit.

Famine's never changes. Rosa brought him here once, bored or titillated. He didn't like it, but he did what she wantified. He always did everything she wantified. But not anymore.

He scrabbles in Vincent's pocket and rips Ember's

bag free, crushing Vincent's hip into the wall with sparkle-ripped strength. No way he'd come down here soberfied. Not after Ember left, practicamally in tears, her disappointment searing his soul like ironfairy rage. If he'd truthed her from the beginning, they could've come here together, and she'd be safe.

He snaps sharp teeth on Vincent's ear, rich blood splashing hot. "This bag hers? Keeping a souvemanir? You make me spew."

"Spew away. I eat my souvenirs. How about your balls?" Vincent snarls, black with oozing hatred, and he coils thick vampire muscles and whiplashes free.

But Diamond's ready. And he grabs Vincent's arm and hurls, letting the cocky prick's momentum do the job.

Vincent stumbles, and spins blindly into that open doorway, and quick as a snakyshifter scumbag, Diamond pirouettes on flashing wings and slams the door shut.

The door rattles as Vincent flings himself against it, raining distant curses. Diamond holds on grimly and forces the rusted iron bar home. "Till you rottify, pus-brain."

Thick scarlet fury spills under the door like blood, and Diamond spits and walks away.

Ahead, the pinklit corridor looms dark, edges wavering in tunnelblack gloom. It's Famine's sick faesight that the glasses show, this shadowy world trapped in spelled fairyglass, outlines and see-throughs and secrets floating on breath. Only they're secrets Diamond doesn't want to hear, rainbowbright like flayed bodies. But he forces himself to look, his blood throbbing tight with rage. She's here somewhere. Can't leavify. Can't abandon her. Can't let Famine hurt her.

He darts around a doorway, where a fat black spriggan in leather taunts a wriggling fairy girl with his
long pointysharp blade. She's tied to a post, her mouth
stuffed with her own severed applegreen hair, and the
spriggan's started on her wings, stabbing the sensitive
membranes with holes while she chokes and bleeds
murky despair stained with blood.

Diamond swoops in on heat-drenched black air, and
kicks the spriggan's head against the wall.

Thunk. The sweaty body drops soundlessly. Diamond plucks the sword up before it falls, and cuts the
fairy girl's ropes, snickersnack. "You okay, darlin'?"

She just thrashes and spits, and flutters off bleeding.

Diamond whirls in midair and searches on, the blade
light in his hand. Darts his glassfae sight through door-
ways and around corners, searching for a spicy Ember-
whiff. Watches on the colored emotion currents for
something familiar.

Hell, he barely knowifies her. Only that she smells
of blossom and her kiss sparkles like peppered honey,
and when she smiles, some coldcrystal thing in his
heart melts like hot chocolate fudge—

His pulse backflips. In the corner, honeyed scent
flowing cherryred, mixed with the musky moonspice
of her blood.

It's Ember, chained hands and feet, spilling fear and
loathing like green vomit. And a cruel-eyed fairy, glowing triumph-blue. Shadows crush around him like dead
ghosts, his spindly hands on her body. She's half-naked,
luscious flesh spilling out, her rich girlscent a bold lure.

Ember, shuddering in pain as she forces back a
scream. And Famine, mindsense maniac, shining with
magic and mayhem and malicious intent. He's tearing
her mind out. Scraping it open for everyone to see.

She's howling and struggling and clawing with invisible will to keep it in, but the air's snaking green with her evil, hate-rich dreams, and Diamond squeezes his eyes shut but he can't not seeify.

He can't stop seeifying her. With Jasper. With other faceless men who hurt her. With a nameless, dying bloodfae boy. But always alone. Feardrenched. Her own shivering prisoner.

Diamond's scarlet rageflash lights the air. She's chained to the bricks, helpless. And even he can't match Famine's spellifications. He doesn't have a prayer.

But he doesn't think. He doesn't hesitate. He just dives for that precious scent, somersaults with his wickedsharp blade scything, and kicks the door open in midair.

23

Metal sliced the air, screeching, and Famine's cruel caress ripped away.

But it wasn't a relief. Only more torment.

I howled, helpless, tension crippling my body with vicious need. My nerve endings screamed jagged, whipped to insatiable hunger by Famine's tricks. Even airflow tortured me, the sensation both too much and nowhere near enough. I wanted pain, burning, flaying, anything to alleviate this awful cramp that shook me rigid. My body pleaded for release, and the loss of Famine's touch was unbearable.

I forced my eyes open. Tears smeared my glasses, and all I saw was an angry scarlet blur.

But I didn't need to see to smell roses.

Crazy laughter choked me, and more tears spilled, washing my eyes clearer. Diamond hovered, a shimmering glass glory on a sparkled crimson pillar of rage. His shining hair scattered the light like jewels. He'd dressed for the occasion, tight black rubber hugging his body, his bare arms glittering in fairy sweat. His glasses flashed golden, fury searing through like flame. A razorcut blade dripped green blood in his hand.

I shivered, hope and dread fighting icy battles down

my spine. I didn't want him here, not with my worst nightmares painting lurid pictures in the air like a sick green horror movie. I didn't want him to see. I wanted to plead with Famine to keep tormenting me, make me shatter, let me rest at last.

Famine hissed, wet blue wings shining, and my desperate longing splashed his mouth scarlet. "Come for a taste, prettyfae?"

Diamond didn't waste time with words. He just arced his blade and dived headlong at Famine's face.

Famine swooped upward, claws raking. The scything blade missed, ruffling his indigorich hair. Diamond somersaulted, rosy wings flashing, and snapped backwards for a reattack. Famine jerked back, black blood splashing from a fresh gouge on his arm.

I wriggled in my chains, the cruel iron a welcome pain. They were both so fast, so beautiful, locked in vicious midair battle like angry angels. I longed to dive in screeching, warble in delight as my muscles stretched. Slice that blade across my skin and feel the hot blood flow. Grab Famine's head, smash it into the bricks until the rotten wormshit stopped sneering.

Famine lunged with razor teeth at Diamond's throat. Diamond leapt backwards and slashed. A hank of Famine's inky hair fell. Swift as a bluebellied snake, Famine latched onto Diamond's wrist, and he jammed his foot against the wall and pulled.

Bone crunched. Diamond lurched off balance, hissing, and the blade tumbled from his hand to clatter against the wall.

My breath squashed hard. Oops.

Diamond's wings crunched into the bricks, and Famine struck in a blue blur. I gritted my teeth, waiting for blood.

But Famine didn't tear his throat out. He just yanked Diamond's head around by the hair and stared into his eyes.

I yelled, fear spilling cold green moisture down my body. "No! Diamond, don't look—"

But he already had, and as I watched helpless, his fury-golden eyes melted scarlet.

Famine grinned and panted, his jewel-pierced chest heaving. "Too slow, shithead. Story of your life. You can't protect them, can you? God knows you're no good for anything else, but you can't even do that."

"Shut it, psychofae. Just let Ember free." Diamond spat, splashing Famine's chin. But he couldn't move. Trapped, pinned immovable by Famine's spiteful spells. And his winedark remorse flooded the air, rippling from his heart like a dead bloodstain.

Poisoned claws slashed at my soul. Not him as well. I could accept my own death, even if it made me thrash and rage at the stupidity of it all. But I didn't want Diamond dead because of me.

Famine sniffed the rich purple flood. "Mmm. I adore self-loathing. It's my favorite, after fear. Did you see Ember's? Nice, wasn't it? But a pretty boy like you? What's there to loathe? You treat your body like a whore. All you've got to give, is that it?"

"Save it, clever-ass." Diamond swiped sharpglass claws, defiance glowing golden in his translucent veins. But the air rippled thicker, bloodier, all that secret emotion ripping free.

My lungs swelled, painful. I didn't want to hear this. It was none of my business. Diamond was so self-assured. To see his heart flayed open was more than I could bear. I thrashed in my chains, furious. "Let him go, you brute."

But Famine ignored me. He inhaled deep, sucking in Diamond's colors, and his wings quivered alive with stolen rose pink. "Give it up, Diamond. You're empty anyway. All those careless affairs, and you couldn't keep the one woman you really wanted."

Diamond lunged, held back by invisible magical bonds across his chest that pressed bright welts into his shining skin. "You're full of shit. Just let her down."

A dark blue laugh, sparkled with golden lust. "You don't care about any of them, do you? You pretend to be so protective but it's all about your ego. You need them to adore you. You're so fucking focused on yourself that you *bored* the love of your life into drinking from a vampire."

Rage rippled white as Diamond snarled, but he couldn't escape, and the ripe red blood of his hatred spilled faster, pooling on the floor.

Famine grabbed Diamond's jewel-studded hair, yanking his head back. "You hurt her, didn't you? Broke her pretty face with your fist because she wouldn't play your self-serving game. You fucking animal. You lie, you trick, you flirt to get attention, but you're dogshit wrapped in a pretty bow. You've got nothing a decent woman would want. And now you can't even keep this one."

"Don't believe him. It's all just tricks!" But I couldn't get free. I couldn't make Famine stop.

Famine smirked. "Your Ember's tasting every lick of this. She knows how empty and hateful you are. She'll die, Diamond, right in front of you, and there's not a damn thing you can do."

Diamond gnashed his teeth, straining to break free. But Famine's spell held fast, and that thick scarlet flood kept on coming. My tongue tingled with the taste of it, honey nectar like desire. Mmm. I swallowed, and my throat sighed in warm delight as Diamond's viscous loathing slipped down, caressing, so filling and warm. . . .

Horror scorched my bones. I was eating him, ripe and ravenous like a beast.

But his emotion sparkled on my tongue, hot scarlet rivers splashing over my chin. Desire savaged my whip-taut body all over again. I wanted to swallow, drink him in, suck his essence down until this cursed hunger stripping my nerves raw was sated at last.

I yelled, flame roaring in my bones. God, I was hungry. Famished. Ravenous for sensation and release and flesh on shuddering flesh. Frantic, I tried to focus, but nothing worked. I throbbed inside, longing for pain, punishment, the desperate relief of a touch. Cruel, kind, I didn't care. This was what Famine did. Reduced everything to evil, selfish hunger. Made greedy beasts of us all.

I raked my lips with hungry teeth, and yelled as the blood burst. I thrashed my head until my hair sprang loose. Sharp wire nipped at my ears, but the evil pink glasses wouldn't come off. I couldn't stop the horrible visions, heartliquid staining the air, mental rape in Technicolor 3D.

Against the wall, Diamond struggled in his magical trap. His face shone, sweat and tears, and as I wriggled and kicked to free myself, his agonized golden gaze fixed on mine.

Fairyspelled emotion punched me, and my breath sucked out, and I *saw*.

I saw, deep into his slinky secret places, so warm and strange and beautiful. And I knew Famine was wrong.

Colors rushed, a telescoping tunnel of truth and mirrors, Diamond's secret heart ripped open to view by the vicious clash of two relentless glassfae talents.

Famine was wrong. Diamond's heart wasn't broken. There it shone, bold and fairycurious and lustful for life. But it hid, bruised, afraid of its own courage. Afraid of what would happen if he let it loose. Like me.

Understanding flashed firebright, and a sob caught my throat. All that contempt, so cutting and cold? It was directed at himself. Whoever she was, this girl of his, he'd hurt her, and he hated it. Whatever passed between them, it'd crippled him.

He wasn't playing with my affection. He just didn't think I'd ever care. Just assumed I'd walk away once I was done with him. Like she did.

He'd given me everything he knew how to share, and I'd thrown it back at him because it wasn't enough. Inside, he felt as worthless as I did, and I'd as much as told him it was true.

I struggled to hold his gaze. "Diamond, stay with me. He's tricking you. We can both get out. Don't listen to him!"

Famine giggled, that seablue stone in his chest flashing lickspit with greed. He caressed Diamond's cheek, and inkblue contempt smeared from his finger.

My veins rippled. Famine was emoting.

Just a smear, a tiny blue leak. But definite. Famine's own colors, bleeding free.

My muscles twisted tighter, agonizing, but I didn't care. Famine just gave himself away. He was as vulnerable as we in this weird pinkglass magictrap. Just a matter of pressing the right buttons.

And with a glassbright flash like crystal, I knew just what Famine was afraid of.

24

Lickerish delight salted my mouth, and I grinned, deathly, tension spilling bumps over my skin. "Go on, shithead. Kill me. I'm gonna run straight down to hell and tell Kane just what makes you tick."

Famine giggled, but for a moment, his fingers halted in Diamond's hair.

"I've figured out what you wanted, see. You and those other four idiots with your stupid gemstones? That vampire kid, glutting himself on blood. Crimson eating pretty boys to stay beautiful. And Jasper, well, he'd do anything to stay alive." I inhaled, savoring Famine's anticipation. "Immortality, right? You're afraid to *die*."

"Nonsense." Famine laughed, but it clanged, false.

"You're fucking terrified, and that's why you've set up this little heartmunching safari down here, isn't it? Because you know you're going to hell. And in hell, *the hunger will never stop*."

"Shut up." Famine's voice rang flat, not his usual delighted lilt. His deep blue wings leaked, fat indigo droplets splashing the floor.

"I know about hunger, Famine. It's the same as loneliness, see? It's this cold empty place inside you, and to fill it, you *consume*. You stuff yourself with sensation and oblivion and meaningless sex and more and worse and lower, until one day the empty place starts eating you."

"Shut up!" Famine gripped Diamond's throat, but Diamond just kept struggling. Famine gnashed his teeth, and the drip increased to a inky trickle, his wings bleeding pale.

That hot salty Famine-essence slicked my tongue, and I spat it out, triumphant. "It already ate all your friends, didn't it? Does it feel good, to strip your lovers bare and drink them up? Everything you care about, consumed. And when you die, you'll go to hell and you'll be all alone screaming in a dark empty hole and every day the hunger will chew through your guts and munch on your heart but no one will *ever feed you again*."

Dirty blue liquid splattered like paint, and Famine whirled in a spray of Diamond's roseglass blood and dived for me.

I squealed, dodging in my chains for a hiding place I couldn't reach. Glass shattered as Diamond's invisible bonds broke, no magic to hold them now Famine had let go.

Famine crashed into me, teeth slashing for my belly. We hurtled backwards, my shackles ripping tight. His vile blue hatred clogged my mouth, sour and chilled like swampwater.

Diamond uncurled with a snap of bleeding wings. He dived for his sword with a crystalline crunch, folded long pink fingers around the hilt, and flung himself headlong.

I yelled. Famine was all over me. Diamond couldn't run him through without stabbing me, too.

But bright bladework arced, whistling above my head. Diamond crashed into the wall behind me with a breakglass crunch. My wrist chains twanged like piano wire, and broke.

I crashed backwards on flailing wings. Famine tumbled on top of me, venting thick blue fury like vitriol. We thrashed in midair, colors spurting like evil fingerpaint as we fought to stay aloft. I gagged, his long hands squeezing at my throat.

Black stars twinkled before my eyes. I choked. My exhausted wings buckled. Blood and spit drowned me. He was too strong.

Famine giggled and dragged me up. I thrashed my legs, but my boots scrabbled just a few inches above the ground. "Wriggle, little girl. I like it that way." And he licked his hot wet tongue up my neck and over my chin, searching for my mouth to suck my life away.

Diamond rolled, and the air lasered bright with magnetic fae directionality. He hurled his sword in a flashing steel curve.

I flung my arm out, and the hilt smacked into my palm. My tendons spasmed tight. The sword held fast, and I stabbed upward with the last of my strength.

Flesh caught, and ripped. Burning blue blood seared my arm to the elbow. And Famine's eyes flashed red hot with fury and pain. He jerked, stained green ichor spilling from his mouth onto my face, and fell on top of me.

I crashed to the ground. Famine's weight crushed me. Blood and mindslime sloshed on the bricks, soaking my hair, griming my skin, thick and greasy and disgusting. Famine gurgled, ghastly, his face draining pale an inch from my eyes.

I shrieked and kicked, desperate to get the vile

creature off me before I vomited. His hair fell in my face, pasting to my lips as it crackled dry. I shoved, palms slipping on brittle flesh, his salty stink covering me, soaking wet into my hair, up my nose, crawling over my tongue, down my throat. . . .

A shining pink hand grabbed his shoulder, and the body heaved off me.

Metal flashed, cutting my chains, and my ankles popped free.

I scrambled to my knees, aching. Famine lay there, fading, his hair crackling dry. Inkyblue liquid leaked out around him, a swelling pool of gore. His skin drained white. The sword wobbled upright, still caught beneath his skinny ribs, and in a fit of rage, I grabbed the hilt two-handed and shoved the blade home.

Famine choked, and his fiery albino eyes blanched white. His chest heaved one last time, and he fell limp, just an empty husk in a wet blue puddle. Dead.

My fingers cramped. I couldn't let the blade go. Sweat ran itchy on my skin, and I longed to wash it off, a cool shower and a long sleep in safety. But I couldn't relax. I couldn't calm my racing pulse, the rasping breath burning my lungs, the shrieking tension his torture had wrought in my body.

An arm floated softly around my shoulders. I jerked, my nerves on a jagged edge. I'd almost forgotten Diamond was there, and now his rosefairy scent swelled deep in my veins, thrashing my blood to a panic-drenched mess.

"C'mon, angel. Let go. Gotta skip it." His voice worked gentle but insistent under my skin.

I couldn't face him. He'd seen everything. I shuddered. "No. There's still . . . gotta get . . ." I couldn't say it. I could only do.

I forced my arms to move. Ripped the blade from Famine's bleeding white body. Dragged his crackling hair from his throat with my boot heel, and jammed the swordpoint into his flesh.

His skin sliced like paper, so easy. Blood spurted blue. I forced the point under the shining blue shard and twisted, and the gemstone popped out with a wet squelch.

The vile demongem shrieked as it clattered on the floor, blue-tinged white skin still ragged around the edges.

I had it. Gemstone number two. And I hoped the sick fuck already burned in hell.

Tremors racked me, sobs without the tears. The sword dropped from my fingers to clang on the blood-drenched bricks. My whisper cracked raw. "Can you . . . I can't . . ."

Diamond scooped the bloody gemstone up and stuffed it in his pocket. He dug swiftly in Famine's gorestained clothes and came up with a rusted key. In his gentle hands, my manacles clicked open, and he unfolded the tight metal from my wrists and ankles and dropped each horrid hinge to the floor. Then, he held out his hand for mine.

My face burned. I wanted to take it. I wanted to faint in his embrace, let him take care of me, carry me up the stairs and out into the burning summer air of freedom. Take me home, bathe me and put me to bed and caress me with his beautiful body until the terror was gone.

But I couldn't. I didn't dare. I was too raw, too exposed, and he'd seen everything. He'd seen the bleeding heart of my fear. If he touched me now, I might never escape.

"You okay?" Diamond brushed my hair back. His fingers lingered on my cheek, and his bright rosy aura made me ache. I was half-naked, bleeding, splashed in grime and gore, my muscles shaking with unbearable strain. He could soothe me. Release me. Make me better.

I tilted my head away.

He swallowed and let his hand drop.

Dumb, I pulled my dress straight. Fumbled the buttons into place. Dragged wet blue-stained hair from my eyes.

I didn't let Diamond take my hand. I just averted my face and stumbled hot and aching for the door.

25

Outside, moonlight drenched my blood with lust.

Engine noise tore my ears, Doppler echoes howling as we hurtled over the bridge. It was late, or early morning, unknown hours vanished. Reflections glittered silver like evil stars in the windshield, not artificial lights but moonshine, gloating over every surface with fat greedy licks. Heat shimmered the darkness, hungry and feral, consuming everything like a monster.

Beside me, Diamond shifted gears, muscles jumping in his arm. I shivered in a sweaty ball in the luscious front seat of his car. My pulse throbbed, my breath rushing in and out too fast. Hunger hollowed my guts. Thirst ripped at my throat. My skin ached to be touched, the deep dark places inside my body screaming to be filled. Famine's foul hunger magic still cackled in my blood like a fairymad fever, wriggling into knots with the savage moonlight until I didn't know where I ended and the madness began.

We shrieked to a stop, and I opened the door with burning fingers. But I stumbled, my feet tangling, and Diamond didn't ask. He just swept me into his arms and carried me, and I leaned my pounding head on his chest, my fists clenched tight over my face.

A rush of breeze and we landed, his balcony shining white under the burning moon. The city lay in darkness, the power unrestored. The place was a graveyard, black and silent, the apartment blocks and offices beside us looming like a dead forest. Diamond's glow shed the only comfort, rippling rosy like underwater lights.

He carried me to the bathroom, smooth black tile and glass, and set me gently on my feet. My heels skidded, and he righted me. "You okay?"

"Uh." Moonlight pierced the window to light the crystal planes of his face. His fingers lingered on my waist. His rosepetal scent swam in my head, awful and delicious. I shuddered, overwhelmed. I wanted to lean on him, let my shaking legs buckle. It was unfair. Famine had taunted him, too. He had wounds of his own that I'd carelessly scraped raw.

But he was so close. I could feel his fever, taste his pulse in rhythm with mine. My desire throbbed. I needed contact, sensation, oblivion. Awkwardly, I stumbled closer, and his ruby eyes burned dark and deep, torturing me all over again. He kissed my forehead, a gentle brush of fairy lips that made my skin scream in agony.

I wanted to grab him. I wanted to run away. "H— how much did you see?"

"Everything."

My heart shrank. I closed my eyes, words tumbling to my lips. "Diamond—"

He stopped me with a gentle claw on my bottom lip, a dangerous caress. "Yell if ya needify," he whispered, and left me there alone.

I'd lost him. He couldn't face me. Not after he'd seen how selfish and horrible I was.

Blindly, I stripped, banging my knees on the bathtub's edge as I yanked my boots off. My dress plopped to the tiles, soaked in sweat and gunk. My bra had Famine's horrid essence on it, and I peeled it off and flung it aside. I'd ripped Famine's devilglasses off, hurled them from the car to smash on the parched concrete. But I could still see the stains. I'd always see them.

I fell past the free-standing glass screen into the shower and slapped the taps on. For a moment, nothing happened, and my foggy brain recalled the blackout with a sick twinge of fear. But then water came, gushing, sickly warm from the sun but clean and clear and refreshing. I ducked my head, spraying, swallowing, drenching my hair, letting the muck rinse from my tortured body and glug like bloodclots down the drain as if that'd make everything Famine said okay.

But it didn't. The tension wouldn't ease. My wing membranes strained taut, droplets plucking them like drumskins. The water's warm slide was too gentle, not enough to ease my pain. My muscles contorted tighter. Moonlight glared in my eyes through the wide window over the bathtub, and it bubbled my blood hot with blind need.

I banged my palm into the shower screen, and the glassy vibration only teased my distress to a higher pitch. Pain, pleasure, hot, cold, I didn't care. So long as I felt something that could drain this evil spell away.

I twisted the shower off and leaned my cheek on the dripping glass. My voice dried to a croak. "Diamond."

Silence. My nerves shredded. He'd already left. Couldn't bear my selfishness a moment longer. Yesterday, I'd dared to dream he could want me. Now I knew he never would.

"Diamond." I tried again, the cracking syllables carrying. "Please."

A tiny rustle, and the door eased open. "Ember?"

"I . . ." I swallowed, my throat parched even though I'd drunk gutfuls. I couldn't get the words out.

He floated inside, claws clinking on the doorknob. His rubylit shadow stained the moonbeams with bloody ripples, his hair shining like fractured starlight. He was barefoot, gleaming, basking in the heat. "You hurt? Can I—?"

"Hit me." It splurted out, stained with anguish.

He stared, eyes burning scarlet. "What?"

My blood scorched hotter. I was naked, raw, my wounds exposed, and his gaze stabbed me deep. "Hit me. I need it. Please."

"No." Quiet, firm, unmovable.

"I have to hurt! I have to feel. Please!"

"No, Ember! I won't. Don't askify." He averted his face, sweat gleaming silver on his neck where the vein pulsed bright.

Tears racked my throat, and a yowl welled up, ripe with anguish that drove my words off an insane, hurt-crazy cliff. "Why not? What about *her*? You hit *her*. Is she so special? Do you love her so much? For me, you can't even . . . Oh, fuck."

I slumped, tears flowing. My words made no sense. They made perfect sense. I was perverse. I was foul. I crouched against the glass, my wet hair plastered to my skin, and the smell of my own skin made me sick.

"Don't ever askify that." Diamond swooped beside me, hands on my shoulders, and his body shook. Tense, hungry, tortured. Like me. "Yeah, I hit her. I hit her because she tore my heart out and spat on it, and I won't ever forgivify me so long as I breathe."

"Then stop trying to make up for it!"

"What?" He gripped me tighter, and his claws sparked hot sensation along my arms, but it wasn't enough. Not nearly enough.

"Whatever you did to her. Whatever she did to you. It can't be made up for. What you had is broken, Diamond. Just let it go."

"I can't." His gaze cracked scarlet, burning inside with despair and hopelessness. "It's all truth. What Famine said. I'm no good for you."

"But I need you." Desperation thickened my voice. "If you won't hit me, touch me. Be with me. Please!"

His breath deepened, rough. "Ember—"

"I know you don't want me like that. I don't care. Please. Just get him off me." I huddled closer, twisting my fingers tight in his hair. His fragrant body heat sprang my nipples tight, my skin breaking out in eager bumps. I was naked in his arms, and my nerves hacked raw.

But he held me away. "Angel, are you blindified? You light me up so hard I'm dizzy. I can't thinkify anything but you. But I'm dirty. Corruptified. You don't—"

"Please. He's on me, in me. I can't bear it!" My voice ruptured into a scream, stupid tears flowing faster.

He covered my mouth with trembling fingers, caressing my face, pressing his forehead to mine, his mouth against my wet cheekbone. "Hushify, Ember. Please. I can't . . . You don't . . . Oh, hell." And he silenced my quivering mouth with a kiss.

His lips met mine, and my blood caught fire.

My pulse thundered. I pressed against him, drinking in his hot roseglass flavor, opening my mouth and pleading for him to come inside. His tongue found mine, sweet and bitter. I squeezed my eyes shut on hopeless tears and kissed him harder, rougher, every rich caress driving me closer to madness.

It wasn't enough. He was too gentle, too restrained. He wouldn't ravish me, hurt me, ease my pain. I murmured into his mouth, dragging him closer.

With a gasp he pulled back, waterdrops glittering in his hair. "Everything he said is truth, okay? I lied to enchantify you. I'm nothing you'd ever want—"

"I want this. Now." And I pushed him backwards and climbed onto his lap.

My parted thighs ached, that tender flesh exposed. A thrill spiked my spine. God, he looked fantastic between my legs, a glory of glowing fairy fire and hard muscle, ripe for taking. His hot gaze raked over my naked breasts, and I felt every tingle. He was dazzling, dangerous, threatening in his beauty. I wanted to be threatened. I wanted to hurt.

I pressed against him, and the heat of his straining cock twinged my muscles tighter. My bones still burned with a demon's awful promises. My blood still heated like fever with moonshine and spelltorture. I was flayed inside, exposed, vulnerable. I didn't care. I wanted him inside me, bruising, thrusting hard, winding me tight until I snapped.

I bent over. My breasts folded onto his chest, and his wings glittered, hungry. When my hair fell in his face, he groaned in surrender and dragged my head down.

"You honor me, angel." His whisper burned my neck, prickling all the way to my toes. He brushed his lips across my sensitive throat, and I couldn't help but moan aloud.

His sharp fairy teeth grazed me, tender but menacing, and the shock stung me hot. His tongue crept out to tease me, tracing hot shapes and dragging out my pleasure until I shivered. My skin was so taut, it throbbed. He kissed my collarbone, licked the crevice under my jaw, tasted my earlobe. Finally, he tilted my chin down to take my mouth, and this time he kissed me hot and hard, his tongue ravishing mine, every demanding sweep of his lips the perfect torment.

I opened my mouth, whimpering, begging him to take me. At my surrender, he crushed my hair tighter in his fists, and his twisted fairy cock swelled even harder between my legs, big and hot and demanding. I was on top, but he owned me, led me, dominated. God, I could kiss him like this forever, his hands twisting my hair tight so I couldn't escape, his tongue forcing me open, taking what he wanted, telling me what to do. But not tonight. Tonight I needed more.

I wriggled up in his lap, pulling him with me. He grabbed my hips and lifted so I could settle myself. I wanted him all over me, his skin rubbing on mine, and I reached behind him to pop his studs, dragging his tight black rubber off to rub my naked breasts against his hard-packed chest. His smooth body felt so good, and my nipples sprang tight. Hungrily I reached beneath me to undo his pants, panting. "Fuck me. Please. I need it."

"No." He grabbed my arms and held me still, his wings bathing me in hot purple glow. "Not like this."

"But—"

"Trustify. Let me touch you." He traced my spine with one warm finger.

My body strained, yearning. But fear zinged my wingbones, and I stammered, undone by desire and the need for raw release. "Don't read my mind. I can't do that. Not after Famine—"

"Trustify. Tell me what to do." His claws trailed

hot tingles over my back, and when he scratched me lightly, my muscles quivered in eagerness. He teased my wingjoints, tracing soft circles, drawing them to delicious hardness, tempting me.

I groaned, my moonstruck blood singing. "Oh, god. Harder. Hurt me. Break me."

He captured my mouth for another bone-melting kiss, and wrapped his long fingers around my joints and squeezed.

"Oh, yes. More." I arched my back, bliss rippling my spine tight. My thrusting breasts ached for contact, my nipples begging. He pulled harder, forcing me backwards in a tense curve that spiked pleasure deep into my sex. And when he swept one stiff nipple into his mouth, my flesh swelled so sharp and sweet, I yelled.

He sucked on me, dragging my nipple deep in his mouth and crushing it with his tongue. Pain and desperate pleasure stabbed, just the elixir I needed. He shifted to the other one, sucking and testing me with his teeth until my sex ached for the same treatment, wetness flowing deep. His hard cock pressed against me, a throbbing promise that made me shiver.

He kissed a sparkling swath down my belly, still massaging my wingjoints to quivering ecstasy as he went. I buried my hands in his scintillating hair as he nibbled my ribs, my hipbone, the curve of my belly, sharp teeth shocking, bruising, caressing. Until at last he could reach no further and dragged me out onto the floor in a tempting patch of moonlight. He hooked my thigh over his shoulder to expose my burning wet flesh. At the sight of me, he groaned and rubbed his cheek inside my thigh, crisp hair caressing hot. "You are so beautiful."

I shuddered, fevered. His moonlit skin prismed,

showering me in fairysparkled delight. My sex ached hard and sharp. My skin flared alive, every glide of his fingertips and lips a beautiful agony. Normally I liked to be teased, for a guy to take his time. Tonight, I just wanted to scream. I scrabbled at his hair, dragging him closer. "Touch me. Please. Now."

He bit me, with a hot snarl of desire, right where my mound swelled under trimmed red hair. Need wrenched my muscles tight, threatening to tear them from my bones. And then he swiped his tongue over me, one hot delicious lick from entrance to tip, and everything I knew about tension melted into a delirious mess.

I groaned, desperate. Too much. Not enough. He delved his tongue deeper, inside where my muscles gripped, exploring all my secret shapes, dragging rich delight as he went. "More. Don't tease. I need to come. Please."

He fastened that clever tongue on my little point, and it felt so hot and good and sore that I writhed, tightening all over with pleasure. God, it was like he'd done this to me a dozen times and knew all my tricks. And he wasn't reading me. He just knew.

I felt so wild and vulnerable, all my nerves afire. And he didn't only lick me. He caressed my hard little bud with his lips, sucking me deep into his mouth and playing with me until my overstretched nerves backfired, spilling hot sensation all through my body, over and again and harder and faster until I screamed, gripping his head in my hands so he wouldn't stop until I was done. My abused muscles strained hard, and with one last hard suck at last I broke apart, fiery relief scorching down my legs and deep into my belly, all my horrid tension melting away until there was only desperate burning pleasure that I wanted never to end.

My limbs quivered, my breath a glorious scorch in my lungs. He licked me, kissed me, his lips gentle and soothing, letting me come down in my own time. My body sighed, blessed relief, the torture in my muscles fading to a rich dark bliss. He slipped his finger inside me, stroking softly, exploring. I stretched, luxuriating, his mouth still on me, and incredibly my pleasure swelled again. He'd make me come again, and this time it built swiftly, dizzy, my limbs crying out in bliss.

He knew how to make me feel good. But I didn't want it. I wanted him, hot and delicious, his skin on my tongue, his hair in my face, the burning thrust of his body into mine. I didn't care if he knew every dark and despicable thing about me. He understood me like no one else because he'd seen that. And I'd seen his own nightmare. I wanted him close.

"No," I gasped, trying to pull him off me. "I want you. Don't—"

But too late. Pleasure splashed like molten glass, sparks tingling all the way to my wingtips, and I shuddered and moaned and let it take me, hot and hard and shattering.

At last he released me, sliding his hot smooth cheek along my thigh, his lips devouring my tender skin like he never wanted to let me go. I dragged him upward to cover me. His body slid on mine, so light, so big, all hot muscle and burning pulse and shining wings. His fairybright skin on my breasts made me gasp. I pressed my face to his chest, inhaling his rosepetal scent, and it fired my blood with honeydark desire. His hair trailed over my shoulder, following his kisses over my collarbone and my breasts and the hollow of my throat.

I wanted more. I wanted to please him, make him mine. I slid my hands over his back, slick with sugary faesweat. My claws brushed his wingjoints, and he groaned and our lips collided, drinking thirsty kisses like we'd never stop. I wanted to do that to him all night, just to feel his pleasure.

But desire struck my body aflame. Moonlight crooned wild melody in my pulse. I'd had my release. Famine's torture seemed a lifetime away. Now, I wanted something different. Something more. This beautiful fairy boy belonged to me, here and now. I wanted him to know what he meant to me.

I wrapped my thigh around his hip and slid urgent fingers between us, desperate to get rid of his clothes and have him naked, touch him, get him inside me. The buttons popped, springing his hot hard cock into my hands. So silky smooth, glowing like burning glass. Hungrily I moved my hips, pressing the tip into my swollen flesh.

He groaned and pulled back. "Stop it, Ember. Can't. You don't want—"

"Do want." His hair spilled moonlit rainbows over my breasts, and I gasped, the pleasure intense. "Whatever she did to you wasn't your fault, okay? You're brilliant and beautiful and so tender, it hurts and I want you, Diamond. Need you. Don't leave me now."

His body strained against mine, hungry. "But—"

"Shh." I silenced him with my lips, and our kiss consumed me like hellfire, deep and desperate, the melting heat not just desire but something more dangerous. And I grabbed it and held on tight, bringing him with me on sighs and whispers and feverish need. "The past is gone, Diamond. I'm here. Love me."

And he worked his hands beneath me to grip my wingjoints tight, and slid slowly inside me, inch by luscious glassy inch.

So smooth. So hot. So tight. I groaned, my body on edge, hungry to take him. I tilted my hips, and he pushed deeper, hard, his lovely twisted length filling me to the hilt.

My wings slammed flat on the tiles, and I cried out, my breath knocked away. Hard, smooth, not fragile but exquisite. He felt so right. We fit, he and I, drawn together like fairy flame, and I couldn't pretend it wasn't happening anymore.

He breathed deep, tense, feverish. "Ember. You feel so . . . Oh, shit."

My cocky fairy boy, lost for words. A breathless smile curled my lips. Now that was really something.

I gripped him to me, caressing his perfect hips, his smooth fairymuscled back, that gorgeous ass. He crushed me against him, muscles flexing in glittering moonlight, and pressed his forehead to mine so I could gaze into his eyes. So hot, so intense and focused, like I was the only thing in the world that mattered.

My heart stumbled, dangerously vulnerable. Surely he did this to all the girls. Made them feel special, safe, adored, not just sex but a gift he treasured. The fluttery foolishness in my belly was just that. Foolishness.

But I couldn't tear my gaze away. Couldn't stop drinking in his weirdlight beauty, basking in the rosy glow of his attention, drowning in the hot ruby depths of his eyes.

And then he moved inside me, slow deep strokes that spread burning delight deep in my belly. My vision blurred, delirious. God, it was unfair. Nothing had ever felt this good. I gripped him, pulled him in harder, claws digging into clenching muscle. Our bodies molded tight, and my wingjoints shivered and swelled in his caress. My sex tightened around him, every thrust lighting fresh flame. I cried out, beyond coherence, my pleasure dragging to an impossibly high peak.

"Hushify. Not yet." His whisper soothed me, and he slipped gently from my body on a soft breath of wings. He stripped himself of his pants with a graceful aerial tumble, and bent to me and held out his hand. "Come with me."

I trembled. Beautiful like an angel, shimmering hair and glowing skin, face perfect crystal, wings a shining stained-glass glory. Only an angel wasn't all rawglowing muscles and rosedark scent, his body slick with sweat and my redstained fluid. An angel didn't have a body I wanted to worship, swelling lips I wanted to kiss, a magnificent cock I wanted to push inside me, slide my lips over, suck into my mouth.

My pulse throbbed, afire. I grabbed his hand, and he lifted me effortlessly like a doll and carried me outside in his arms on an easy swoop.

On the balcony, heat slicked over me, my lungs burning. No lights shone, the city a desert of blackness and moonshine that caressed my skin so sweetly, I gasped, my blood sparkling. But still my palms flattened on his chest, tense. I'd done it in public before, with Jasper, but we were always sparkled out of our minds. Tonight, I was high on something far more dangerous.

My whisper cracked, fragile. "I'm naked."

"Good." Diamond tumbled us over the edge into shimmering moonlit night. His strong arms held me close. His glamour wrapped around us, light and shimmery, and his hot lips teased my ear with shivers. "I love you naked."

The air caressed me, running like warm water over my nakedness. I fluttered my wings and laughed, and my wet hair tumbled free as we dipped and dived in an urgent embrace. Tongues mingling, hands searching, limbs entwining as we sought closeness. He licked one nipple, then the other, suckling them to swollen points, and I squealed in delight and flipped over to wrap my fingers around his cock, stroking, ducking my head to lick him, his dark fairy taste and his burble of pleasure at my touch driving my senses to rainbows with desire.

I took his cock deeper into my mouth and sucked. Mmm. So hard, so smooth on my tongue. He groaned, low and hot. "God, Ember, you'll kill me." For a moment he worked with me, thrusting gently, his delicious flavor swelling in my mouth, and then he shuddered and pulled away and dived beneath me to settle me in his lap.

Warm updraft lifted us, and our wings swelled on bright moonlit breeze. I wrapped my legs around his hips, urging him. He pushed inside me, hot and hard and so big, like the first time only deeper, more intense. I groaned and arched, rich dark sensation flooding. Again he slid teasing hands around my wingjoints, easing me backwards so my spine curled. Just like before, only this time he was inside me, and it felt so good, my wings juddered. He thrust into me hard, his mouth on my breasts, suckling me until I moaned. God, he could fuck me so deep like this. Slow and forceful and endless, just how I liked it. And his cock was the perfect shape, stretching me tight, rubbing me with hot hard flesh in all the right places.

And then warm glassfae talent caressed my mind's edge, a spritz of fresh excitement, not intrusive but beautiful. He shifted me upward an inch or two, changing the angle, and I groaned with delight, an urgent ache rippling my inner muscles. I was wrong. *That* was the right place. "Oh, god. Yes. Right there. Harder."

"Uh-huh." He obliged me, muscles clenching. His long hot tongue on my nipples made me ache, and when he bit me my hair slapped my butt, spasms of delight straining me hard.

He didn't mean to trick me. He just wanted to please me. That was all he'd ever wanted.

Diamond murmured, dark with desire, tonguing my nipples to desperate agony. "Mmm. So gorgeous on my cock. Love the way you beg."

"Not begging . . . oh. Oh, fuck. More. Please. Let me . . ."

He gasped in time with me, our hazy sighs melting into the night, and when another orgasm gathered and tightened inside me like a storm, I didn't care who saw us or heard me. He crushed me to him, his mouth both hungry and so tender on mine, and with my pleasure about to erupt in flames, I gasped and quivered and kissed him back like I never wanted him to let me go. Our senses mingled, brilliant fairy magic glittering in my eyes. His scent intoxicated me, his kisses drowning me in affection and emotion and closeness I'd never felt before.

Moonlight seared hot delight deep inside me, and I split apart, like lightning exploding in my sex, the thunder rippling outward, juddering along my limbs, tingling my scalp, stinging my palms, igniting delicious fire in my blood that burned on and on.

He came after me, gasping into our kiss, his last thrusts so deep, I quivered all over again. His cock swelled hot inside me, spilling his essence deep in my body, and our liquids mingled with a magical sparkle that I felt all the way to my heart.

For long seconds, I panted in his arms, limp, my limbs refusing to do anything but jibber in helpless pleasure. The air scented sweet and smoky with our sex. My skittering heartbeat matched his, a shared rhythm that throbbed through us as one.

His chest still heaved, his breath torn, his cock still hard inside me. He shifted against me, tweaking loose hair from my forehead with his sharp nose, fairy contentment burbling in his throat.

Summer breeze cradled us, filling my wings with warmth. My thoughts scattered in bliss. Like a dream, everything perfect and strange. Startlingly clear, his taste fresh like berries in my mouth, his skin a glowing caress on mine. Like I'd imagined us, a beautiful fantasy just the way I wanted it.

My blood jerked, fearful, and I kissed him again, and again, desperate, terrified he'd vanish. It wasn't real. Just some cruel trick of Famine's, and in a moment I'd wake up covered in blood and tears with all my raw emotion splattered on the air for him to drink. My lips bruised on his, and I whimpered, helpless.

"Shh. S'okay." Diamond folded me in his warm embrace. He soothed me with kisses, slowing and gentling his lips until I clung to him and buried my face in his chest with sobs cramping my throat.

He stroked my hair. I inhaled, wet. God, I was crying like a silly girl. He'd think he'd hurt me. That I didn't want it. That I'd insist it was all his fault, say *it was a mistake* like some haughty teasing bitch who can't make up her mind.

I sniffled, mortified. "Sorry. I just . . . shit."

But he only rubbed his cheek against the top of my head, holding me tight as we floated on hot summer currents between buildings. "Real, angel," he whispered, "it's real," and my fragile heart overflowed.

I wrapped him in my limbs, folding my wings around us as far as I could. His empathy, accident or not, tore my soul bleeding. I didn't want this to end. Didn't want to wake up and remember I was going to die, that I still had one more gemstone to go and this strange, sad, beautiful fairy boy, who delighted my body and tempted my heart stronger than any demon's ashen kiss, wasn't mine.

That he'd still use my blood to help that other girl. That no matter how she'd hurt him, he still wanted her more than he wanted me.

Nothing that happened tonight had changed anything. How could it? She was the girlfriend. I was just the whore. With her around, I'd never have his heart. This . . . thing between us, however rich and lovedrunk, was just a fleeting dream.

26

Diamond kissed me, bittersweet, and eased himself from my body, leaving me empty. He drifted us down on banking wings and landed us softly on his balcony with a glassy thunk.

It clanged like cold reality. I stepped back, my legs wobbling weak, and folded shy arms over my kiss-swollen breasts. My nakedness scorched me, raw under the moon. This wasn't dreamworld now. Surely now, he'd realize we couldn't do this anymore.

Diamond just gazed at me, his roseglow tinted golden with our pleasure, and his rubylit eyes burned.

My wingtips curled under the intimate heat of that gaze. Ideas smoldered there. Hot, breathless *oh god more* ideas. I swallowed. "Umm . . . can I have first shower?"

He nodded, silver glitter shedding from his hair, and glided a single roseglass claw along my collarbone, tempting. "Want some helping?"

My treacherous pulse throbbed. *Say yes. Take him. Make him yours. You're the whore, so act like one.*

I backed off, dizzy. "Uh. Nope. I'm fine." And I turned before he could mesmerize me with that devilpink smile, and darted inside to safe darkness.

* * *

Blindly, Diamond whirls and collides with the railing. His bones clang, glassy, and he stumbles gracelessly to his feet so he can kick it again, make it hurt more. But the pain doesn't feel good. It just hurts, raw and scarlet. Like inside.

Shoulda talkified. Shoulda said the words.

He's never been very good at talkstuff. Too many wordyjumbles, stutterfications, sounds colliding in his head that mean nothing. And the truth has always been glassy, to be smeared and foggified, tinted to his whim.

What wouldn't he give for one whisper of truthtalent now.

He doesn't want to look back for her. Doesn't want to remember the delicious madness of making love to her. But his bright glassfae sight seeks her out all by itself. She's in the darkened shower. Water spills down her skin, spraying her wings, sliding soap bubbles over her breasts and between her thighs. Her long scarlet lashes flutter closed, her slender throat tilting back, and it's all he can do to keep still.

Comfort her, kiss her hair, slide his arms around her, lift her naked body against him, ease her thighs apart . . .

Sweat trickles on his chest, and he looks away, spearing his gaze sharp over the darkened city. But it's no use. He can still feel her. Still taste her, lovely girljuice sweetifying his tongue, her soft hot mouth a delight. Her spicy nipples between his lips, springing hard, her slickwet cleft sliding hot on his cock, which even now aches and hardens just dreaming her.

But the most compelling memory is the achesharp pain in his heart.

Her hot green eyes dazzle him. Her toothy smile

stops his pulse. Her touch befuddles his senses and wobbles his legs weak. The rich purr of her voice makes him crave chocolate cake. And dreaming of her lying there in his bed, satisfaction wafting from her moon-dusky skin, fills him with delight and pride and honest-to-hell passion he can't explainify away as sparkle-fueled lust.

He rarely wants a girl more than one time. But he'd happily make love to Ember over and more and forever again. . . .

But she doesn't want to keep him. She's clearified that enough. Even though she'd said things that glittered warm over his heart like starshine. He wasn't empty. He wasn't broken. For a few crystalprecious minutes in her embrace, he'd believified.

Shit. He crunches clawsharp fists, and his palms split, lustgolden blood flowing. But that pain doesn't soothe either. His nerves still spike sharp, and he can't concentramate. All he can see is Ember, sugarcocoa-candy girl, the woman who cleans his spirit and overflows his heart, and he knows that this time, guilt isn't going to make him forgettify.

It's not just infatumation. Not just afterglow from insanely good sex. She's enchantified him, sure and dangerous as a faetainted hellbrew, and it's too late to spit it out. Loving Rosa hurt him like acid for so long. He doesn't remember it being like this, bone-shivering and painful and delici-yous to the point of delirium.

When Diamond falls, he falls hard.

And he just faceplanted the pavement like Wile E. Coyote from a thousand glorious, honey-scented feet.

Goddamn it.

He wants to laugh, somersault, dive on the air in glittering pink gladness and warble his exultation to the stars. Either that, or scream scarlet rage and clawify his eyeballs out. She's a delight. A temptation. A trap. Standing there in the shower with her pretty wings all mussed from their loving, her pulse throbbing slow and hot. He's lied to her. Used her trust against her. And it's too late to backtake.

Rosa's dirtysilver bracelet cackles in triumph on his wrist. The sharp points cut in, and bruises already dim his skin purple. The stone glows, violet evil-eye, and bright anger sprays along his nerves. He could free Ember from the demon's debt right now, if he could offget the damn bracelet. And if he wanted to die doing it. When she finds out he's had it all along, she'll never forgivify him.

He doesn't love Rosa anymore. His feelings for her were venomsick, destructive, a plea for punishment. He knows that now. *Stop trying to make up for it,* Ember said, and screw him with a cactus if her words hadn't laid him on his ass like a steelcored gutpunch.

Upmaking what he'd done was useless. Rewindifying fixed nothing. Time he started living his life in forward motion.

But his soul is shackled by this craftyvamp gift. If Ember is to live, Rosa must die. And if Rosa dies, so does he.

Why the hell would he give his life for a candycute girl he's only just met?

Because she's got her whole life in front of her, and you've already wastified yours.

Because you can't bear to see her cry, to watch the emerald hateflare in her eyes when she realizes you've betrayed her badder than she ever knowified.

Because you're already in love with her, you pissheaded glassfairy idiot.

He kicks the rail in a useless burst of anger, and glass clangs.

Love's no fucking use when you're dead.

I staggered into the bathroom, dizzy. Soft moonlight shone, his toxic scent lingering. I could still see my wet wing imprints on the dark tiles, a pinklit smear of my arousal where he'd licked me until I shuddered and broke apart for him.

I pushed the door shut and dashed under the shower, rubbing my arms and body and legs, letting the water splash over my wings, run in my hair, sudsing his woodfragrant soap between my legs to get his glorious smell off me. But it wouldn't budge. His pinkglitter fluid washed down my thighs and gurgled down the drain, and though nothing remained, the stain burned all the way to my core.

My own stupidity throbbed in my skull. Big Em's sarcastic scolding stabbed me like pins. *What were you thinking, Ember? To touch him like that? Let him touch you? So he's got a cute fairy ass and a big cock. He wants to feed you to a vampire, for fucksake. Just because Famine hurt your poor widdle feewings doesn't give you an excuse to act like a dickhead. So get over your stupid little crush and get on with the job.*

Embarrassment flushed me raw. Away from Diamond's hypnotic smile and tempting pink skin, it was a no-brainer.

The water trickled weak, its pressure almost exhausted without power. I stumbled out and dried off with a towel I found folded on the bathtub, trying not to imagine this fluffy purple cloth sliding over his chest, his muscled thighs, the hot skin of his cock. . . .

I bent over to dry my legs, and pain wrapped my

spine like evil flame. I grimaced and stretched, waiting for it to subside.

It did. But only a little.

My skin wormed cold. The fire in my bones was getting worse. Kane's deadline loomed inexorably closer.

I didn't have time to be precious or squeamish about how I got the last gemstone. I didn't have time for any of this.

Diamond could help me. But his help didn't come for free. Why should it? He didn't care for me, not really. Not beyond a few sweet caresses. And the last thing I needed right now was to owe him anything.

But guilt still chewed my nerves ragged. I'd known he wasn't mine. I'd used him, used his body and his desire for me to scrub away the memory of Famine's abuse. I hadn't meant it like that at the time. But that didn't make it right.

Even with the blessed delirium of loving him still afire in my blood, I couldn't help feeling like the dirty selfish tart who just screwed someone else's boyfriend.

I wrapped the towel under my aching wingjoints and around my body. My wet hair dripped in scarlet hanks. I tiptoed out, dreading the look in Diamond's eyes. Words tangled, an impenetrable jungle in my head, knotting my tongue sore. How could I explain? What could I say that wouldn't make him think I'd used and discarded him?

The kitchen benches gleamed, pale and warm, his green poison vial glittering at me from the breakfast bar, mocking. But Diamond wasn't inside. I could see his pink-rimmed shadow, still on the balcony, wingtips shimmering in the first light of dawn. He was already avoiding me, and my sated flesh ached in memory.

Stiffly, I walked up to the open door. He didn't turn.

Didn't acknowledge me. But he knew I was there. I could tell from the red flush in his wings. I swallowed, our future sour like ash in my mouth. *Keep it together. Don't give in to him.* "You know who she is, don't you? The bloodpetal girl?"

"Yes." His voice was soft, certain. "Her name is Rosa. Ember—"

"Okay," I interrupted before I could change my mind. "It's a deal. Help me get my gemstone, and then I'll help you free your girlfriend." My lips trembled, and I had to force the words out. "I . . . I think it's best we don't see each other anymore after this."

Still he didn't move.

"Did you hear me? I said I'll do it." Dread watered my limbs.

A scarlet ripple as he sighed and turned. "Look, you don't understandify—"

"Don't." I backed inside. If he touched me, I'd crumble. I stumbled over a pile of his stuff and fluttered. "You don't have to explain. I get it. I'm a big girl. You've got someone else and that's okay. I'm sorry I don't . . . that I'm not her."

He lighted after me, a spring of wings. "Don't want you to be her, Ember. Want you to be you."

I couldn't let him talk me out of it now. "Yeah, well. I'm me, all right. Watch me." I grabbed his glittering green vial from the bench, ripped out the cork, and upended the poison into my mouth.

It sparkled over my tongue, warm and numbing, and I swallowed, dark sweetness like syrup, until the vial was empty.

Diamond stared, his rosy face draining ashen.

My stomach frothed, and delicious hunger spread

through my limbs, sparking my nerves alive. "Holy shit," I gasped, thirst throbbing in my blood. "Thought you said this was vampire poison."

He flew to my side, easing the glass from my fingers and putting it aside, brushing hair from my sweating face. "What'd you do that for?"

I tried to shake him off. Too close. Too much. "I can handle it, okay? I'll poison Ange for you. I just want this to be over. I want my life back!"

"I know, angel." He gripped my shoulders, as if to force his words under my skin, deep into my body where I already wanted him too much. "I know. But I gotta tellify—"

"No." I jerked away, fevered, images of our love rippling rosy in my memory. My wet hair slicked my skin, a hot dark echo of his lips. "We've talked enough. Get off me—"

"Rosa is my girl, Ember."

Denial hardened like rock in my throat.

His wings flared golden with glittery despair. "My girl. Bloodpetal. They're the same person. This shiny on my wrist? It's her gemstone. She's bindicated me, just like Jasper did to you. If I rescue her, you die."

The truth dazzled me. He was bound to Rosa in ash and fire, like I was to Jasper. And he'd never told me. I staggered, blind, and a cruel whip of disdain lashed me wild.

I'd been such a fucking idiot.

How long had he known? All this time, he'd been using me to save her. And when he did, I'd die.

I hugged the towel tight to my body, shaking. I felt hollow. Empty. Like he'd sucked out my insides and left only my skin. Like only my falsebright shell remained, the Ember who smiled and flirted over her champagne glass while she was screaming inside, only the inside had melted away and nothing was left.

"You knew," I managed at last, dry like dead leaves in my throat. "You knew all along. You kissed me and held me and let me think . . . God, I'm so dumb. You *fucked* me when you knew you'd have to kill me?"

He flushed dark merlot, the color of vampire blood. Just like he had at Famine's. The winedark hue of guilt.

I laughed, crazy. "You know what? Everything Famine said about you is true, Diamond. You're dead inside."

"No. Once maybe. Not anymore. I feel. Because of you." He didn't drop his shimmergold gaze. Didn't let me look away.

"Screw you." But tears burned my throat, and I choked. Maybe it was just the moon, or that glittery green poison making me emotional, but I'd thought him as alone and lost as I. I'd thought he needed me to make him whole.

But he'd just needed me to die.

He swallowed, bright veins aglitter in his wings. "Look. Tonight's our chancy. Ange's place, some partyfication. He's trappified her there. We'll workem something, make her cut me free—"

"Yeah, right. And then what? You feed me to Kane and piss off into the sunset with her? Awesome. Thanks so much." I wrapped my towel tighter, scanning the messy floor for something I could wear. My fetish dress was in pieces. Jesus, I was stuck here naked. . . .

"No no. Can't doify. Not now never."

Laughter coated my throat with bile. "Oh, right. Like you give a shit what happens to me. Spare me your big bleeding heart."

"I don't. Care. About her. Anymore." He bit the words out slow, careful, like he fought to keep them in line, stop the syllables flowering. "I care about you."

The intensity in his gaze shivered my skin, and I shook it off. "Give me a break. What do you thin! just happened here? We screwed, okay? After what was maybe the shittiest night of my life, and not exactly a party for you either. I mean, wow, thanks for being there and everything? But now I'm supposed to believe you're all gooey and sentimental about me? I don't think so—"

"I think I'm in love with you, Ember."

My mouth opened, speechless.

For once, his gaze held no deceit. No lie. Nothing but determination and heat and glitterfire truth.

He didn't come closer. Didn't touch me. Just stood there and stripped me naked with his eyes. "You betterfy me, angel. I know that don't sayem lots, for a rotten heart like mine. But I'm peacified when I'm with you. You're wildsweet and precious and beautiful like . . . like sunshine, and you're so far above me that . . . I just want to deserve you. Let me try."

His scent washed over me, roses and glass, still spicy with a whiff of our pleasure, and with it came a glassy flash that paralyzed me. His talent, raw and bleeding with pain and confusion and secret golden wonder, and all my hard-won composure drained away like blood from an open wound.

My legs wobbled, and I righted myself on numb wings. It felt so real. He sounded so . . . sincere. He'd said everything I'd ever longed for, deep in my most secret places where I loathed myself.

And his fucking arrogance spiked cold fury into my bones.

Too good to be real. Too glassy perfect to be anything but a lie. And for a glorious, heartstopping moment, I'd fallen for it.

My chin trembled, and I pointed a shaking finger at him in accusation. "That is a low and dirty thing for you to say to me."

He stared, flooding crimson.

"I'm not an idiot, Diamond. You think I don't know how you've played me all along?"

"Angel—"

"Shut up." Viciously, I wiped my eyes, wet hair flying. "I don't mean just your lousy magic tricks, either, which oh by the way are getting *totally* obvious, so you can just give up if it's all the same to you, but Jasper probably told you all about me, didn't he? What makes me laugh, how he talks me around when I'm upset? What I like in bed? Jeez, I'm a gangland girlfriend, Diamond, I've seen it all. I've learned my lesson. I know when I'm being conned. Don't you *ever* say that to me again."

His lovely lips quivered, and he inhaled, wincing like I'd bruised him deep inside.

My eyes burned, but I swallowed on a lumpy ache, and kept it together. He deserved whatever I did to him. Too many lies loomed between us. Too late to kiss and make up.

Trouble shadowed his eyes violet. "At least let me helpify tonight."

Tonight. Yeah. My thoughts collided, dull. He needed me to poison Ange. And I still needed him to get my last gemstone, though I was damned if I could see how that'd work out. It wasn't like he could just take it off, not with his soul still chained to Rosa's and headed for hell.

Like it or not, we were stuck with each other.

Great.

My heart jittered. He was a lying asshole who'd betrayed me in the worst possible way. But that didn't mean I didn't ache for him. That I couldn't still feel his lips teasing my breasts to aching pleasure, his powerful heat as he thrust inside me, the desperate, dangerous thrill in my heart when we made love.

"Okay. Whatever. Just don't talk to me for a while, okay?" I fluttered to the bed and curled there, hot satin burning my cheek.

I closed my eyes in encroaching dawn, and darkness heaped dry and stifling like dirt. My skin still tingled with his lost touch. I wanted him here to hold me. I could still taste his rosedrenched kiss, feel his hot fairy caress on my body. I could get up, bring him inside, lay him down beside me. . . .

I sighed and rolled over. I needed rest. Long heat-soaked hours stretched until tonight. I'd never sleep.

But I did, and I dreamed of Famine, ripping my skin off with a sharp blade, peeling layer after layer in search of my heart, only to reach the center and find an empty space.

27

Early evening hung thick and scorching, no respite falling with the sunset, and the redbrick wall before us loomed tall and forbidding. My skin prickled with anxious sweat. Diamond pulled open a jasmine-draped wooden gate, and we walked in.

I sucked in a breath. Wow. Like a Tuscan palazzo, terracotta and cream stucco covering arched gables and balconies, a pergola draped in shiny vine leaves, red and black tiles tracing pathways through the torchlit garden. This house went on forever.

I stepped through the archway, heels clicking. Insects buzzed softly, moonlight shining down through tall hedges and walls covered in jasmine. At last the moon shone full, and excitement pierced my blood sharp. Only a few hours until perilune. I felt like a princess in a children's story, trapped in the magic garden to wait for my prince.

But my nerves snaked, and my skin was clammy. Tonight, I'd feed a vampire. And not just any vampire. Ange Valenti, Diamond's boss, old and cold and scary. But whatever. Vamps were all the same. All spellbound to dumb lust by my blood. I'd feed him. Distract him while Diamond rescued his girl. And then . . . what?

Doubt seared my heart like hellfire. Diamond had promised it was over between them, that he was doing this for me. That he'd make Rosa release him from the spell, and bring her gemstone to me.

I wanted to believe him.

But he hadn't said he'd kill her for me. I didn't know whether to be grateful or disappointed that I didn't inspire murder, and my confusion maddened me. Was he still hoping we could weasel out of this, do a deal with Kane, keep all our lives? Fat chance of that.

At least, he hadn't said he loved me again. He'd been cold, in fact. Distant. Avoiding conversation.

Probably for the best.

I'd dressed for the occasion, a long black evening dress in Chinese silk, with subtle cleavage and a halter neck that left my back bare. A slit up one side let my thigh peep out. I'd pinned my hair in a simple twist, and I wore a black evening bag with a slim strap to carry the gemstones in. Elegant. *Just be demure but sexy,* Diamond had advised. *He likifies that.* But discomfort wriggled under my skin, like the whole world stared at me.

Awesome. Dressing to please a hungry vampire ganglord. So much classier than dressing to please Jasper. I sure was moving up in the world.

Diamond walked beside me, silent, a hand's breadth away. Too close. Not close enough. He didn't look at me. He wore deep ocean blue, soft pants and a smooth sleeveless top that made my fingertips itch to touch, and like any cocky fairy show-off, he wore everything muscle-hugging tight. He'd coiled and plaited his shimmerglass hair like some weirdpink elfin warrior, and his wings gleamed iridescent like oilpolished glass. As usual he moved easily, graceful to a fault. Only his eyes betrayed his discomfort, burning a smoky purple that tingled my spine weak.

My belly warmed. He looked gorgeous, a smolder-ing roseglass prince, and no doubt he was doing it to make me miserable. Fine. He could be like that. Even if we got out of this alive, sex with him was a mistake. Obviously he knew it, too. End of story.

Not looking at each other, we walked under a jasmine-draped pergola into the garden.

Torches flared, replacing the dead electric bulbs that laced the trees surrounding the whitepaved patio. Tall ladies in glittering dresses, guys in suits or bright fairy colors, jewels and gold flashing under warm glam-ourbright haze. I recognized a few of Jasper's friends, a grinning blue boy who winked golden lashes at me, a skinny green spriggan with gold rings and a nasty grin. Drinks clinked and poured, bright music tin-kled, chatter and teasing and vibrant laughter. But it all seemed false, the smiles forced, the glittershine eyes just a little too bright.

My heart sank. I'd attended gang parties before, though never at Ange's house. Everyone so polite and nice to each other, swapping gifts, complimenting each other's girlfriends, fussing over gowns and jewels to make sure everyone saw how rich and successful they were. They'd all have pistols under their jackets, knives in their clutch bags, a mouth full of ego-bright fangs. In a few hours, everyone'd be off their faces on sparkle, and there'd be fights and pissing contests and hot fum-bling sex with strangers in the dark. Not for me, of course. But Jasper would punch at least one guy for looking at me the wrong way, and when we got home, he'd assume I wanted to sleep with him to say thank you, no matter how drunk or bipolar he was.

Only Jasper wasn't here.

My wings shivered, and I painted on a smile as I tucked one hand over Diamond's arm, clutching my bag tight with the other. I'd agreed to pretend to be with him. No one would ask questions that way, but it irked me rigid that they'd assume he'd picked me up in turn like a discarded paper cup. Did they even care that Jasper was dead? He'd put his ass on the line for them enough times to warrant at least a tear or two.

But as we threaded through the crowd, it was as if no one knew or cared. They all smiled at me, complimented my dress or my hair, sent Diamond a smirk or a dirty wink, made inane comments about the heat or obscure gang business I didn't understand.

Diamond slipped a champagne glass into my hand, bending close to whisper. "S'okay. Chillify."

But disgust flowered warm and salty in my mouth. I tried to cool myself down, but the moonlight and Diamond's fragrant muscled arm under my palm weren't helping. I wanted to flap my wings, punch someone, climb the flowering hedge and rain leaves and sticks down over all these liars.

We turned a corner, and Diamond pulled me close in the flowering hedge's shadow, his rich scent making my head swim. "Ember, I can't do this no more." He wrapped warm fingers around my wrist, and his voice chimed crystal with urgency. "Can't make silences when I want to scream. Kiss me." And his lips collided with mine, hot and heart-melting like all our kisses had been from the very beginning.

I gasped, my defenses dissolving in sweet delirium. He tilted my chin up with his thumb, deepening the kiss. His berry flavor unhinged my reason, and I leaned into him, tasting his lips, inhaling his gorgeous scent, his magnificent body a hot tease of desire against me.

Throbbing moonache scattered my thoughts useless. God, I wanted him to be mine. I wanted all this to go away.

He pulled back, breathless and glowing, his mouth still seeking mine like he couldn't let go. "Fuck, I wanna rip Ange's skin off for touchifying you and he ain't even done it yet."

"But . . . it's the only way." I leaned my head against his cheek, and my heart stumbled, lost. "Kane's deadline runs out in a few hours. I can do it. Ange doesn't scare me."

"Well, he should, angel." Diamond kissed my hair. His heartbeat thudded through me, comfort and restless longing. "He should. Fuck. I'm so sorry."

"It's okay." I closed my eyes, let his fragrant warmth envelop me, protect me. "None of this is your fault. I'll keep Ange occupied. You go find Rosa, make her undo that spell." If she could. If anyone could. And if Diamond wasn't deceiving me with one last, horrid trick.

I felt warm and safe in his arms. It couldn't be real. I didn't deserve it. Surely, this would turn out badly.

He held my face in his hands, caressing my cheekbones with light claws. "Swearify my life, Ember. I won't let him hurt you. I'll come for you. Trustify." And he dizzied me with one last kiss and pulled me around the corner into the light.

My vision blurred, vague images mingling of figures, faces, black suit, dark curls, flashing gold links.

Diamond's smile dazzled me, rich with deceit. "Hey, Ange. Nice party. I bringified you a gift. This is Ember."

I focused with a jolt, spilling my champagne.

My pulse trembled. Hulking shoulders in expensive couture, damp dark curls cut close, a darkly good-looking face and a fang-tipped smile.

And Angelo Valenti kissed my hand, gray eyes intense on mine. "My pleasure, miss."

My fingers burned icy like Jasper's ring. His lips were cold. So was his hand. Or maybe I was just too warm. I wanted to recoil. So he wasn't staring at my cleavage or checking out my ass like every other guy. I didn't care. His old-fashioned manners made me shiver, and the reality of what I'd volunteered for shook me cold. This was Angelo's house. His party, his sycophantic guests.

And his insatiable vampire appetite I was supposed to feed.

My stomach twisted. Not just some starved vampire kid with a hard-on who'd come in his jeans from a taste. Not even a virus-mad psychopath like Vincent DiLuca. At least with Vincent, it'd be over quickly.

But Ange Valenti, 350 years old with patience and savage hunger to match. I'd heard about Ange and his pleasures. He could make it last all night. And not in a good way.

Bile boiled in my throat, and I forced a smile. "I've heard a lot about you."

"And I haven't heard a thing about you, miss, which makes me wonder what other secrets your fairy boy's keeping." Ange's flat local Italian accent made him sound like a steroid-dumb muscle guy from Brunswick. I wasn't fooled for an instant.

"Nothing you need knowify." A dangerous undercurrent darkened Diamond's grin. "Don't break anything, okay? She's expensamive."

My nerves chilled. How could Ange not see Diamond's deceit? Or was I just spelled by Famine's ripping emotional torture to forever see nothing but the truth on Diamond's face? Either that, or Diamond truly became a different person with me.

You betterfy me, angel. I'm peacified when I'm with you. His words echoed in my mind, tart with desire and regret. We'd become so close so quickly, colliding in some beautiful, magical world where I felt like I'd known him forever.

But surely not. Magic didn't happen. I was just a bloodfae girl, and not a very bright one. I couldn't bring anyone peace. I didn't know him. We'd fucked. That was all.

Ange smiled tolerantly, his grip still possessive on my hand, and he spoke to Diamond but never shifted his gaze from mine. "Wouldn't dream of it. Did you fix up that vermin problem we talked about?"

"Not yet." Diamond shrugged, easy. "I'll get 'em for ya. No sweat. But I wanted to introducicate you two first. Show I'm meanifying well."

"Kid, you've outdone yourself. Go get a drink, have some fun. And don't p—Don't annoy Tony. He's got a real bug up his . . . well, ya know what I mean. Sorry, miss."

A homicidal vampire ganglord who didn't curse in front of girls. Cute. I affected a smile. "That's okay."

Ange crept cool fingers up to my wrist. My pulse jerked. I couldn't hide a gasp, and I saw his real smile for the first time. Cold. Slow. Hungry.

I swallowed, and fear swallowed with me.

Ange glanced slyly at Diamond. "Oh, and Rosa's here. Dying to catch up with you. Just keep your hands off, she ain't yours no more."

Diamond glanced at me, that hotpink gaze for once impenetrable. Then he flipped Ange a mock salute and a grin, and sauntered off.

And the most dangerous vampire in Melbourne pressed my hand once more to his lips, his gray eyes backlit with crimson anticipation. "Ember, is it?"

Ice brittled my spine. Diamond had left me. Whether he'd told me the truth about Rosa or not, I'd no one to rely on now. I didn't want to be afraid and alone.

But I was. No one could help me but me. And I should have realized that a long time ago.

My mind thrashed for an idea, a plan. Stall. Scream. Run.

But I couldn't run. Ange would never let me escape. All I could do was hope Diamond's vampire poison wasn't a lie.

I tried a smile. "That's me."

Ange stroked my cheek with a cold finger. Only it wasn't cold anymore, that calculated caress. It was warm. Flushed, with my pulse's trembling echo and a vampire's hateful lust.

I shivered, and sharp white teeth glinted in Ange's smile. "Well, Ember. How about we get to know each other?"

28

Diamond walks away, hot fairy anger afire in his veins, and it's all he can do not to whirl back to her and drag her to safety. He saw the ravenous delight in Ange's eyes. His glassfae sight sparked like electrificated wire with the hitch in Ange's pulse when the vampire inhaled her moonrich scent. Diamond's palms itch to clawify the virusrotten shitsmear's face off.

Ange fell for his Ember-trick without a blink. Too easy. Everything Diamond thought he wantified. But all he wants to do is dive back there and rip Ember away.

But he stills his shaking hands and strides through the crowd like nothing's amiss. Just stick to the plan.

Find Rosa while Ange is distracted. And make her reverse this stupid binding thingy. Make her give him his worthless soul back.

Because it's not Rosa's to keep. Not anymore. And then, he can get back to Ember, where he belongs.

Dying for her would be simply-snitch. Just hand the gemstone over, let Ember go, let Rosa's binding suck him down to hell. It can't be crappier than this. And facify facts. Diamond's led a rotten life. With or without Rosa's spellings, he'll likely end in hell one day anyway.

But he's always done the easy tricks. Walk away. Blame someone else. Never riskify.

Not this time. He doesn't want to die for Ember. Any useless creature can die. He wants to live for her. It's the only way he can prove he's worthy.

He scans the crowd for Rosa's darkflowing hair, his glasstalent piercing hedge and creeper-stained wall. Figures move in hot translucent darkness, torchlight boxed in an eerie cube where the walls should be. He hops around the dryparched fountain, scorched blossom bobbing dead at his feet. Nothing.

His eyes swivel towards the house, and a familiar spicy whiff quivers his nose alive.

In a dark flash, he dims before he darts through the crowd. A whipsprung hop and swoop, and he's scaled the balcony, lighting in a stucco archway's shadow. Rosa's sharp scent guides him, and he slashes the walls aside with faesight and searches with razoredged eyes.

There. A slim shape, huddled beside a shining steel bed frame. He yowls, fairybells echoing like sonar, and his directional sense plots a swift path of unresistificality that doesn't involve crashifying through walls.

Through the French doors he skips, fairy-light. Up a dim corridor and around a corner and he's in an opulent bedroom, moonlit from an open clerestory where the garden's jasmine fragrance spills in.

Rosa's slim body lies motionless by the bed, wrapped in a whitesatin robe, dark hair flowing free. He dives to her side, urgency silvering his veins. Finish this, get to Ember before Ange gets too far into it. "Rosa. Wake up."

She jerks, her voice stripped tense. "Diamond? Oh, thank god. Get me out of here." She scrambles to sit, and chain clanks, one ankle and one wrist bound to the curled iron bed frame.

Diamond's mouth sours. Her pretty leg's bruised, her hair all tanglified, fatigue circling dark under her eyes. Her wrists are slashed, half-healed fangmarks scabbing over, and when her robe slips off one creamy shoulder, it reveals more fresh bites.

He waits for scarlet rageflash, the cruel imperative to avenge, crush, kill.

It doesn't come.

Because she's not worth it. Do dealings with her and get back to Ember, where you belong.

Her hellbracelet bites into his wrist, and he swallows, tight. "Not so fast. Promise me first."

Her violet eyes—sure, right, how'd he forgettify?— her eyes darken with impatience. "Over on the dresser. The key. Quickly."

He stares her down. "Promise you'll unlock the shiny and let my soul go."

Rosa stares, broken. "What? I can't do that, Diamond. You know I can't! I'll go to hell if you—"

"You'll go there sooner if Ange deads you." He stares her down, cold. "Promise, or I swearify, I'll leave you to bleed."

"Please, Diamond, I'm begging you. . . ."

"No, Rosa." Tears. They used to hurt him. Now, he feels nothing but disgust. "You had your chancies to do this easy. You fucked it. Promise."

Rosa's mouth trembles. "Oh, god. I've seen that look in your eyes. You're in love with her, aren't you?"

Diamond laughs, crystalbright. "Don't pretendify it hurts. I know you don't give a fuck. But yeah. Meanifying, I don't give a fuck about you either. So promise, if you don't want me to deadify your lying ass right now."

She sobs and gives in. "Okay, okay. But promise you'll let me go if I do." For once, her gaze bears no deceit. Just empty despair. "Please. I know you've no reason to care. Just . . . don't let me die like this. Give me a chance to fight."

"No."

"Please! If we ever had anything, Diamond. Don't let me spend my last few hours chained to a bed."

Urgency itches under his claws, but warm compassion glimmers in his heart, too. He's too timeshort to argue. Rosa will drown in hellfire soon enough. And cruelties aren't his style, not these days. Let her see the stars before she dies. "Okay. I promise."

"Show me your arm."

He holds it out to her, impassive.

She rips her bracelet from his wrist. It tears free, ruby blood splattering her fingers. The gemstone flares scarlet with angry hellfire, and ash litters the floor. The spell's broken.

He flexes his forearm. It feels . . . different. Cooler. The tiny flame in his bones gone. Yes. "Now givify."

Trembling, she hands the bracelet over. He takes it. Sparks prickle his palm, but he holds it tightly.

He plucks the key from the polishwood table and unlocks Rosa's wrist shackle. Flesh squelches. He drops the bloody manacle, disgusted. Images flood of Ember, shuddering hot in Famine's dungeon, the tight metal unfolding from her soft bruised wrists. . . .

He gnashes angry teeth and bends for Rosa's ankle.

And swift like a serpent, Rosa dives for the empty shackle and locks it tight around his wrist.

For a dazzled moment, he's too slow to figure it out.

She snatches for the key. He jerks back, but the chain drags him up short, and she grabs his wrist and rips the key away with a laugh. She stands, and with a wrench of vampire-strong muscles, tears her ankle chain free.

Cruel disbelief rots his blood, and for a stunned second he closes his eyes.

One day, that bleeding heart's gonna get you killed. Goddamn it.

She rakes him raw with a cunning smile and rips the bracelet from his grip. "Thanks. You're so predictable. I like that about you."

He scrabbles for the key, but she's already tossed it out of reach. He yanks the chain and flexes his forearm hard, sweat springing, but the manacle won't budge. "You ungratefulicious cow."

She slips her robe back onto her shoulder, bloody marks already healing. "Hardly. It's your little blood-fairy bitch who's been hunting me and my friends down. With your help, I might add, and fuck you very much. So nice of you to bring her to me, and all her gemstones, too."

Useless fury ripples his muscles aglow, and he jerks on the chain but it won't come free. The bed's bolted to the floorboards. "She's worth a squillion of you, trash-bitch. If you hurt her—"

"Oh, I should think Ange is doing fine with that, don't you? What a thoughtful gift. Maybe I'll go have a taste. But he doesn't like to share. Hope she doesn't get broken." Her clever eyes narrow cruelly, her glint-white fangs mocking him.

His glassy wing panes crawl. Once, he'd thought her beautiful. "You inventified the whole thing, right. He's not hurting you."

"No more than I want him to, pet. And he's so much better at it than you ever were." Rosa leans over him, breasts swelling. "Still, you do smell good. Wonder what you taste like?" And she licks a scorching trail over his collarbone and sinks sharp teeth into his shoulder muscle.

Agony spikes. His wings jerk hard against the bedframe, but he can't escape. She sucks, blood forcing out through muscle and skin, and he grits aching teeth. Like white-hot blades in his flesh, and his blood screams afire.

He yanks her hair, strands ripping. But no use, until she groans and drags her head back, blood splashing gembright from her smile. "Ahh. Very nice. Fairy blood makes me horny. Want a quick one, for old times' sake?"

Diamond opens his mouth to tell her to go fuck herself.

"Enough of that." A shadow slips from darker shadows, and that flat lizard voice slides scaly on Diamond's skin.

Tony LaFaro caresses crusted yellow hands into Rosa's hair, his flatnosed face twisted with triumph.

She tilts her head back for his kiss. "Mmm. Don't be jealous, baby. He's all yours."

Diamond laughs, sick. "You've got to be shittifying me. You really will fuck anything."

Tony grins, and Rosa snakes forward and snarls, spitting lips an inch from Diamond's. "I do what I must to get ahead. Don't be so damn superior."

"Least I'm not whorifying my dignity away." But images flash of Ember, pretty skin slashed all over, her blood dripping jewelbright over vampire lips, and heat springs ugly beneath his skin. Whatever dignificality he had left, he's lost it now by letting Ember do this.

Rosa snaps at him, lashing his lips bright. "Like

you've never screwed your conscience blind to get what you wanted—"

"C'mon, kids, play nice." Tony drags her off, her dark hair flying. "Why don't you leave the grown-ups to talk, love?"

She tugs her robe straight with a scowl. "Fine. Think I'll go check on your fairytart girlfriend. She should be bleeding nicely by now." And she flounces out.

Diamond snarls and thrashes, aching, but it's tame compared to the chill in his heart. If Ember dies because of him . . .

Tony's grin spreads wider. A spring flicks in his hand, and a wickedsharp blade pops out, jagged edges glinting feral in the moonlight. "So pleased you could make it."

Not now, you sickity fuck. Not with Ember alone and bleedified.

Diamond swoops upward, wings flashing. But his chained wrist yanks tight, and he tumbles hard to the floor. His wingtips shatter, excruciating, but the pain just steels his nerves tighter. "Too scaredy-lizardfreak to fight fair? Let me free and I'll chew your scaly-ass throat out."

Delighted sweats glistens on Tony's flat yellow face. He bends closer, and the hot stink of sand and reptilian skin parches Diamond's tongue. "Think I'm stupid, fairyshit? Not likely. Anyway, I've got a friend who'd like to talk to you."

And a slim hard figure slinks from the shadows. Jeans and diamond earrings, wet hair in jagged silhouette, silverflash fangs.

Vincent DiLuca grins. "Surprise."

Diamond stares. The kid's clothes are smeared scarlet and blue, and his eyes gleam bloodshot, a crazyfied glint that outshines even his usual psycho glare. His hands shake, his fingers bitten raw. Whatever happenated him in Famine's dungeon, it wasn't pretty.

Tony cackles, delighted. "Ha ha. Amazing what you find lying around in Famine's trash. Thought you girls might like to talk. Go ahead, kill each other. I really don't give a fuck who wins." He slinks away, his dry lizard chuckle fading.

And Vincent licks spitslick teeth, and crouches on quivering thighs, one palm balanced on the floor. His voice scratches, ripped raw like he's been screaming. "I've had a really shitty night because of you. And I'm gonna make you bleed for it before you die."

Diamond yanks his chain harder, crushing his wrist. "Lizardboy's using you, DiLuca. Too shit-scared of Ange to do me himself. You really gonna kill me for his funnification?"

Vincent grins, hungry. "Nope. I'm gonna do it for mine. And when I'm done, I'll hunt down your little bloodfae bitch and eat her. If there's anything left."

Clarity dazzles Diamond like crystal. He's never cared too much about dying before. Always seemed inevitmable. But he never had anything to live for until now.

She'll never forgive him for betraying her. No matterficality. To keep her safe isn't dying for nothing.

But this is.

He crouches tense and ready, springing his claws tight with a crystalsharp crunch. "Bring it, fairybait. I'm gonna carve your throat out. Don't say I didn't warnify."

29

Ange held the door for me, and with chills jolting my spine rigid, I walked in.

Candlelight reflected on the white-framed windows, gloating over polished floorboards and smooth mahogany furniture. A bedroom, not a lounge, dark linen and cushions so the mess wouldn't show, framed modern art I didn't like on the creamy walls. Above, an electric chandelier hung dark. I wished it was on, even though the moon shone bright and crazy, thudding my pulse to madness. Warm perfume drifted, flowery and light, but it didn't fool me. I could still smell the blood.

The door clicked shut.

I tried to relax, but my body knotted tight. After Jasper, I'd vowed I'd never do this again. Yet here I was, whoring my blood on a fairy boy's say-so. I'd never learn.

I had to get out of here. I sidled backwards, gripping my bag tight in my lap. "Uh, I'm sorry. I've really gotta go—"

"Don't think so, love." Air rushed, and Ange was behind me, solid and immovable. I jumped forward, but he gripped my wrist with lightsteel fingers and tugged me back.

My pulse galloped, crazy. His casual strength made me shiver. I wasn't getting away. I'd just have to get it over with as quickly as I could. Hopefully, he'd choke on the poison and die, sooner rather than later.

Diamond will come for you, Ember. He said he would. Trustify.

Ange's warm fingers stroked the back of my neck, and I shivered. He didn't waste any time. I could feel him inhaling, tasting my scent, the shadow of his lips only a fraction from my skin. "You smell fantastic," he whispered, dark with promise.

He traced my wing's edge, and my membranes crawled hot. I wanted to scream, leap away, run. My mind clammered as fast as my pulse. What happened now? Did he expect me to sleep with him, or did he just want to eat? Was I supposed to participate? Fake it like a prostitute? Or just stand here and let him do what he liked?

Demure but sexy. Diamond's advice echoed. *He likifies that.*

I turned, no effort required to lower my gaze or let my lips tremble. "Do . . . do you really think so?"

He lifted my hand to sniff inside my wrist, the faintest of kisses breaking my skin out in bumps. "Love, I've lived a long time, and you are the sweetest thing I've met in years."

I forced a blush, moonblood heating my cheeks. "Oh, well, I'm sure I'm n— Oh!"

A tiny sting scraped my wrist. I jerked, mortified at the heat that flooded along my arm.

He held me, fingers like iron. "Shh. Quiet now. It'll hurt a little bit."

Blood beaded along the scratch, luminescent in hungry moonlight. His tongue dipped, lapping, and the sting deepened to a soft ache that tingled my fingers and crept slyly up to my elbow.

Horror oiled my throat, but the greedy moon cackled rich in my ears and wouldn't be silent.

No. I'm not listening. That didn't just feel good.

"Oh, that's superb." Ange closed his eyes on a slow sigh of desire. He kissed my wrist, teasing the thin skin with tempting fangs, and I quivered rigid with disgust and strange eagerness. No one ever did this to me before. They'd all just bitten me and sucked out what they wanted.

Was he actually trying to make it good for me?

Could it be good?

Moonfever bubbled in my blood, and my pulse skipped faster, harder, Diamond's poison tainting my wits with evil curiosity. I burned to know. I didn't care. I wanted to flee before I embarrassed myself. I wanted to stay here and let him do whatever he wanted.

Helpless, I tugged, trying to break free. But Ange held me, capturing my other arm as I fought, and before I knew it, my aching wings were pressed tight against a wall and I couldn't escape. His body held mine, hard and frightening.

And irresistibly, he bent my wrist back until the tendons pulled tight, and sank hot fangs into my skin.

His lips burned me, no longer cold but feverish. Softly my skin broke, a sparkling pain that deepened and spread as he forced slowly inside. My moonthick blood pulsed hot, eager, oozing fresh into his mouth. He closed his lips and sucked, not hard but tempting, his tongue caressing the blood as it spilled, and reckless compulsion stabbed me hard.

I sobbed and averted my face, loosened hair falling. The intimacy made me retch. It hurt. It felt disgusting.

But with the moon lurking fat and greedy overhead, that silverneon heat throbbing deep in my pulse, my blood ruled me. And my blood didn't care about the pain. It just wanted more. More sensation. More pleasure. More thrills. More.

Ange pulled back, licking the bright spill, and as his teeth slid out, my flesh cried. He nuzzled the bite, blood smearing on his lips. "You like that?"

"Uhh." I didn't trust myself to talk. The sight of my blood in his mouth flushed me rich with dirty desire, and acid sloshed in my throat.

He trailed hungry kisses up my forearm, and grazed hot teeth inside my elbow. A single blood-drop swelled, and he smeared it lightly, licking his lips. "How about we try a little more?"

I trembled. This was grotesque. And Ange had barely begun. He'd taken only a mouthful or two. If Diamond's poison was affecting him, he wasn't showing it. Maybe it was slow-acting. Maybe it just didn't work.

I swallowed, ashen, and forced a nervous smile. "Look, I really should be going. . . ."

Ange sucked a glowing ruby droplet from his lips, his eyes alight with hunger, and with a twitch of impossibly strong fingers he flipped me around so my breasts pressed into the wall.

He crushed me, his hard weight both threat and promise. His kisses on my shoulder made me quiver. "Honey," he whispered, his fangs a seductive graze on the back of my neck, "you're not going anywhere. I've got all night. And I'm gonna taste you all over—"

"Oh, Angelo, you're not starting without me?"

The voice slid in behind me, low and purring, female. I jerked, involuntarily pressing against Ange, and he bit my spine softly with a lustful snarl. Blood trickled down my bare back, and he licked it up, one long shivering caress up my spine. "Go away, Rosa. I'm busy."

My pulse leapt tight, and I forced my head to look.

Pale and slender in a white satin robe, syrupy dark hair flowing as she sauntered in with one hand cocked on a shapely hip. Perfume drifted, expensive and heady. Her violet gaze sparkled over me, fangs glinting in a red-lipped pout. "Don't be greedy. We can share. Diamond said I could have some."

Rosa flipped shiny silver over her fingers, and I recognized Diamond's bracelet. His blood crusted the edges, dried rosepetals. She brandished it before my eyes, and a jewel embedded in the silver flared, dancing with unholy scarlet fire.

My stomach hollowed cold. I'd always thought that flame was just a reflection from his luminous skin. But it wasn't. That was the gemstone. She'd taken it from him. I was screwed.

Or maybe he'd given it to her.

My reason juddered and broke under a blast of rage and denial. He'd betrayed me. Given me up for her. He'd lied to me, and yet again, I'd believed it for the sake of a few scorching kisses. Fuck, I was so dumb.

I wanted to wail my anguish to the hungry moon. Stupid bloodfae whore, thinking I was worth something. Even to a cruel-hearted glassfairy gangboy with shit for a conscience.

I'd never learn.

Rosa wrapped her hand around my bag's strap and ripped it away from me. All the gemstones, hers. Except for the one screeching frosty laughter on my finger.

My mouth trembled, treachery souring my tongue.

She was beautiful. More beautiful than I. No wonder Diamond wanted her. Her eyes' cruel glint made me shiver, even in a vampire's embrace. They were welcome to each other.

But still my heart scorched like acid that he'd choose a rapacious bloodsucker bitch over me.

Maybe a taste of poison would do her good. If it was even real.

Or I could tell Ange the truth.

My skin tightened. Tell him I was poison. Tell him Diamond was trying to kill him. Maybe, Ange would let me go. I had nothing against him. Why not?

Sure. Because vampire gangsters were notoriously forgiving. He'd just break my neck, and then he'd kill Diamond, too.

Yeah? So? What did I care? Diamond had betrayed me.

But my veins spiked warm with denial and sparkling fear, and I realized I didn't want him dead.

I shivered, heartsore. God help me, but I still felt something for him. Deep in my shattered soul, where for a few precious moments in his embrace, I'd gazed into the mirror and hadn't loathed what I saw.

For that, I owed him something, however small and futile.

My determination firmed. My life had been so pointless, a tawdry scrap for affection I couldn't win and meaning that just wasn't there. So if I had to die with my soul trapped in a cursed gem, let it be for a purpose.

To kill this evil, toxic woman who'd crippled Diamond's heart. To set him free.

If I can feed one sick vampire maniac, I can surely feed two. Let them both drink the poison, and good riddance.

I arched back against Ange, moonflushed desire mixing flame into my blood. "I don't mind sharing if you don't."

Ange slid warm palms over my wings, sniffing my damp scent with a sigh. "Maybe when I've finished. Till then you can watch, Ro. You like to watch, don't you?"

Rosa chuckled, hideous, and settled herself elegantly in a plush dark armchair. "You know I do."

My halter neck popped open in his fingers, and he pulled me from the wall and stripped my dress down to my hips, unzipping me to let it fall to the floor. I could feel Rosa's gaze sliding over me, calculating, and somehow it was worse than Angelo's hungry stare. The hot moonlit air stroked my breasts, pulling my nipples tight, and I shivered with anticipation and disgust. Wetness slicked between my legs, hot and horrid. If he touched me there—god, if he bit me there—I'd scream.

But I couldn't help wondering. What would it feel like when he finally lost his patience? Hard and fast and painful like the others? Or . . . something different?

Ange lifted me in his arms, light as a cloud, and when he dropped me softly on the bed and started brushing hot wet lips over my ankle, my body shuddered in confusion and delight.

Moonlight shone full and hot onto the bed, caressing me wild. My veins pulsed hard under his kiss. My legs slipped apart, honey fragrance erupting, and my spine arched on curling wings, willing him closer.

Delirium throbbed through my body, awakening vile desire. I wanted this monster to drink me. I wanted him to go down on me. I wanted to claw his eyeballs out and run shrieking, find Diamond and cling to him in warm rosescented safety and never let him go.

Or slap his arrogant roseglass face and fly away.

I didn't know what I wanted.

I just squeezed my eyes shut and waited for the sting.

30

My cheek prickled hot, and I jerked awake.

Violet eyes stared at me coldly, and rich perfume made me retch. Another slap, throwing my head back. "Wake up, bitch."

I cursed and shook myself, and hair tumbled wet in my face. Hot glare blinded me. I hooked up a hand to drag my hair aside, but something rough and tight held me back.

I jerked my arms again, and looked down.

Rope. Thick and wrapped twice, cutting into my bitten forearms. I kicked my ankles. Same. My wings crushed behind me, the ends jammed under my butt against hard wood.

Tied to a chair. Naked, except for a familiar blood-stained white robe. And scarlet cuts slashed my body everywhere, blood seeping from my legs, my arms, my torso. I hurt all over, my skin raw, and my head ached dizzy like I'd slept too long in the sun.

I struggled and cursed, and memory flooded in. Hot delirium, the slick slide of blood, teeth hard and rapacious in my skin. Ange had taken his own sweet time with me, and with the moon playing its lustful tricks with my desire, pain had contorted darkly with pleasure until I didn't know one from the other. I'd screamed, moaned, thrashed as he and Rosa swallowed blood from every part of my body. Excruciating, luscious and prolonged, until I'd finally slipped into welcome blackness. And now they'd tied me to a chair in some dirty basement, boxes and piles of junk and dust creeping in the corners.

My wounds crawled and squished, the dying virus in their spit already doing its healing work. I hissed at Rosa, baring angry teeth. I hoped Diamond's poison killed her quickly. "You've taken what you wanted, you greedy whore. Let me go."

Rosa grinned, her creamy skin flushed with satisfaction. She'd showered and put on a shimmering blue gown. An oil lamp burned on a dusty table, orange flame wavering. She dragged my head back and forced a cup of tepid water to my lips. "Drink. Can't have you dying on me yet."

My head wobbled dangerously, and thirst parched my throat. I wanted to spit in her face. But I wanted the water more. I gulped, liquid spilling over my chin. It tasted like dirt.

"That's enough." Rosa tossed the cup away and gave a wet, hacking cough. She wiped her mouth swiftly, but not before I saw the dark smear.

My smile tweaked. I'd expected something more dramatic. But maybe the poison was working after all.

She waved my bag before my nose, taunting me as she tucked Diamond's silver bracelet into it and snapped it closed. "Thought yourself pretty clever, didn't you? Stealing all those gemstones. Quite the master thief."

She cleared her throat again, and I glared. *Cough until you choke.* "Screw you."

She slapped me again, slamming my head back. "Shut

up, fairyblood. The gemstone's mine now. You can keep yours, if you like. It doesn't matter." She leaned in, her smile cruel and fragrant with my blood. "Because I don't owe Kane! I don't need to beg for my life with him like you do. All I care about is making sure you never come after me again."

I swallowed hacking laughter. I'd met Kane, and I didn't like Rosa's chances of getting away scot-free. She was welcome to him.

Strange calm settled me. I'd already been bitten so many times. At least this time it'd be quick. "You talk too much. Just kill me and get it over with."

"All in good time." She plucked a plastic packet from the table and popped it open.

Bugs jittered under my skin. A syringe? What the hell? Truth serum? Drain cleaner? A deathsparkle hit?

She flicked the plastic cap, and the needle glittered sharp. I shrank, my pulse gibbering. But she pumped her fist and jabbed the needle deep into her own bulging vein.

Thick vampire blood leaked into the fat plastic tube, rich like raspberry syrup. She gritted her teeth, breath short, and held on until it was full. And then she pulled it out, a tiny red bead glimmering on the needle's tip, and stepped toward me.

I thrashed, but the chair was too heavy. I couldn't move.

Rosa grabbed my bulging arm and shoved the needle deep into the crease of my elbow.

Pain spiked. I yelled. She pushed the plunger, and hot vampire blood surged into my vein.

Horror pierced my burning bones. They'd kept away from my mouth earlier. I hadn't swallowed any, at least not much, and it took a lot to get you infected that way.

But now she'd squirted the vampire virus deep into my blood.

That needle was fat and full. More than enough to infect me. Already, fever munched my blood, attacking my cells, pumping to every part of my body. And soon I'd be mad and ravenous like Vincent, no control, no care. Nothing would matter but insatiable hunger for blood.

And if the hunger didn't finish me, Diamond's poison would. Surely no longer immune, not with the blood-fever burning in my veins.

A scream scraped my parched lungs, and I let it free.

Rosa just laughed, tossing the syringe away. "Diamond is gonna love this. His pretty new girl, a vampire. Just like old times . . . Oh, wait. I gave him to LaFaro to play with after I took my gemstone. He's probably already dead! Never mind. I honestly believe it's the thought that counts, don't you?"

I yelled, bloody sweat springing on my skin. He hadn't lied. He was true to me. Rosa had tricked us both, and in spite of everything, my bones ached in sympathy with my lurid fairy prince's broken heart.

Anguish ripped me raw. He hadn't betrayed me. I knew that now. Maybe he'd even meant it when he said he loved me. Either way, I didn't have an excuse to push him away any longer, and it delighted and terrified me at the same time.

I wanted to claw Rosa's smug face off for hurting him. To be with him, to wrap him in my arms and kiss him and promise it'd be okay. I wanted to curl up in the warm glassy shadow of his wings and drift away.

But too late. Rosa had probably already killed him.

My heart swelled tight. I wished I could grab the hours we'd spent together and bottle them so they'd never be lost. Even the bright torture of Famine's dungeon seemed a treasure. Diamond had seen the abject depths of my soul there. He'd come face-to-face with the darkest, most rotten part of me, and he hadn't turned away.

I couldn't wipe him from my thoughts. His eyes, his crystal laugh, the strange bliss of his touch. I needed him with me. I felt safe in his embrace. Without him, it all seemed pointless. Jesus, was I in love?

I felt like howling. Why did this have to happen now? With the moon and vampire hunger raging in my blood and hell only a few hours from claiming my soul?

But I'd known what I was in for. I'd had my chances to leave him, forget him, push him away. If I'd fallen for him, I had only myself to blame.

Rosa clicked her tongue, stifling a cough. "Wouldn't waste your energy, pet. You'll get quite hungry very soon. Pity you won't be able to get out." Her beautiful face hardened. "Stay here and starve, bitch. And when you die, that pretty ring will drag you to hell and you'll burn forever. Good fucking riddance."

She flipped me a wave and sauntered out, slamming the rough wooden door. Metal clanked as the bolt drove home.

I wriggled and yelled, but the rope wouldn't give. I was trapped.

The oil lamp flickered and puffed out.

Leaving me in stifling hot darkness, with hellscorched bones and sickdirty fever already simmering in my veins.

31

Diamond grips a jagged shard of his own broken wing-glass, and jams it with a rotting rip into Vincent's throat.

Vincent chokes, blood frothing scarlet. Diamond twists the glass, hacking it deeper. Razor edges slice his palm. "Toldified ya, shithead."

The vampire jerks between Diamond's thighs, but the fairy holds him down grimly with bloodsoaked hands and tears the glass free.

Vincent slumps, bloodshot eyes fluttering. Rich arterial blood gushes from his throat, spreading in a bright red puddle on the floor.

He's not moving.

Diamond lets the glass drop from numbcut fingers, and collapses, oozing blood and exhaustion.

Seems like hours he and Vincent fought, metal slashing, claws raking, the iron manacle hacking into his wrist. His skin is torn, his wings cracked, his shirt fangslashed away. His shackled arm aches, hyperextendified from dodging Vincent's fangs. In a delirious haze, he slams his shoulder into the floor over and again, until the bastard pops back in and he yowls in bonegrating torture.

Panting, he drags himself to hands and knees. Blood

puddles on the floor beneath him, blue with fatigue from what seems like a thousand screaming cuts. His wings ache, edges splintercated sharp. He wants to curl on the floor and sleep forever.

But urgency scrabbles holes in his skin. Long time since Ember went with Angelo. She could be dead already. Could be unconscious, alone, bleedifying out slowly. . . .

He drags his bruised forearm into the light. Chain rattles, dripping blue and yellow. Key's lostified, gone with Rosa. But he has to get out.

The manacle is misshapen, metalstrip curled from stress. A smidgin bigger than before.

Fuck. This is gonna hurt.

He squeezes his eyes shut and slams the heel of his hand down on the iron bedstead.

Hollowglass bone cracks, a spike of red-hot bad.

Diamond yelps, his thumb crumpling, and he squeezes his hand from the manacle before it unhurtifies. Bone heals faster in the heat. It'll get better. Forgettify.

He lurches up on chipped wings, crunches on his wavering faesight, and staggers out.

Corridors wobble and dissolve, bright outlines glaring golden. Ember's echo is everywhere, screaming like a curse, a ripe accusation bleeding scarlet down the walls. He tumbles down curved white stairs from the mezzanine into the entrance hall. Out in the garden, spectral guests still laughymingle, glasses and jewels edged in fiery purple. Moonlight pours in the top-story windows to light his way, and the moon's perilously close to full.

He follows her scent's bright scarlet twist, curling

smoke from a lost candle, and it leads him deeper, darker, into the bowels of the old house where his skin creeps and strange smells twinge his nose in corridors undisturbed in a long time. Heat swallows him, sucking his breath tight. His glow flickers bloodstains on the cream-papered walls, his shadow leaping like a ghost.

A scream pierces the air, needlesharp.

His ears prickle in agony, and his skin ripples scarlet. They're torturing her. It's Famine's dungeon all over again. This time, let him not be too late.

He skids around a corner, the sound still scraping his heart raw, and another scent slicks his tongue like grease.

Perfume, delicate and expensive, the hot splash of spice.

He stumbles down one last hidden stairwell. Glowing shapes mingle and confuse. At the bottom a door stands bolted, and the timber rattles with a brittle fairy scream.

His wings flare, ready to jump, slash, fight. Last night, he almost got his head slicified, leaping in fastways.

Lesson learnified?

Hell, no.

He blasts the bolt off with a vicious bloodspattered kick and dives in headfirst.

The door imploded, wood splintering, and Diamond crashed through in a hail of blood and glitter.

My fairy was alive. And he'd come for me after all.

But I barely heard it above my shrieking ears. My throbbing veins. The awful gnawing hunger. The vampire virus had me in its jaws, and it was ravenous. Unless I drank blood real soon, my insides would melt with fever and I'd die screaming. But the virus didn't want to die. It wanted to feed, and its rampant thirst consumed me.

Light slashed my eyes raw. Fever shivered me rigid, and I strained against my ropes. Sweat streamed off me, precious moisture I couldn't afford to lose. My skin swelled clammy. My hair plastered my shoulders, unbearably hot.

Already fresh sharp teeth slashed through my gums, ravenous, and my mouth streamed with hungry spit and blood. The bloodfever had gobbled me up frighteningly fast. Maybe because Rosa's vampire blood was already mixed with mine. Maybe the full moon. Maybe blood-fae essence and the virus played hard. I didn't care. I just wanted it to end.

Diamond scrambled to his knees at my feet, lumi-nous. Shirtless again, muscles quivering tight with fa-tigue, his sweat-slick skin slashed blue and scarlet in a hundred places, sliding wet with lusty fairy blood.

And the virus's delirious urge to survive seized my brain with famished claws.

Spit splashed down my chin. My hands quivered in talons, and the rope bit into my arms as I struggled to be free. I had to eat. Now.

He spoke soft and swiftly, bleeding fingers work-ing at my ropes. "Ember, it's me. You're okay. Let's get outta here."

His dusky crystal voice sparkled dark desire in my flesh. His bloodstained scent inflamed me, running on my tongue, his skin's rosepetal flavor blotting my mind with lust. Kiss him, take him in my mouth, taste his pulse throbbing under my tongue. My gaze zoomed in on his throat, just above his collarbone where the vein swelled, and his heartbeat drowned my ears wild.

I wanted to suck him dry. Fling him down and sink my teeth into him, tear his skin open and let the blood flow, swallow and swallow and swallow. . . .

A dying animal's howl pierced the air, and I realized it was me.

"Hushify, angel. S'okay." My ropes swelled tight with sweat and blood, and his murmur twinged with frustration as he couldn't get me undone. He hadn't seen it. Didn't know what I was.

His breath's tiny caress tortured my skin raw. I screeched, terror clawing me bloody inside. "Go 'way! Please. Don't set me free." I lisped, my new teeth slashing my lips, and blood spurted onto his fingers.

His gold-flashed gaze jerked up, and he stared at me, his face paling pink.

I sobbed, thrashing my head aside. He'd seen my deepest shame at Famine's, and he hadn't deserted me. He'd nurtured a flame inside me I'd barely known was still alight. I couldn't bear his disgust, not now. But I'd become the thing he despised most. The monster we both hated, the thing that had ruined his life and made a fearful misery of mine.

But he wrapped strong arms around me, and his whisper broke with sorrow and rage. "Ohmygod, Ember. This is all my bad. I was stupid, I couldn't . . . Fuck. I'm so sorry."

His hot body made my skin scream. His hair brushed my face, tempting me to touch, bite, devour. His blood-scent maddened me beyond sense. Hunger shrieked and cackled inside me, tainted rich like moonshine but a thousand times worse.

I couldn't help it. I couldn't stop myself. I dragged my tongue up his knife-slashed cheek.

Bright fairy blood tingled on my tongue, and my

nipples jerked tight. My sex flowered hot and wet, deepest pleasure stirring inside.

I moaned and licked again, arousal hacking my nerves to a ragged mess. Disgust skewered me on a hot iron needle, but I couldn't stop. I wanted my mouth full of him, dripping with him, swallowing him. "God, get away from me. I'm so hungry. I can't . . ."

But I didn't mean any of it.

He pulled back, gripping my head in his hands, and planted a kiss on my mouth.

Deep, hot, fleshscented. His lips slid wet on mine, swollen with desire. The inside of his mouth was so slick and hot. I groaned when his tongue met mine, and helplessly I bit down.

Blood burst into my mouth. Thick, delicious, tingling with life. I swallowed, desperate with longing, and the sparkling fluid spilled down my throat.

Oh, god. It was like sex, the pleasure flowering deep inside me. Was this what it was like for them, tasting me? My body swooned, the ache deepening, intensifying. Hunger tingled inside me, stroking me to shivering fire . . .

He pulled back, his breath ragged, and tugged harder at my ropes.

I choked, my mouth sticky. I wanted to lunge for him. I wanted to hide my face forever. "What you doing?"

"You'll die if you don't eat." He yanked my ankles free, tossing the rope aside.

Dismay threaded my veins with hot wire, and I wriggled, trying to get away even as the hunger thrust my snapping teeth forward, frantic to reach him. "No. Don't! I can't stop. I'll hurt you—"

He scraped my hair back and pressed his forehead to mine. "Don't care. Love you, Ember. Takify."

I strained to bite at his wrists, desperate, even as I sobbed, tears a fresh fever on my face. "But—"

"Takify. Drink me. I'm yours." And he slashed my rope one final time, shredding it with bloody glass claws, and I was free.

Insane lust jabbed my muscles aflame, and I burst from the chair and dived for him.

We fell to the floor, thrashing wings and sweat and blood. His hot skin slicked on mine, but it wasn't enough. I tore my robe aside to rub myself naked on him, thrusting his thigh between mine where I was wet. God, he was hard, his swollen cock pushing against my leg, and my breath rasped faster. He was already bleeding, and it tingled my skin all over like hot kisses. His glorious rosy scent scorched deep inside me. I grabbed his hair and dragged his head back. The glassy fibers slid a silken caress around my fist, every sensation a torture of pleasure. He didn't fight me. Just exposed his throat, strong and beautiful, the veins pulsing and glowing with hot fairy desire.

My wings trembled, afire. Hunger rushed my blood burning, and I bared my infant fangs and struck.

Flesh crunched, and my teeth forced in. He bit back a yowl, shuddering beneath me, and I shuddered, too, the sensation overwhelming, his skin's delicate pop in my mouth almost too much to endure. He gripped my waist, yanking me closer. Unbearable sweetness twinged my tongue, and I bit harder, urgent, digging for the vein.

At last, it broke. Blood exploded in my mouth, hot and bubbling and glorious. I groaned. So delicious. I swallowed, dragging him into me, filling me with him. Blood spilled sticky over my chin. I didn't care. My body tingled alive with thirst. I sucked harder, and this time it flowed easier, pulsing in time with my heartbeat, all resistance gone.

Delirium throttled me. This rich intimacy of feeding made me ache inside. It was like joining, melting together, an endless mingling of blood and flesh and heart that stripped my fear away, and hunger's rich madness drowned me.

Eager, I crunched my teeth harder, drinking him in. Diamond growled, in delight or agony. "Yes, Ember. Drink me."

His heartbeat throbbed in my mouth, swift and strong. He reached between my thighs to caress me, and I gasped as he touched hot wetness. He found my pleasure easily, stroking my secret places, and my nerves cried out in delight.

I murmured, blood splashing in my haste. His touch vanished for a moment, and I whimpered, lapping desperately at his throat while he shifted underneath me, and then his hot naked cock pressed hungrily between my legs and I bore down.

He thrust into me, hard and deep, and we both cried out. Now he really filled me, blood and body, and frantically I sank my teeth into the wound again, seeking more, harder, hotter. Blood pushed into me, too, like our sex. His pulse drove stronger with his pleasure, sparkling the luminous fluid with life. I moved my hips, and he rose to meet me, forcing me down harder, impaling me deeper. My claws scrabbled helpless at the floor, it felt so good.

I sucked and swallowed, his bright fairy blood washing down my throat. The intimacy swelled like moonshine on my heart. I felt so close, his skin sticking to mine in a hot glow, his hair in my face, his skin in my mouth, his heartbeat echoing through my veins, the delicious friction of his cock deep inside me. He groaned my name, and it vibrated through my lungs, my breasts, into my blood, down between my legs where I shuddered and swelled, tension throbbing tight.

This was home. This was love. And I'd consume it all.

He thrust harder, and I felt him start to come, his flesh throbbing in mine, pressing on delicious places that made me moan. I drove my teeth deeper, swallowed him with mouth and sex, dragging him into me. He gasped and let go, his fluid sparkling into me. His blood pulsed hard and fast into my mouth, salty with his pleasure. I cried out with my mouth full as I broke apart.

Fast, hard, the intensity whiplashing my spine. Tension exploded like fireworks in my belly. My limbs melted hot, unbearable delight, and my muscles milked the last drop of his pleasure while his blood still gushed down my throat.

I swallowed and groaned, hot fluid spilling, never wanting it to stop. Emotions dizzied me, a heady mixture of terror and delight. Before, I hadn't believed him when he said he loved me. But now I could taste it, shimmering like flame on his blood, and it felt so good inside me, I wanted it all. I'd swallow him whole if I could, keep drinking until there was nothing left.

Beneath me Diamond groaned and shifted, weak. His chest heaved swift and shallow. His pulse thrummed on my tongue like a hummingbird's, and the bright magenta glow of pleasure in his wings dimmed.

I pulled back, panting, my body sated but virus-mad hunger still chewing inside. The rubyhot blood leaking from the wound I'd made in his throat mesmerized me. It pulsed luminous over his skin, pooling in his collarbone's hollow, trickling over his chest, drop by glowing drop. . . .

But I couldn't. I was killing him.

My stomach gurgled, stuffed with blood, but already the burning essence filtered through my strange new digestive system. Soon, I'd be ready for more. And the hunger raked my skin like claws, demanding, begging, screaming at me to feed.

He smiled, breathless, and even though his glitter had faded, his beauty still tore my heart. "S'okay," he murmured, licking his lips. "More."

"No." I buried my face in his wetstained hair, sobs crippling my chest. His scent watered my mouth. His blood still stained my lips. "God, I'm sorry. I didn't mean—"

"Don't cry. S'okay. Moon's nearly full, candy. Better go gemmify." And feebly he pushed me away.

My nerves screamed, jagged. This wasn't fair. We'd known each other for two short days, and already I was thinking about forever. I should be running away as fast as my wings would fly.

But I didn't care. Our closeness crippled me. His reluctant honesty stripped me raw. The way our bodies sang together made me weep with loss.

And now I'd eaten him like a beast without care or conscience. Taken my pleasure from his body and left him empty, just like Jasper and Angelo and all those men I hated had done to me.

My heart howled in agony, and I clutched at him, kissing his cooling lips, wishing with every glamour-spelled cell of my body I could undo what I'd done.

But I couldn't put the blood back in. I couldn't re-light that fading rosepink glow in his wings. I couldn't repair that aching sore in my heart.

He kissed me back, weak and warm. "Go, angel. You're strong now. Gettem gems from Rosa, come back for me."

"I can't! What if you—?" I choked on tears. I couldn't say it.

"Without another kiss? Get real." Laughter wheezed in his throat, and he pushed me away, coughing. "Go on. Save it. Gettin' all tearyfied here."

I swallowed, and caressed his face one more time, his skin so smooth and warm under my fingers. His fading ruby gaze locked on mine, and my heart lurched. So much I wanted to say. So much he deserved to hear.

But I couldn't think of a single word.

Blindly, I stood and stumbled out.

Her footsteps fade, and at last, Diamond lets his eyelids flutter closed.

A breathless smile aches. Simply-snitch, in the end, to die for her.

It's weird. He's always spitfired rage at death, unwilling to let go and get what he deservamates. Done any shitty thing to stay kicking.

But with Ember sobbing in his embrace, dirtyfever burning her life away, nothing ever came more easyfied. His life did her no good. This be the next bestest thing. At least now, she's got a chance.

Hs heartbeat stirs, sluggish. He's bleedifying, the hot liquid spilling ever more weakly from his throat. He's so cold. Numb. He should lift his hand, stop the leakification.

But he doesn't. Weakwater floods his muscles. He pictures her, the fiery glory of her hair, the emerald lifelight in her eyes, and his slowing heart warms with a glimmer of pride. His lady makes a beautiful vampire.

But still his throat swells tight, and tears spill hot on his cheeks. They had such a short time.

Strange. He doesn't cry, not him.

Sounds ghost distant, and fade to nothing. Blackness seeps thick. He breathes and chokes. No fair. He can't smell her anymore. He wants to smell her. Taste her. Sleep in her candysweet embrace forever.

But she's gone.

He lets go, and drifts, waiting for hell.

32

I reeled into the corridor, my feet sliding numb. Hot air swirled, rich with vile bloodstink. Heartbeats addled my newly sharp ears, mixing into a fierce drumbeat. I weaved toward the sound. My stomach lurched, sick, all that blood oozing into my virusparched body. Already, fresh hunger chewed in there, a rabid beast I couldn't chain.

Light dazzled my eyes, the moon glaring brighter and brighter through the open clerestory. I stumbled on, dragging my robe around me. I had to find Rosa, give myself one last shot at Kane's prize. Otherwise I'd have killed Diamond for nothing.

I couldn't give up and die now.

Unsteady, I walked out, beneath the tiled archway into the garden. Heat tore my breath away. Moonshine blazed on my skin like silver sunburn, and conflicting tides struggled for supremacy in my blood. I wanted to dance under the moon with wings afire, curl my spine back and howl, grab the nearest boy and rub our naked bodies together until we melted. I wanted to dive on the nearest party guest and rip her pulsing throat out with my teeth.

I wobbled among jasmine hedges and wilting flower

beds, sniffing the crowd with my alarming new sense of smell for Rosa's perfume. My shadow made a small dark ring around my feet as the moon strove higher, and the hellborn ache in my bones scorched hotter than ever. Scents washed over me, a fleshstinking rainbow, blood and skin and hair, the heady ache of alcohol and rich food. A green fairy in shiny purple silk stared at me, her slanted yellow eyes rounded in shock. A sniggering brown spriggan with wirebrush black hair and a potbelly did the same, his beer glass halting halfway to his pointy-toothed mouth.

I lifted my chin high, defiant. I supposed I wasn't exactly dressed for this occasion, in a stained white robe to midthigh and covered in glowing glassfae blood. At least my wounds had healed, a lucky side-effect of the vampire virus. Awesome.

Hot fingers wrapped my wrist and yanked me off balance.

I thudded sideways into the white concrete fountain. My wing scraped the wall, ripping, and my nose stung with that hateful dark perfume.

Rosa snarled, jabbing her long nails into my throat. Her eyes gleamed sickly, her skin clammy with evil sweat. Poisoned. At least, I'd gotten that right. "Get away, did you, slut? Too bad I found you. What did you do to me?"

My vampire hunger yowled like a fighting cat, aroused, but my belly crunched tight with stupid fairy fear. I choked and scrabbled for her wrist, knowing it was useless.

But she cursed, and in my fist her grip broke.

Fresh vampire power sizzled though my muscles, and delight burned my skin. I was stronger now. She was weak from the toxic blood she'd sucked from me.

And my strength would only increase the longer my
bloodfever burned.

I snarled, and shoved her in the chest. She stumbled
backwards, but recovered swiftly, slashing scarlet nails
for my eyes. I ducked, and instead she caught my hair,
and yanked. My scalp ripped, and I tumbled to the
ground on top of her.

We rolled in the crackling grass, limbs thrashing
and fangs snapping for a hold. Her virus-rich blood-
scent thrilled me. Her pulse tempted me, throbbing like
dark wine under her pale skin, her wrists, her throat,
her curving breasts. My wired-up muscles gloried in
the fight, and I pinned her hips down with mine and
clawed for her eyeballs. She yelled and fought me, her
eyes wild, and ravenous spit filled my mouth in anticipation.

But iron hands grabbed my ribs and tore me off her.

I whirled through the air, wings flailing, and landed
with a skull-sickening crunch against the wall.

Angelo's steelgray eyes glinted dangerously a foot
from mine. He grabbed my shoulders and smacked my
head into the concrete again. "Hands off, b— Holy
mother of Jesus!"

I scrabbled to get away, but he didn't hit me again.

He was clean, dressed, neat, no trace of my blood. No
trace of sickness, either. Ange was tough and hundreds
of years old. Was the poison not strong enough?

He took in my healing bruises, the freshcut fangs,
pressed the back of his hand against my cheek for fever.
His face tightened. "What the fuck happened to you?"

I panted for breath, and spit dripped onto my chin.
Dumbly, I flushed, the fever shocking me hot. I shouldn't
be embarrassed. But I wanted to cover my face, hide
myself, deny the thing I'd become.

Rosa clambered up, yanking her dress straight. "Cheap slut bitchjumped me. Looks like she's been whoring around. Let's get rid of her."

I stammered, and nothing came out. A roaring ache split my skull, and I tried to hold my head up and pull my loosened robe to cover my breasts at the same time. I didn't want to be naked in front of Angelo again.

Not that it mattered. Surely, he'd kill me now. Can't suffer vampire vermin on his turf, especially not a whore he'd already used and discarded.

Angelo glanced at me again and turned to Rosa with a slick-fanged snarl. "Tell me what you did."

Rosa smiled and waved a negligent hand. "Nothing. Maybe we made a mistake. Accidents happen."

In a vampireswift flash he loomed before her, his fingers cruel on her shoulder, and his calm, cold voice spiked fear into my veins. "This is me you're talking to, slut. No mistakes. No accidents. Tell me what you did."

"It wasn't me, Ange, I swear." Rosa trembled, her lips aquiver like a schoolgirl's.

Admiration soured my mouth. She was good. No wonder Diamond fell for it. My heart bled for him, that he'd loved such a venomous viper. I knew what it was like.

Ange snarled, sarcastic, and turned to me, cool and courteous as any rich-ass businessman in a suit. "Don't be afraid, love. Who infected you?"

Nervous laughter spilled out, and I swallowed it. This was surreal. I hugged my robe tight, sweat slicking the satin to my thighs. If I accused her, surely he'd chew my head off and eat it.

Rosa laughed, too, angry. "You'll believe her over me? A snarky little bloodtart? Come off it."

Her insults slashed my heart raw. Just another conceited tramp who thought she was better than I, assumed me good for nothing but blood and sex.

"She did it." I pointed a shaking claw, reckless. "She tied me to a chair in the basement and injected me and left me to starve. I only got away because Diamond set me free." Satisfaction settled, and I waited for him to laugh, hit me, tear my throat out in a hot scarlet gush and end it all.

Ange's eyes flashed black with centuries-old wrath, and he whirled and backhanded Rosa in the face.

Bone crunched. She flew backwards, blood pouring down her chin.

He'd turned back to me before she hit the ground. "Love, I am so sorry. Did Diamond fix you up?"

"Excuse me?" I still goggled at Rosa, groaning on the grass in a scarlet stain, her blue satin gown awry. Her bag had fallen from her shoulder, and it lay a few feet away, a dark smear on the grass. It looked familiar.

Ange flicked a fat roll of cash from his pocket and folded some, counting it swiftly before offering it to me. "For your trouble. Believe me, I'll make her regret it. You need a job, come see me."

I stared. Green and yellow, a lot of money. More than I'd taken from Jasper. Surreal indeed. For a greedy vampire gangster with back-asswards morals, Ange Valenti was a half-decent guy.

Pity the other half was cold, mercenary, misogynist, and downright creepy. As if money could ever make up for what she'd done.

I shook my head, my voice steady. "No, thanks. Keep it. But there's one thing I'd like."

He flicked sardonic eyebrows and tucked the money away. "Whatever."

I pointed next to Rosa, who was only just crawling to her feet. "That bag. It's mine."

Angelo shrugged and glared at Rosa. "Give it to her."

Rosa scowled as she dusted off her bloodsoaked dress, her split lip already healing, but this time real fear shone dark in her violet eyes. "What for? She's a useless bloodwhore."

For the first time, impatience sparked Ange's voice hot. "At least she's making an honest living. You're a lying daughter of a demon, and you will not splash virus around without my say-so. Give it to her."

She grabbed it and held on, defiant.

Ange sighed and yanked the bag from her grip. He was cruelly strong. Too strong for her. And he dipped his dark head with that creepy old-fashioned politeness, and handed the bag to me.

Rosa screamed, and dived for it, but too late.

My hand closed over the velvet. Rosa crashed into the ground, missing me by inches, and on my finger, Jasper's ring burned with frosted flame.

Gemstones. Mine. And not a moment too soon.

High overhead, the moon lit the sky like daylight.

33

I clutched the bag to my chest, triumph blazing fireworks in my veins. Kane's deadline was up. And already I felt the magical pull of my thrall, dragging me to him.

I'd given him my soul when I accepted Jasper's cursed ring. But I'd done my part. I had the gemstones. I could only hope Kane would keep his promise and set me free.

I stretched my arms, inhaling, exalting to the silvery light. My bones burned deep, the promise of hellfire alive. Moonshine spilled over me, lighting my skin with a metallic glow. My wings swelled hot and tingling. I'd won.

My only regret was I'd never told Diamond thank you.

"Ember. How lovely to see you."

That warm velvet voice coated my spine, tainting my tongue with charcoal.

I turned, shivering. Kane stared at me, black eyes flat with my reflection. Black suit, bow tie, his golden hair spilling loose.

What had I expected? To be dragged to his lair in

hell? Nothing so sordid for my elegant demon lord. He was already at Ange's party. I wasn't getting away.

Rosa cowered on the ground, tears swelling her eyes. Angelo just glared at me, dark. "Kane, look, if there's an issue here I'm sorry. I didn't know she was yours. No slight intended."

"None taken." Kane didn't move his gaze from mine. "Just the little matter of a debt."

I scrabbled in my bag. The gemstones leapt and giggled, smarting in my palm with malicious glee, and I dragged them out. Moonlight glittered on the jewels, winking red and blue and yellow like evil eyes. I thrust them out to Kane, my pulse wild. "I got them. Look. They're all here."

Kane's face gleamed, and he reached for them.

"No!" Rosa screamed, and launched herself at him, clawed nails scratching.

Kane glanced at her and blinked. A wave of black hellspell shimmered the air in rich sulfur stink, and Rosa fell, her mouth and nose exploding in blood. She hit the ground at my feet, unmoving.

Ange's brow flickered, but he didn't protest.

Kane didn't even look. He just scooped the gems from my hand.

A tiger's eye for Crimson. Famine's dark sapphire. Rosa's violetpink on silver. All there. Except one.

He held them to the hungry moonlight, twirling them in neat fingers. "I like the blue one."

My throat parched, but I held my voice steady. "I did everything you asked. Now give me what you promised."

Kane smiled, scarlet. "But there's still one left, cindergirl."

I held out my hand, shaking. Kane gripped my fin-

ger, and in a flash of awful scarlet flame that seared
my flesh, Jasper's ring pulled free.

My bones flared hot, one last agonizing warning,
and the fire inside them died.

I gasped, staggering. I felt light, clean, unburdened.
Like I'd dumped some nasty baggage.

Kane stuffed the gems in his pocket and turned
away.

"Wait," I gasped. "Is that all? Am I done?"

"Yes, Ember. All done. Much obliged." Kane
grinned, playful like a wicked child. "Unless you'd care
to go another round? There must be something you
want. You've got a little virus problem, I see. I could
make that go away. Or . . . something else?"

Memory stroked me hot, his sly touch in my mind,
hunting out my desires. Before, he'd tried to tempt me
with visions of me and Jasper, and it hadn't worked.
But I had a far more compelling desire now.

Wildly, I clamped my jaw shut, fighting to clear my
mind, think about something else, not let my sorrow
show. Not picture my roseglass fairy prince, bleeding
out in glowing puddles on the floor with my teethmarks
in his throat.

But Kane inhaled, sniffing me, and crafty knowl-
edge lit his eyes blue. "Well, that's new. And an easy
one, as it turns out." He traced a seductive finger across
my lips, branding me, and his whisper sucked evil desire from my skin. "I can give him back to you, Ember.
Alive and unharmed. All you need do is give me your
soul."

His compulsion dived deep inside me like an evil
serpent, coiling around my resolve until it gasped and
shuddered, weak. I choked. My lungs filled with Kane's
thunderstorm scent, and I sobbed. I wanted it. Wanted

to say yes, beg for Diamond's life, let my soul slip away into blackness if it meant I could have him back.

Diamond would hate it. I knew that. It'd tear him in two that I'd cursed my soul for him. But I didn't care.

Fuck doing the right thing. I was selfish. I was reckless. I'd make Diamond's sacrifice mean nothing. It didn't matter. I just needed him to hold me so I could pretend I was okay. I needed the guilt to go away.

Kane stroked my hair, his lips teasing mine. "Last chance, Ember. I won't offer again."

Charcoal licked my bones raw, and I opened my mouth to say yes.

And beside us, Angelo doubled over with a rich groan and heaved up a gutful of blood.

I jerked back, shaking, yanked from my hellish fugue back to reality.

Kane stared, his nose wrinkling. Ange spewed again. Blood. My blood, glimmering alive with moonshine, but clogged with lumps of darker, poisoned meat.

My breath caught. Shit. The poison had worked. And I had *I did it* written all over me.

Ange gasped, blood and saliva dripping from his nose, and his hard gray glare snapped up onto me. "You dirty fucking bitch."

Blackness shimmered like heat haze, and Kane's wrath staggered me dizzy.

I fell to my knees, and the demon dragged my head up by the hair. His claws sprang out, slicing hot hell-wrath into my scalp, and his black eyes swirled scarlet. "Look what you've done!"

I fought, grass scraping my knees. "I didn't—"

"Not that one. No no no. That one's mine. I *need* that one *alive*." Kane grabbed me by the throat, and my flesh scorched alight with his vengeance. "I'm disappointed in you, Ember. I gave you every chance."

"I'm sorry!" His grip squeezed my voice to a croak. "Please. Don't. I'll make it up to you—"

"Oh, yes. You will." He dropped me, ash scattering like snow, and fury sprang his hair blue. "You want your precious fairy boy so much? Go and get him."

And the fire in my bones blazed high and triumphant.

I howled, despair hacking my heart in two. The stink of my burned flesh sickened me. Already grasping spectral hands crawled up my ankles, dragging me down. I kicked and hauled upward with my wings, panic flashing my nerves like electric shock, but they wouldn't let go.

Hellfire scorched me, dragging my breath away. Agony flared sunbright. Already, charcoal simmered my lungs dry. The air howled and funneled inward, a dark vortex sucking me into emptiness. My limbs folded, and grass smacked into my cheek as I fell. My vision bubbled and faded, a dying film reel.

A scream pierced my lungs. I scrabbled blindly, fighting to stay. But a gritty ashen whirlwind sucked me away, and blackness stuffed my throat silent.

34

Scorching wind buffeted my wings, and my head thudded into red dirt. Stormclouds boiled the sky, black and scarlet like bruised flesh, shedding bloodtainted shadows that crawled and hissed. Thunder threatened, dark and steamy, and somewhere unseen creatures cackled and moaned.

I rolled in choking dust, coughing, and ash glued my mouth sour. I dragged myself to sitting, palms scraping raw. Ange's garden was gone. A red gravel plain stretched before me, warped in the heat like a lurid planetscape, and dust swirled, obscuring the fiery horizon, stinging my wings and raking my eyeballs hot.

My bones ached, aflame, and my new vampire senses fired hard with warning. Hell. Kane had sent me to hell for defying him.

And I wasn't alone.

Beside me, Diamond choked and crawled to hands and knees. His wings dragged bright ruts in the gravel. Red dust coated his battered body, and pinkglow blood seeped from a hundred cuts and scrapes. But he was whole. Real. Alive.

Relief drowned my spluttering heart, and I cracked an exhausted smile, my newly long teeth scarring my lips. I hadn't bled him to death. It didn't make sense. I didn't care. "Hey. Prettyfae. You okay?"

"Like you care." Diamond's tone razored me raw.

I gaped. "What?"

He dragged himself to his feet, and his accusing berry eyes scorched me cold. "I said, like you give a shit. This is hell, Ember. I'm dead. You killed me."

Hot guilt squeezed my guts. "I didn't mean it! You know that. God, if I could take it back, I w—"

"Sure. Whatever. You didn't *mean* to let Jasper screw you, either. Didn't *mean* to kill your little blood-fae boyfriend. Hell, I'll bet you didn't even *mean* to sleep with me so you could screw me over." He leaned closer, stained with blood and dust and the scorching red glitter of disgust. "You're just one big useless accident, Ember. Fuck you."

I stammered, but inside my soul howled in denial.

Lightning scarred the sky, a rage-filled crack of thunder, and the earth shuddered and tilted beneath me.

I yelled, scrabbling for a hold. Rocks and dirtclumps rained as the ground broke open, a deafening rumble. A dark chasm split wide, the other side groaning away behind me into stormy blackness.

Gravel scraped my belly as I slid downward. I clawed in sick terror, desperate for something to hold. Rocks jabbed bleeding under my claws and ripped them away. I strove with my wings for lift, but swirling wind and falling rocks slapped them churlishly aside.

At the top, Diamond watched me, unmoving.

"Please. Help me." The wind tore my words from my lips, hurling them up to him stained in terror and bloody remorse.

But he just wiggled his fingers in a wave and walked away.

I screamed, torn raw with anguish and fear. My elbow struck a rocky ledge. I clutched wildly, and at last my bleeding fingers found purchase. I hugged the ledge and hung there, legs flailing, and beneath me the hell-chasm boiled scarlet and black in the bloody stink of charcoal. Frightful screams of torment ripped on the wind, souls trapped in eternal torture.

My nerves shrieked, and I fought to control my breath. *Don't look, Ember. Don't look down.*

I looked down.

Flesh rending, blood spurting, the throaty rip of muscle from bone. My stomach lurched, and I tore my gaze away.

I struggled until my biceps screamed in frustration, but I couldn't haul myself up. The wailing wind tore at my wings, threatening to drag me into dusty oblivion. Fatigue weakened me, and in my grip rock crumbled. I couldn't get purchase. Even with my new vampire energy, I wasn't strong enough.

I collapsed against the shuddering wall, dirt in my face, clutching the crumbling ledge under one weak, agony-crippled arm. Kane's words to me slithered in my bowels, cruel torment. *Want your precious fairy boy so much? Go get him.*

Tears sizzled dry on my cheeks. Kane had taunted me. Let me think I still had a chance to keep Diamond alive. But Diamond had left me here. I'd killed him to save my own useless skin, and he hated me for it. I couldn't blame him. And now I was in hell, alone.

No one could save me but me.

Hell howled beneath me, the pit bubbling and reeking like a witch's foul cauldron, rank with the screams of the damned. Charcoal clogged my nose, and thunder rumbled the stormy air with the sick stink of inevitability. My wings hung limp and useless. My muscles cried for rest, silence, death, and I stared up at the chasm's distant edge and my heart quailed in despair.

It looked so far. So difficult, all bumps and sharp edges and sheer beyond-vertical rock. I'd never make it, not on my own.

It'd be so easy to let go. Fall into the pit of torment. Take what I deserved.

But in my head, Big Em snorted in disgust, wild scarlet hair flaming bright. *Get a grip, Emmy. You've beaten Famine. Survived the virus. Lived through a vampire's cruel appetite. And you've got a beautiful fairy boy who thinks you're the shit, god help him.*

"He's dead!" I gritted the words out over guilt like broken glass, tears slashing my cheeks. "He hates me! You heard him. What's the point?"

Yeah, I heard him. Big Em stared me down, glitter-bright and hard. *Eloquent, wasn't he?*

"Don't you dare make f—"

Think, Little Em. He said "you killed me." When did you ever hear him talk like that?

Dust clotted my teeth in doubt. *You killed me.* Not *You deadified* or *I'm cactus* or anything else weird and jumbled like he'd say.

Bingo. How many cute little Diamond-isms did you hear in that speech? That's right. None. That wasn't him talking, Emmy. That was you.

I sucked in gritty air, ashen hellstink like acid, and understanding burst like sunlight.

He wasn't real. This wasn't real. It was all a dirty demon helltrick. And I'd come this close to falling for it. To letting myself drop into the pit, where Kane could eat my soul.

I hadn't succumbed to Kane's temptation in the garden. He didn't own me yet. He'd sent me to hell, but he couldn't make me stay. Not unless I surrendered. He was still trying to trick me into saying yes.

Well, fuck that.

Big Em smiled and winked at me, her green eyes sparkling. In the scorching light of hellfire, Big Em looked a lot like me. She always had. I'd just been too afraid to let myself be her.

Yeah. That's right. So screw you, if you can't even crawl a few blinking yards up a wall by yourself. Do you want to save your soul and get back to your boy before he dies, or not?

I gritted my teeth and dragged myself out of the pit, hand over shaking hand.

My claws ripped. My muscles screeched in protest. But I made it.

And when I reached the top, and my cheek thudded exhausted into the dust, the air shrieked with Kane's bloody frustration, and on an angry crack of sulfur-tainted lightning, I whirled flashblind into the sky and tumbled back into the real world.

35

I slammed into the floor facefirst, my skull rattling.

Cool air caressed my hellscorched skin. The screech of wind subsided, replaced by the steady rush of rain on iron.

My skin was clean, no dust, no grazing rocks. And the hellfire eating my bones was gone. No pain, no itch, no evil ashen stink. Like it never burned.

I blinked, dizzy, and wobbled to my feet. The basement where Rosa had infected me. Dusty boxes, junk, the chair where I'd sat with my ropes still stained with blood.

Beside me, Diamond sprawled bleeding.

My heart lurched. I dived to my knees, cradling his head in my lap. His hair spilled lifeless over my thighs, that rainbow glitter faded. His vital scent wafted weak, even with my new vampire senses. I rubbed my cheek over his lips, and faint warmth greeted me. Hope shone dim on my heart. He was breathing. Just.

My pulse gibbered cold. I'd beaten Kane's lies. Diamond couldn't die now. I stroked his face, his hair, burying my nose in that fading rosepetal glory. His eyes jerked left and right under fluttering lids, and he murmured and fidgeted in his sleep, some vile dream

that shivered his spine and broke his skin in sweat.
Maybe Kane taunted him, too. Tried to make him believe I'd deserted him.

Desperate emptiness pressed cold inside. I'd escaped damnation because I'd believed he didn't hate
me. Because I wouldn't let my fear destroy me. And
now, I wanted him more desperately than ever.

He unlocked me. Dissolved the prison of my fear,
and now I walked free under the stars. He'd shown me
the best part of myself, and I didn't need anyone anymore.

But being without him thrust hollow despair into
my heart.

He was crazy, ridiculous, a wild fairy madman with
a killer smile and fuck-'em-all courage that melted my
defenses to mush. Such a bright, glittering star, to flicker
out in a dusty basement because of me.

We'd known each other such a short time. This
melting need in my heart couldn't be love.

But without him, my peace lay shattered in shards.
Whatever this was, it was stupid. It was insane. It was
beautiful. And I wanted more.

Wildly I shook my head, tears flowing faster. I
pressed my lips to his, seeking his warmth, his love,
the warm comfort of his pulse and his skin on mine. I
bit my tongue, pain slashing, my vampire blood trickling between his lips and linking us like a lifeline.
Only a little bit, not enough to give him the virus. It
had healed me. Maybe it'd heal him, too.

The wound in my mouth healed, and desperately I bit
again, over and over until the blood flowed hot down his
throat.

It hurt. I didn't care. I'd vowed I'd never share my
blood again. Never give myself so completely to any-

one. But Diamond could have it all, to the last shimmering drop if it'd bring him back.

I kissed him, desperate. "Wake up. Come back to me. I can't do it without you."

And he choked and gasped, and his wet ruby eyes sprang open.

Hot tears spilled gratitude down my cheeks, and I folded against him, my muscles at last giving out.

Breathy laughter shook his chest, and his fingers slid weakly into my hair. "I'm guessifying this inn't hell, then."

I couldn't speak. I just held him, and he held me, and outside the rain fell.

36

I tilted my head back, hot nightclub lights blinding me, and emptied the glimmering scarlet vial into my mouth.

Liquid slimed my tongue, salty and warm, tingling like fairyglitter but thick as blood. It crawled and slithered in my mouth, an animal searching for food. I gagged, my eyes watering. But I forced my lips shut with my fingers, and with a gritty squirm the antidote to Diamond's vampire poison uncoiled like a hot worm and dived down my throat.

My stomach cramped, and I doubled over, panting. "Fuck a duck. You sure this stuff works?"

The blue fairy spellworker simpered and giggled, coppery wings jittering in glee. "Worky work, yes yes. No more poison." He stroked a claw down my cheek, and sniffed my hair, his curled nose twitching. "Curious. Bloodfairy bloodsucker. Make a fine sparkly or three. Sure I can't have a tasty?"

"Don't you tryify." Diamond snarled, glassy teeth flashing, and pushed the blue fairy off me. Strobes glinted bright magenta warning in his eyes. We'd fed him, gotten his strength back. It didn't take long, not with that hit of vampire blood. He was tough, my handsome fairy prince.

The blue fairy stumbled and scowled, witchy fingers wriggling in a mock hex. "Snarkypoo you. There's gratitude for you. Fixed your girly, didn't I?" And he poked out his pointed green tongue and turned away.

"Wait." I swallowed and touched his arm. "The bloodfever. I . . . can you cure it?"

The fairy smirked, twirling long bronze hair around his finger. "Maybe. What's it worth to ya?"

Diamond slid his smooth arm around my shoulder, tugging me with him. "He's gaming. Don't hearify."

But my strength almost matched his now I was a vampire. I resisted, my veins twitching. I had to know. "What's your price?"

The fairy leaned closer, and sniffed my collarbone, licking wet green lips. "Mmm. Blood, of course. It'll make some fine spelltricks. And I'll need a lot. Testing, you know. Mixing and stirring and sipping the tastiness." His eyes glittered greedy yellow. "You've got plenty. Just a bottle or two a week. No loss."

I jerked back, sick. "No, thanks."

This time, I really was done selling my blood. Even if it meant I'd have to live like this forever.

The fairy shrugged. "Suit yourself. Change your mind, let me know." He blew Diamond a sparkling green kiss, and fluttered into the dark.

Diamond glanced at me, hot ruby eyes unreadable. "You sure?"

I swallowed again, dry and hungry. "No. Who the hell was that weirdo?"

"No one. Just a—"

"Business associate? Right. I get it. Let's go." His

business had just become more complicated, what with Ange sick and vengeful and Kane sullen that Diamond and I had gotten away from him.

Were we hiding? Not exactly. It's hard to hide when you're a six-foot-three flashypink gangster and a blood-fairy with fangs. What we'd do next, who knew? But I'd never known Diamond at a loss for an idea. Even if it was a crazy, irresponsible, fuck-the-rules idea. Part of what I liked about him.

We wandered, his hand hot and smooth in mine, and uncertainty slid cool into my bones. Sweet nightclub smoke misted, vibrating with the steady beat, lasers spearing bright. It hadn't taken them long once the rain cooled everything off and power was restored to get the club started again. Bodies crushed, a fleshy temptation, the sugary scent of breath and sweat and sex. Dancers flashed snapshots in the strobes, flushed rainbow wings, shining limbs, glittering jewelpierced skin and painted lips. The smell of blood watered my mouth, and my hungry fangs sprang tight.

I gripped Diamond's hand harder, his rosy scent a not entirely safe distraction. The fever wasn't as awful as I'd feared. I think my vampirebait blood tamed the virus faster than a human's would. Maybe Diamond's poison helped me fight back, too. Perhaps in time, the virus might die and I'd be back to normal. After all, I'd never once met a bloodfairy vampire.

I didn't know. But for now, wild hunger still gnawed at me, and my skin burned, and I wandered dazed in a perpetual state of confusion and horniness.

Which brought me to my current problem.

I tugged him into a corner, worms wriggling in my belly that had nothing to do with fever or poison or slitherweird fairy cures. I tried to look into his eyes, but my gaze kept slipping, my belly warm. He wore faded jeans and a scruffy slashed-off shirt, and he looked gorgeous. Lord, he was beautiful, those curving glass cheekbones and glowing skin, his hair a glittering glory. Too beautiful for me. His face still shone pale, tired, his translucent veins shining purple with fatigue. But he'd be okay. Luckily, I hadn't taken too much.

At least, I hadn't this time.

But I didn't trust my hunger. I didn't trust my desire for him. Next time, I might not be able to stop.

I wrung my hands in my lap. I'd been working up to this conversation with Jasper, but I'd never imagined this. "Look. Umm . . . This isn't gonna work. You and me, I mean."

His pupils glittered silver. "Uh-huh."

I stuttered, dazzled. "I— that is, I like you and everything. . . ."

"Uh-huh." He drifted closer, warm and rosy.

I swallowed, my skin tingling, and backed off, but my wings pressed against the warm metal wall. "Yeah. And I've had . . . kind of a good time. . . ."

"Uh-huh." He brushed hair from my cheek, a gentle caress that quivered me hot.

"Mmm. Y'know, except for nearly dying. That wasn't so great. But—"

"How 'bout the kissing?" He glided his body against mine, curling his wings over us in a roseglow cocoon. "The kissing part was dead awful."

"I wouldn't say *dead* awful—"

"And the sex. All that lick and touch and suck. I really hatified that bit."

"Mmm." My mouth watered, and heat flowed tight in my belly. He was even more irresistible with my new vampire senses. His pulse throbbed in my hypersensitive ears, his scent a luscious torrent. He felt so warm and smooth against me, his strong thighs, his chest, the warm insistence of his hardening cock. God, was he ever not hot for me? "Yeah. Rotten. Listen, about that—"

"And the part where you swallowed my blood with me inside you." He dipped his head to brush soft lips on my shoulder, and the warm tingle of his breath made me shiver. "Dunno how I bearified that."

I gasped, breathless as he trailed kisses under my chin. "But . . . I nearly killed you. I can't—"

"Still alive, inn't I?" He leaned into me with a satisfied murmur, and the way his cock pressed against my thigh, he clearly was.

I wanted to kiss him, strip and feel our bodies naked. Pin him down, crush my teeth into his throat and drink until I died. "But . . . didn't it hurt?"

"Like a motherfucker. Not the pointificality."

"But . . . but I thought you hated it. Bloodsuckers, I mean."

"Not when you do it. See this?" He caught my fingers and pressed them to his palm, his wrist, where tiny scars sliced his hot skin. "Hurting is good. It's how I do. I can takify."

My fingertips tingled over the light bumps, not straight like razorcuts but rough clawmarks. I swallowed, strange desire melting my belly. "You do that yourself?"

"Not anymore." And he slid long fingers into my hair and pulled my mouth to his.

His lips tempted mine, all hot and smooth and soft, and when his tongue brushed my lips, my resolve dissolved in molten wanting. I opened my mouth, letting him inside one last time. Tingling delight spread from our kiss all through my body. I ached, hunger and desire stirring together, burning bright until I couldn't tell which was which.

It didn't feel like one last time. It felt like the beginning.

His kiss dragged such desperate need from my heart that I tore away, gasping. My fangs pricked sharp in my gums, straining for contact. "Diamond, stop it. I'm trying to tell you it's over."

His mouth quivered an inch from mine like he didn't want to restrain himself. "Do you wantify it over?"

"Do you want a vampire girlfriend?"

"You're not a vampire girlfriend. You're you. And I. Want. You." He pinned my wrists to the wall and our lips collided again, hard and passionate until glitter blinded me and my body thrilled tight with desire. He searched for my teeth, raking his tongue across my hungry fangtips, and blood burst into my mouth, glowing rubyhot with his glorious fairy flavor.

I groaned and sucked on his tongue, feeding on the twin gifts of his blood and his pleasure. My mouth burned mintbright, flavor seeping down my throat, and my stomach growled in satisfaction. And then he gentled the kiss, slowing me down until I could breathe, and our lips caressed together over and over, so sweet and close and warm, I shivered.

His tenderness burst like sunlight in my heart. Tears pressed my lids, and I swallowed, stupid. God, I was crying again. A moment of compassion and I'm in pieces.

He kissed the wetness away, his fingers sliding between mine. "Sayify you don't like me."

"Huh?" I licked my lips, breathless, his heady flavor intoxicating me.

"Sayify I'm a lousy gangbanging freak and what I do for a living sickifies you."

"Huh? No. I mean, we're all on the game here—"

"Or I just don't do it for you and making love to me was dead-rat borificating."

I goggled, confused. "What? No, I—"

"I smell bad? You don't like pink? Glass itchifies your skin?"

"Don't be ridiculous."

"Then I guess you're all out of excusificality."

"I'm not making excuses—"

"Then what?"

"It's just—"

"Just nothing." His smile turned wicked, sparkling my spine with desire. "Gotta warnify, though. I kinda like you. Offscaring me won't be easyfied."

I laughed. "Just you wait. I'll irrit your flashy pink ass off until you're dying for a moment's peace."

He swept me close, his lips an inch from mine, and his whisper vibrated through my body, so warm and safe. "Is that a yes?"

Such a beautiful, crazy fairy, all mine. To think I'd imagined him shallow.

I nodded, and locked my wrists around his neck, and whispered into his mouth on a kiss. "Yes."

He responded, lingering, and rubbed his cheek in my hair, a contented fairy burble warbling in his throat. "Don't be fearified, angel. I'm not."

I tilted my head up, his glittering glass hair falling over my shoulders, and gazed into his hotflash eyes.

And I wasn't either.